Severe

Carolina Hell Reapers MC

Book #1

By:

Keta Kendric

Severe – Carolina Hell Reapers MC

Copyright © 2023 by Keta Kendric

Cover: Cosmic Letterz

Editing: A. L Barron, One Last Glance Editing and Tammy Jernigan, publisherchick1@gmail.com.

ISBN: 978-1-956650-08-2

Table of Contents

Prologue	1
Chapter One	5
Chapter Two	17
Chapter Three	27
Chapter Four	37
Chapter Five	43
Chapter Six	57
Chapter Seven	73
Chapter Eight	91
Chapter Nine	117
Chapter Ten	139
Chapter Eleven	149
Chapter Twelve	163
Chapter Thirteen	173
Chapter Fourteen	191
Chapter Fifteen	205
Chapter Sixteen	217
Chapter Seventeen	231
Chapter Eighteen	239
Chapter Nineteen	247
Chapter Twenty	265
Chapter Twenty-one	269
Chapter Twenty-two	281
Chapter Twenty-three	293
Chapter Twenty-four	303
Chapter Twenty-five	309
Chapter Twenty-six	317
Chapter Twenty-seven	329
Chapter Twenty-eight	341
Chapter Twenty-nine	349
Chapter Thirty	367
Chapter Thirty-one	383
Chapter Thirty-two	403
Chapter Thirty-three	411
Chapter Thirty-four	415
Epilogue	423
Acknowledgments	427
Author's Note	429
Other Titles by Keta Kendric	431
Connect with Author	435

Dedication

To all the readers who asked for more of this character and for those who support and continue to support me and my literary work. You are my best motivation.

Synopsis:

Jade McKenna, raised by a drug kingpin, abducted at fourteen, and caught in a drive-by at sixteen. You would think she would be intimately familiar with chaos, but the roles in her life were flipped after her father's death. Boarding school, owning businesses, and mingling with the social elite became her norm.

Until one day, the chaos returns.

Severe, a biker-assassin, shows up out of the blue and takes her, tells her she's coming with him until...*Until what?* She ends up at Ground Zero, his motorcycle club compound, and has no choice but to figure out how to live among a group of legendary death dealers, biding her time until she can escape or until death. Her choices are dismal, but she learns that there are worse things than death, and it's been lurking over her shoulder her whole life.

Warning: Warning: This book contains graphic violence, explicit sexual content, and is intended for adults.

Prologue

Hunger twisted my stomach into a roaring knot, the pangs a relentless monster that gnawed at my insides. A low whistle called my attention, along with that of Pope, my always upbeat dog, his breed a mystery. Currently, he was suffering the same fate as me: hunger, thirst, and the never-ending torment our devil and keeper unleashed on us.

Like me, Pope breathed harshly after a round of lashes with a belt neither of us could avoid. The leashes around our necks prevented our escape and kept us from reaching the one thing that would take away the ache in our bellies.

Our devil ordered us to fight for the chicken leg she tossed just out of our reach. Her attempts to make us turn against each other failed despite her taunts and yells. When exhaustion took my will, and Pope beat me to the chicken leg, our devil took it away from him and tossed it out of reach again.

We lay there, starving, with food in front of us. He or I would rest and build enough energy to stretch our bodies to reach for it, but nothing worked. The metal leashes would pull too tight, crack our skin, and induce the una-pologetic sting and stabbing burn of pain.

Raw, chapped, and bleeding, our hunger continued to entice us to add to our injuries. Pope was suffering because of my weakness and inability to give the devil what it asked for, a fight between us. My failure to inflict pain on Pope, the one thing that I loved, the one thing that kept me going, would be the death of us both.

This time we were tied up, but what would happen to us the next time? This punishment was the result of Pope snapping at our devil. He'd bitten our tormentor, barely breaking the skin, to protect me.

Lifting my head, I stared at the dirty chicken leg the devil had tossed aside as another form of punishment. I needed to be strong for Pope. With gritted teeth, aching muscles, and a throaty groan, I managed to lift my shaky arm and pull against the metal around my neck.

I focused on the piece of meat, setting aside the trimmers of hot pain racing through my neck, my stomach, and my back. I made it go away. There were no more stomach cramps, only a dark rage that boiled inside me. And I allowed it to take control.

Ideas of how I wanted to kill the devil settled in the deepest and darkest place in my head. It was a place I was learning to accept, to embrace. It was an escape from this reality where I didn't experience hurt and wasn't a failure.

I pulled, stretched, twisted, and kicked out my legs. Three times. Seven times. Ten times until my big toe touched the tip and inched the meat closer. Three more tries, and I nudged it over to Pope, who snatched it up by extending his paws.

I collapsed, exhausted and faint. Tears that would have come had I any left to cry remained elusive. The blur of exhaustion threatened to pull me under, and I welcomed it to avoid the ache of defeat.

Why didn't the devil just kill me?

"Because I love to fuck with you, to see you in pain, to make you hurt."

The demon always answered my questions, and I couldn't discern anymore if the answer came from inside my head, from my own mouth, or from the one who liked to inflict physical pain.

My eyes fluttered against the dust floating away from my face before it was sucked back in with each harsh drag of air I took and released.

A warm, wet swipe against my dirty cheek pulled me back from the brink.

Pope.

He sent another lazy lick across my cheek before he turned his head away with a flop against the hard ground. When he turned back, he dropped a piece of the chicken leg on my face, giving me half of the prize.

Pope understood humanity better than the human devil who tormented us. I was too weak to lift my hand to shove the meat into my mouth and unsure if thirst would hinder my attempt to chew and swallow.

Pope nudged the meat with his nose so I only had to open my lips to grip it. The gritty, dirt-covered morsel was the only source of nutrition he or I had eaten in three days.

The lingering presence of death hovered above us like a dark cloud, eagerly waiting to snatch us away from this hell. At this point, death may be our only savior.

CHAPTER ONE

Severe

Fifteen years later.

My current target, Jadis McKenna, was a mystery. She was the question mark that stained my otherwise self-assured nature where my job and executing my tasks were concerned. She fed an insatiable need to know more simply because a question had developed in the first place.

She had me holding conferences in my head. I'd been studying her for a month now. She didn't sleep, and when she did, it usually ended with her on the floor in the fetal position.

Nightmares. Naps. Eighteen-hour workdays. She functioned on coffee and tight schedules. Fundraising and campaigning for money for the needy was the foundation on which she'd built her reputation. The notion left a question burning through my brain. Why was she under a kill order?

Her file played on a loop in my head. There was enough dirt in there to kill her twice, dig her up and murder her a few more times. However, something kept tugging at my gut and prevented me from executing this kill order right away.

I didn't choke her to death with my bare hands when I was in the elevator with her yesterday. I didn't stab her twenty-eight times to see how long it would take her to bleed out a week ago when I was in the bathroom stall next to hers at the center she runs.

"What the fuck is wrong with you? She did the crimes, and her death order was approved by the Six. What more do you need?"

"I don't know," I answered the demon who'd taken up residence in my head and refused to leave. "She doesn't fit. No matter what the evidence says. I can't enjoy the kill if it doesn't feel right," I surmised in an attempt to make myself understand.

"Fucking pussy. Fucking idiot. Fucking kill her already. You've killed women before. Is that it? She's got a pussy, so you've decided to express some form of empathy all of a sudden?"

I ignored the sick prick whose voice kept stabbing at my brain stem and telling me to go through with something that didn't make sense.

"Shut up," I muttered through gritted teeth.

"You're a fucking sociopath who gets off on killing. You sick fuck. You used someone's entrails as your jump rope a month ago, and now you're putting yourself in timeout. What the fuck? Kill her!" he demanded, his voice roaring angrily in my head.

"You're getting on my nerves. Shut up," I grumbled. A deep breath did nothing to provide an ounce of relief. There had to be a way to get him out of my head. I tapped the side of my temple with the palm of my hand, hoping it would quiet him, if only for a minute.

"You don't even have a body. You live unwanted in my head. So, why don't you shut up and let me, the one who actually uses brain cells, figure this out," I said under my breath, although I couldn't help my facial expressions and hand gestures that indicated I was speaking to someone.

On occasion, I answered myself in the presence of others. I didn't care what people thought of me. It was the best thing about having a freeloading demon in your head. It kept people away with their questions and noise and irritating conversations I didn't want to hear.

Jadis McKenna didn't fit the definition of *my* usual targets. I was overkill for someone like her, which leads me to believe that there was something off about her and this death note. In the seven years that I've been a member of the Order, this was the first time I seriously questioned the validity of a kill order.

My instincts haven't failed me since I became a member of the Hell Reaper MC, nor had they failed me when I graduated to a Reaper under the Order, a secret society of assassins.

"Where's your weird ass cousin?"

The question pulled me back into my current reality as well as made me slink farther into the dark corner in which I stood, eavesdropping.

"No disrespect, and if I ever go to hell, I want *him* with me. However, I execute people for a living, and he gives me the fucking creeps," Popper, one of my Reaper brothers, told my cousin, Micah.

There was no other person in this building they could have been talking about except me.

"He's not weird. It just takes an advanced brain like mine to know how to read him," Micah replied.

A loud snort-laugh was Popper's response.

"Tell that to the last ten poor fucks he's killed. Most of his shit makes national news. It's the kind of shit not even the Order can cover up. They are calling him the Antichrist."

Popper dropped his head and lowered his voice, but I read lips better than most. "I got a few screws knocked loose myself, but him, he fucking talks to people who aren't there. Aren't you worried he might snap one day or some shit?"

Micah chuckled. "Nope. My cousin has his shit together better than you think."

Popper's quick side-eye said he wasn't convinced.

Micah, as well as my cousins, Israel and Eli, were the only people who advocated for my sanity. They didn't believe my mind was compromised. They were blindly optimistic when it came to me due to our blood relationship—my long-lost father was their uncle. However, they, as well as others, should have been afraid, very afraid, because there were times when I wasn't altogether sure I could control what was living inside me.

Like now, instead of mingling with the rest of my club brothers, I was lurking, listening, and observing their behavior. Studying them while they were unaware was how I learned the proper mannerisms I needed when I faked my way through certain impromptu work issues.

I enjoyed the way most people regarded me with caution. It gave me a sick sense of pride to scare those who were labeled monsters themselves. Social gatherings or anything that involved people, laughing, and drinking made me want to swallow gasoline-soaked razorblades and chase them down with a lit Zippo.

An order from my cousin, Micah, also the president of our motorcycle club, was usually the only reason I attended any events. Locally, we were known as the Carolina Hell Reapers Motorcycle Club. This particular party was the club's annual birthday celebration. The party was being hosted at the armory, the location known as our official club campus.

The women, the drinking, and the public displays of sexual acts that took place at our parties turned my stomach. The usual hang-arounds and 'community pussy' as my brothers called them, knew not to approach me.

People. They were too self-absorbed, talked too much, were emotional for no reason, and were too needy of attention. I craved solitude. Doing my job and doing it well was all the ego-stroking I needed.

I stepped from the shadows of the thick dusty curtains hanging from the floor-to-ceiling windows in the lobby of the old military barracks my cousins had converted into a ballroom. This old armory was the perfect clubhouse, hang-out spot, and stand-in for our real motorcycle club compound.

Ground Zero was like Area 51. Those who speculated about it would never find it, and the ones who believed it existed or knew of its existence were probably dead. The Order, who trained and funded us, didn't even know about Ground Zero.

"Hi, handsome," one of the newest hang-arounds slinked up to me, smiling like she could see my face through the brim of my black cap.

I reached out a hand to keep her from getting too close. She glanced at my pale hand before angling her neck up, attempting to get a peek at my face.

"Want to have some fun?" she asked, poking out her chest.

She left nothing to be desired in a red tube top and baby blue mini skirt she kept pulling down her legs.

"I want to know if a woman's uterus will go into rigor if she dies while we're fucking and I keep going while she's dead."

The smile melted from her face before she gulped down a hard swallow.

"Wh-what?" she asked, like her brain had trouble processing what I'd said. I took a step closer, towering over her, my low cap obscuring my face from her view. She was smart enough to step back.

"Would you like to be my test subject? My curiosity is getting the better of me," I whispered, noticing goose bumps peppering her arms at my questions.

Mouth hanging open, she backed up, turned, and marched away so fast her heels wobbled under her quick steps.

"And there goes another one," a familiar voice said behind me. I turned to meet Micah's smiling face. "When are you going to stop scaring all the women away and actually fuck one of them?"

He was forgetting that I didn't turn down all the women he and Israel sent to me for sexual gratification. I fucked them, just not with my own body parts.

He lifted a hand and squinted at whatever image had entered his mind. "Don't answer that. The few you did touch never returned to any of our parties," he said, shaking his head. He'd also tracked down a few to make sure I hadn't murdered them.

"We're having church tomorrow instead of Sunday. I also need to talk to you about something," he said.

I knew what that *something* entailed, and the last thing I wanted to do was talk about the kill order I hadn't executed yet. I nodded and stepped off, sensing my cousin's eyes on my back as I sought the comfort of another dark corner.

***

The next day. Ground Zero.

The path cleared when I walked into the club's cabin where church was set to be held. I hated these meetings. Though necessary, I didn't like being closed in a tight space with a crowd.

A nod or quick eye contact was all I offered while members stepped aside, most unwilling to allow me too close. I was the walking definition of what the Hell Reapers represented. Where I differed was the black cap I preferred and my antisocial temperament.

The sum of my personality was what I didn't have control of others seeing. A six-foot-three, two-hundred-ten pound, and black clothes wearing menace. With seventy percent of my body covered in art, the visible parts of the seventy tattoos I sported couldn't be hidden. My willingness to put in work at the drop of a dime, especially wet-work, was also a characteristic I couldn't hide.

When I did speak, it was usually to myself and sent normal people running in the other direction. It gave my brothers more excuses to call me crazy. My internal clock was permanently set on a time I would be less likely to interact with people.

I worked most nights and slept days, so my skin, the parts that weren't covered in ink, could use some sunlight. My social interaction skills were lacking on purpose, and I didn't plan to do anything to improve them.

Simple conversations and pleasantries were my torture. Why pretend to have a good day if you weren't? Why pretend you cared about how someone else was feeling when you didn't?

I tugged at my baseball cap, pulling it lower over my eyes while marching through the entryway where more Reapers had gathered. I pushed the door to the sanctuary open and stepped inside.

"Cousin," Micah called out in greeting when I entered the room. The ranking members of the MC were already gathered around the table. Some cast quick glances while others offered nods in my direction before they returned their attention to Micah.

"Pres," I returned with a head nod, giving him the respect he deserved before standing to the left of the door and away from the rest of the crowd congregated around the table. Others were in chairs pushed against the wall on either side of the table. I belonged at the table but rarely took my appointed seat.

Despite my propensity to make sure everyone stayed at arm's length, members always listened intently on the rare occasion I did speak about business.

An hour later, and before Micah could get out the words, "Meeting adjourned," I was prepared to turn out the door and escape all the chatter that erupted.

"Severe," Micah called, his voice chasing me down and ending my escape attempt.

He flashed me an expression, his eyes squinting so slightly you'd miss it if you didn't know him. He wanted to talk to me alone. The inflection in his tone insinuated that he wanted to talk about business and, thankfully, not about me, my feelings, or my state of mind like he normally did.

Once the room was cleared and the door was pulled closed by the last man, Micah's face softened, and his smile surfaced. He was one of those people who could smile and talk you into believing all was right in the world right before he snatched your soul out with his bare hands. His road name wasn't Spyder because arachnids were cute and cuddly.

"How's your latest contract going?" he asked, standing to the left of me now when he'd just been sitting at the head of the table a moment ago. His catlike reflexes and speed made him one of the few people who could sneak up on me.

"I'm studying it," I replied. It wasn't a lie. I needed more time with this one. It was odd for me, but not unusual for a Reaper to want to get to know his target.

"I've never known you to take this much time before giving a target your *time*. Is it because it's a wom..."

"No," I answered quickly, cutting him off. He didn't need to know that for the first time in my *career* as a merc, I had serious doubts about the authenticity of the contract. My gut kept telling me something wasn't right. And although I didn't let my cousin get the word out fully, my target being a woman wasn't my problem.

"I have a lead on the dentist," I updated, shifting the subject.

Micah lifted a dramatic eyebrow.

"Your list?"

I nodded. Micah and my cousins knew about my personal hit list. They knew the true reason why I needed it and therefore had never protested against me periodically wiping names off the list in my spare time. The list was a part of my self-prescribed mental health medication.

"How many do you have left?" he questioned.

"Eight."

Although Micah and my cousins were only four years older than me at thirty-two, they were the only father figures I'd had in my life. In all the ways that mattered, they helped me find a purpose and gave me a life, two things I never envisioned for myself growing up.

Micah's wise eyes remained locked on mine.

"With you, it goes without saying, but I'm going to do it anyway. Be careful and reap well, brother."

I nodded and took off for the exit with Micah's laser-locked gaze drilling a hole in my back. It wouldn't be too long before he forced me to talk about what was taking me so long to fulfill my order. Unlike anyone else, my cousin had the uncanny ability to see right through my dark nature to read what simmered below, and it was never pretty.

CHAPTER TWO

Severe

New York.

September produced the perfect temperature with enough heat to keep your energy buzzing while the whispering coolness of the breeze chased it down.

The temperature made my five-hour spy session a pleasant time of deep contemplation, and it helped me reach a conclusion to my annoying dilemma.

I breathed in the anticipation filling me with fire. The notion of impending death always set my pulse ablaze and teased at what was left of my ravaged soul. Spying on my target at a distance was one thing, but I needed to see her. I wanted to see her up close again. I needed to breathe in her scent. I needed to taste the air she breathed. I needed to stare into her dark-brown eyes.

The sickest part of me always wanted to know more about my prey because it was one of the vices in my life that gave me a spark of joy.

Creating death wasn't vile, disgusting, or ugly to me. It was peace and quiet, a final solution to a lifetime of problems.

I was also a sick freak who wanted to play with his food before eating away her life. Many death scenarios had played out in my head during my wait, and I had narrowed it down to two.

Easing up from my perch, I stretched as the city view widened before me. The roof of the Smithfield building on Pinecrest Street gave me an excellent view of her twenty-first-floor studio apartment.

She, like many others, believed their high-rise apartments and luxurious accommodations were the security blanket that never came off. They were blissfully unaware of what lurked within the rise of elevation and the perfect folds of comfort.

Her tinted glass and safety windows were pointless as I was in possession of X751 binoculars. They were a new prototype that allowed me to see through the glass, regardless of the tint.

Ten minutes later, I had stored the equipment. Now, I schooled my face to that of a normal person. I was finally prepared to do what I should have done weeks ago.

"Can I help you, sir?" a cheery tone rang out from the front desk attendant.

"I'm entertainment for Mrs. Roland," I said with a wink. I aimed my finger down the hall where I'd witnessed the woman go in with a man young enough to be her grandson. The attendant waved me off with a pinched smile and one eyebrow stuck in the air.

"If you hurry, you can catch her before she climbs into the elevator," he said, pointing me in the direction of the woman and her boy-toy.

For the past few days, Mrs. Roland had entertained several men, a few of whom she'd asked the desk to send to her room without question. I took off, pretending to catch up to the older woman and her current date.

When I studied a target, I also considered their surroundings as well as the behavior of the people with whom they liaised. It's how I knew exactly where to walk to avoid the cameras. Thanks to Mrs. Roland, I was now in possession of a keycard and the code for the elevator.

After climbing into the elevator and pressing the twenty-first floor, the taste of death grew heavy on my tongue, and it kept growing the closer I got to the floor and near my target.

Jadis McKenna built a persona that made her a modern-day Robin Hood in the public's eye. However, her contract portfolio revealed a she-devil with her hands dipped in one of the most elicit businesses known. It was her dirty business practices involving children that pulled her into the deathly magnet of our specific order of assassins.

Although I hadn't made the purpose of her kill order connect specifically to her while studying her, the evidence compiled against her justified the contract. Since none of our contracts were less than a quarter million payout to the Order, it meant a high-profile customer had requested and paid the hefty sum.

My hesitation on this specific woman, I'm sure, had many in the Order questioning my timeline.

Getting to her floor and her small apartment was a breeze. She used this place as a temporary residence. For such a high-class place, they were lax in their security measures.

Pitch dark, I crept through her space, the scent of honey-infused lemon permeating the air. There wasn't a door to her bedroom but a hand-painted thick wood divider.

The woman had impeccable taste and was wealthy enough to have whatever she wanted, so I didn't understand her sick side hustle, which had landed her on a Reaper's radar.

The gentle slide of my blade from its sheath put a smirk on my face, one of the few things in life to make my lips turn to the sky. The all-consuming exhilaration of knowing life and death was about to collide into a single line at my hands was an indescribable rush.

The demented ideas swirling in my head gave me a dose of warm exhilaration. The preparation for death and the lead into the act could be just as satisfying. Death had a way of providing me the comfort I didn't seek in others.

People made me uncomfortable. They easily irritated me. They didn't hesitate to diagnose me while dishing out the perfect remedy that would *fix* me. However, it was their eagerness to interact that I preyed on, giving them a little of what they wanted so that I could acquire what I needed.

Tonight I needed to get into this apartment, and here I was, walking through my target's front door like I was on the lease agreement.

There she was, lying half-covered, her brown skin glowing even in the dark moonlit room. Her face, one I'd memorized, crinkled as her internal awareness let her know that something was amiss.

A monster lurked a swipe away from slitting her throat wide open. A lone vein poked at the delicate skin of her neck, teasing me, forcing me to swallow the lump that formed in my throat.

"Kill her now."

"Kill her slowly."

"Make her bleed."

The sick demon in my head kept shouting demands I'd been fighting to ignore for the past thirty minutes. He was so loud in my head that now my temples throbbed.

The idea of how it would feel to see the blood rushing from that severed vein while she gasped for air and fought the undeniable truth called death gave me a warm and fuzzy sensation. The elation of the kill was like a shot of the most expensive high-end drug injected straight into my veins.

She would suffocate on her own blood, claw at her throat, pray, curse, and beg. The sweet torture of seeing it unfold made me inch closer.

"Kill her now!"

"Hurry!"

My eyelids dropped and remained closed in an attempt to temper the taunting words in my head.

"No, please."

"Please don't go."

That wasn't my demon's voice. My eyes popped open at the rustling of sheets, of her turning. Sheens of sweat glistened against the specks of moonlight that highlighted her face in her new position. She faced me now, eyes shut tight, body clenched in stress.

I backed off, easing into the easy comfort of a dark corner.

"Daddy, please."

"Don't die. Don't leave me."

The agony in her tone and the horror scraping along every syllable of her words gave me a chill, something that had never happened before. I was usually the one who made others shiver with just a glance.

She jumped up in a rush, reaching in my direction.

"Daddy!"

She screamed and gasped so hard, the rattle in her chest sounded. Her hand remained lifted in my direction even when she opened her eyes, her chest rising and falling hard with each long breath.

After two minutes of her staring at the wall straight ahead of her, she reached behind her and pulled away a pillow, dropping it to the floor beside her bed.

She slid from the bed onto the floor. With a small portion of her head touching the pillow, she balled into the fetal position.

"The bitch is about as crazy as you are," my demon pointed out. His voice was one I'd taken prescription drugs for, had talked to head doctors about, and subjected myself to medieval shock therapy to get rid of, but nothing worked.

By most people's understanding, hearing voices labeled you crazy. Since I was functional in all the ways that mattered, I wasn't sure about my official label.

This was unexpected. The death of her father was noted in her records. He'd died when she was sixteen in an unsolved homicide. The way she just called out for him made me believe she saw him die. Her records clearly stated that he was alone, his car riddled with bullets, eleven of which were plucked from his body.

Had she seen her father die?

Was there more research to be done? A month in or not, this kill order kept taking unexpected turns. Twists that kept my instincts on high alert. My Reaper brothers assumed I enjoyed the sweet torture of making myself wait, but this time I didn't have the same burning ache that drove me close to the edge, drove me to the point of making the kill that much sweeter.

"Fuck research. Kill the bitch and be done with this shit. I need to see blood. Lots of it."

She dealt with rich sharks in her everyday life, which probably made her tougher than the average woman. Based on her willingness to walk into dangerous neighborhoods unprotected and interact with anyone and everyone she encountered, I concluded that she wasn't easily scared. Her upbringing of having a kingpin for a father also gave her an edge that made her tougher despite the entitled life she now led.

A prolonged torture was a more suitable fit for this one. Two days? No. Maybe four. She would probably last about five days in a torture scenario. Knife play. Bloodletting. Nails. Tips of fingers.

"Take away her sight, her sound, and fuck her pussy with your blade. She had a dream, so what? Kill her. The order was sound. Kill the bitch now so that we can move on."

The voice could be a comforting companion sometimes, but right now, I wanted silence to think in peace. Death intrigued me, but it excited him. Every time I reaped someone, I learned something new about death.

What would my new target's death teach me? What knowledge would Jade McKenna give me that I didn't already know? She turned, releasing a low groan. I'd spied on her enough over the past weeks to know she didn't sleep well, probably the demons of her own creation hunting her.

My demon had a point. The kill order was sound. I freed my blade, my hands shaking with anticipation.

I ached to experience the feel of ripping into her perfectly toasted skin, painting it red, and decorating it with deep slashes. The more beautiful a canvas, the more I wanted to paint it, to destroy it, to turn it into a proper representation of death.

My hand inched across the darkness, the blade catching a stray strain of light and gleaming across the prone silhouette of her body. It took a while, but I found the perfect beams of light that allowed me to see the tip of the blade. It sat less than an inch from that beautiful vein thumping against her skin, beckoning me closer. Pleading for my attention. The knife sat centimeters from her throat now.

"Please. No," she whispered. The action caused her neck to move in such a way that the tip of the blade nearly nicked it.

While remaining in my low crouching position, I stepped across her balled-up form and eased into a prone position beside her. I lay there next to her, assessing, contemplating, and thinking for a beat before I decided to slide half under her bed and a few feet away from where she slept restlessly.

"Please. Please. Please," she panted low and desperately.

The low ocean sounds playing from some electronic device on her bedside table edged into my focus. The constant ticktock of the large clock on the wall she slept facing joined the sounds of the seagulls and crashing waves.

When she shifted this time, she flipped, facing me. I froze, expecting a scream, but her warm quick breaths breezed over my face. I slid farther under her bed with my knife tightly gripped in my hand. The tight space didn't allow for much movement, my chest scraping the metal frame with every easy breath I took.

I'd witnessed her go through this dream sequence many times before, but this was the first time sound had accompanied her actions. The knowledge that it was her father's death haunting her gave me something else to think about with this target.

The decision to kill her should have been an easy one. Indecision was a rarity for me. It had never taken such a strong grip on me like this.

"What the fuck is wrong with you? Will you kill this fucking woman already? This back-and-forth shit is not you."

I already had doubts about this kill order, and now her nocturnal musings were pouring more questions into my brain. My eyes began to droop while observing her fight demons in her sleep.

If she woke up and saw me, I'd have no choice but to kill her. It was a plausible plan since my instincts had me questioning my duties for the first time. I allowed sleep to consume me, taking advantage of the gift as sleep was as elusive to me as it was to my target.

CHAPTER THREE

Jade

New York.

I hated everything a person was supposed to love about charity events. Therefore, I pretended my way through them. A humble attitude on my part and the promise of public praise convinced the rich to give up their money for a worthy cause. The monetary donations made them feel better about themselves versus the charitable causes their donations supported.

Tonight, over two hundred had come out to show off their expensive attire and brag about their latest accomplishments. I stroked their egos every chance I got, my way of earning the ten-thousand-dollar-a-head cover charge they paid to get into my event.

I ran a hand through my freshly pressed, black, lengthy hair that many assumed was a weave since my skin tone was darker than a brown paper bag. Doing a once over, I skimmed a hand down one side of my satin, royal blue, one-shoulder dress. The skirt flared and swept the floor and was in direct contrast to the flirty slit that kissed my thigh and flashed a teasing glimpse when I walked. The material played a cute game of peek-a-boo with my toned leg and gold gladiator stilettos.

The money for this event would stock the warehouses of the five food banks I'd worked tirelessly over the past four months to establish. We'd created an app that allowed individuals in need to select the food and personal items they needed, and it would be delivered to their address. For individuals who didn't have access to the app, word-of-mouth sent them in person to one of our data centers, where their information was collected for the services.

There was no such thing as a refund in this business, but it didn't stop me from bowing my head in silent prayer, requesting that this event turn out to be one of the most successful to date.

The hundreds of applicants counting on this service were set to receive weekly deliveries as early as a few weeks from now. Therefore, the cause was well worth the frayed nerve endings I would undoubtedly suffer tonight. I planned to kiss ass with gusto and hand out compliments like they were freshly minted one-hundred-dollar bills.

When I made the decision to jump down this rabbit hole seven years ago, I was wet behind the ears and only twenty-two years old. Since then, I've picked up many tactics that allowed me to suck up donations like a car wash vacuum.

I never believed my first small event to get school supplies and computer equipment for my old high school would lead me to spearheading multi-million-dollar humanitarian projects that garnered local and statewide notoriety. Two of my current projects that raised money for scholarships and homeless relief had even gone nationwide.

My first smile of the night surfaced at my assistant, Jana Dupree, escorting my uncle in my direction.

He believed he was being a gentleman by taking her by the arm, but I knew my assistant well enough to know that she was the one leading him where she wanted him to go and introducing him to the select people we had on our list to impress with his presence since he was a senator.

His face lit up at the sight of me. His wide smile and perfect white teeth matched the gleam of joy in his eyes. I opened my arms and walked right into his warm embrace. He squeezed hard and gave me a little shake that made me release a squeal of delight.

"Senator Jaxson McKenna," I addressed him teasingly. He preferred me calling him uncle, no matter the type of setting. "I mean, Uncle Jaxson," I corrected to see his famous gap-toothed smile. For a man in his mid-fifties, he could put most thirty-year-olds to shame with the tall, lean stature he maintained with a proper diet and exercise.

I eyed him up and down like I didn't already know how impeccably he always dressed and groomed himself. As a public figure, his suit game was top-notch, and his grooming schedule was followed religiously.

"You are looking as handsome as ever. Don't make me have to beat these women off you in this place. I might be in this expensive dress, but the Harlem streets are in my blood," I said, making him chuckle.

Although my uncle managed his life well enough to master the politicking game and become a senator, my father had chosen to master a different type of game: the dope game. Unfortunately, the streets had claimed his life when I was sixteen.

My uncle Jaxson had taken me in with open arms, although Loretta, his nosey wife at the time, didn't get along with me. She was the one who convinced my uncle to send me away to boarding school. And as much as I hated to admit it, it was one of the best things that could have happened to me. The top-tier school enticed me to lay down the street mentality that had been instilled in me and embrace the other talents and capabilities I was unaware I possessed.

"I see eyes on you," my uncle stated, glancing in the direction of said eyes. "We'll chat later. I know you have to put some work in with this crowd. He bent his elbow to Jana after giving my shoulder an affectionate pat. "I'm so proud of you," he muttered with emotion flashing in the depths of his wise gaze.

"Thank you," I mouthed before Jana got them moving again.

A deep inhale, a concealed eye-roll, and I turned in the direction in which I sensed the most intense staring.

"Mr. and Mrs. Williamson, good evening." I greeted them, offering a smile I knew could melt a heart in two seconds. "You two are blessing my vision with grace and class tonight." I placed a tender hand over my heart. "Your presence humbles me."

If the couple's smile grew any bigger, the whole room would end up blinded by the gleams bouncing off their bleached teeth. They both edged up to me, the wife invading my personal space, as they lifted their flutes of sparkling champagne.

"Ms. McKenna, you warm my heart," the woman returned. The excitement in her tone while speaking had me fighting to keep the wattage of my smile at the right voltage.

"Always a pleasure to see you. You're such a lovely young lady," the mister expressed with glee.

I was used to most crowds addressing me as *young lady* or *kiddo*. It meant they didn't know my first name or hadn't taken enough time to read my bio, which was blasted all over the internet along with my demographics. However, the way they addressed me didn't matter as long as it was respectful and would eventually lead me to get into their pockets for some donation money.

"I can't tell you how proud I am that you've attended three of my events this year. I feel honored and blessed," I continued.

I was laying it on thick, but with true narcissists, there were never enough compliments, and I was stocked with enough to start my own dictionary of statements to make people like this smile.

Durwin, the husband, had put his trust fund to good use, building a chain of profitable vegan restaurants and prepackaged meal plans that made him and his wife, Barbara, multimillionaires.

Many of the couples in attendance weren't nice to me because I was their gracious host. Many didn't attend my events because they were particularly good people who cared about helping the less fortunate. Most attended because I possessed a specific key that opened the doors of enlightenment to their egos and popularity status.

Once a year, I named a humanitarian of the year. The televised event would be received nationwide because the state governor and the senator, my uncle, were keynote speakers and presenters of the accomplishment. It was one of the ways I kept the rich on a leash, so to speak, and lure them with the prospect of vast repute. Most of the people I rubbed elbows with possessed more money than they could spend in one lifetime, so I didn't have an ounce of guilt for finding clever ways to make them give up some cash for a worthy cause.

"Ms. McKenna, you look simply ravishing," Mrs. Williamson voiced a late compliment."

"Thank you. This old thing," I said, releasing a fake laugh that matched the woman's. We dragged the pleasantries out, talking about our attire, and the tone of the conversation made me shut my ears off somewhere around Mrs. Williamson's updates on her winter wardrobe.

She harped on and on like a swarm of gnats about the activities they *claimed* to do with the ten-year-old twin boys they had adopted a few years ago. Rumor had it the nannies were raising their children.

"You do such an amazing job with these events," Mrs. Williamson complimented. I wasn't aware when she'd switched subjects which spoke to how well I'd managed to tune out her words.

"Thank you. I…"

"Excuse me, Ms. McKenna. I'm so sorry to disturb you, but I have a situation that needs your immediate attention," Jana interrupted, cutting me off.

She was bubbling with enough excitement to nearly pop herself right out of the little black dress she wore. Her interruption undoubtedly drew the attention of the couple.

"Pardon me for a moment," I smiled, excusing myself before I turned to face Jana. I took care to remain within earshot of the Williamsons.

Jana and I leaned into each other like we were whispering a well-kept secret before I jerked my head back, eyes wide and sparkling. I belted out a gleeful squeak.

"Are you sure? He's pledging an additional fifty thousand dollars?"

My assistant gave the same bubbling performance as I did. I'm sure sensing the couple's eyes on us and aware of them eavesdropping.

"We must make a formal announcement tonight. We can't let that kind of generosity go unnoticed."

"I agree. Oh, and WNTZ is here," Jana pointed out. "I'll work him into our short program and write an announcement speech to make sure he shines like the star he is."

"Thanks so much for letting me know," I told her, giving her shoulders an affectionate squeeze before she walked away.

When I returned my attention to the Williamsons, the hunger in their eyes almost made me laugh.

An hour and fifteen minutes later, it was the Williamsons on stage beside me, pledging a hundred-thousand dollars versus the fifty thousand from the fake rich donor Jana had made up.

Many assumed I lived off the millions I collected in the name of helping the needy, but that wasn't true. I was the daughter of a man who was once street royalty. My father may not have gone the legit route in life, but he'd been smart enough to stash away enough money on behalf of my brother, my sister, and me to ensure we never had to work a day in our lives.

Although I lived with my uncle after my father's death, my brother was eighteen at the time. He chose to follow in our father's footsteps to become the next king-pin. And my sister, well, she was still missing.

Despite staying under my uncle's roof until I became an adult, it was my father's drug money that paid for my schooling. It eventually paid for the first non-profit I created and the few businesses in which I invested. I continued to double down on my investments until the ten million dollars my father left in my trust fund was washed clean.

By the time I was twenty-seven, I was as wealthy as the people who attended my charity events. I'd made myself the owner or silent partner in over thirty businesses throughout the boroughs and surrounding areas.

"Oops!" I sputtered, unable to keep some of my drink from spilling over the top of the glass as I careened into someone. Thankfully, it hadn't spilled on the man's suit.

"I'm so sorry. I wasn't watching where I was going," I apologized, steadying myself, the glass, and the bubbly liquid threatening to leap over the top.

"It's okay," he said, already stepping away from me. His shoulder-length hair hid his face, but there was an alluring warmth emanating from him that had me wanting to chase after him to see his face.

His skin, the little peek I got of his neck and chin, was pale but not ghostly, more like a warm porcelain color.

His scent was as mysterious as he was, not allowing me to piece together a specific flavor.

Strangely intriguing, the encounter had me standing and staring long after he was swallowed by the crowd. I couldn't see him, but I sensed his magnetizing aura.

I've rubbed elbows with many people, but the vibe he'd passed along to me wasn't like anything I'd ever experienced. His was uniquely unexplainable and left a lingering pull that kept tugging at me like the air around me was kissed by his spirit.

"You okay?" Jana sneaked up on me. Her face was pinched in concern. I didn't know how long I'd been standing there thinking about the seconds-long encounter I'd just had with the man.

"I'm fine. Is everything in place to start shutting this event down?"

"Yes. The crew is on standby until the last of the guests leave."

Now that the night's events were over, all I wanted was to rescue my feet from my heels and have a *real* drink. I never drank at any of the events I coordinated. I merely nursed different drinks throughout the night to enable me to spice up egos with a clear head.

After a final chat with my assistant, I ensured the ballroom inside the Jardine Plaza Hotel, one I was a contributing partner in, was being cleaned and shut down properly before I headed to the bar.

No one was the wiser or had any reason to suspect that I maintained a small apartment inside the building. It was one of the studio apartments on the top floor. I slept here when I was too exhausted to make the hour-long drive outside the city to my house.

"Hello, Ms. McKenna. What can I get you?" the bartender, Ramsey, asked.

"Surprise me. Give me something that lets me know I've done a good job and deserve to be rewarded."

His big smile made me give up one in return.

"I have the perfect thing," he said. "I'll be right back."

I breathed in deeply and exhaled, grateful for another successful turnout, but more so, I was glad it was over.

CHAPTER FOUR

Severe

Studying a target was both frustrating and exhilarating at the same time. The task sometimes required a set of unique skills I possessed but hated using. The necessary evil of becoming another person for the sake of the mission made every part of my brain ache. At times, it even made my stomach queasy, knowing I'd have to interact with people in a civil manner.

Mr. Sylas was my alter ego, the civilized one who painted over my exposed tattoos and appeared normal enough for people to talk to me and even trust me. One of the reasons for my shoulder-length hair was to maintain some vanity that allowed people to deem me *approachable*.

Although I'd ditched the suit, I still felt restricted by the mere act of pretending to be normal. Everything within me, namely my demon host, screamed that I was a unique personality that couldn't be acted away no matter how often I practiced normal people's behaviors.

My target was currently at the bar having a drink. Although it was difficult for me to admit it, I found her interesting. My demon's urge to kill her remained, but that was to be expected of him.

Although I'd had to kill a few women who possessed reputations as vicious as any man, this one, based on her everyday interactions, didn't give off any duplicitousness. She didn't match the portfolio that necessitated her kill order.

The Six were the faithful leaders of our organization. They managed our contracts and training so meticulously that it was rare for a contract to be overturned. They refused to accept anything that would cause a Reaper like me to cast doubt on who we were set to reap. However, there were warning bells going off in my head about this one.

Although Jade's portfolio was a book of graphic secrets and horrific crimes, I continued to possess a need to hold back. This order had created an insurmountable amount of uncertainty that rendered me incapable of reaching my execution delivery point.

In layman's terms, this case wasn't giving me a hard-on. Unless I found a way to connect this woman to why she was slated to be eliminated, I would have to return the contract so another Reaper could execute the order.

My cousins had introduced me to the multilayer organization that eventually gave my life structure and purpose. Many didn't know how deep down the rabbit hole our *Reaper* title went.

In order to become a member of the Hell Reapers Motorcycle Club, locally known as the Carolina Reapers, you had to go through an initiation process as a prospect and prove your loyalty to the MC by completing your first reaping. The first reaping was the prerequisite that led you deeper to the shadow organization that funded the Reapers and six other branches that made up the Order, or more accurately, a secret society of assassins.

My target's movement dragged me away from memory lane and put my thoughts back on the path on which I'd set myself.

Why her?

While studying her over the past month, I'd found myself asking the question *too* often. In me, most people saw a killer, a sociopath, or a scary motorcycle club member. I was a combination of those things and more, but I was also thorough.

In Jade, I didn't see a money launderer for the drug organization her brother ran after her father's death. I didn't see a child trafficking seductress of which the Six had provided adequate proof. The crimes she'd committed on paper checked all the necessary boxes, and she qualified for one of my most vicious reapings. But *something* wasn't adding up.

Jadis "Jade" McKenna was the daughter of the notorious crime boss, Jace "Trigger" McKenna, who died in a fatal shootout about fourteen years ago. Jade's brother, Jace Jr., had taken over the family business, which her father had done his best to shelter Jade and her sister Jasmine from. Naturally, Jade remained close to her brother despite him being the head of the Ruthless Disciples.

The question remained. Do I carry out this hit, or do I stall it until I am satisfied with the authenticity of her crimes?

"You or I won't enjoy the kill with this doubt in your head. Fucking get your shit together already. If I take

over, I'm killing everyone *in this fucking building,"* my demon spat, making my head ache.

"Dammit," I hissed. How much more time was I willing to spend on Jade before my or my demon's patience ran out?

Now, she sat at a bar alone, sipping a drink, no doubt celebrating her victory over the rich pricks she'd convinced to give her ungodly amounts of monetary donations. Tonight, I saw firsthand how she'd become the *it* woman where raising money for worthy causes was concerned.

How could she do so much for the poor and unfortunate and turn around and piss all over the goodness she created?

Were her philanthropic exploits genuine like my gut kept convincing me they were, or was my gut wrong, and her actions were a cover-up for the dirty deeds she orchestrated for reasons I didn't understand? Reasons I haven't borne witness to in all the time I'd been studying her?

She was a very wealthy woman, so money wasn't her motivator. It was only a matter of time before her secrets were revealed. As of today, I had two weeks to take her out until the Six nullified my contract and re-assigned it.

There were no extensions if you exhausted the forty-five days you were allowed to carry out the order unless *they* found or were presented justification. No contract had been overturned since I'd been a member. The Six were meticulous about the contracts they vetted and issued.

After lurking for fifteen minutes and seeing her nurse her drink at the bar while fingering the keys of her phone, likely working, I walked up and took the stool two down from hers. The place wasn't packed but had enough people scattered around to allow me to sit close to her while blending in with the crowd.

I sensed her glancing my way while she sipped and allowed one hand to type over the surface of her phone at an impressively rapid pace.

"Can I have what she's having?" I asked the bartender when he walked up with a friendly smile, reflecting the one I'd plastered onto my face. My question drew her attention, and I acknowledged her with a quick glance.

"It looks interesting," I said, nodding toward her drink.

"You won't be disappointed," the bartender added quickly. "A *Violent Death* coming right up," he announced before stepping away. Fitting name.

She lifted her drink in my direction, the gleam in her eyes telling me it wasn't her first.

"It's tasty but watch it because it will sneak up on you," she warned.

I gave a quick nod, ensuring she didn't see too much of my face and hoping she didn't have a nose for scents, like me. I possessed the ability to sniff out almost anyone I'd met before by scent alone. Since I'd slept so close to her a few nights ago, I'm sure my scent had found its way into her memory whether she knew it or not.

A sharp ache in my head made my left temple throb.

"Are you going to kill this bitch or not? If not, sit this one out and let me do it."

CHAPTER FIVE

Jade

The second celebratory drink was a little too much based on the way I wobbled on noodled legs when I stood up from the stool. The stranger, who'd never shown me a full view of his face, offered a strong hand, steadying me. He didn't let go until he was sure I was steady on my feet.

"Thank you. I believe I've overindulged," I said, not drunk but tipsy enough to lean on the stranger more than necessary. His body was solid, strong, and addictively enticing in a way that made me want to touch him…everywhere.

Straining my eyes and my neck wasn't enough to get me a good view of his face. His shoulder-length hair, though it smelled good and was impressively healthy looking, got in the damn way.

Was he purposely hiding his face? We hadn't exchanged any more words aside from him confirming that the drink was good after the bartender had brought it to him. I'd greedily taken down my second while he nursed his first. He'd been more interested in what was on his phone while he sipped the drink than where he was or who was checking him out.

However, I'd been aware of him the whole time. He released me and turned to the approaching bartender. He placed some bills down and pointed at my empty glasses to indicate he was paying for my drinks. The bartender picked up the bills before a wide smile broke out on his face. The stranger turned back to me.

"Good evening," he said, his tone soft and kind of refreshing. When he walked away, it was the second time tonight I'd wanted to go after a guy. I stood there for a few moments, wondering what could have been. I was old-fashioned when it came to dating and wouldn't have minded him being more engaging.

"Oh well. Que Sera, Sera." Whatever will be, will be. The lyrics from the old Alfred Hitchcock movie were totally fitting to match my bad luck with men lately.

The last man-child I'd dated was a thirty-five-year-old starving musician who was stupid enough to let my assistant catch him telling his friends he'd hit the jackpot. His plan was to find a way to get me to finance his band's interests as well as use my platform to promote them. It goes without saying I never saw him again after we *talked*.

I wasn't even thirty yet and already had men attempting to make me their sugar momma. I stepped away, regretting that I'd have to go to my car to retrieve my computer. Most people in my condition would have enjoyed the cheap thrill the liquor was bestowing, but I was a true workaholic who wasn't willing to let any spare opportunity get away.

***

It took me ten minutes to run up to my apartment and retrieve my car keys. Half the time was spent searching for the keys after setting them down to go to the bathroom.

The buzz from earlier was now a dull hum to my rapidly recovering bloodstream. I was already primed and ready to work.

When the elevator doors closed me inside, the air became suffocatingly tight in the small space. An eerie vibe made my skin prickle while the elevator lowered me to the fourth-floor parking structure. The beep signaling each floor grew louder the lower I dropped. I glanced down at the keys in my hand.

"Better safer than sorry," I muttered, positioning the key fob so that I could at least poke out an eye. Although I'd gotten rid of my heels, I hadn't changed my dress and had to grip a fist full of the material to keep from tripping over it.

The garage wasn't pitch dark, but the lighting wasn't the best either. I made a mental note to bring it up at the next board meeting since I was a partner of this hotel.

When the doors slid apart, I peeked my head out first before taking a quick glance in each direction. I'm sure I was the only person crazy enough to be up after midnight, contemplating working.

I stepped off the elevator and relaxed when a crisp breeze tickled my skin. My steps echoed off the concrete floor, my slippers scraping across the rough surface.

My car was straight ahead, parked at the far end of the garage. The click of a car door opening and then slamming shut drew my attention to the right.

At the halfway point, I picked up my pace, although I didn't detect the sound of footsteps. I didn't notice how fast I was walking until I slammed face-first into a solid chest. The man had stepped out in front of me so fast I barely caught a glimpse of him before I smashed into the wall of his body.

"I'm so sorry," the words rushed out before I backed away from the man in black.

The gleam bouncing off a speck of moonlight caught my eyes before the shiny barrow of his silver-plated gun found its way into my view.

Cautiously, I lifted my hands like that would deter this dark figure from taking my life. My eyes bounced between the shadow of the man's face and the gun now aimed steadily at my head.

"God, let it happen fast," I prayed furiously, the words echoing inside my head. *"I hope I've done enough in this world to earn your grace and mercy."*

"Aren't you going to beg me not to kill you or something? Are you not afraid?" the man asked.

"I'm very afraid," I told him, my voice shaking. "I don't want to die, but the scariest and most tragic thing to ever happen to me has already happened."

My heart hammered, my chest rising and falling fast to keep up with the loud thumps beating against my eardrum and thrumming through me.

"You're a beautiful woman. Nice smooth skin. Real tits. Lashes. Hair." He looked me up and down before he shook his head and pursed his lips. "It pains me to separate you from this world."

The metallic click of his gun when he cocked it sounded like a bomb going off. It would be the last sound I would hear before I died. The scent of his citrusy-spicy cologne, the faint sound of traffic in the distance, and the fading scent of car exhaust trapped inside this garage would be my last living experiences.

The man's eyes left me and lifted up and over my shoulder. Although I didn't hear any footsteps, I sensed someone behind me. Sudden death stood in front of me while an uncertain danger approached me from the back.

Someone was creeping up behind me, but the distraction could also save my life. I leaned in the direction I wanted to sling myself as the man in front of me rushed forward.

"Not so fast," he whispered harshly, spinning me so that my back was pinned against his chest. One of the fluffy slippers I'd traded my heels for slid a few feet away, leaving the pad of my foot to scrape against the scratchy concrete finish.

"Let me go!" I shouted, struggling to break free of the tight grip he kept around my neck. My self-defense training wasn't working. The more I squirmed and twisted, the stronger his grip grew until it was so tight I heaved, struggling for air. The cold hard press of steel to the side of my face made me freeze.

"That's it. Be cool. I'll make this quick and painless. And..."

He left the statement open, freezing at the shadow approaching us while I was choking on my heart since it pumped like the pistons of a revving engine.

"Why are you doing this? You don't have to kill me?"

"Sorry, beautiful," he whispered before placing a kiss on my cheek. "Your little mind games are not going to work on me."

What the hell is he talking about?

"Is that one of your goons coming to fail at rescuing you?" he asked.

The metal pressed deeper into the side of my temple the closer the shadow came to us. Whoever this was, he moved like a phantom, like he possessed the ability to float across the floor. Unlike the man holding me at gunpoint, this one didn't allow any part of his face to be seen.

All I could do at this point was fight and hope for the best. I stomped on the foot of the man at my back, but the impact my bare foot made atop his boot was useless. Another hard snatch from him, and I was back in his deathly grip. The cold metal reclaimed its position, pressing hard into the side of my head.

Eyes clamped shut, I braced for the impact of the bullet when it slammed into my skull. A loud hiss sounded before the bullet exited the chamber and whispered a deathly lullaby into my ear.

Blessedly, I'd been spared the pain. I feared the unknown aspects of what awaited me beyond death. Like I told him, the scariest thing to ever happen to me had happened already. I ran the reminder through my head repeatedly while I lingered on the precipice of my impending death. What part of my brain had the bullet damaged to dull the pain I expected? Was I still standing?

A dose of reality crept back into my system. It dawned on me to open my eyes. Was the shot fired meant for the shadow man who'd been approaching and not me? My eyes sprang open wider, but the image of what I believed was a man was no longer in sight.

Where had he or it gone? Maybe I'd finally allowed my mind to wander too far off the deep end and was hallucinating this whole scene.

The hard breaths of the man holding the gun to my head were my reality check. A hard yank back was followed up by a shoulder grab before I was spun away from the death trap in which I'd been pinned. I staggered away on shaky legs and glanced back in time to see the shadow man fighting with the one who'd had me in his grip.

Fists pounded flesh, hard punches echoed off the ceiling, and muffled grunts sounded while two human shadows went toe to toe. How had the other man approached the one holding me without being shot? How had he snatched me away without either of us being shot?

Was the shadow man on my side, or were they fighting to see who got to kill me?

With them both shrouded in darkness, I couldn't tell who had the upper hand, only that they were struggling to get the gun. The one who'd captured me before snatched the gun up and aimed directly at my head.

Me?

He still wanted to kill me. All I saw was the muzzle flash, and in the millisecond I had left to live, my life flashed before my eyes. My father's death, my abduction, never seeing my sister again, my brother taking over the streets, living with my uncle, and finally finding a purpose for my life.

The impact of a hard body knocked the wind out of me before I was spun in the opposite direction of where I was standing.

What was...hap...pen...ing?

The idea evaporated, and I gasped from the hard shove that sent me flying in the direction of a thick concrete beam. Blessedly, I had the presence of mind to lift my hands and stop myself from slamming face-first into it.

Chips of cement flew off the concrete a few feet away. There was no warning since the gun was fixed with a silencer. I dropped and scrambled behind the same column of concrete I'd avoided a collision with.

Footsteps echoed off the walls, growing closer. The one who just saved my life chased the other who was determined to kill me. My dark savior fired at the one still aiming to get me.

Was this really happening right now? Someone was trying to kill me.

My stalker finally dropped, leaving the other one standing over his body with his gun still aimed at his head.

Two quick muzzle flashes and the man's body jerked violently. Fear slid down my throat fast and hard, causing me to gulp and clamp my lips shut to keep a scream from flying free.

The silence that followed came alive like death himself had stepped into this garage with us. The man who'd had a gun to my head went still.

I cupped both hands over my mouth, and instead of running like I should have been, I was stuck staring and unable to move. The one who'd saved my life leaned over the dead man, his darkly silhouetted body stooping to get a better view of him.

"Is he dead?" I questioned, peeking from behind the column, my eyes wide and searching. "Did you kill him?"

The man didn't answer, and although he'd shielded me from a bullet with his own body, I was as afraid of him as I was of the one lying before him. Where had he come from? Why was he bent over the man and now searching him? Was he about to rob him?

Although I remained in a crouching position, I left the safety of the concrete pillar and inched closer to the scene.

Why was he taking a picture of where he'd shot the man? What did the tattoo on his chest represent?

A few cautious steps drew me closer. My neck stretched, and my eyes gleamed through the darkness to see what he was doing. This was a train wreck or a situation I couldn't avoid seeing.

"Are you a cop? If not, are you going to call them?" I questioned but received no answer. He continued to conduct a thorough examination of the dead man, lifting his shirt and taking more pictures. The dark pool of liquid circling his head told me where his fatal wound had landed.

The shadow man wasn't wearing a hoodie, but a black baseball cap was pulled so low over his eyes that he shouldn't have been able to see anything at all.

He lifted the cell phone he'd been snapping photos with to his ear. The sight eased some of my tension.

Thankfully, he was calling the cops. Still hopped up on adrenaline, I inched closer, taking easy, catlike steps.

"Yes. I'll send you the pictures. Three teeth, no eyes, no blade." The words didn't make any sense but were ominous enough to make me stop my approach. I believe he was referencing the man's skeleton tattoo, visible on his upper chest area. I got the impression that he wasn't on the phone with the police after all.

He hung up and shoved his phone into a pocket at the side of his leg before he stood. Compared to me with this one slipper on, he was tall like a skyscraper and lean, although being in all black in a dimly lit area could be warping my sense of his true size.

He stood unmoving and staring with no visible face. His predatory stance made me take some steps back. Had this man saved me, or had he taken out his competition?

As soon as my brain convinced me to run, he came stalking in my direction.

The tiny parts of his face I did see were a white blur that streaked through space to come after me. I blinked rapidly and squinted, preparing for an attack, a hit, or even a rough snatch, but none ever came. He simply stood towering over me, face in shadow, the bill of the cap aimed at my face.

"You're coming with me."

His voice, although low and way too calm for this situation, sent a chill up my spine.

"But–" I lifted my hand to point at the body. "We have to wait for the police. He tried to rob me. He was threatening to kill me with a gun to my head, and you shot him to help me. You saved me from being shot."

Standing in front of this man and talking to him was like standing in front of a dead guy in a casket. There was no life there like he didn't register on the life meter. Was that even possible, or was I in shock?

"He's dead, and you're not freaking out, not running for your life, or not attempting to claw my eyes out. Instead, you're standing here calmly having a conversation with the man who killed him. How are you going to explain that to the cops, especially when it's all been caught on camera?"

I'd been betting on the cops reviewing the video. But he had a point. I wouldn't appear to be a victim to whoever reviewed this footage. If anything, it may appear that I'd set the dead guy up to be killed.

"I can't just leave the scene of a crime. This man had bad intentions, and he's lost his life."

A few rays of light bounced off the shiny chrome finish from the gradual rise of his gun. He didn't point it at me but simply kept it at an angle to allow me to see it.

I choked down a gasp, and the fear I'd managed to set aside came back with a vengeance.

"Let's go. Now," he said in a tone so low and authoritative it felt like it had initiated inside my own head.

I knew not to challenge him. He hadn't put the gun away, but he didn't turn to walk away either. And as soon as he did, I took off in the opposite direction, my bare feet slapping the concrete when I lost my second slipper.

"Aww!" I yelled when he appeared in front of me like some dark Marvel villain. He'd run me down in seconds and turned in front of me like a fast-moving car cutting off my highway to freedom.

The sight of the gun put a dead silence in the air, stilling me.

"I am darkness. The unseen danger that gives you a chill. The icy prick that makes your skin crawl for no reason you can see. The hell that invades your dreams and gives you nightmares. Do you want to find out what happens when I get upset?"

His words were the bullets he'd used to load his gun. The barrel of the cold metal touched my forehead, and my internal prayers blasted off like the vocals of the Mississippi Mass Choir.

"Come, or I can leave you lying here with him. It's your choice."

He turned and walked away, not even worried about me taking off again. Reluctance gnawed at my bones while I took shaky steps to follow this harbinger of death.

"What do you want with me? Why can't we wait for the cops? I don't understand."

My rescuer may not have rescued me at all. Had I traded one nightmare for another? This situation made me think of one of my favorite movies, the Terminator, when Sara Conner was so afraid of Reese, who turned out to be her savior and one of the best things to happen to her.

I prayed this was one of those times because there was no doubt this man had saved my life when the one he'd killed was a millisecond away from taking it. Despite what this man had done for me, I continued to glance back at the area cast in darkness, where we were stepping away from a dead body.

When the surveillance footage was finally accessed, I prayed the officers reviewing the footage were smart enough to see that I wasn't being given much of a choice of staying behind to give my statement. Hopefully, being forced to leave my slippers and apartment key near a crime scene was another hint in my favor.

Every instinct I possessed was telling me to run, while a little nagging voice in my head kept reminding me that even though he'd held his gun on me, he'd first saved my life.

CHAPTER SIX

Severe

This was a turn I didn't expect to take and one I should have never made, but believed I was right. My goal tonight was to end this once and for all, but like the times before, something deep within tugged at my instincts and prevented me from pulling the trigger.

"What the fuck is wrong with you? Why the fuck didn't you kill her?"

"Shut up and let me think," I muttered.

We were on the sidewalk now, and people passing by intentionally put distance between themselves and me the moment they saw me talking to myself. I sensed her behind me, hesitant and contemplating running.

"You got between her and a fucking bullet. What the fuck were you thinking? Is there someone else in here making decisions that I don't know about?"

"Shut up. You're not even *something,* much less *someone.* Shut the hell up already," I muttered through gritted teeth, causing the next man I walked past to speed up.

This contract had gone sideways real quickly. Instead of taking out my target, I rescued her from what I first believed was a simple mugging until I saw the telltale signs of a mercenary. The way he moved and fought suggested he'd had extensive training. However, my hackles went up when I noticed him with eyes on *my* target.

The decision was made without me even realizing it when I saved her from certain death. This would have been the most satisfying reaping yet, but damn, that wasn't the case now.

A sinister smile crept across my face while marching her toward my bike. I was breaking some major rules of the Order. It wasn't the first time, and it wouldn't be the last. I needed to find out who the person in the garage was, who he worked for, and why he was a third wheel in my assignment.

I approached my black Ducati while Jade marched soundlessly about ten feet behind me in a shadowy alcove. Her fight or flight instinct was on high alert, but she hadn't run yet, nor had she approached anyone on the streets for help.

"Why?" she asked, her tone shaky. "What do you want with me?"

"We can do this the easy way or the hard way," I replied, replacing my cap with my helmet. She stood about six feet away, considering her options.

"You don't need me. If you need to leave, I understand. I'll talk to the authorities. I grew up on the streets of Harlem and understand street code better than most. The most important one is that we don't rat. You took a risk saving me, so now I can repay the favor. Considering I haven't seen your face and I don't know who you are, I couldn't rat you out either way."

She had a point, but leaving her meant that others might come to take out what was mine to take, not theirs.

"We can do this the hard way or the easy way," I repeated.

"But."

She glanced down at herself.

"I'm wearing a dress," she pointed out, trying to buy time.

When she figured out I didn't care about what she was wearing, she gathered the dress in her fist and took a few choppy steps closer.

"Are you going to kill me?" she asked, fidgeting and looking around. The idea of running or screaming or even fighting me was playing out in her head and reflected in her erratic movements.

"You would already be dead, and I'm sure you know that. Don't make me repeat myself. I don't like doing that," I told her.

A few more hesitant steps brought her closer. By now, the security footage should have already been deleted after a copy of it was sent to a Reaper-owned secure server.

She was close enough now that I was able to turn and grab her, but I didn't. She had guts. I'd give her that much. Most women in her situation would be running, screaming their heads off, and calling all sorts of unwanted attention. Her attitude in this situation must be a reflection of her upbringing.

I reached out and took her arm. She didn't wiggle and squirm as I expected but allowed me to take a firmer grip to assist her onto the back of my bike. I enjoyed the fighters over the timid ones. Although she wasn't putting up a fight at the moment, she was definitely a fighter, even more so than I originally anticipated.

This was set to be a glorious death. I sensed it like the marrow stirring in my bones. Now, all I needed to do was figure out why a possible member of the Order was cutting into my contract when there were two weeks remaining. I wasn't the only one breaking cardinal rules that were punishable by death.

***

Jade

The chill in me was growing colder by the second. It was seventy-eight degrees, and I was shivering while sitting smashed against and gripping the torso of a cold-blooded killer. My cheek lay pressed against the skeletal face of the large grim reaper patch sewn into the black leather of the vest he put on before climbing onto his motorcycle. He'd gripped me by one arm and used sheer strength to sling my hundred and fifty-pound body across the back.

His baseball cap had been traded for the helmet, so I hadn't seen anything but a small glimpse of the bottom half of his face.

We took off so abruptly I had no choice but to cling tightly to him. I tensed around him, my fist gripping his black leather vest. My legs were pressed snugly against him. The wind whipped against my face, making my eyes water and leaving only his body to protect me from the elements.

The heavy dose of awareness that weighed me down didn't stop me from noticing the strong lines of muscles cording his legs and flexing against his black cargo pants to caress my inner thighs.

This man took wearing black to a whole new level. Hands gloved, arms covered, face always obscured, black boots and pants. The little glimpse of flesh I did spot was all that let me know he was Caucasian, his skin pale.

City lights and the head and taillights from other motorists blurred, making it impossible to pinpoint exactly where we were now. All I knew was that we'd left Manhattan and were heading toward Brooklyn.

The speed at which we traveled added to the multiple levels of anxiety racing through me. Had I been rescued? Was I being taken from the frying pan and thrown into the fire? There were too many questions and no answers.

This dark avenger hadn't harmed me physically, but he had threatened me with a gun. He'd also saved me from someone I believed would have killed me with no remorse. Therefore, my logical reasoning kept swaying back and forth where it concerned my safety.

He was obviously a criminal or mercenary based on the way he fought with that guy in the garage. They both used a high level of martial arts and handled their silenced weapons with advanced combat training.

The most intriguing thing about them was their unusual ability to use the dark like it was another article of clothing. The more I thought about it, the more I'd say mercenary over criminal, although in most cases, they were one and the same.

My mental musing only led to more questions. Why would a mercenary want to kill me? Why would this one risk injury or death to save me?

This guy's demeanor was sharp. It was cold and calculating, and I sensed he had intimate knowledge of this situation before it occurred. Was the inevitable my death? Was it being postponed so he could take me someplace else to finish the job?

Did he have beef with the man he'd killed, and I happened to get in the middle of it? My teeth sank into my bottom lip. It was the most logical conclusion since there was no reason I should have been targeted by mercenaries in the first place.

What if this was an attempt to ransom money from my brother or to blackmail my uncle, both powerful men on opposite ends of the spectrum where right and wrong were concerned?

My brain was on overdrive and had allowed me to easily forget that I was snuggled up with a death dealer. There was no longer any doubt that this man was the bringer of the end.

For now, I was alive, which meant I'd have to do everything in my power to stay that way, even if it meant cozying up to a living nightmare who wasn't showing his hand, literally and figuratively.

The salty taste in the air, combined with the sulfur scent, suggested that we were getting closer to water.

When moonlit waves shimmered across my view and the masts of distant boats took shape against the night sky, there was no doubt we were at the Brooklyn Marina.

Once we stopped and the bike was parked in a designated spot, Mr. Shadow man hopped off. He gripped the underside of my right arm to help me off. Thanks to the darkness, I was saved from flashing him a quick glimpse of my thin panties when I tossed my legs over the bike.

Reluctantly, I followed him while contemplating if I should take off or believe that there was an ounce of goodness hidden deep within him.

I believed my best bet at surviving this was not to do anything to upset him until I found a way to free myself. My goal was to escape without catching a bullet.

I picked up the hem of my dress and padded along the wide wooden deck. My savior-captor never glanced back one time. Like he was sure I would follow him.

No one, not even a nosey neighbor, was out stirring. Aside from the dark waves of the ocean, an odd calmness blanketed the area like it was presenting the quiet before a vicious storm.

Taking inventory of my captor from behind, he was tall, lean, and fit, not someone I was stupid enough to fight with my limited self-defense skills. With his gloves off, I finally saw more skin. Portions of his hands were covered in tattoos, leading me to believe the rest of him sported more ink. He'd managed to switch out the helmet for his baseball cap and created another failed attempt of me getting a glimpse of his face.

Darkness clung to him like a moving cloak. I possessed the ability to read a room filled with all types of rich men and women, but with him, my brain picked up radio silence.

He was an illustrious trick of the mind. He wasn't someone you sensed like others. He registered on my visual cues but not my sense of knowing like he'd found a way to hide what we as humans should naturally sense. *Weird.*

He kept the same long-legged stride, and although he hadn't glanced back, I believed he had an eye on me the whole time. The idea of running or yelling for help had me snapping my neck around in every direction, searching and praying for the right path that would give me the best chance of escaping.

"Running would be a mistake. You wouldn't get far."

His smooth voice didn't match his dark demeanor. When he finally did glance back, I wasn't sure if it was a smirk or a frown on his face. It mingled within the darkness of the night, a blur of pale white under the brim of his cap. He had me glancing around myself for the same shadows that surrounded him.

He proceeded to our destination. His steps remained soundless while my bare feet made clunky slaps against the hard deck.

He finally turned into the last spot in the darkest corner of the marina. The name 'Reaper5' was spelled out in big white letters against the wide blue body of the large boat. Was this his boat? Was 'Reaper' his name? If so, it fit his dark personality.

I stared so hard at my surroundings that I tripped over a catch on the boardwalk. I was too overwhelmed with questions and my impending status to worry about the sharp ache that shot through my foot like an explosion of bullets had gone off.

Was I his prisoner? If his intention were to kill me, he'd have done it in the garage, as he'd already pointed out.

He sprang the door to the boat's cabin open and waited. The sight of him sent a shiver through me, and my shoulder cracked at the involuntary jerk I failed to suppress.

I stepped past him, being careful not to touch him. When I stepped across the door's threshold, I couldn't help thinking, *Am I going to survive this?*

Although I wasn't sure what to expect, my assessing eyes took in a tidy, neat, and well-kept interior. Were bikers and mercenaries hiring housekeepers these days, or did this one have obsessive-compulsive disorder?

The boat was no older than ten years, maybe, and the setup and even the built-in furnishings were factory standard. Not cheap or expensive, but presentable. Neat, glossed wood finishes with a comfortable-looking leather couch as the centerpiece of the small living room area. The ocean-blue walls gave the room a dark vibe, yet splashes of white and cream from the paintings and lampshades saved it from being too dark.

If not for his shadow, I wouldn't have known he'd walked in after me. I spun away from checking out the place to face him. His tall, hawking frame sparked intimidation, but I did my best not to let it show. He glanced down, and I sensed his eyes piercing me, although I couldn't see past the darkness surrounding his face.

"Give me any problems, and I'll enjoy dismembering your body, tossing it into the water, and seeing the fish rip your flesh into tiny pieces."

Yikes.

A hard swallow made my throat bob. The hard clap from the door slamming shut may as well have been the slap of chains around my wrist and ankles. I was locked inside a floating prison with a killer intent on keeping me at the edge of my fear. I had no disillusions that he'd make good on his words and gut me like a fish if I decided to act up.

He pointed a stiff finger at the couch and walked away, leaving me frozen in place. His shadow and his soundless steps made me bend at the waist and strain my neck to see him before he disappeared down a dark hall-way. Was he not worried about me making a run for it and getting away? Was he testing me?

I turned, staring at the front door, but was too afraid to even reach for it. Running would give him the reason he needed to finally kill me. I walked over to and eased down on the couch, never taking my eyes off the front door.

His shadow breaching my sense of awareness was what jolted me awake and alerted me to his silent ap-proach. I stiffened at the sight of him, stunned and unable to determine how I'd managed to doze off. How had I found enough peace in this situation to drift off?

Sleeping around someone like this guy wasn't a good idea. However, and in my defense, I'd only gotten a few hours of sleep in the last day and a half due to my final preparations for the event.

He stepped into the small kitchenette, but I couldn't see the inside fully to know what he was doing. I recalled the memories of my current situation and how I'd arrive here. Why hadn't I gone up to my room, showered, and climbed into my bed?

"Here," he said, making me jump. What was this guy, a magician? How could I not have seen him approach?

He'd shoved a flimsy white paper plate in my face with the most disturbing-looking peanut butter and jelly sandwich on it I'd ever seen in my life. I chanced a glance up and into his face, curious despite my anxiety.

I caught his defined, clean-shaven jawline, a set of deep pink, flirty lips, and a shadow of his nose. His eyes were lost in total darkness. He knew I wanted to see his face, and I believed he enjoyed that I couldn't see it.

I finally reached up and took the sandwich and the bottle of water from him.

"Thank you," I said, being polite in an effort to broker peace between us. I hadn't eaten at the event, or all day for that matter, and although I was hungry earlier, tonight's events had sucked my appetite into the dark abyss of terror into which I'd been snatched. His offering meant he wanted me alive, but for how long?

"I need to wash my hands," I said, reaching in front of me to set my sandwich and water atop the glass coffee table. I may have been stuck between a rock and a hard spot, but it didn't mean I was abandoning the good manners my father and uncle had taught me.

He didn't reply vocally but pointed at the same dark hall he'd disappeared into earlier. I sensed his eyes on me when I stood and walked in the direction he'd pointed out.

I pushed the door open, stepped into the dim, moonlit room, and scrambled around until I flipped on the lights. A queen-sized bed draped with a pale blue comforter and four fat, fluffy white pillows sat against a lux blue shade of the paint on the walls. Small bedside tables with lamps atop them sat on either side of the bed, and a dresser that matched the gold trimming of the headboard sat along the passage to the bathroom.

Once in the bathroom, I slid the door closed and took a moment, glancing at my reflection in the mirror. What was left of my usually flawless makeup looked like I'd applied it in the dark. My pupils had disappeared and blended into my dark brown eyes. It looked like I'd morphed into some wild creature who's energy matched that of the one in which I was currently stuck with.

My full lips were dry and cracked like I'd held a blow dryer to them for an hour. My dress was eligible to be entered into the most-wrinkled contest and was beyond being salvaged by even the best dry cleaner.

I turned on the water and waited until it was steaming hot before pulling a towel from the small standing rack and soap from the mirrored cabinet. I scrubbed my face, arms, and neck areas free of the dust and light sheen of sweat coating it.

Once the towel was rinsed clean, I applied more soap before sitting on the closed toilet to clean my dirty feet. A long hot bath would have been better, but coming up with a plan to prolong my life was more important. I needed to think.

When I stepped back into the living room, he was sitting on the opposite end of the couch I'd vacated. I sensed his eyes following me, making my uneasiness around him return with biting force. It also made me indecisive about sitting on the same piece of furniture as him.

Reluctantly, I took the seat, reminding myself that I'd already faced my worse fear and survived it. I would make it through this situation as well.

His black attire highlighted his light skin tone, and it bothered me that I hadn't gotten a good look at his face yet. I picked up and sat the thin plate over my lap and prepared to eat my sandwich since my stomach had decided to come back to life.

I ate under the vigilant eyes of the devil, and it hadn't occurred to me until I was halfway through with the sandwich that he could have handed me poison and was waiting to bear witness to my horrific demise. Inadvertently, I glanced straight into the abyss of where his eyes should have been.

"It's not poisoned. Besides, poison is too easy. It's not messy enough."

My hard swallow followed his words. What the hell was that supposed to mean? He sounded like evil reincarnate and read me like he was in my head. Did the man with no face have a soul?

I took another bite of the sandwich to distract myself from his all-consuming presence. At first, it was like he wasn't even in the room, but now that he'd spoken, the sound alone sucked the room of all of its air.

Was he going to sit there and ogle me like I was the prey he was intrigued by?

"I'm Jade. What's your name?" I asked. My words tumbled across my lips, surprising me with how calm they sounded. However, they received what I believe was an arched brow.

After a long silence, I shrugged my shoulders. It was safe to assume he wasn't going to answer my question. I took another bite of the sandwich, glancing down at the plate sitting in my lap for something to do.

"Severe," he said before he removed his cap and tossed it on the coffee table. Was *Severe* his name, or was he telling me there would be severe trouble if I made another escape attempt?

He leaned back and rested his head on the back of the couch, closing his eyes. There was no way he didn't sense me staring at him. I'd forgotten all about the sandwich because the man's face was that of a sculptor's dream.

His light complexion complimented his strong angular features, and without the cap, the light glowed against his ivory skin. There were tattoos at his hairline, but I was unable to make out what they were unless I chanced getting closer. Although I hadn't gotten a look at his eyes, he was definitely hiding a face that would get a lot of attention.

Why the hell was I sitting here admiring the face of a man who'd killed without an ounce of remorse and had taken me as his prisoner so I wouldn't report the murder? This was another of my scenarios for what my current situation may be, and the notion put a damper on my internal compliments of his features.

I was afraid to ask the questions eating a hole through my brain because I was too afraid of his answers.

When can I go home?

Are you going to kill me?

Were we spending the night right here on the couch? He hadn't even bothered to take off his boots, although his motorcycle club vest was gone, leaving him in a long-sleeved black shirt and black cargo pants. I didn't see the gleam of his pistol I caught a glimpse of earlier, holstered and resting under his arm, but I was sure it was there.

Lord, if you hear me, please don't let this man find a reason to kill me. Please let us find a way that we both can at least go our separate ways.

CHAPTER SEVEN

Severe

The nuts and bolts holding my sanity together had been greased and loosened. This wasn't the first time I'd questioned a reaping, but it was the first time I was stalling one to satisfy the roaring sense in the back of my mind that something wasn't right.

I was fully aware of the terrified woman next to me while resting my head against the back of the couch to think. I needed to apply reasoning to my actions to understand better why I'd created this situation for myself.

Instincts. A sixth sense. Whatever you choose to call *it, it* was what made me take her and not indulge in the one thing that would have given me satisfaction. The kill was my drug of choice, my food. It fueled my need to live. It gave me purpose. I obsessed about it like an addict dreamed of their next hit. Yet, my next fix sat next to me, and something wouldn't let me take the hit.

I *was* the monster many labeled me. But I don't believe I'd ever reaped anyone who didn't deserve it. My brain wouldn't allow me to believe this woman deserved it despite the write-up on her. It wouldn't allow me to believe she was that harsh. It was as if the evidence presented against her belonged to someone else.

My eyes opened to a view of the ceiling, and the sound of deep breathing told me she'd fallen back asleep. The top half of her body was in a deep lean, with her head resting against the arm of the leather couch. She'd found a way to tuck her legs into her dress, despite the blanket sitting at our backs.

I squinted, staring at her sleeping form. She was relatively calm for someone who'd witnessed a murder, been kidnapped, and repeatedly threatened with death. Her calm in my presence was a feat that not many outside my MC or my order could pull off.

I made people nervous. I scared people. I was the living representation of the thing that haunted their dreams, and I liked it.

The first thing I needed to do was find out more about the crimes this woman was accused of because her background was too clean to fit any of them.

***

Jade

I turned to get comfortable and almost spilled over onto the floor. I caught myself, my hand gripping the edge of the couch. My fear of falling off the couch ceased to exist when I glanced down, focused, and noticed I'd nearly fallen on top of him. *Severe?*

He was lying down there on the floor between the couch and coffee table, with no cover and not even a throw pillow under his head. A thin blanket spread across the floor was all that separated him from the hard wood. He looked dead, eyes closed, face aimed at the ceiling.

"Planning on staring at me all morning?"

I stifled a gasp at his sudden words. He hadn't even moved, not even a flinch.

"No," I finally answered before backing into the couch and noticing through the window that the sun was aiming for a higher climb.

I live to see another day.

I released a long exhale and lay there staring at the ceiling, waiting for him to move. Waiting for something to happen. What though?

Why was he sleeping down there on the floor? Was that his way of keeping me from running? I lifted back up, letting the warmth of the sun streaming through the small window wash over my face.

"Aww!" I yelled, jumping back hard enough for my back to smack into the couch.

Hard and fast blinks and my hand covering my chest were all that kept me grounded. He didn't react to my loud yelling. He sat on the coffee table staring. The black cap was back.

How had he gotten off the floor, put on his cap, and sat on the coffee table, all without me noticing or hearing it? The man was a living ghost, so silent I'd forgotten he was in the room.

"You're staring again," he pointed out.

How could I not when he was clearly doing magic tricks? At least that chilly edge to my senses from last night wasn't as strong. I did believe that he wanted me afraid of him, but he'd shown me that, at least for now, he wasn't going to kill me since he'd had all night to do it.

I tossed my legs over the side of the couch so I was face to face with him now, our knees almost touching. He had no face most of the time but was no longer as intimidating since I'd gotten a glimpse at what he kept hidden.

"Why am I here? The cops are processing or have processed that scene from last night. I'm sure they've found my slippers, room, and car keys next to the body. They will start looking for me, and they'll find out that I didn't kill that guy or have anything to do with his murder?"

He aimed a finger in the direction of the coffee table to the left of him. I glanced down at the area where he pointed.

"How?" was all I managed to say while my wide, unblinking gaze was on my keys and slippers.

He shrugged.

"You're connected? You know people? Your motorcycle club brothers?" I questioned. Everything about this man and this situation created questions upon questions, and I wasn't getting any answers.

I wasn't as green as he likely assumed. I made sure I at least knew a little about a lot and knew enough to know that some motorcycle clubs were well-connected outlaws that lived by their own rules.

"You saved me, and your friends probably cleaned up that murder scene, so why am I here with you? What am I missing? Are you going to let me go?"

"Not right now." His voice barely registered before he stood and walked in the direction of the kitchen.

I chewed into my bottom lip, wanting to scream at him for being so damn stubborn and non-responsive.

"I didn't grow up under the umbrella of privilege like you may think. Street code 101. So, last night I went to my room after attending a charity function I sponsored and slept in late. Last night in the garage never happened."

He clapped three hard times, and I swore I heard the sarcasm in the sound.

"Good for you," he called from the kitchen.

"What's the point in keeping me around? We can go our separate ways and never have to see each other again."

My eyes were glued to his boot-clad feet, and I was struggling to figure out how he'd learned to walk with such a strong stride without making a sound.

"Thank you," I told him, taking the awful-looking PB&J sandwich and the bottle of water he handed me. *At least he's not going to let you starve*, I told myself.

I ate the sandwich with gusto, guzzling water the whole time, not realizing how ferocious my hunger had grown overnight. Severe sat on the other end of the couch, glancing in my direction like I was the savage one.

"So let me get this straight in my head. You saved me from a situation that could have ended my life. You live outside the law, and your club has more than likely already covered up what happened. You're keeping me with you until you're comfortable that I won't rat you out? And what happens if you never get that warm and fuzzy? Are you going to give me the ax even though you helped me? It makes no sense. You could have left me to die if that's the case."

I didn't see his expression with that cap pulled so low, but the way the cap lifted a little on his head suggested his brow raised while assessing me and considering my words.

"That's it. That's all I can get from you? Silence. I hate to sound ungrateful, but I didn't ask for your help in the first place. Now, you're punishing me because you decided to stick your nose in my business."

Nothing.

"Aren't you going to say something?" I said in an elevated tone. I considered myself a person with excellent self-restraint and patience, but this guy was ticking me the hell off. I aimed a stiff finger at him.

"Maybe I've got it all wrong, and this has nothing to do with me. Some of you motorcycle clubs believe in living by the gun and dying by the gun. I'm starting to think that I wasn't even supposed to be in this equation. You and that guy were probably already engaged in a battle, and me going to my car at the wrong time gave him a chance to add more drama to the situation."

I leaned over to glimpse into the darkness masking his face. I was throwing out scenarios, hoping he'd react to one in a way that gave me a clue that would explain why I was with him right now.

"Is that what it is? If so, I grew up with a drug-dealing father who taught me about the streets before I was speaking complete sentences. I've seen dead bodies. I knew that he murdered people. I saw him get murdered," I said, choking on the sentence, the only one to get his attention.

He glanced in my direction. I assumed he'd show some sympathy or at least confirm one of my assumptions about why I was with him.

"Do whatever you need to do mentally, but you will stay with me *until*."

"Until what?" I asked, although I didn't want to know the answer.

"Until I give you the most gruesome death this city has ever seen or until I let you go. I'm still deciding."

I swallowed the mountain-sized lump in my throat. The statement, plus the sinister intent emanating from him, shut me up, maybe indefinitely. He was weighing his options for my life, and if he let me go, would that truly be the end?

He'd murdered someone, saving me in the process, but I didn't know what kind of chaos he and that man had brewing between them. Logically, I wasn't safe away from this guy or with him. He could pretend to let me go just so that he could later sneak up on me and snuff me out.

There was also another idea that I didn't want to manifest in my head, yet it roared loud and clear. Both these men could have been attempting to collect on a bounty put out on me and were willing to kill each other to collect the reward.

"There are some female clothes and shoes in the bedroom. Get dressed. We need to take a trip," he ordered.

I wanted to mouth off at him, but considering my dilemma and his deadly threat, I decided to walk into the kitchen, toss my empty water bottle and paper plate into the trash, and head to the bedroom.

Once inside the bedroom, I found women's clothes in the drawers and closet. Coincidentally, most of them were my size.

I was still unsure if *Severe* was his name, but it was what he was getting assigned. The women's clothing came to mind. I didn't believe he was the type to bring random women back to his house. He looked more like a fuck-them-once-without-knowing-their-name type of guy.

There was no way I was wearing another woman's underwear, so I decided to wash mine in the sink and use the hair dryer I found to dry them. I used the hair products that lined the side of the counter, which were surprisingly made for black hair, and slicked my hair into a neat ponytail.

The purple and black bonnet I spotted under the sink let me know that a black woman had been on this boat and based on the number of products and clothes left behind, it wasn't for a random sleepover. Did Mr. Judge, jury, and executioner out there have a thing for sisters?

Hmmm. I didn't see it, but it may well be the only reason he was contemplating my fate. While he thought it through, I took a quick shower before jumping into a pair of stylish jeans, a fitted T-shirt, and some comfortable slip-on sneakers.

Stepping back into the living room, I stopped short at the sight of him on the couch. His shoulders were back, head aimed straight ahead, fingers pinched to the ceiling, and eyes closed. His black hat sat on the table.

Meditation?

Nothing about this man made sense. I meditated often. The notion of getting lost in nothing always helped me relax and find my center. I walked over to the couch and joined him when he didn't acknowledge me.

When I opened my eyes, Severe was standing at the front door. He hadn't made a sound when he moved, so I didn't know how long he'd been waiting, but I did take note that my short meditation session was the first time he'd given me an ounce of any sort of respect.

A meditating, killer-biker-mercenary?

There were weirder things in the world, I attempted to convince myself.

The sun peeked from thick patches of dark clouds as rain posed a threat it may never deliver. My gaze made another pass over the Marina, disappointed that there wasn't anyone within range that could help if I ran. I swallowed the idea because I wasn't altogether certain if he would shoot an innocent if I dragged someone else into our drama.

"Where did you say we are heading again?" I asked, hoping for more than two or three words at a time.

"I didn't," he said.

"Aww!" I yelled in my head, wishing I could shake him.

He walked with his head aimed straight ahead at an easy, long-legged stride like he didn't have a care in the world.

When we approached the bike, he tossed his long legs over and readied it for our unknown trip. Once the bike was straight up between his legs, he reached out a hand to me to pull me aboard.

Although he'd performed a similar action last night, the sun helped me get a better look at his hands. A tattoo spilled from beneath the black, long sleeve shirt he wore. The black ink branched out all over his hand, some even spilling into his palm.

When I finally stopped staring and stretched my hand over his, I froze for a second time, and so did he before he initiated the pull. When he tightened his grip around my hand, the aches of sensation pulsing through my hand and marching up my arm intensified.

His touch chilled me down to the bones while heating my skin enough to make me sweat. Our connection was flaming ice, gripping and unnerving enough to make me forget the extent of my situation. The chill of the impact continued to tingle up my arm and ache in my palm when he pulled harder for me to hop over the seat.

The tight fit of both of us in the seat left me pressed snugly against his back. What was up with this uneasy sensation consuming me while observing him seated between my legs?

There was none of this craziness last night. Was I attracted to this man whose face I'd seen once? Whose eyes I still desperately wanted to see. The same man who'd threatened to kill me multiple times and wouldn't explain why he wasn't allowing me to leave his sight?

"No," I mouthed silently, telling my inner slut to calm down. My inner slut was a card-carrying member of the Club of Whorish Intentions. She loved the bad boys and often partook in short exploits, happily content with not going further than a weekend max.

I reached under his arms while he stood to start the bike, and I froze at the sight before me. His comment about the dead man's skeleton having three teeth and no blade slammed into my brain at the sight of the reaper on his back. I was sitting eyeball to eyeball with the thing that had a full set of teeth and not one but two bloody daggers through the skull.

It had to have been some kind of code, which meant that he did know the guy he'd killed last night. The bike shot off like a rocket, and two things happened fast: I gasped and deadbolted my arms around his strong torso.

In a matter of seconds, I did my best to distract myself from the way being this close to this man made me fidgety. I didn't want to feel anything, but my body and mind were on opposite plans when it concerned this scary, weird, and hard-to-read man.

I was responding in ways I was ashamed of while fighting to remain grounded enough to stay on an even playing field. The tug of war between mind and body was why I'd meditated in the first place.

In the case of this man, I was determined to keep either from making a decision for the other. Staying on neutral ground in this situation may be the way I survived it.

A quick peek around one of his sturdy shoulders every once in a while allowed me to see that we were driving down Pike's Boulevard.

After what must have been an hour, watery eyes, and my body still on a mission to slut me out, we turned into an RV park. The crooked and chapped wooden sign presenting the faded words, Yellow Pines RV Park, was one hard gust of wind away from falling to the ground. The lonely road leading into the park had a thin line of trees on each side, along with congested and overgrown weeds.

The space opened to dozens of RV's, some old, some new, some on four flats and parked indefinitely. We weaved our way through the winding path, much like traveling through a maze, before we stopped at the end-row RV in a line of five in the back. A thick patch of forest loomed behind the mobile homes, allowing the sound of insect calls to blend in with the sound of the energetic flow of the interstate behind it in the distance.

Severe traded his helmet for his cap without casting a glance in my direction. He didn't offer up his hand to help me down this time but kept the bike steady so it wouldn't tip over when I climbed off.

I hopped off the bike and followed my new keeper to the front door. The RV was new enough to have a glossy shine on the black and gold exterior. It was large with expandable sides. The well-kept surroundings and neat appearance outside suggested a proud owner.

The interior door was open, but a glass storm door allowed you a look through for a view of the inside. Severe delivered three solid knocks on the door and waited.

I jumped as a monster sprang into the doorway, barking and growling loud enough to vibrate my insides. Part of my scream escaped before I clamped both hands over my mouth.

A Rottweiler, the size of an adult tiger, answered the door. He stood on the other side of the glass with his teeth bared, but he wasn't looking at Severe. Those vicious eyes were pinned on me. I considered myself a dog person, but seeing this beast made me question myself.

"Satan, go to your room!" an authoritative female voice called out before a series of hacking coughs sounded and grew louder at her approach. The dog took off, and the owner, a woman who looked like death's sister, appeared at the door.

I couldn't tell if it was drugs or some kind of sickness that had a deadly hold on her. And like the dog, she wasn't looking at the man standing in front of her. Her gaze was glued to me. The prolonged stare had me ready to inch closer to the demon in which I was familiar. Despite the uncomfortable tension racing through me, I stood my ground, keeping my gaze pinned on hers.

She swung the door open, and I followed Severe up the three narrow steps. The RV tipped slightly when we climbed aboard. Once inside, the woman headed for her couch. I stood at the door, silenced by the huge rebel flag hanging above the couch on which she was seated.

I'd been to all manner of slums, hoods, and ghettos because that's where the money I raised was most needed. However, being inside this racist woman's house stirred up my anger and a touch of sadness. And not knowing where Satan had gone also had my nerves going haywire.

"You can have a seat. If you're with my nephew and haven't been dismembered yet, you must be much tougher than you look and have one hell of a story."

Her one run-on sentence had given me more information about the man I was with than he had given me within the day that I'd known him.

I sat on the loveseat next to Severe. He didn't bother making any introductions.

This was his aunt? Why were we at his aunt's house? More questions, no answers.

"Did you find out anything?" he asked her, pulling her wandering eyes away from me. Was she fascinated with me? The way her eyes probed and assessed suggested she'd never had a black person in her house.

One of the two laptops she'd picked up from the coffee table in front of us sat across her lap. While typing, she pulled a cigarette from the pack sitting next to the extra laptop.

She lit up, and the long drag she took from the cigarette breathed a burst of toxic energy into her system. Once she'd pulled up whatever she'd been searching for, she handed the computer over to Severe.

I leaned over, and he didn't turn the screen away. My attempt to decipher the text, as well as several pictures he was scanning, was useless. It was like observing him shuffle a deck of cards. I did catch a glimpse of some crime scene photos of the man he'd killed last night.

This wasn't my first time seeing the digitally captured aftermath of a gruesome crime. My father had the police in his pockets. He reluctantly allowed me to follow him like a shadow when I was growing up. Until this day, I wasn't sure if he wanted me to be a ruthless kingpin like him or if he was simply giving me the toughness I'd need to survive in the world in which I was raised. Whichever it was had impacted me in ways I'd been struggling to overcome with sporadic therapy sessions, meditation, and focusing my energy on helping the people who were once my father's prey.

Back then, I was obsessed with his wicked lessons because I wanted to be him. I was determined to become the fiercest Kingpin in the game. I'd even learned the locations of his trap houses, stash houses, and codes to the three safes of his that I knew about. Inside one, I'd run across crime scene photos multiple times. After experiencing death live and in living color, seeing it in photos didn't bother me like I knew they would the average ten-year-old.

When Severe stopped scrolling and focused his energy on the photo of the man's tattoo, I knew it was a clue to something big and maybe the reason he kept me.

I couldn't be upset at him for wanting to keep me close. If it were one of my father's enemies back in the day or one of my brother's enemies now, they would have killed me along with the guy in the garage.

Three teeth. No eyes. No metal. The tattoo was bare compared to the one on the back of Severe's jacket. Was it some sort of ranking system for him and his people? Was the guy in the garage a member of their motorcycle club, or was he an enemy of their crew?

I was tangled in this mess now, and unless he solved the mystery surrounding the dead guy and somehow became convinced that I was no threat to him or his club, my hope of getting back to my life anytime soon was slim to none. The quicker I accepted that cold hard truth, the better off I would be at thinking of a way to save myself.

He scrolled through some text, but I was unable to make out the words. At this point, I was leaning so far over to be nosey, I may as well have been sitting in the man's lap.

A glance revealed the darkly shrouded face of Severe, who ignored the fake smile I presented.

My gaze turned to the aunt next. The cherry on her cigarette was blazing as much as her eyes were burning a hole through me.

She squinted and kept bouncing her assessing glance between Severe and me like she was in the middle of solving a complex math problem. Both their eyes on me gave off more of a physical vibe than a mental one.

"I can't figure it out. How are you still alive?" The aunt blurted, unable to take the suspense anymore.

"I can't figure it out either. How are you still alive?" I questioned, putting my eyes on the cigarette in her hand and then the oxygen canister sitting next to her.

Her eyes widened, and her lips parted at my question before she glanced at Severe, to put me in my place, I supposed. So much for keeping my mouth shut. There was only so much I was willing to take before my mouth took over and my mind followed.

A look was exchanged between the aunt and Severe, and she lifted her non-smoking hand in surrender, giving up her investigative quest for why Severe hadn't killed me yet.

My gaze crept up to the big rebel flag that took up most of the space on the wall behind her head, and she noticed.

"It's a big blaring reminder of why I poisoned my husband and, ironically, one of the few things that keeps his asshole friends from suspecting me of his untimely demise."

I gulped. Had she just confessed to murdering her racist husband like it was no big deal? Yes, she most certainly did. I'd also seriously misjudged her. Maybe she wasn't a card-carrying member of her hate group of choice.

Severe handed her the laptop, breaking up her continuing assessment of me while I reeled over her confession. She took the laptop, her thin arm looking like it would snap with the weight of it before she sat it in her lap.

"See how far you can dig. Use CCTV to see if I was followed at any point last night or today," he told her.

The old murdering auntie was a computer geek. She nodded at Severe's request, but her curious gaze strayed back to me. I was apparently more interesting than her nephew asking her to cover up a murder. Severe stood and made his way to the front door. I followed.

We went through what was becoming a routine of climbing aboard the bike, except this time, we had an audience. The aunt and Satan stood behind the glass, gawking at us. Severe took my hand to assist me on the bike this time, and I fought like hell to keep from reacting to the unusual sensations that rushed through me.

The bike roared to a thunderous start after he climbed aboard. We jerked off, zipping through the narrow passage at a speed that made images swipe past my vision like I was looking through a view finder.

Where were we headed now?

CHAPTER EIGHT

Severe

Merlin, my mother's sister, was as mean as my mother was, just in a different way. Her husband's flag was all that was left of the racist bastard. It was once displayed in her window until her neighbors campaigned for the park owner to make her remove it.

She had married a nationalist who introduced her to the environment and put his foot in her ass every chance he got. When she had a spiritual awakening of sorts, brought on by her cancer diagnosis, she acknowledged his way of life was a joke. Killing him was her way out.

After liberating myself from her evil sister, Merlin attempted to connect with me, but I wasn't interested. However, when I found out about her knack with computers, I was the one who gave her pointers on how to put her husband down like the rabid dog he'd become.

When her husband's brother suspected her of his brother's disappearance, he beat her and put her in the hospital. Her dog had saved her life. Her brother-in-law showed up at the hospital later that night to finish the job, unaware that she'd called me to help her.

She stood by as I dismembered him, the same as she'd done while I dismembered her husband after she'd poisoned him and didn't know what to do with the body. Both brothers were buried around the perimeter of her RV, fertilizer for her small flower gardens.

She traded her tech skills for my help and the RV I purchased when the double-wide trailer she and her dearly departed were living in got repossessed. She'd inherited her skills from her father, who was once a famous hacker for the government. He died in prison while serving a double life sentence for selling national security secrets.

There wasn't any emotional connection between my aunt and me. Our relationship was purely transactional. I gave her money, and she was one of a few of my hidden secrets outside the Order with skills that were useful in my line of work.

She knew how demented her sister had been to me. Saw evidence of my abuse when she visited once a year and did nothing about it. She called herself my aunt, but she was nothing more to me than someone to use.

In the case of my suffering, most of it had occurred before I'd gotten a chance to unleash my demon on anyone. Suffering humbled you even when you were freed from it. I made a vow to only unleash my demon on the monsters who deserved it.

Jade tightened her grip around my waist, the action reminding me she was there. Having her pressed so tightly against me filled me with an uncomfortable tension that left me fighting hard to maintain my unflinching posture. Everything about her unsettled me. She had the ability to scrape along the edges of my senses and drag down my well-crafted mental walls.

"You like her. You like her. You like her," my demon taunted, singing the shit in my head.

"Shut up! You didn't pull the trigger when it was time either," was my nonverbal response.

"We're going to kill her violently. Therefore, making friends with the prey is not a good idea, not even for you," he reminded me, ignoring my comment.

The sick bastard went radio silent after leaving his comment about killing Jade echoing inside my skull. I released a long sigh due to the tugging in my core from her closeness.

There wasn't much in my adult life that moved me. *She* was inadvertently finding a way through the sludge of sick energy surrounding me to reach *me*.

Did she deserve my wrath? It was something I hadn't figured out yet. If I found out she did, then she would get what was coming to her. I was stuck with her until I got to the bottom of this situation. It was the only way to enjoy my kill.

My one source of relief in this world was being overshadowed by my burning need to find out who wanted her dead badly enough to interfere with my contract. The hitman's tattoo with three teeth marked him as a new recruit, fresh out of training. Each tooth represented a kill. Eyes represented five kills each. A dagger represented fifty kills. Other than my dead uncle, my cousins Eli, Micah, and Israel's father, I was the only Reaper with two daggers.

Our organization thrived on order and discipline. Integrity was its lifeblood despite its deadly objectives and tasks. How was it that someone, possibly an impostor, breached a contract that wasn't executed yet? Whoever it was may as well have spit in my face.

For the sake of the Order, the man from the garage needed to be an imposter out to make some extra cash. He wasn't from Kansas or Nevada, the only other locations with Reapers like us.

It wouldn't be the first nor the last time that money had motivated men to make stupid decisions. If it were a bonafide member of the Order that I killed in that garage, my crime for taking the life of a fellow Reaper would be punishable by death. However, considering he was operating under an illegal order, it made his death null and void by the Order's standards.

My questions were stacking up. Was the unshakable structure of the famous Order crumbling? Issuing illegal kill orders and instructing members to perform illegal actions didn't just happen overnight. I needed answers before my contract truly expired. Once my time ran out, I'd have no choice but to kill Jade or send her on her way to be taken out by another Reaper.

The hairs on the back of my neck stood up before a chill gripped me.

"Death." *My* demon roared to life.

A quick glance in each mirror didn't reveal anything amiss. However, I recognized the cold hand of death when it lurked nearby. I steered the bike with one hand and placed the other at my waist while my eyes searched for what threatened to creep up on us.

We could make a pit stop and lure them into the bowels of the hell they were asking to go to by disturbing my already splintering mission.

"Murder."

"Kill."

"Blood."

The screech of tires sounded before I saw the midnight black, darkly tinted G-wagon approach about a quarter mile back at my five o'clock. Jade must have sensed something because her arms clamped around me so tightly, they shook like she was back there bracing herself for war.

The sun reflected off the vehicle's dark windshield, blinding me to the imminent threat barreling down on us. I decelerated, allowing the dark vehicle to catch up to us. Jade's nails clawed into the front of my cut like a cornered cat. I suppose it was her nonverbal way of asking me what the hell I was doing.

As soon as I saw us reflected in the driver's side window and in the shiny glossed finish of the side of the G-wagon, I stomped on the breaks, causing the back of the bike to lift and slam back down with a loud belching screech along with Jade's long echoing scream.

The rear view showed a car breaking and coming up behind us at a rate of speed that would have crashed right into us if I hadn't already mapped our sharp right turn from its path.

Jumping lanes in front of a semi a few car paces from striking us was a calculated risk I was willing to take. The driver stomped the brakes like he was avoiding a stunned deer that decided it was a good idea to jump into the path of a speeding truck. The driver was still breaking by the time I pointed the screeching bike onto the exit.

"Where are you going? Kill them. Kill them all!" my demon yelled loud enough for me to clamp my lips shut to keep from shouting the words.

"Shut up. I don't even know how many there are yet," I muttered through gritted teeth.

I searched my surroundings, calculating different scenarios in my head and around my demon's insatiable hunger to kill. Despite it being a much more skilled killer than me, it didn't know how to stop or control its desire to see blood. *It* took shit way too far and had everyone thinking I was the devil's spawn.

"Stop calling me a fucking 'it.' I'm the best part of you, you fucking idiot!" he yelled, leaving his voice rattling inside my head.

At this point, Jade may as well have been another article of my clothing. She was wrapped around me so tightly that I was convinced she was doing her best to climb inside my body.

In my peripheral, I saw the G-wagon make an erratic right turn to get off on the exit I'd taken. The area I sped through now was an industrial area with a few businesses scattered here and there but mostly large car manufacturing warehouses.

The G-wagon crept up in the background, attempting to avoid alerting me to their presence. I drove at a leisurely pace until I spotted a building that was locked down for the weekend. We zoomed past the building, leading them, so I would know how far the ones inside the vehicle pursuing us wanted to take this.

"Death?"

"Yes," I answered my demon truthfully. This had the makings of *its* favorite pastime.

"Call me an 'it' one more fucking time," he warned. *"I'll kill everyone on this fucking block, including your new girlfriend back there, just for spite."*

For someone who was a sociopathic parasite, my demon sure was sensitive.

We made a quick left on the next street and another left onto the little alley that led to the back of the closed warehouse. At the second set of dumpsters, I stopped the bike and helped Jade off.

She was talking a mile a minute, her wild eyes searching the distance for the G-wagon I knew was coming. I pushed the bike from view along the side of the dumpster.

"You don't think they're coming, do you?"

The sight of me screwing the silencer on my Beretta M9A3 shut Jade up quickly.

"What are you doing? What have you gotten me into? We need to call the cops," she said, eyeballing my gun before lifting her gaze to meet mine.

She was just as bad as the monster in my head with all that talking. Now, she was back on the subject of cops. After the way she'd grown up with a kingpin father, you'd think her faith in the cops would have all but died, but her view let me know she'd been reprogrammed by society.

Not me. I was never inducted into what people considered normal societal functions. I mimicked their behavioral patterns when I needed them, which suggested there weren't many out there truly being themselves.

I noted that about five shots should disable the lock on the back door.

"They're coming. I hear them," Jade said, standing so close behind me that her warm breath was a brush stroke against the back of my neck.

"What if they want to talk?"

She almost made *me* laugh. It would have been a sarcastic one, but it was something I never did. I glanced back at her.

"Did I say one word to you last night when I pulled the trigger and killed a man?"

She didn't reply, catching my drift of who was coming and their intentions. I reached back and placed a firm hand against her stomach and eased her back to give me some room.

I leaned against the side of the dirty brick wall and, with a concentrated aim, fired off multiple rounds. At our angle to the door, the ricochet, if there were any, wouldn't come back our way.

"Four shots," my demon reprimanded me for getting the calculation wrong.

Once the box and strike plate that kept the lock in place came apart, I sent a swift kick into the area. The door swung inward with a hard wind-whistling sound. There was no use telling Jade to stay close as she had stepped on my bootheels twice already.

Her harsh breath revealed her level of anxiety. I shared a similar breathing pattern but for a different reason. A kill was one of the few times me and my demon could act as one, agree, and compromise until he'd go off on one of his tangents and take shit too far.

"This way," I called back to my new shadow. The faint sound of the G-wagon pulling up close to the front doors of the building found its way to me. I pulled in a deep inhale and released it gradually, allowing myself to go into kill mode.

***

Jade

My heart pumped so fast I was afraid it would alert the bad guys to our location. What kind of drama had this man pulled me into? Last night, you couldn't have convinced me I would be depending on him for my life.

For a split second, the notion hit that I may have actually been the target of him, the guy from the garage, or both of them. Now, I didn't know what to believe. I was getting pulled in so deeply, I was starting to believe I was stuck with the danger I knew and prayed he would find us a way out of this current disaster.

Instead of going deeper into the warehouse, we stood in a dead-end hallway near the front door. Severe placed me about five paces behind him. My shoulder kissed the wall while prayers were being fired off in my head like fireworks.

You've already survived the worst, I reminded myself. No matter how much danger I was currently in, I didn't believe anything else would come close to what I'd already lived through, or what I'd endured at fourteen and two years later at sixteen years old.

The low thump of footsteps alerted me to someone's approach. They wouldn't have expected us to be standing in the hallway, so they would likely walk right into Severe if they decided to pay a visit to this area that housed the offices.

The barrel of a big silver gun appeared first. The person wielding it used the wall for protection. The next thing I knew, Severe caught and snatched the man before he jabbed him in the throat. The quick, hard thrust stifled the man's ability to speak.

Severe twisted his gun arm fast, and at such an odd angle, it appeared the man was waving from behind his own neck. His gun clinked to the floor before I got the chance to even duck.

"Walt," one of the man's buddies called out. His voice sounded distant, like he was crouching low and searching.

Large red and angry marks marred the man's flesh when Severe adjusted his grip around the man's neck. He stared into the terror shrieked glint in the man's eyes while choking the life out of him. He tightened his grip, keeping the man still.

Severe's hand moved in a blur, and the next thing I saw was a knife embedded so deeply in the side of the man's head that the black handle was the only part visible. The man's body jerked in Severe's arms, and his legs gave while Severe bent with ease to lower him to the floor.

Both my hands were clamped over my wide-open mouth. Growing up, seeing the aftermath of death and dead bodies wasn't new to me, but I'd never seen someone die in real time while I was a spectator.

I peeked under my lids while Severe dragged the man farther down the hall like a lion dragging prey after the kill. He tossed the dead man aside like a bag of trash.

With a grip on the handle of his knife still sticking from the side of the dead man's head, Severe picked that moment to glance in my direction. Without dropping his gaze from mine, he jerked the knife free.

His face, in a rare moment where he lifted it, caught the light, and it set his skin aglow. The expression on his face shone with a spark of contentment. I believe this deadly situation was giving him some sort of satisfaction.

How the hell had I ended up *here*?

The echoes of rapidly approaching steps made him crouch lower. I folded my body in on itself while in my stooping position. My eyes kept going from Severe's back to the man, who, according to the blood pouring from his head, wasn't dead yet. It pooled around his shoulders, the gash at his temple gushing the thick liquid like a pressure valve inside his head had been released.

The next man came into the hall at a rapid rate of speed. Severe was unable to catch him in the same manner as he'd caught the first. However, he did manage to deliver a vicious chop to the top of his gun hand, knocking the silenced pistol to the floor. The gun clinked hard and skidded in my direction.

Although my father and brother took me to the gun range and taught me how to shoot, I often questioned if I would have the guts to pull the trigger if my life were ever on the line. It looked like today may be the day I found out.

"Walt," the man managed to call out when he spotted his dead friend. Severe sent a fist slamming into his face. The impact sounded like a brick landing on hardwood and cracking it. There was no way he hadn't shattered his jaw.

The man staggered but managed to keep fighting. Like the guy from the garage, he had advanced combat training. They traded kicks and punches to gain the upper hand. While they struggled for dominance, I remained low to avoid a stray bullet while crawling toward the discarded gun.

I swiped the gun up, made sure the safety was off, and repositioned to my spot on the wall as Severe and the man tumbled to the floor. Multiple sets of footsteps approached this time. Unfortunately, the struggle playing out before me didn't give me a clear shot at my low position. I aimed at the opening anyway.

The other two ran up, and I froze. Severe sliced through the neck of the man he had placed in a chokehold. He made the move so effortlessly that I wondered if his struggle with the man was staged to lure the others to his position.

The thick black knife had sunk so deep, the man's blood bubbled from his neck and splattered onto the floor like thick red sauce. The others' eyes widened at what was happening to their friend. Their faces transformed within seconds before they lifted their weapons.

A small red hole appeared on one of the men's foreheads before he staggered back, tripping over his own feet before he hit the floor with a hard thud. All movement ceased. The bullet had short-circuited every bodily function.

Severe tossed the same black knife he'd used to slice the man's throat open. The speed and precision it was thrown with caused it to land deep in the last man's throat.

He clawed at his neck, his expression one of terror, shock, and regret. The color drained from his skin like his soul had packed up and vacated his body before it hit the floor.

I took in the scene, my eyes wide and my lips parted. I couldn't move, and the gun sat limp in my hand. This level of death, involving trained assassins, wasn't something I believed I would ever encounter. It wasn't something any *normal* person was prepared to encounter.

Severe shoved the man he'd had twitching against his forearm away with a huff. His face was awash with a glow I believed was happiness. This was the type of scene he lived for. This was his livelihood.

Four men were gone within a matter of seconds. I'd never seen anything like this in my life. This scene would join the collection of horrors that invaded my dreams.

The empty eyes of the two in crumpled heaps near the hall entryway were aimed in my direction. Why couldn't I turn away from the carnage in front of me?

I let my legs slide out with my back propped against the wall. I was crouched so low that I'd slid to the floor somewhere between the two catching the same knife with vital parts of their bodies.

Severe checked each man, looking through their wallets and collecting their phones before dragging and tossing them into one pile.

"Stay here while I check for more," he told me while walking out. I rushed to my feet, unwilling to stay in this hallway-turned-tomb with four fresh dead bodies. Hopping and jumping over the splayed lifeless legs, I failed to avoid those dead eyes, gaping wounds, gunshot holes, and the chill of death that filled this space.

When I edged closer to the wall that turned into the warehouse, I peeked into the open space. The hairs on my neck were standing, and a creepy chill in the air made them prickle along my skin.

My knowledge about the spiritual realm was basic, but I believed that the spirits of those in this hallway were at my upper back, and I sure as hell wasn't waiting around to meet any of them.

I peeked around the wall once more and jumped back, bumping the wall when the front door flew open and released a loud screech. Severe walked in carrying a small, palm sized electronic device. I lifted the weapon in my hand, aiming it at him.

"What the hell have you gotten me into?"

He proceeded to walk right past me like there wasn't even a gun in my hands. I glanced down at the gun and back up at him. I lowered the weapon, knowing it was a foolish move to make after what I'd just witnessed. Besides, Severe appeared to have been born without the fear gene.

Since he was walking around like he didn't have a care in the world, I assumed he'd killed all the men from the G-wagon.

I stood in the doorway of the hall, observing him use the device with blinking red lights and emitting a low sound.

"What are you doing?" I asked, praying he would articulate more than a grunt or a one-word answer.

"I'm cloning their phones."

"Are these people your enemy?"

No answer. Not even a grunt.

"Are they my enemy too?"

If they were, the question now would be, why? Did it have anything to do with my father? My brother? Whatever the case, was it bad enough to warrant my death?

"What's going on? Why are they trying to kill *you*?"

He continued his task, sparing me a quick glance. Like with the man in the garage, he snapped photos like he was a crime scene expert.

"Hello," I said, louder than I intended. Careful not to attract further attention, I took cautious steps closer so my voice wouldn't carry so loudly.

"Please," the word came out as a whisper and got Severe to at least look at me.

"You have to tell me something. When will I be able to go home? By now, people will be looking for me."

"You are in this now until I figure out how to end it. Do you want to be alone when more like this group come storming into your house or into your place of employment?"

I shook my head absently, struck dumb by his suggestion.

"Are you saying that I'm on their radar now?"

"Yes. My people extracted the surveillance footage from the garage, but it wasn't destroyed until an hour after we departed, which gave others a small window of opportunity to observe what happened."

Words formed in my head and dissolved into earth-shattering mist before I pushed them over my tongue. Gun limp and hanging heavy in my right hand, I used the left to squeeze and massage my throbbing temples.

I was stuck in a nightmare I wasn't sure I would wake up from. Bodies were dropping around me like rain from clouds. If I returned to my life with this type of heat hanging over my head, the possibility of encountering more men like them was guaranteed.

I couldn't risk my staff, my friends, or my family by going home. There must be a way to rectify this, but without knowing all the puzzle pieces, I couldn't figure out what I needed to do to end this.

"What about the cops? They can put me in protective custody?"

Severe aimed a finger at the men. "They own the cops."

"What am I supposed to do? I have a life and people depending on me."

"They can either wait, or you can let them be dragged into this because of your impatience."

I clamped my lips shut. Was I being unreasonable to want to find a quick resolution to a problem I'd stumbled into by happenstance? Was I stuck with this killing machine of a man?

If I walked away from him right now, there was a chance I might die. If I stayed with him, there was a chance I might die. What was I supposed to do? Did I have enough resources to protect myself? These men were mercenaries with one objective. *Kill.*

Once he had the phones cloned, Severe stood and walked past me, not even casting a glance at the massacre he was leaving behind. I was unable to stop myself from taking in a scene that could very well be the entryway into hell.

I had to speed-walk to keep up with Severe. My face creased when he walked past his motorcycle and headed for the G-wagon. I hadn't noticed the keys in his hand and didn't have the strength left to ask any more questions. I simply walked to the other side, opened the door, and climbed inside.

Severe backed the vehicle out of the alley, driving it as recklessly as he did his bike. I wanted to ask him about leaving his bike, the dead men, and even where we were headed, but I didn't want to hear his not-really-an answer, answer.

I laid my head against the seat and closed my eyes. Prayers had worked in the past. Although not a fast method of solving a problem as immediate as mine, it was all I had and likely all that would get me out of this mess.

"Will you prepare Reaper1?"

The phone was to his ear. When had he dialed it?

"Yes, make all the notifications. I also have a vehicle I need you to destroy," he said before he grew silent.

"Thank you."

Until now, I didn't know his lips were capable of forming words of appreciation.

When Severe searched the men back there, I hadn't seen any skull tattoos on them like the man from the garage. What did any of it mean?

My face crinkled into a tight knot when we left the city limits and didn't decelerate until we were turning onto a lonely road that led to a private airport.

"Why are we here?"

"I need to go home where I have the resources and the army I may need if this situation progresses any further."

I swallowed the lump in my throat and pushed my question out.

"Where is home?"

"South Carolina," he replied.

"South Carolina!" I yelled. "You expect me to get on a plane and travel all the way to South Carolina with you?"

I waved my hand absently in front of me.

"Of course, you do," I answered the question for him.

I eyeballed the small terminal we approached. Severe parked the stolen G-wagon outside one of the three hangars. What was he planning to do, drive the plane himself?

I climbed from the vehicle and followed him into the hangar. Two planes were parked inside. Severe walked into a small office with me trailing him.

A man, who appeared middle eastern, handed him a set of keys and documents on a clipboard. The man focused his attention on me, and one brow lifted swiftly.

He glanced at Severe but didn't question him. When the man got over seeing me, he and Severe began to speak with so much aviation jargon that I barely followed the conversation.

Severe turned to walk away, and the man's curious gaze fell on me again. His twitching lips indicated he wanted to say something, but instead, he gave a friendly nod goodbye. I returned the gesture with a wave and followed my inherited trouble.

When Severe walked up to the small plane and marched up the steps, I stopped at the foot of the stairs. Was there a pilot onboard already?

Reluctantly, I marched up the steps and ambled into the cramped hall that led to the cabin. I stopped and turned to the empty cockpit, observing it before I shifted to the interior body of the plane.

Severe was walking back to my location. He bypassed me and proceeded to pull the entry door closed. Once the door was secured, he stepped past me again and ducked into the cockpit.

I stood at the cockpit door, glancing at the blinking control panels.

"You're flying this plane?"

He placed a set of headphones over his ears and proceeded to flip switches.

"Yes, unless you want to do it," came his smart reply.

I inched forward until I'd walked past the threshold into the cockpit. He must have sensed the way I was staring at him because he pointed at the co-pilot's seat.

After all that had just happened, the sight of him about to fly this plane made me smile. I had severely underestimated him, assuming he was this heartless killer who knew nothing other than putting people in the ground and bossing me around.

We eased from the hangar smoothly, the engine revving once we cleared the structure. After snapping myself into my seat, I took in the low rolling landscape in the distance and the hangars and terminals that made up the small airport.

Severe read off information I didn't understand to the local controller. He continued to press buttons, turn knobs, and check panels while I gawked. We coasted until we were aligned on the single lane of the airstrip and came to a stop.

Silence lingered in the air like a heavy curtain of uncertainty before the engine roared and breathed life back into my altered reality.

"Reaper-1 is cleared for take-off," the voice spilled into the cockpit, loud and clear. My heart pounded. Was I about to be flown to another state by a mercenary I'd met last night, one I wasn't sure was protecting himself or me from other mercenaries?

We took off, the strength of the pull sending me back and into the seat. The landscape zoomed by until it became a blur. The air swished and traveled along the nose of the plane, visible due to the speed of the wind.

The lift-off made my stomach drop, and my forehead was pressed into the side window, taking in the dwindling sights before it settled.

The cockpit view allowed me to experience flying in a way I never had before. I was like a kid experiencing my first plane ride despite me being a frequent flyer.

"Severe," I called, casting a roving gaze around the cockpit before it stopped on him. "I'm impressed. Where did you learn to fly?"

"We're all experienced in multiple forms of transportation," was the generic answer he gave.

"Your motorcycle club?" I questioned.

"Yes," he replied while flipping more switches and steering the plane. It banked hard and set me on a lean to the left. A view of waving water was revealed before the first hints of cloud dust *whooshed* past the window.

"Is it safe to say that your motorcycle club doesn't fall under the typical definition of what a club embraces?"

"What do you classify as typical functions of a motorcycle club?" he asked. This was the longest string of words I believe he'd said to me since we'd met.

"Forgive me if any of what I say offends you, but all I have to go on is speculation, hearsay, and what I've read. It labels most motorcycle clubs as outlaws who live by their own rules. It is suggested that you often break the laws set by normal society. I'm aware that not all, but some clubs are notorious for illegal activities and are often involved in illegal business practices, like drugs, prostitution, and gambling."

He glanced in my direction, and despite his cap pulled down over his eyes, I sensed them assessing me. I was already becoming familiar with the notion of knowing when his eyes were on me.

"From what I can discern from being around you, I don't believe your group has anything to do with selling drugs or guns. I don't believe gambling is your thing. Selling women or any of the usual illegal activities don't appear to be your thing either. Unless you're masters at hiding it."

"The services we provide are paid for by the organization that trained and represents us. There are more rules than you could possibly imagine," he stated.

This was news to me, and it sounded like he hated the rules. The way Severe dropped bodies without stressing or cleaning up the chaos he left behind spoke for his organization, their reach, and their depth. Based on the boat, him leaving expensive bikes behind and picking up planes like they were taxis, their financial backing was also top-notch.

A smile tugged at my lips when I pictured Severe working a nine-to-five. He was a lot smarter and more resourceful than I'd initially assumed, but him working at a coffee shop, stocking shelves, or even working a toll booth would never fit.

"What does your motorcycle club do for money?"

My curiosity had me leaning closer, praying he wouldn't be his normal uncommunicative self.

"We are trained and educated in the art of dispensing death. We take care of those who your criminal justice system let slip through the cracks. There are many. Those who get away with buying out of their punishments. Some skirt the system through technicalities, clever attorneys, and by many other means."

The already deep crease in my forehead tightened. Was he saying what I thought he was saying?

"Are you saying that you all are trained assassins? Bad guys who take out the bad guys?"

His stringent stare, although I couldn't see it, gave me the answer I wasn't sure I knew how to process. This meant my little trip to my car last night had delivered me into a mess I wasn't sure could be smoothed over by influence or money. The only thing that was straightening this out was death.

"So the guy in the garage. Is he an enemy of your club?"

"That is a question I need to find the answer to," he replied.

"Are you going to kill me?"

He stared. The chill I expected to feel under his watch didn't dig in as deeply as it had last night. Since he hadn't left me to fight off the guys we'd just encountered on my own, I don't believe his intentions were to kill me. However, when you're dealing with a man who'd confessed to being an assassin, my fate, as far as I was concerned, remained in question.

"I don't know the answer to that question yet," he finally responded, after I'd talked myself into believing he didn't want to kill me. My face creased into a tight knot.

"You don't know if you're going to kill me? I don't understand."

No answer.

"Don't get me wrong. I'm not ready to die, but if you plan to kill me, then why haven't you done it already?"

The question was supposed to stay in my head, but my curiosity was a raging beast I couldn't control under these circumstances. I could be a bit mouthy when something ticked me off.

"I need more answers," he replied.

"Answers to what?"

His answers to my questions were cryptic enough to make me believe he was purposefully not telling me something.

"What aren't you telling me? Why save me only to turn around and kill me later? I don't understand. Besides, it doesn't feel like you want to kill me? You had all night to do so while I slept only feet away from you."

Silence.

"Is it your club? Will they order you to kill me if they knew you took a stray with you?"

More silence.

I blew out a long sigh. I'd known this man for a day and already knew that when he went deadly silent like he wasn't alive, there was no getting anything out of him. I turned my back to him and peered at the thin sheets of cloud smoke breezing by the window.

The landscape below was lush and green, with lines mapping the highways and off-white dots and squares marking structures. The beauty of this world wasn't admired enough, especially by me. The matter of not knowing what lay ahead of me made the scenery a more enchanting view.

My popping ears were what dragged me from my nap. The clicking and turning of multiple buttons and the bottom falling from my stomach alerted me to our descent and of us nearing our destination.

The sky had darkened with thick low hanging clouds. The promise of rain in this city was one that wouldn't be broken.

I'd passed through South Carolina a few times via the airport. Nothing about the landscape was familiar, but it didn't stop me from being captivated by the sky view of the city and the ocean that kissed a large portion of the land.

I was once again impressed by Severe's ability to fly this aircraft. The smooth landing had me glancing out at the ground zipping by to make sure we'd actually touched down.

I wasn't in any hurry to meet any of his fellow club members. A motorcycle club full of assassins. Had Severe freely divulged the information as a warning that I wasn't safe?

"What now?" I questioned, unbuttoning my seatbelt when we pulled into the back of a hangar like it was a garage. He cut the engine.

"I find answers and wait to see if any more come begging me to meet death," he finally replied.

He ducked to pass under the cockpit doorway and walked away. However, the statement held enough weight to keep me sitting in place before I gathered my wits and exited the cock pit. At this point, I didn't know if Severe was my protector or my executioner.

CHAPTER NINE

Jade

There was no checking in or checking out of the airport terminal or calling a taxi or Uber. Severe simply punched in a code and stepped inside the door that looked like it was about fifteen feet tall. He proceeded to walk across the wide-open hangar floor where several vehicles, motorcycles, and a plane smaller than the one we just flew in, sat.

I had trouble keeping up with his long-legged stride because I was too busy being nosey. Was this all owned by his motorcycle club? Was murder for hire that lucrative a business? What type of organization was this to furnish their members with so much convenience?

I was acquainted with many wealthy people, but I didn't know any who could walk into an airport, hop on a plane, and get clearance to fly to wherever they desired.

I jerked at the sound of a motorcycle engine revving. It ripped my eyes away from the layout of new equipment.

The Harley appeared to have never been touched. Was it silly of me to expect a biker to pick a car over a motorcycle?

Severe strolled closer, this time with a black helmet to match his all-black attire. He stopped, pulled another helmet from the handlebar, and handed it over.

It fit perfectly, but getting the face shield to close was more challenging than I expected. After seeing me struggle, Severe beckoned me closer with a wave of his inked-up hand.

He gripped a portion of the helmet at my neck and tugged. He dragged me closer until the front of me pressed into his muscular thigh, stretched taut from holding up the bike. His fingers scraped my neck where he gripped, making the pulse point his finger sat against thump faster. I glanced into the blackness of his helmet. Was he watching me watch him?

Why did being this close to him set my skin ablaze? I wanted to, but I couldn't drop my eyes, even when the voice in my head yelled for me to look away.

What was up with this fierce tension between me and this deadly man? Was I attracted to him or to the dangerous swagger he projected?

He snapped the shield into place, securing the helmet on my head. His hands dropped, and he offered me one, waiting for me to hand him mine.

I sat my hand inside his, and like before, a cool burst followed by a spark of radiating warmth exploded in my palm, shot up my arm, and spread out in tiny surges of pleasing energy all over me.

I stared, unmoving. He hadn't even flinched. There was no way he didn't feel the exhilarating rush. I ignored the sensation marching its way through me and tossed my leg over the back of the bike.

He did most of the work of pulling me onto it. I slid into a perfect fit, my front melting into the back of him. The strength of his leather-clad torso and black jean-clad lower body dominated the front of me. His fresh clove scent added to the sensation that was growing in intensity the longer I touched him.

The elongated screech of the big hangar doors sliding open was what drew me from the mind fog clogging my brain.

We strolled through the doors, and a quick glance over my shoulder revealed the large doors sliding back into place as we drove farther away.

The city of Charleston was small compared to what I was used to, but it had an inviting vibe about it that took the sting from my hyped anxiety over the situation that was wrapped like a vice around my life.

The first stop was at a small house where I was instructed to wait with the bike. I considered running, but with no purse or means to take care of myself, I remained at the mercy of a man I didn't trust.

Severe stepped out with his phone to his ear. The dim rays of sunlight allowed me to see enough of his face to notice him frowning. I memorized the address to the house as he spoke, a just-in-case.

We drove for another fifteen minutes and ended up at an office building in the old downtown area of the city. There were flags of several different nations billowing in the breeze out front. It had double-sided tinted windows and no identifying signs visible to give me a hint as to what was inside. Since Severe was paying it a visit, there had to have been illegal business of some kind happening inside those walls.

I'd been instructed to wait outside again, but I wasn't about to stand out in that heat. Despite the earlier promise of rain, the sun hadn't stayed hidden long. Sunbathing while Severe continued to hide things wasn't about to happen.

I approached the building cautiously before I eased the front door open, grateful I didn't run into anyone. With no receptionist at the front desk, I crept behind the nicely decorated raised counter and snooped.

The stationery read: Todd Bradshaw, Attorney at Law. This bit of knowledge led me to believe that whoever this Bradshaw was, he was as crooked and illegal as the Hell Reapers Motorcycle Club. I left the reception desk and tiptoed into the single hallway, where voices projected and drew me closer.

"I've checked with the Six. None claimed to have deployed anyone," a deep male voice said.

"He was a year old at the most. Is it possible someone in the chain of command has gone rogue, cutting side deals and skirting the guidelines they're supposed to set and enforce?" Severe asked.

What the hell did any of that mean?

"This is the second time in three months that a brother cutting his teeth was killed doing something that wasn't sanctioned by the Six," the other man said.

"Could it be a retired member? Whoever's doing this must be deeply connected. They know too many secrets. Too many orders of operations."

The Order. The Six. Disrupting orders of operations? What were these guys, corporate executives of the assassin world?

"I don't know, but I've got some eyes and ears on this to see if we can make head or tail. I'll notify you as soon as I know more," the voice said.

The sound of Severe's footsteps let me know he'd just walked off. I ran on tiptoes back to the lobby and out the front door. I took a seat on the steps since they were shaded by one of the big trees in the small stretch of land out front of the building.

Severe stepped out, flashed me a quick glance, and kept walking. He stopped one step below the one I used for a seat. His face was aimed straight ahead, but his question may as well have been whispered into my ear.

"Did you find out anything interesting?"

I shook my head. "No. Half of it, I didn't understand."

He maintained his stance, but his pointer finger tapped lightly at the outside of his black jean-covered thigh like the action helped him think.

"One more stop, and I should have some answers by tomorrow."

With that, he stepped down the rest of the steps, and I stood to follow. Again, the little voice in my head urged me to run and take my chances with the authorities. However, my father was the main one who preached religiously about never trusting cops in situations like this one. He said the streets always righted wrongs and eventually laid straight the most tangled messes. My gut was telling me that my father's advice was sound in this situation based on the way it began.

The last stop was another house. Presumably a safe house due to its discrete location. It was nestled in the middle of an upper-middle-class neighborhood bearing freshly manicured lawns and happy-go-lucky families enjoying Sunday barbeques and pristine sunshine.

After we did our routine dismount from the bike, Severe helped me out of the helmet without me having to ask.

We walked side by side onto the shaded porch, where I was pointed to one of the two cushioned wicker chairs. I sat without protest and recalled the vacations I planned to take once this was over. I closed my eyes against a merciful breeze that brushed lightly against my cheeks until a mental jolt made my eyes snap open.

The invisible nudge from beyond my scope of knowledge kept pushing. This strange sensation had possessed me many times before, especially when I was younger and shadowing my father's every move. The feeling was usually accompanied by trouble.

I bent to stand, and a blacked-out BMW came creeping down the block, displaying the signature approach for a drive-by. I glanced at the front door and back at the car, figuring they would have a chance to take me out if I risked running for the front door.

I sensed eyes on me from within the car. It crept along, keeping me planted in my chair but ready to dive onto the wooden porch and hide behind the large ceramic flowerpots for protection.

"Please let it be paranoia," I begged in a low tone as the car continued its crawling pace. Directly in front of the house now, they hadn't accelerated or rolled the windows down, but it didn't stop me from keeping my gaze pinned and my body primed and ready to dive for cover.

The car crept past. The sight allowed me to release my paranoia and speculate that the people were probably lost or looking for a certain address.

"Phew." I blew out a long-winded breath of relief.

My body and mind had gotten all keyed up for some drama to pop off, making it difficult to relax. I scanned up and down the street to make sure the car hadn't doubled back. After five minutes of me allowing my paranoia to get the best of me, Severe exited the house.

I was too busy gawking to see his face clearly from my seated position or to take the water he was handing me. He ended up having to wave it in front of my face before I noticed it. Taking it and opening it, I guzzled, not acknowledging my thirst until I was drinking.

Severe waited until I'd drunk every drop before he took the bottle and sat it on the little table next to the chair I vacated. I proceeded to follow him to the bike and handed over my hand. He pulled, but I didn't move.

"At some point, can I at least call my assistant to take care of things? She will not hesitate to call the FBI or any other agency that will listen concerning my whereabouts. She can also let the rest of my family know that I'm okay."

"Yes, later, when we arrive at our destination. Don't give your assistant any location information. She's better off thinking you're still in New York."

My lips twisted into a smirk that I didn't understand. I climbed over the bike and attempted to shake off the warm flow of energy Severe's touch poured into my hand.

After twenty minutes of lying horribly to myself about not being attracted to this man I was snuggly wrapped around, we arrived at the parking lot of another marina. The sun had dropped and was leaving burning hues of orange tracks across the horizon while flirting with the water in the distance.

This time the name painted on the boat read, "Snake Eyes." This boat was bigger and more luxurious than the one harbored in New York. The inside of this one was newer, updated, and sported a touch of elegance I didn't expect from someone who labeled himself a biker-assassin.

Severe closed and locked the door, shutting me in with him. Only the lord knew when I'd return home. I prayed it was soon. Before I got the chance to ask him if this was his boat, he took off down a dark hall, and a light from what I assumed was a bedroom popped on.

"You'll have to give yourself a tour, Jade," I said low to myself. I walked past a soft tan and leather couch and stopped before entering the dining and kitchen area. Something that appeared out of place caught my attention.

There was a pair of female slippers resting under one of the small in-tables accenting the couch.

Hmmm.

I eased into the kitchen and found the cabinets stocked with canned goods. There was bottled water, eggs, milk that hadn't expired, and condiments in the fridge. The boat gave off a homey vibe like the city of Charleston.

The kitchen opened at a different angle to the same hall Severe had disappeared down. I crept closer to the room and peeked inside the open door. The sound of the shower revealed what Severe was doing.

Unable to keep my curiosity at bay, I eased open one of the dresser drawers and found women's clothes like in the boat in New York. The small collection of black hair care products sitting atop the dresser had my curiosity soaring through the roof.

Was this where he and his club entertained women? Severe came off like a piece of burnt toast, but maybe he was more interesting than I was giving him credit for. Was it possible he and his club brothers were into black women? This was the second time I'd found black hair care products. I didn't want to offend him by asking, but I'd assumed clubs like his had rules against interracial relationships.

I shrugged.

What the hell did I know? I'd been away from street life for so long that I'd all but forgotten that my father was one of the most feared kingpins in the country.

The water shut off, and I crept my nosey butt back to the living room. I picked up a magazine, a *Black Hair Magazine*.

Somebody's got a thing for chocolate. My smile spread at the idea and grew wider as I thumbed through the magazine.

Severe walked in with basketball shorts and a T-shirt, all black, of course. His feet were bare, and his dark hair scraped his shoulders, still damp. I couldn't believe my state of irrational behavior, but my eyes would not be denied.

"You look comfortable. Not trapped in deadly assassin mode anymore," I said, not hiding that I was checking him out. He was lean, not skinny but solid, with a defined tone that let you know he was in great shape.

He took a seat on the other end of the couch before throwing his head back to relax.

"You can use the clothes you already saw in the bedroom if you want to take a shower," he said casually.

I released a sigh. The man didn't miss a thing. I didn't have a comeback, so I stood and walked away.

The clothes fit me perfectly. There were even a few pairs of panties that remained in the packaging. Packaging or not, I washed them in the sink and blow-dried them. The last thing I needed was an STD from whatever skanks Severe, and his biker brothers had in this boathouse.

In a comfortable T-shirt and shorts, I redid my ponytail, brushed my teeth since there was a new spare toothbrush, and padded back to the living room. The circumstances were horrendous, but not having to worry about work was a relief: no phone calls, complaints, schedules, or meetings. This situation was forcing me to take the break I kept delaying.

Instead of joining Severe on the couch, I headed into the kitchen. With a rumbling stomach, I figured I'd make myself some eggs before he made me another of his raggedy peanut butter and jelly sandwiches.

It took a few minutes to scramble some eggs and toast bread. I stepped into the small living room and handed

Severe one of the plates I was carrying. He glanced up, staring from me to the plate like it was a stick of dynamite I was handing him.

"You haven't eaten all day, so I figured you'd want some too. You don't have to eat it. But I'll point out that scrambled eggs are one of a few things I know how to make."

He took the plate, glancing at me with a blank expression that I sensed he was working hard to maintain.

"Thank you," he finally said, lowering the plate of fluffy eggs and two pieces of toast so that he could eat. I was grateful I hadn't burned the meal as I'd gotten used to my assistant ordering my food or the cook, I'd hired who came in three times a week.

I sat my plate on the coffee table and stepped back into the kitchen to get two bottles of water. I sat his water on the table, and like the food, he stared at it. He eyed me with pinched brows like no one had ever done anything like this for him before.

After taking the seat, I pulled one leg up on the couch and faced Severe.

"Are those your girlfriend's clothes in the bedroom?" I glanced down at myself. "That I'm wearing?"

He choked on the food in his mouth at the question, coughing a few times before clearing his throat.

"This is my cousin Israel's boat. Those clothes are his old lady's."

I did remember that a biker's woman was called his *old lady*.

"Oh," I said.

"Your cousin's old lady is black?"

He nodded since he'd put a fork full of eggs in his mouth.

At least he had manners.

"I thought motorcycle clubs like yours didn't approve of that sort of thing, interracial dating."

"We're not the typical motorcycle club. It's usually the 1%ers who believe in and implement those types of restrictions and rules."

I nodded, although I didn't fully understand.

"What about you? Have you ever dated outside your race?"

He stared, forehead pinched. I believe I understood the look. I was out of line and all in his personal business. However, this was an unusual situation, so proper decorum didn't apply.

"You're nosey." He paused for a long time before adding, "I. Don't. Date."

"Wow. That sounds so final. Why don't you date? Is it because of what you do for a living?"

He sat his empty plate on the table and picked up the water.

"That's part of the reason."

"What's the other part?" I questioned, genuinely interested in this man's life for some odd reason.

"My job is a small part of the reason I don't date. The biggest part is that I don't...like...people. They reveal to you all of their good parts and the ugly parts you have to coax from them, most times discovering they're monsters."

"You have a warped view of people. Not all of us are monsters. Some of us may come off as monsters, but some of us have to become monsters to fight the worst monsters."

The statement got his attention based on the way his gaze shot up to capture mine.

"If you truly want to know someone, I believe all you need is the patience to share yourself and accept the parts they share with you until you have gathered enough to truly know them," I said.

I shrugged off an unpleasant idea that crept into the most pleasant conversation we've had so far. "Some things are too painful to talk about. Therefore, it may take time to truly know someone."

We grew silent. Had he noticed how my voice had cracked when I mentioned painful things? The silence dragged on and made me a little antsy, so I gathered the dishes and took them into the kitchen to wash them.

I thought about home, but I didn't miss it. Once I'd cleaned up, I walked back into the living room and flopped down on the couch. I was closer to him this time but not close enough for him to think we were friends.

"Can..."

As soon as the first word floated across my lips, he handed over the phone. I turned the ancient thing over in my hand a few times. It was an old flip phone, a burner.

"Thank you," I said absently. My brain had already committed itself to turning my assistant's number over in my head until I was sure I remembered the right sequence.

"Hello."

Jana answered on the first ring.

"Jana, it's me."

"Me who? It can't be my boss calling me after going missing and ignoring the rest of the world," she replied.

I placed the phone on speaker, knowing Jana would speak her mind and get whatever she had on her chest off without taking one breath.

"There's no way this is my always dependable and hardworking boss who's never ditched a meeting in all the time I've been working for her. The lies I told on your behalf today were lying to each other by the time it was all said and done," she stated, finally taking a breath. "Jade, where have you been? Are you okay?" Her voice was cracking with concern now that she'd dispensed all of her sarcasm.

"I'm okay. I apologize for not calling sooner. After the event, I went home, and instead of being happy about how well it had all turned out, I was kind of sad. And lonely. Mentally, I'm drained. Physically, I'm just tired."

She hadn't mentioned anything about the dead man in the garage. It suggested the local authorities were keeping it under wraps if they even knew about it.

"How long have you been feeling this way?" she asked.

"For about a year now," I replied. It wasn't a lie.

"Why didn't you say anything before now? I would have grabbed Taylor, and we'd have come over with weed, junk food, and all the liquor you could stand."

Taylor was her ten-year-old bong.

"I appreciate that, but it wasn't that kind of lonely. It was more along the lines of me not having anyone to share my proudest moments with. And Camden doesn't count. He was a decision born of desperation. This is about me having a heart-to-heart with myself about not taking time for myself, not resting long enough to figure out what I want or need, and about how I keep putting off pouring some effort into finding my person, someone I can be self-ish with."

Severe's face was lifted to the ceiling, his eyes closed, his head resting against the couch. However, I sensed him dissecting my conversation, which was long overdue. What better time to have it than when my life was flipped upside down? This specific conversation was also a good lead to me getting what I wanted from my assistant with-out too much of a fight.

"I know what you mean," Jana said. "I've been trying to get you to take some time off for two years now. Even presented you with man candy on a platter so you can go on and have that fling or two I've been telling you that you need and deserve."

"You were right. I believe I've let the stress go on for so long that it's caught up to me. Right now, I don't believe I'm mentally ready to come back to work," I blurted and prayed she'd buy it.

"Say no more. I've got your back. You know that I've had a backup plan ready for years now, praying you'd let me sit in the chair for more than the few days you travel away for business."

I bit into a grin, hoping Jana didn't hear the smile in my voice.

"Are you sure? It's a lot to dump on you out of the blue?"

"I got you, and you know this. Now, book yourself a nice island vacation and make sure you fuck anything sexy with a pulse. You deserve it. Especially after that douchebag, pretty boy, preppy asshole, Camden, who actually believed he was smart enough to play you for a fool. With his engaged-with-twins-having-ass."

I chuckled. My love life had its ups and downs. My downs, I took in stride because Jana was my pit bull. It didn't matter if I dated the president. Jana was that friend who would make sure he treated me right and didn't have too much shade in his background. If things with Severe weren't so deadly, I'd have Jana all over this situation.

Severe was being a little too tightlipped. However, this was one mystery I would have to solve for myself.

"Thank you, Jana. I don't know what I'd do without you. Also, please call my uncle and my brother and let them know I'm taking some time off. I'll check in with you from time to time."

"Okay. Have fun. Don't think about work. As a matter of fact, pretend like you don't even have a job."

"Done," I said, hanging up. I sensed those mysterious eyes of Severe's on me before I lifted my gaze.

"She knew you were lying about why you couldn't go back to work, but she let you do it because she genuinely wants you to be happy," he said nonchalantly.

My forehead crinkled before an inquisitive brow lifted.

"And you know that based on the conversation we just had?"

"Yes. You love your work, so you weren't planning to take a break, no matter how badly you need it. And you probably are lonely, but you deal with it because work is your coping mechanism. Your assistant will eventually figure out why you've suddenly veered off from your norm."

I flashed him my fiercest side-eye, part impressed and part wondering how the hell he could read Jana and me so well. If there was one thing I knew, it was that Jana wasn't going to let me off that easily.

"I see flying lessons aren't all you learned in assassin school," I pointed out.

I swore I saw a hint of a smile, but it disappeared so fast I may have imagined it.

"So, Severe. Tell me about yourself."

His head snapped in my direction.

"You're not here to get to know me. We're stuck together until it's over. That's it," he said with finality.

My lip twisted dismissively at his comment.

"You see. That's my issue. I can't put all the pieces together to figure out what you've dragged me into. I believe you're stuck with me like the burden you're not sure you want to carry in the midst of the sort of drama that can happen in your line of work and with your organization."

He remained still, thinking about my words, I suppose. Since he wouldn't talk, I was planning to fill in the blanks every chance I got so he'd help me close the gaps one word at a time.

"Although I know I have no control over when my time comes, I'm not ready to die. I didn't come with you because you threatened to kill me. I came because I believed you when you said the assassin had ties to something dangerous enough to keep coming after me and anyone I know. I also believed that going with you would help me stay a few steps ahead of death. Many people don't know their purpose, but I believe I was put here to help those that can't help themselves. Maybe you are here to help me."

I leaned over so he could look into my face.

"Me being around you could lead to my demise, but at this point, I believe me being alone will get me there faster."

He turned his face away, dismissing my concerns, but his voice came low and steady anyway.

"It's my job to end life. I enjoy it. Like your job, mine fulfills my loneliness. It's my choice of substitutes for the many activities I skip because of my lack of social skills."

He leaned closer to me, giving me a little dark peak of his eyes. Were they blue or green? He'd distracted me that quickly.

"With me is the safest and most dangerous place you could be. I don't believe someone who doesn't deserve to die should be taken by one of us. I believe they should die naturally. Accidentally, if that's what's meant for them, but never by one of us."

What was he saying? I slid closer, my knee brushing the side of his leg. The slight touch, for reasons I'd have to figure out later, filled me with a warmth that was hard to ignore, just like when he helped me onto his motorcycle. It took some mental gymnastics to reconnect with my train of thought after the touch.

"Are you saying that the guy in the garage was a member of an organization like yours, and the one reason you saved me was because you didn't believe I should die by his hands? Was he your club's enemy?"

He didn't answer, and since he'd taken a life and saved mine, I assumed the latter. The guy in the garage had to have been his organization's mortal enemy.

"Would your enemy truly come after me because you chose to save me? Will they keep coming after you now? Why keep me with you? Why go through all these extremes when you don't know me?"

At this point, my leg was pressed harder into his, and I was leaning in, prepared to dissect every word. He glanced down at my knee, pressing into the side of his leg, allowing his gaze to linger at the connection.

Even though he no longer had the hat on, the light from the lamp behind him obscured his face from my view. This man possessed an intimate relationship with the darkness.

"I'm tired. I'm going to sleep," he finally said.

"But…" I stopped short when he took one of the throw pillows and one of the thin blankets from the couch back. He spread the blanket on the floor in the space between the couch and the table as he'd done last night. The pillow was tossed on the floor before he proceeded to lie down, nudging my foot aside with his shoulder to claim his spot.

"There is a perfectly fine bed in the other room. If you think I'm going to run away from you, I can't. No phone. No money. I'm not even in my own state."

He fluffed the pillow under his head like that alone could compensate for him sleeping on the hard floor with nothing but a thin blanket under him and no covers.

"I prefer to sleep on hard surfaces. The bed is too soft," he finally answered one of my questions.

"I can take the bed so you can have this couch," I told him.

"The couch is too soft too."

My eyes searched through the space around me to make sense of him.

"So, let me get this straight. You always sleep on the floor, no matter where you are?"

"Yes," he said, his tone so low I barely made out the word.

I got more comfortable on the couch, pulling the other thin throw over my legs.

"Why? Were you raised in a cave?"

"Something like that," he said before he turned on his side and away from all my probing questions.

The parallel between his habit and mine floored me. I spent many nights sleeping on the floor, also. My reasons for doing so were scattered throughout my brain in pieces. The trick would be putting the pieces back together.

What kind of upbringing would make someone sleep on a cold, hard floor? The longer I was around this man, the more the intrigue surrounding him grew. There were so many questions, and at this point, they were starting to build a wall around me.

CHAPTER TEN

Severe

"Wake up!"

My eyes snapped open at the shrill voice in my head. The light prickle on the surface of my skin was another alert system. Something was wrong. I reached under the table and drew my gun, the silencer already attached.

I scanned my surroundings, not seeing or hearing anything out of the ordinary after giving the dark living room a once over. Jade was sitting up on the couch, her attention aimed at the front door like she was expecting someone to knock the door down. She didn't move or say a word. I assumed she was asleep until she blinked.

She finally glanced in my direction while I got in a stooping position. I placed a finger to my lips, letting her know to stay quiet before pointing at the bedroom. Understanding my silent instructions, she slid from the couch to a position behind me, staying low.

Boom!

The front door came open with a thundering blast. I caught a glimpse of the man who'd kicked it in before he ducked back behind the outside frame.

I sent two silenced shots to the area he assumed would protect him. The armor-piercing rounds I was firing didn't have a problem cutting their way through the front wall of the boat or his body protection if he were wearing any. The intruder cried out before his body hitting the outside deck sounded.

"There are more," my demon called.

I stood, gun aimed in one hand, and yanked Jade up and behind me with the other. I backed us up in the direction of the kitchen, taking silent steps. I couldn't hear the others, but I sensed them lurking, waiting for their opportunity.

Once I'd backed Jade into the kitchen and had her pinned behind me, I reached around her to open the pantry door. Three dark figures came rushing in the front door before I could get Jade into the pantry. I clipped one in the shoulder while the others dove for cover.

I pulled Jade down low. Using the light that came through the small window in the living room, I scanned our surroundings, and I eyed the open front door.

"Get in the pantry and lock yourself inside. Don't come out unless I call you out," I barked the command.

Without protest, Jade pulled the door open with as much ease as she could muster, but the squeak it released drew too much attention. A few wildly fired shots slammed into the door. However, the shots didn't stop Jade from scrambling into the pantry, crawling on her hands and knees before she slammed the door shut.

The pantry was a designated safe room. The devious smirk on my face represented my state of mind. It was time to again satisfy the insatiable itch I'd not been able to scratch ever since this situation manifested and metastasized, disrupting my warped peace of mind.

The loud thump of boots sounded, letting me know that at least three more had entered the boat. These people would die, there was no doubt about that, but my question was, who were they here to kill? Me, Jade, or one of my club brothers?

Since this was Israel's boat, there was no telling who they wanted, as my cousin had a penchant for stirring up deadly drama.

I climbed up and hopped over the counter, diving through the opening that earned me four shots from multiple locations, whizzing past me. One bullet clipped me, grazing the skin of my shoulder. The searing ache that emanated from the wound added to my need to see blood.

I took off in a dash, heading into the storm of bullets waiting for me. My actions were a calculated risk but necessary.

After landing behind the couch, I rolled a few times, yanked my cousin's spare hunting knife from the bottom back of his couch, and low-crawled to get closer to the front door. More shots came in my direction, but the couch and my low positioning gave me the cover I needed to unclip the flash-bang grenade from the bottom of the small end table next to the couch. My cousin and any of my club brothers who had houses outside the compound were always prepared for anything.

I lifted up enough to peek into the area that led to the bedroom where I'd seen the most muzzle flashes. As soon as my head broke the surface of the couch, three shots went off, the silencers making them sound like light taps on a drum.

The flashes gave me a good idea of where the two were hidden. I closed my eyes and allowed calm to claim my headspace, picturing where I needed to aim and how much time they'd need to react if I released two quick bursts.

I lifted, aimed, fired, and ducked in time to hear them return fire, striking and splintering the wall behind me. The loud grunts of the man I'd hit let me know that my calculations were accurate. His distraction gave me time to roll across the opening and nearer to the front door. Shots came my way due to the moon giving them a view of my dark silhouette.

I dived out the front door, slamming it shut. Expecting more to be waiting outside, I aimed, ready to fire into the walkway. If there were more, they were smart enough not to give up their positions.

I crawled on my hands and elbows until I found the latch that led to the skylight above the bedroom. They would expect me to enter the obvious one over the living room.

It was me who'd help Israel rig this place for moments like this one. By my estimate, there were at least four still inside. I popped the latch and eased the little window open. I snaked through the opening, and instead of lowering myself from the roof, I used the little sliding rail system we'd anchored to the ceiling. It took me a moment to strap my legs and waist to the tracks, but once I did, I was able to slide along the ceiling. I eased the space open above the door that would allow me to slip from the bedroom and into the hallway.

Once I was hanging over the edge of the hallway that led into the living room, I spotted the first lifeless body.

He was bleeding out, with dark liquid pooling around his head.

I scanned and found others, one sitting against the wall, gun at his side with his friend attempting to administer help due to a chest wound. Although they were wearing body armor, the bullet's powerful punch had sliced through it. The trajectory indicated he had a lung full of blood or a heart that was squirting blood into his chest cavity.

Sliding movements put me in the area over the top of them. The silence and darkness were their greatest threat. Hanging above my prey, I scanned for their friends who, if they were predictable, would be protecting these two.

"*Amateurs*," my demon said when I spotted one man with his gun aimed at the skylight in the living room and the other with his aimed at the front door. With ease, I holstered my pistol so I'd have both hands available to undo my straps.

I gripped the thick metal hook with my left hand and undid my waist with my right. I dangled from the ceiling while holding myself in place with my hands.

By the time my feet touched the floor behind the one kneeling and giving aid to his injured friend, his brains were all over the chest and face of the injured man. The shout didn't make it off the injured man's tongue because the shiny blade of the hunting knife was planted deep enough in his open mouth that the tip struck the back of his skull.

The friends weren't aware that they were two men short. I backed away, fading into the darkest corner of the living room.

I tracked their movement since my eyes had adjusted. One ran and ducked behind the couch, his aim remaining on the door. He called out to his friends in the hall, looking in my direction.

"There are two of them," he said, getting the attention of the one who gave up his position in the kitchen near the dishwasher. There was another, who was aiming at the skylight, but he'd been smart enough to reposition himself.

"Hey, how are you guys doing over there?"

"Not good," I whispered, answering for the dead men. "Come and see," I said, acknowledging that the man was clueless as to who he was communicating with.

"Jay, cover the door," the man called out before easing from behind the couch and jetting in my direction. Their movements had given up the last man's position.

When he walked up on his friends in the hallway, slumped in the deadly tangle I'd left them in, he was already gone. I walked up behind him, slipped my left forearm under his chin, and used my right hand to split his throat from ear to ear.

His arms shook uncontrollably, the gun falling to the floor as he attempted to lift his hand to his open throat. A clicking sound came from the gaping wound. The warm flow of blood over my arm while I was laying his convulsing body on the floor was like a fix being injected into my veins. His feet knocked hard against the floor, drawing the attention of the last two.

"What's going on over there?" another whispered.

"Shh!" I returned, so he would stop worrying about the business of the dying and keep concentrating on the wrong area.

My current victim was lying in his final resting position, with wide, unblinking eyes aimed at me. No one was home, even as light spasms continued to run through his body. I stepped over him and positioned myself flat on my stomach before sliding to the edge of the hallway.

From my position, I was unable to spot the final two. They were unusually quiet, waiting, and ready. Using my hand as a sound funnel, I rolled onto my back and shouted toward the ceiling.

"He's in the bedroom!"

I lifted, aimed, and released two rounds in the direction of the bedroom. Multiple sets of thumps beat up the marble floor, heading my way in a mad dash. The first one to reach me came from the kitchen area.

He moved fast enough for the bullet's momentum to slam into his head and send him back, but not enough to keep him from falling and forcing me to roll away from breaking his fall. His throaty moans and him wiggling like a worm made the last one stop and take cover before I got a shot off.

The one wiggling on the floor near me found me staring down at him. I lifted a finger to my lips, indicating he should be quiet, but he didn't see the humor in my attempt at being funny and continued his cries. I shrugged, lifted my gun, aimed at the spot right between his eyes, and let the bullet introduce him to a permanent nap.

The last one must have been their leader because he was smart enough not to be where I expected. When a noise came from the kitchen, I turned in that direction and stopped in my tracks.

"Fuck," I mouthed.

"Told you. You should have killed her," my demon taunted.

The last one had Jade tucked securely against him with his forearm around her neck and his gun pressed against her right temple.

"Shoot him! Shoot him!"

"I can't. No shot," I replied to the evil bastard in my head that didn't care about my target dying.

"Drop your gun and kick it over here," the last one demanded.

"Fuck her. Shoot him!"

I tossed my weapon in his direction, and it landed at his and Jade's feet. The split second it took him to glance down at my tossed weapon hitting his foot, I reached behind me, pulled my Nighthawk, and took out the top of the man's head. The reaction on his face didn't fully form as his body dropped, almost taking Jade down with him.

She jerked herself from the man's grip and ran over to me like I was the good guy hero she desperately wanted to believe I was. I did nothing to stop her when she threw herself around me, not caring that I was standing there with a gun in my hand.

"Get her the fuck away from us!" My demon shouted. *"What the fuck?!"*

I allowed her to have a moment while I scanned the area for the more of them I prayed were coming so that I could quiet the riot taking place inside my head.

At fifteen seconds, I peeled Jade apart from my body.

"I'm not the good guy in this situation. Look around," I suggested. "The last thing I need you to believe is that we're friends or that I wouldn't do the same thing to you if and when the time comes."

She took a long leisurely look around at the dark terror lying about the boat, swallowing hard like she was keeping down bile.

"I told you not to open the pantry door unless I told you to," I reprimanded her.

She stared with an expression I couldn't read. "What was I supposed to do? A muffled voice called out, asking if I was all right. I thought it was you."

I released a long sigh before walking over to Mr. Top Less, checking his body for any signs of who he was or may be connected to.

There was no identification, not even a wallet.

"We have to go. If they aren't already here, more will be coming if these guys don't send confirmation back to whoever's running this show."

"Can I pack a few things since I don't even own the clothes on my back?" she asked, her sarcasm not missed.

"Yes. Hurry," I told her while heading to the pantry for more ammunition. Instead of going in the direction of the bedroom, Jade remained in the kitchen staring while I opened the false wall at the back of the pantry. She padded closer until she was standing inside the door. Her wide gaze took in the wall of weapons and equipment inside.

"When I'm finished here, I'm leaving with or without you," I warned her, sliding into a pair of black cargo pants and not bothering to take off my shorts."

"The hallway is blocked. I can't get through," she said.

I glanced down at her legs. "You look like you're in good shape. Jump over them."

Was she afraid of the dead? She was the daughter of a drug kingpin, and she already admitted she'd seen multiple bodies growing up. All those years of living the good life had softened her.

Reluctantly, she walked away.

"Oh my God," she mouthed before a thump sounded from her having to jump over the bloody bodies in the hallway.

She returned a few minutes later in snug-fitting jeans, a fitted T-shirt, and tennis shoes. There was a backpack thrown over her shoulder. I was in the process of cloning another of the dead's phone and checking the body for more clues. I didn't believe this group had anything to do with Jade, or she would have been dead the moment she opened that pantry door.

This was some Hell Reaper mess. The good thing about Reaper mess was that they would eventually have the whole club coming after them no matter what Reaper was in trouble.

CHAPTER ELEVEN

Jade

Instead of going through the front door, I followed Severe through the hall of death, jumping over bodies thrown about like ripped-open bags of trash. The darkness wasn't dark enough. I still managed to see the carnage this man was leaving on this boat. The scent of blood was so thick, I swallowed hard to keep from throwing up.

Once inside the bathroom, Severe locked us inside. The wall behind the standing dresser holding the towels concealed the hidden trap door. Severe shifted a level on the wall, and it opened a half door that revealed a view of dark waving water kissing moonlight.

A hard knocking sound found its way to us, which I assumed was coming from the front door being kicked. Severe turned back to me.

"Outside the door is a ladder. Climb down into the smaller boat below. Be quick about it unless you'd like to stay for another show," he stated.

I shook my head rapidly, stooping and taking a quick assessment of the small black motorboat below. The ladder, a portable metal one, looked like it would be hell to climb down, but once I turned and positioned myself just right, I inched down the ladder quickly.

There was about a six-foot drop between where the ladder stopped and the boat. The last thing I wanted was to land in a bad position and break something, so I took the time and turned around before jumping into the boat.

I landed with a hard thud. My left palm slapped the hard plastic coating of the boat's interior, but thankfully nothing was broken.

Severe's long legs stuck out above before the rest of him followed. He stepped down two steps but then stopped.

Why was he...

Tap. Tap. Tap.

The echo of the shots he released sounded before he ducked, and small blazes of fire traveled over the area where his head was a second ago.

He lifted and released another burst of shots. He was taking on gunfire, and it occurred to me to start the boat's engine.

I yanked at the handle, not knowing what the hell I was doing, but my efforts only made the boat sputter. Severe lifted and fired three more shots before he stepped down twice and jumped into the boat, landing on his feet like he was a stunt double in a movie.

He took the handle from my hand, gave it one long crank and the boat roared to life. He moved the control handle into gear and steered the boat expertly when it shot off like a rock skipping across the water.

The backpack broke my fall when I was thrown onto the floor of the boat. The speed and wind kept me in place on my ass, and after a minute, I was able to finally sit up.

"Stay down, "Severe called back, steering the boat and ducking. Had those been bullets whizzing past my head and not insects as I'd assumed?

Now, I understand his erratic driving and why I needed to stay down. More bad guys had arrived and were outside the bigger boat and on the deck, firing at us. We were apparently far enough away that their bullets didn't have enough impact to injure us because Severe wasn't returning fire and no longer ducking for cover.

After about five minutes of lying there while Severe drove, I lifted and took in my surroundings. We were in the wide-open ocean, motoring along the coastline, where night provided the perfect cover and moonlight the trusted guide.

It could have been minutes or hours later when the sun began to crack through the sky in the distance. The orange and yellow beams flirted with dancing water. The areas that bore a tree line and the coastal land were a beautiful sight that I took the time to appreciate.

I breathed the fresh wind-tossed air allowing the breeze to freely rock my swaying body from left to right. My eyes snapped open when the boat's motor idled, indicating we were decelerating. Severe turned us into a little cove, barely big enough for the boat to squeeze through.

Trees hung low over the boat and sent me back to my sitting position to keep their thick-leaved branches from clawing into me and tugging me off the boat.

Once we cleared the trees, the channel widened, but we trudged along at a sluggish pace since some areas were congested with thick brush, and in a few places, we had to stop for Severe to remove enough foliage for us to continue.

When he opened a compartment on the boat and removed a large machete, I didn't know what to think until he was hacking at the low-hanging vines and thin branches like a madman. I believed he lived to destroy things.

Another hour and my butt was going numb. The sun had risen enough to show me a sliver of its bright surface over the treetops. This area was thick with trees surrounding the narrow waterway, reminding me of the wetlands I'd seen on nature television programs.

A fleshy thump sounded, and I turned in the direction of the sound.

"Aww! Oh! Oh, no! Get away!" I yelled at the top of my lungs, skittering back on my ass to get away from the monster slithering its way in my direction.

Severe glanced uncaringly at the thing before his brow pinched like he didn't understand my distress. Did he not care that I was about to be eaten alive?

"It's just a snake," he said like I didn't see the big black creature whose yellow eyes were locked on me and whose pink tongue kept tasting the air like he couldn't wait to get his mouth on me.

"Kill it! Oh, God. Kill it!" I shouted to Severe, holding my chest to keep my heart from bursting free. At this point, I'd backed myself all the way up to Severe's legs and held on to one of them for dear life. The damn thing kept coming, so I amped up the horrid sound of my continuous screams, hoping it was enough to make it turn away.

Severe set the boat, stopping us. He turned with me latched onto his leg. When he reached down and picked it up, my screams intensified because his action brought the thing closer. Its wagging tail was so close to me, I kicked at it.

Severe blessedly tossed the thing in the water, putting me out of my misery. He shook his head, pitying my display of cowardice.

"How are you more afraid of a four-foot non-poisonous snake than you are of me? I don't understand," he said, turning back to get the boat going again. My fingers were still digging into his leg, and I continued to shake as my fear hadn't subsided.

I laid my head against the side of Severe's thigh and blew out shaky breaths. He may have had a point considering he'd recently massacred at least six men and left his cousin's boat a floating tomb filled with blood and gore. Yet, the sight of that snake coming my way was ten times more frightening. I released another long breath in an effort to calm my pounding heart.

"Where are we going?" I finally asked when I was sure I hadn't suffered a minor heart attack.

"Ground Zero," he said.

"Am I supposed to know what that is?"

"It's my club's compound and the one place I can think of where we can avoid unwanted guests until I figure out the mystery behind these attacks."

"You truly don't know why these guys are coming after you?" I asked.

He shook his head.

I believed him. He was being hunted, didn't know why, and I'd gotten caught in the middle of the drama. Now, he was stuck with being responsible for my life. I suppose he was under more pressure than he revealed.

I eased my tight grip on his leg, noticing too much how toned it was. I sat up higher and took in the environment with a more inquisitive eye, noticing the vast difference in the vegetation and denseness of the plant life.

Moss hung from low-hanging tree branches that reached for the water like long boney arms. The view had a rhythmic quality as the trees all swayed to an invisible beat. The insect calls grew louder and more intense the farther we drove.

"Those guys in New York and on your cousin's boat were determined to kill you. Are you confident that no one will be able to find your club's compound?"

He nodded. "No one has found it yet. And even if they do, they'll never live to tell anyone else about it."

My brows lifted. It sounded a bit cocky, but based on Severe's skills alone, if there was a compound full of others like him, I believed his comment was true.

Something big slid into the water ahead of the boat, followed by another big black thing.

"What is that?" I asked, pointing at the other black log-looking one sliding into the water.

"Gators," he said, unbothered.

I damn near swallowed my tongue.

"What? And you're going to drive over them? What if they try to get into the boat?"

"They can't climb, but here, take this if it will make you feel better," he said, handing me one of his guns.

My gaze darted back and forth between him and the gun several times before I took it, expecting him to pull it back at the last moment. With the gun in my hand, I stared at him like he was crazy.

"You do realize you just handed me a gun, right? Is it loaded?" I questioned, ejecting the magazine and finding it fully loaded.

My gaze met his stare. Was he daring me to aim it at him? I may have been a city girl, but that didn't make me slow. He had another gun, so even if I did feel the need to try my hand at killing him, he probably wanted the excuse to get rid of me. Besides, he'd already proven in New York that me having a gun was of no consequence to him.

I sat the gun across my lap and stopped looking ahead and now faced back, hoping not to see any of those gators trying their luck at finding a snack.

***

Exhaustion had sneaked its way into my bewildered mind and allowed me to fall asleep. Severe's strong leg kept my teetering head from falling off my shoulders, and I think he'd even saved me from tipping over a few times.

As deadly and as scary as Severe was, there was a quiet calmness about him that I wasn't sure he was aware he possessed.

The plush environment, although filled with all types of swamp monsters, maintained an undeniable beauty. A hungry mosquito would launch a sneak attack on me every once in a while and I scratched like I had fleas, but it wasn't as horrifying an environment as the one I'd programmed in my brain about wetlands.

The insect cries teamed up with bird song and the call of any number of other animals to produce a volume of tunes that played tricks on my eardrums and hummed against my skin like dull pinpricks.

Trees grew from the water, which made me think about how tall they actually were and how deeply the roots had to go beneath the ground to keep them from floating away. Moss swayed from the branches; the long veiny strings resembled tree ornaments and gave a natural festive view like the area was host to a never-ending party.

The natural music was alive, not something that was pre-recorded. Insects, mammals, and all animals contributed to the chorus.

When Severe decreased the speed again, we floated past a small break in the trees, much like the one from six or more hours ago that led us into this swamp. He brushed back a few tree branches, and we floated under a canopy of trees that reached across the area so the branches hugged and formed a tunnel passage.

My heart beat a mile a minute. This passage was dark, and I expected a snake to fall into the boat at any moment. Trees came into view when we finally cleared the passage an hour later. Beyond the line of those trees was a wall of vegetation so thick, I was looking for where we could turn to avoid hitting it.

Instead, we floated between the trees that were more evenly spaced for the boat's easy passage. Once we pulled up to the wall of vegetation, I finally noticed that it covered metal. It was a fence line.

When the trees in an area above the fence moved, my hold on Severe's leg returned and tightened despite the gun sitting across my lap.

"Severe," a voice called coming from the moving trees. It took me a wide-eyed moment to understand that what was swaying wasn't a part of a tree but a man dressed to blend into the environment. I'd only seen something close to this in movies.

"Who's that with you, brother?" the voice asked.

Severe reached down to me and opened his palm, and I knew to hand him the gun back.

"This is my guest," he said.

"Has she been cleared by the Pres?" the man asked.

"No. She's a *special* case. It has to be cleared here or…"

Or what?

I believed I knew the answer but didn't want to admit it to myself.

Was he going to have to kill me if he didn't get me cleared?

"I'll radio him that you're on the way," the man told Severe. He nodded.

The wall of vegetation-wrapped metal began to move, opening enough for the boat to pass through. Once we began to float through, I saw that there were more men dressed in camouflage posted at different locations along the inside of the leaf-covered thick metal fence.

Was it me, or were the four men I made out staring like I was the first sighting of a captured bigfoot?

More trees opened up to land with cabins scattered in the distance. This place was huge, and some areas formed walls thick with trees and vegetation that hid secrets behind them.

Once we'd coasted to an area to dock the boat, Severe cut the engine and hopped onto the deck. He tied the boat off before he reached down to help me up. Once I was standing on the deck, I swayed, attempting to adjust to being back on solid ground.

Severe waited until I was sturdy on my feet before he began his trek down the dock and toward the cabins. I trudged along beside him, fiddling with the straps of the backpack to temper my nerves.

When we cleared the trees and the first cabin came clearly into view, my eyes widened and feasted on the scenery. The place was beautiful enough to be a vacation spot where couples could rent cabins for a weekend getaway.

The first man I saw who wasn't dressed like a tree sat at a picnic-type table with a gun in parts that he was cleaning. When he spotted Severe and me, he forgot all about his gun, a part falling from his hand and clinking to the table. He gawked, his gaze tracking our movement.

Severe finally glanced his way and greeted him with a nod that he returned. The man's curiosity about us, or maybe it was concern on his face, stirred my own.

The deeper we walked into this biker's metropolis, the more men we came in contact with. Black was all they wore. Black shoes and boots. Black shirts under their black leather cuts. Black jeans and cargo pants. Some even sported black nail polish. I wore the only pop of color in faded jeans, a purple t-shirt, and a pair of tan slip-ons.

And these men didn't stare—they gawked without restraint. They wanted to know who the hell I was and why I was on their property. At least, that's what I think I was reading in their expressions. They stopped working on bikes, abandoned drinks and food in front of them, and even abandoned each other's conversation to get a look at us.

"Brother," one man said with a nod in Severe's direction, his eyes darting back and forth between us.

"Chopper," Severe returned, greeting the man.

Some returned my wave, but I swore I saw one man gasp before letting his observing eyes follow us along the heavily vegetated path we walked.

I leaned into Severe's shoulder.

"Why is everyone looking at us like we just murdered a bunch of puppies or something?"

"This is not the way to bring someone into the compound. But I'm sure they are looking at us because I'm the last person they expect to see with a woman."

"Why? Are you gay? I don't get a gay vibe from you?"

"No, not gay. Like I told you before, I'm not a people person."

He said it like it was the most elaborate and detailed explanation he could give. A cheesy smile surfaced despite all eyes on us. This probably wasn't the time for sarcasm, but I couldn't help myself. I leaned closer to Severe's cap-shadowed face.

"You, not a people person. Didn't get that vibe at all."

He leveled me with a deadly side-eye I narrowly made out.

"Most of them probably think I brought you here to torture and kill you before I skin and cook you," he stated.

My face squinted.

"They don't know the real you. That's all," I replied, attempting to make light of the comment that he managed to make sound like a promise.

"And you think you do?" he replied without glancing in my direction.

More stares and greetings of "brother" came *our* way.

"I'd like to think that I'm a good judge of character. This is one hell of a situation I'm in with you. I don't like it, but I've always been someone who does my best to work through my issues with patience. I've also come to the conclusion that I don't feel towards you the way your brothers do, based on their looks."

"You should," he said before veering in the direction of the cabin I believed we were approaching. A few men were sitting out on the small porch, one shielding the sun from his eyes while attempting to get a good look at us.

Something told me to look down, and when I did, I barely missed stepping on a monster that had blended into the plush green grass.

"Severe!" I yelled and jumped like the grass had caught fire. I took hold of him, desperately scrambling to put some distance between me and that crawling nightmare.

"What's wrong?" He glanced around us to see what was attacking me. At this point, I was latched on to him so tightly, he had to pry my nails out of his forearm and unhook me from his body.

"You're making a scene. It's a baby garter snake, probably lost," he gritted out and proceeded to unhook my arms from around his waist.

"I'm from the city. They are all monsters to me," I muttered, sensing all eyes on us now that the immediate threat was gone.

He released a long sigh.

"Let's go before you create another nightmare you don't want."

"What's that supposed to mean?" I asked, walking but glancing back, looking for that hideous thing. I didn't care if it was a baby. I was afraid of snakes, all colors, shapes, and sizes.

CHAPTER TWELVE

Severe

We stepped inside the cabin, nearly empty except for a couch, a small table, and a plant in the small waiting area, compliments of some of the old ladies that lived on the compound. Any delicate touch this place had was from them. Although most of the guys didn't admit it often, they appreciated it.

I didn't care. I lived off what I needed. Having pretty decorations wasn't going to impact my life. It wasn't going to improve my job performance. Since I'd never had what I wanted and rarely got what I needed growing up, I grew into adulthood doing fine without *wanting*.

"What is this place?" Jade asked. She was the kind of trouble you didn't want but dealt with because of the deadly turmoil her presence had the capability of creating.

"This is where we have church," I told her.

"Church? You shared with me what you all do for a living, and you still manage to be church-going people?" she asked, staring around like we were in a museum.

"Not that kind of church. When our club holds church, it has nothing to do with religion."

My explanation didn't take the pinched expression off her face. I enjoyed seeing her thrown off guard. In her personal life, everything was organized and planned. She needed some disorder in her life.

I pushed the thick double doors open and stepped into the short hall leading to our sanctuary. Jade followed, and although she wasn't saying anything at the moment, I sensed the hundreds of questions she would ask eventually.

"Kill..."

"Shut up," I hissed through gritted teeth, cutting my demon off, not interested in hearing the same old tired line.

When I stepped into the sanctuary, Micah was the only one there, sitting at the head of the table. Ignoring me, his eyes lit up at the sight of Jade.

I took a seat. Jade didn't. She continued until she was standing face to face with Micah, who'd stood to greet her. The action was an unusual one because he wasn't usually this receptive to anyone.

The only other time I'd witnessed him this way was with his brother, Israel's old lady, Zyana. Did my cousin have a weakness for women I'd not noticed before, or was it a specific type of woman that swayed his otherwise terse demeanor?

"Jadis McKenna," she introduced herself.

Micah took her hand.

"Nice to meet you, Jadis. I'm Micah, but you can call me Spyder," he said. Why wasn't he letting go of her hand? My eyes drew into a squint at the sight of their connection. I swallowed, not understanding or liking the way the sight made me feel.

"I understand that I'm a bit of an unorthodox occurrence around here, but I hope that you'll consider granting me acceptance until, well, I honestly don't know enough to determine until when," her voice cracked, and Micah looked in my direction with one eyebrow stuck in the air.

He hadn't let her hand go, and I was trying to figure out why the sight of it bothered me so much. I wanted to curse and spit and break something, and the crease between my eyes just kept getting deeper.

"Well, Ms. McKenna, will you wait outside for a moment until I chat with my brother? Then, we can discuss the situation further with you. She glanced in my direction as if seeking my permission before nodding at Micah. "Of course," she said, answering his question.

He *finally* released her hand before she walked away. Why did the small gesture of acknowledgment from her make pride swell in my chest? The unusual sensation was dashed away by the evil eye Micah was flashing in my direction.

The rest of my club brothers may not have known who Jade was to me, but Micah knew who she was the moment she gave him her full name.

"Severe. This is unacceptable. What the fuck is going on? She's your fucking target," he said under his breath while glancing at the door Jade had just exited. "This not only goes against our rules, but it also goes against the laws of the Order. I'm a big bad motherfucker. I've taken down bigger and badder, but the Order has two hundred years of secrets and power behind it that even I can't defend without an army. You've given the middle finger to about ten laws I can think of off the top of my head. Do you know what kind of hell this can bring down on us?"

Although we were a legit motorcycle club, we also fell under a bigger umbrella of a secret order of assassins that dated back over two hundred years. The organization was headquartered out of Wilmington, Delaware, and chaired by the Six, also known as The Handle. The Six represented each of the six branches of the organization. Vetted for years and voted into their seats, a few inherited their slots if they passed certain screenings. Some even graduated through the ranks to earn a slot if and when one opened.

Micah was our motorcycle club president as well as the mediator between us and matters of the Order. He was also as vicious with politics as he was with delivering death, so he could sway them to allow us to bend the rules, some with punishments as harsh as death.

"I believe something crooked is going on, and one of the Six may have something to do with it."

He laughed.

"When you informed me that you had possibly taken out a Reaper, I was confident that we would find a resolution quickly or that there was a possible imposter out there mimicking us because there are only two other chapters. What you didn't tell me was that you took your fucking target with you," he stated, sighing hard and shaking his head. He closed his eyes, and I knew he was fighting not to curse my ass out or throw something at me. He dropped his hand and sent a squinted-eye glare in my direction.

"I've been shaking some trees to see what falls out, but I haven't found anything worth following. Therefore, *cousin*, you need to come up with something better than shady dealings. I know you. For you to take shit this far, some deep shit got stirred. What more aren't you telling me?" he asked, waiting.

Despite my never-ending attempts to protect my solitude and be the loner I believe I was born to be, my cousins, Micah, Israel, and Eli, who was currently in prison, relentlessly stayed on my ass, making me adapt to some of life's norms.

Micah had a unique ability to read things in people that no one else even saw. It didn't matter what my capabilities were, Micah was my protective older cousin. He was undoubtedly the reason I wasn't being hauled off into the deepest, darkest hole the Order could find to dump me in for breaking organizational rules.

I had issues expressing basic human emotions like gratitude but knew that Micah knew that I was grateful.

"I did what I normally do," I finally answered him. "I studied my target. From the start, her kill order wasn't adding up to what I saw in her personality. It never did. Still doesn't. A few nights ago, I made the decision to finish my reaping, despite my instincts telling me not to do it."

I shook my head at the difficulty I'd faced in making the decision since I rarely doubted myself.

"I ended up getting intercepted by another suspected member of the Order who was sent to reap my target before my contract expired. The events caused me to pause any further action on my task until I was able to make sense of what was happening. Who was behind the shadow hit? Why do they want her dead badly enough to undercut my reaping weeks before it expired?"

I saw Micah thinking, the information churning in his head. I called up photos of the dead man on my phone before sliding it across the table.

"Who the fuck is this?" Micah asked, referring to the man from the garage.

"I was hoping you knew. You have the ears of the Six. You've seen most, if not all, of our training records." I pointed at the photo. "He has all the markings of a trained Reaper. You know how long it takes to become one of us, the extensive training, the education, the breaking and re-building, and if there are members running around that you or the Six are unaware of, it means something big, bad, ugly, and above our heads is going down."

Micah's face wore a deep frown as he eyed multiple pictures of the unidentified suspected Reaper member.

"Who the fuck?" he muttered the question to himself. If the crease between his eyes grew any tighter, the idea swirling around in his head would merge into a single-cell organism. He peeled his eyes away from my phone.

"When you first told me this shit, I didn't know what the fuck to think, but now, seeing this…" he pointed a stiff finger at my phone. "I know something has to be up with the Order. Maybe even corruption at the top with one of the Six."

He dropped his gaze back to my phone, shaking his head at what he saw.

"The ones that attacked me on Israel's boat, I don't believe they were from the Order, or at least they didn't have the markings of a member. I haven't figured out what they wanted, but I don't think they were after my target. They had a chance to take her out but didn't."

"Hmmm," Micah said, drumming his fingers on the hardwood table.

"We need to work off the grid on this shit. The Order cannot find out what we're up to. We'll use every offline connection we have to see if we can piece this shit together."

"I already have someone working on it offline. In the meantime, my target needs to stay off the grid."

"I agree, but…" Micah said. He leveled me with a pointed gaze. "What happens if she *is* supposed to be reaped? Will you be able to do it?"

My face squinted into a tight irritated knot. Did my cousin read hints of doubt in me?

"Of course, I will. Why wouldn't I?" I told him.

"Are you sure about that? She's not afraid of you. Which means one of two things? She's crazy, or you like her enough to treat her like anything but the person you're assigned to kill," Micah stated.

"I don't like people," I spit the words at him, feeling offended all of a sudden.

"I know that. Hell, everyone in this compound knows that. But, with her, you're…different. I saw what happened out there with the snake. She trusts you enough to think that you'd protect her. She doesn't look at you like others do."

He was pointing out some things I didn't want to acknowledge about myself with Jade and the way she acted around me.

Micah released a low snicker.

"Hell, I can certainly understand your position. She's classy, even while dressed down, and pretty enough to charm the skin off the snakes she's so afraid of. Does she know what you are to her? Did you tell her? Does she have any idea what you may have to do to her?"

I released a long sigh, the action causing Micah to lift a brow. He'd never seen me in a contemplative state where I wasn't sure about what I needed to do.

"I tried to tell her. She's wired differently and, for some reason, is not the least bit afraid of me, no matter what I threaten her with. Gun in her face. Told her I'd dismember her and feed her to the fish."

Micah's brow lifted high on his forehead before a grin spread wide on his face. I didn't care for the way he kept staring, like he was reading something I couldn't understand. The accusation in his gaze made my frown grow deeper. He shook his head.

"Did you fuck her?"

The question made me jerk my head back.

"What?" I eyed him with a cocked gaze.

"Did..."

"No," I answered, cutting him off before he could spit out the absurd question again. He stared down his nose at me like a professor gearing up to drop some interesting knowledge.

"When it's all said and done, this will be a fucking mess, and I'm not talking about the Order either. Never in a million years did I think I'd have to tell *you* this, but be careful, cousin. Keep your dick in your pants and your mind on the mission. There are some things you can't overcome once you cross a certain line."

Before I could tell him to go fuck himself, he stood.

"She stays until we figure this shit out. Mace keeps the guest cabin looking like a five-star resort. She'll be happy to keep Ms. McKenna company since she's always complaining about being bored."

I nodded and walked around the table when Micah walked toward the door.

Jade stood from one of the chairs in the small waiting area at the sight of him, her eyes gleaming with hope.

"Ms. McKenna," he addressed.

"Jade. Please call me Jade," she replied, drawing an easy smile from him.

"Jade. You're going to stay with us until we straighten out some things. Unfortunately, I can't give you much information on what goes on behind the scenes within our organization, but I can assure you, we already have people working to iron out the issues."

"Thank you. I appreciate you letting me stay, and I hope you'll consider sharing more information. I'm much more resourceful than I may appear."

If the smile on Micah's face got any bigger, his lips might stretch to his ears.

"I'll consider it, but for now, all I ask is that you be patient and, despite this situation, try to relax and give nature a chance."

She nodded.

"Nature is scary to a city girl like me, but I'll try," she replied, smiling at him like he'd promised her the world.

CHAPTER THIRTEEN

Severe

"Are we going to your place?" Jade asked, breathing hard to keep up with my fast pace since she hadn't acclimatized to the humidity.

"No," I answered, feeling a lot more asshole-ish than usual.

"You need to kill her. That's why you're feeling off."

"Shut up," I mouthed.

"What did you say?" Jade asked.

"Nothing. We're here."

I pushed the door open and allowed her to walk in first.

"What the hell did you do that for? Now, she's going to think you do that type of stuff all the time. Opening doors and shit," my demon grumbled.

Mace glanced up from the magazine she was reading and stood from the recliner she was curled atop. She and some of the other old ladies used this place as their clubhouse since we'd hosted only five guests in the years since the place was built.

Her big, bucked eyes caught the sight of me before her petite body grew tense. During most of my interactions with the women on the compound, I offered them words of wisdom. I'm sure the last time I saw Mace, I mouthed to her something about the benefits of collecting internal body parts from the dead.

When she or any of the other women saw me, they didn't approach. They avoided eye contact or turned in the opposite direction.

"Can I help you?" she asked in a tone way too timid for a woman I personally knew had killed before. She was the old lady of my brother who went by the name Toe Tags. That she was mated to someone as vicious as Tags and afraid of me spoke volumes about my dark temperament. Mace avoided my eyes and sent concern peeks at Jade standing next to me.

"She needs a place to stay until she doesn't anymore," I blurted, pointing at Jade. I didn't have to look in her direction to know that Jade was flashing me a serious side-eye.

"Oh, my goodness. How rude?" she huffed at me.

Jade stuck out her hand, and although Mace reached for it, she missed grasping Jade's hand the first time due to how hard she was staring between us.

"My name's Jade McKenna. We've worked things out with President Micah, and he's agreed that I'll be a guest here until some important matters are handled."

"Oh," was all Mace said, her mouth agape for a few seconds before she composed herself.

"I'm Ma-Ma-Mace," she spat her name out like she didn't know it. She, like most of the rest of the compound, was having trouble figuring out what Jade was doing with me.

"I can tell from this day room that this place is accommodating, but *Severe* is my sponsor, so I should stay with him."

Jade put serious stress on my name, and her sarcasm wasn't missed. Mace's eyes grew wide, and whatever words she intended to spit out got lost between her throat and tongue.

"Kill her now. She's going to have this whole compound thinking you're a fucking saint. She's still your target. Remember?"

"You're staying here," I told Jade in a calm, even tone. She was becoming more of a thorn in my side than she started out being.

"No," Jade replied.

Her arguing with me made Mace's eyes grow even wider than they already were. She swallowed hard while attempting to contain her nervous composure as no one had witnessed anyone standing up to me. Most of the people on the compound had never seen anyone other than my cousins hang around me, much less interact with me on this level.

I lifted my unblinking gaze, aiming it at the wall ahead of me, struggling to summon the strength to deal with this situation. Jade tilted her head in my direction and set her gaze on the part of my face visible below the brim of my cap.

"You dragged me into this, and although I know I'm probably the greatest burden that's ever come into your dark life, you should do the right thing and see this through till the end. Whatever *this* is," she said, in a tone laced with attitude. "Even if it means being stuck with me."

My eyes closed, and I breathed while ignoring all the vile shit my demon was yelling.

Why the hell would she want to stay with me? I was rude and obnoxious. I was the deadly toxin she knew I was but was too naive to accept.

"You should stay here," Mace suggested, taking hold of Jade's hand the way women do when they think another needs saving.

"If he keeps being this mean to me, I'll come back," Jade told Mace, who appeared ready to jerk her away from me and take off running.

I didn't have the patience or the time. I wasn't worried, however. Jade would run back to Mace once she saw my place.

"She'll be back," I promised Mace before I turned and headed for the door.

"Nice meeting you, Mace," Jade called back like she was hosting one of her benefits and talking to one of the rich pricks she manipulated.

***

Jade

We had come this far, so I believed it was too late to start separating now. Being locked inside a compound with a bunch of trained assassins urged me to make the most logical choice I believed I needed to make. Hell or high water, I was sticking with the devil I knew.

Despite his terse demeanor, Severe had never laid a harmful hand on me. I was already used to dealing with his threats and rude attitude. Besides, I didn't see an easy way out of this place, so as far as I was concerned, I was in prison, and he was my warden.

Trekking back to his place, we strolled past the point where we'd docked the boat and took a sharp left onto a narrow path between brush and trees. The thick, wooden bridge cut through the dense forest and allowed us to travel above land, some covered by greenery and not all on solid ground.

Certain areas appeared to sway like the ground was waving, letting me know that water waded below the surface of the thick vegetation. Fascinated, I admired the convergence of human and nature, mingling in an intimate way that I'd never witnessed or experienced in person.

My ears were finally starting to adjust to the insect and animal calls as they were becoming a dull hum along my skin. The volume teased my eardrums now, rather than strumming them with its wicked tunes like it did when I was first introduced to the sound.

While walking along the bridge, the leaves shimmied on low-hanging branches and swept a light breeze along that licked my skin with a sweet warmth I enjoyed. I wasn't an outdoorsy person, so this was my first experience with nature at such an intimate level.

"I thought areas like this would be teaming with mosquitoes and all types of insects," I blurted, noticing our walk kept stretching on and getting farther off the beaten path from the rest of the camp.

"It is," Severe said. He pointed at one of the small, plastic, round objects affixed to the wooden rail of the bridge we walked along. The objects were attached like green bulbs about every six feet."

"We keep those filled with repellent. It helps, but nature has a way of making its presence known."

"That's pretty cool. I like this place. It's disturbingly peaceful if that makes sense," I told him, stunned that I liked something I would have assumed was outside my comfort zone a few days ago.

We turned along several connecting bridges that drove us deeper into the woods, to the point that all I saw under the bridge was dark waving water carrying patches of vegetation.

When the cabin finally came into view, it looked like all the others, except the porch ran the expanse of the front and wrapped around the side.

"Oh wow," I said when we broke the tree line, and I saw a more expansive water view, not obstructed by moss-covered trees and tall green grass.

"It's so cozy," I stated, taking in the scene while Severe twisted the knob and eased his front door open. The door hadn't been locked.

I suppose I'd have to take the grand tour of the outside on my own later. When I stepped into the living room, I nearly stumbled over my own feet.

What the hell?

"Where is the furniture?"

Mouth open, eyes peeled, I glanced around the living room, which contained a large brown couch and a basic standing lamp. A long wooden coffee table sat in front of the couch. The place was clean but desperately in need of some furniture. No pictures. No plants. No personality. It was the type of dwelling I pictured for a monk or a priest.

A neat stand posted up near the front door caught my eye. I'd missed it when I first stepped into the near-empty cabin. The stand was a small animal's house.

"You have a cat?" I couldn't help flashing him my waiting side-eye.

He nodded before stepping farther into the space. I followed. It was a cat's play and sleep area based on the carpeted area at my eye level.

"*You?* Have a cat?" I couldn't help asking, pointing between him and the cat's little home.

I wasn't intending to be sarcastic in repeating the question, but I found it difficult to believe *he* had a cat. He didn't answer. Instead, he approached, sat, and tilted his head against the couch back. It must have been his favorite thinking position.

"What's its name?"

"Her name is Scrappy," he said without glancing in my direction.

"That's cute. Why do you call her Scrappy?"

He lifted his head and leveled a mean side-eye in my direction.

"Would you be quiet for the rest of the time you're around me?"

No, the hell he didn't.

"Why do you call your cat Scrappy? And where is she?"

His head fell back against the couch, and he rocked it side to side like my questions were torturing him.

"That attitude probably drove her away," I said under my breath, answering my own question and knowing he'd heard me. I dropped my backpack and took a seat on the other end of the couch as him, expecting dust to fly up from the cushions.

"I was on an assignment in New Mexico, sitting on a location, when I spotted a family of cats."

My face lit up at the sound of his voice and at the notion that he was willing to talk to me despite my irritating him.

"It was a mother and her five kittens crossing an open field that would lead them to where they were probably staying in the back of an abandoned bakery. The mother was cognizant of a hawk that lurked above, so when the hawk flew away, the mother believed it was safe for her and her kittens to cross. The big red-tailed hawk must have been somewhere lurking because it swooped in and picked up the runt of the litter."

Riveted, I pulled my feet under me and turned toward him on the couch, pressing my shoulder into the back of it to get more comfortable. It was one of the few pieces of furniture in the living room and ugly as hell, but it was comfortable.

"The little black cat fought, clawing and scratching at the hawk even while being whisked away with the hawk's talons tightly gripped around its neck. The little cat put up such a fight that it disrupted the hawk's ability to take flight properly. At this point, the mother and the other four kittens were gone. They had deserted the little one to fend for itself or figured it was dead the moment the hawk scooped it up."

Fully invested in the story now, I laid my head against the couch, focused on Severe.

"The little cat continued to give the hawk a good fight, so much so that the hawk had to drop it from at least a fifty-foot drop. The cat landed hard but on its feet. It was bleeding from the neck and injured from the fall. It tried to limp away to safety but was far out in the open."

Noticing it was wounded, the hawk came back for it, but even while injured, the little cat took a stance against the much bigger animal, scratching and hissing with such a fierce determination that it didn't give the hawk another chance to grab it again. The bird attacked a few more times and finally accepted that the scrappy kitten wasn't going down without a fight."

The smile on my face was set, wide, and lit with happiness for the little cat I couldn't wait to meet at this point. I loved a story of an underdog beating the odds stacked against them.

"After the hawk flew away for good, the little cat limped its way under a broken piece of plywood and lay there. I ended up completing my mission an hour later, and when I noticed it was still there and that its mother and family hadn't come back for it, I took her. Started calling her Scrappy. That was three-and-a-half years ago."

My damn tear ducts released a few drops that filled my eyes but didn't fall. A warm and fuzzy feeling overcame me at this story.

"I can't wait to meet Scrappy. She sounds like my hero," I said with a huge grin that grew wider during the time he was telling the story.

For someone who came off as a tyrant, who had everyone so afraid of him, Severe had some well-hidden, but redeeming qualities. He was not all dark. He was not the evil-killer vibe he enjoyed putting out. The idea made me feel safer being around him even though I couldn't fully put together the jigsaw pieces of our situation.

I sensed that he didn't know what to do with me, but at the same time, he didn't want to let me go either. Did my presence bring him some level of sick joy that assassins sought?

He stood up without warning and walked off toward the bedroom. I supposed he'd had enough of me sitting there staring at him.

The faint sound of the shower sounded. I was starting to get the vibe that he may be a germaphobe based on the frequency of his showers and the clean emptiness of his place.

The shower was the place I wanted to be most and would be as soon as he was done. The part of me that made me a good leader and savage businesswoman was the part I needed to embrace during this situation, especially with someone like Severe.

I'd never met a darker, more mysterious person in my life. And why did I find his dark nature so interesting? Not in a perverted sort of way, but in an intriguing way that made me want to know more.

I stood, releasing a heavy sigh before I stepped off to look around his place, hoping to find anything that would give more clues as to his identity. At this point, all I knew was that he was a member of the Hell Reapers Motorcycle Club. He had a dying tech-savvy aunt in New York. He referred to Micah as his brother due to their club affiliation, but I believe they may have been blood-related based on their appearances. And I hadn't missed the deep affection in Micah's eyes when he looked at him.

There was no mail or anything to give me more insight on Severe, the person. A loaf of bread sat inside the refrigerator, and peanut butter and jelly were atop the countertop. There was one pot and one frying pan. There was no mistaking what I'd have for lunch today.

The shower cut off, making me tip-toe-run back to my spot on the couch.

I jumped. The sound of the bedroom door opening caught me off guard, even though I was expecting it. Like on the boat, the sight of Severe coming out in a black T-shirt and black basketball shorts was jarring. He almost looked *human*. The black material made his inked porcelain skin glow under the lights in the ceiling.

He'd rarely shown enough human qualities that would allow me to surpass his grim reaper mentality. He cast a quick glance in my direction and maintained a smooth, silent stride into the kitchen. His footsteps were like those of a cat, and if I weren't tracking his every move, I wouldn't have known he was moving at all.

Of course, he was making PB&J.

"Do you eat anything besides peanut butter and jelly sandwiches?" I called into the kitchen.

"Yes," he answered without any additional comment.

"I'm going to go take a shower," I informed, standing and walking away without awaiting his reply. If he wanted to treat me like his greatest irritation, so be it. There were better things to do, like obsess over how to go about resuming my normal life without goons from hell coming to kill me. I wondered if this rival group thought I might have had something to do with the guy from the garage.

My eyes lifted and remained on the ceiling. My life was meaningful in that I helped people, but personally, I was a mess. I rarely attended therapy because I didn't want to talk about the demons that showed up every time I closed my eyes.

I didn't want to talk about my inability to connect with men and forge a relationship with them. I didn't want to talk about my sexual desire, which was probably born from the hellish sexual trauma I'd suffered. Nope, my personal life was an explosion of trauma and heartbreak that I wanted to ignore. The kind of emotional stress I wished I could delete from my brain, sweat through my pores, and purge from my heart.

Professionally, I was a star to anyone who knew me. Personally, I was slowly dying, and no one noticed because I didn't want them to see me that weak. Most nights, my customary drink would be all that helped me get a few hours of sleep.

Now that the thoughts had materialized, getting back to my life wasn't as pressing. I didn't want to admit it, but

I didn't miss the long hours, making decisions all day, calls, or meetings.

If I were being honest with myself, being thrust into this chaos gave me a new appreciation for life. It made me forget most of the personal baggage I didn't want to remember in the first place.

The first steps into his room showed me bookcases filled with books. His bed looked like it had never been touched. There wasn't even a comforter or sheets on the mattresses. Not even pillows. This was why he was so adamant about me staying with Mace at their boarding cabin.

Searching around his drawers was as exciting as listening to my own disjointed ideas.

Black.

Everything he owned was black. I pulled out a black T-shirt and a pair of black shorts that should fit me since he was trim and toned. Hips and a plump ass had always made the waist of my jeans ill-fitting, but they kept my pants up without my needing a belt. At this point, I didn't care how the clothes fit since being clean was much more important than my wardrobe choices.

I remained in the shower until the water ran cold, scrubbing everything from top to bottom and back again. I expected to see black soap. Instead, it was a spicy-sweet, peach-colored liquid that wasn't labeled.

A smile cracked my lips at my frosted reflection of what I sensed was a new me in the mirror. I threw on my new outfit and washed my bra and panties out in the sink before slinging them across the shower rod to dry. If he had an aversion to women's underwear hanging in his bathroom, he could take them down.

I strolled back into the living room and plopped down on the couch.

Severe glanced in my direction. His gaze zoomed in first on his shorts I was wearing before he glimpsed his shirt. I believe the side-long glance was all the reaction I was getting out of him. If only I could read minds.

I picked up my sandwich that he'd sat on the coffee table with a bottle of water. There was no television or visible radio, the things I usually used to distract myself at home.

"So, Severe's your club name?" I blurted, flashing a hard stare like I was the one in charge. He looked over from the dark trance he'd allowed himself to fall into. Yesterday, his stare scared me. Today, the chill up my spine was cold but not icy.

"What's your name?" I asked again, allowing my curiosity to seep through the question. "Severe," he replied, never dropping that spine-tickling gaze of his.

My face tightened. "Severe? Is that your road name or call sign like bikers and assassins use?"

"No," he replied, and that unblinking, dark-as-hell gaze kept my eyes centered on his, although I couldn't see them clearly from the shadowed angle due to his positioning.

"Severe is my legal name," he reiterated.

For reasons I couldn't think of, I liked the name. It fit him. It also meant he'd given me his real name the first time.

"So, you're a member of the Hell Reaper's MC? This compound. Was it built and financed by the Order you serve?"

He shook his head. "This compound is Reaper owned. The Order doesn't know about it," he answered, not giving up any extra words. That bit of information could go into my collection plate.

"This place. It's beautiful. You say that you're not like other motorcycle clubs, but you all profit off of illegal business. Doesn't that make you outlaws, just like other motorcycle clubs?"

His face ceased into a tight knot before he leaned over and got in my face. "There is no other motorcycle club like ours, so keep your opinions to yourself."

I lifted both hands. "Okay. Okay. I apologize for offending you."

The statement appeased him enough to back off.

After about an hour of me talking and him replying with stiff, yes or no answers, I was ready to get away from his depressing mentality. His non-communicative company would end up killing me way faster than his enemy's bullets. After boating through the swamp all day and nearly getting eaten by snakes and alligators, I welcomed the shadows outside, taking possession of the sky.

"Where am I sleeping? Couch or bed?"

He pointed at his bedroom before laying his head back on the couch. I released a long sigh and rolled my eyes at the ceiling.

If weird was a person. I stood and spared him a quick glance before jerking one of the blankets from the back of the couch and walking off.

"Good night, Severe," I called back over my shoulder.

The statement made him lift his head, but I didn't wait around because I was sure he wasn't going to reply.

Before I crossed the threshold into the bedroom, he murmured, "Good night."

The greeting made me crack a wide grin that I kept until I was under the covers and using my backpack as a pillow. I believe I was growing on him.

***

The memories of the last twenty-four hours came back in a rush. I didn't want to deal with my recent past, nor did I want to think about what my future would hold. I slid from the cold bed and tip-toed into the living room and found the light on.

I peeked around, searching for my new keeper. A few more careful steps, and I froze. Like he'd done on the boat, he was lying on the floor between the couch and the coffee table – no cover and a small throw pillow under his head.

This specific location must have been his designated sleeping spot in any location. Was one of the blankets I'd taken from the couch the only spare he had in this place? He was lying flat on his back, and it took me a moment to make out that he was staring back at me.

This man had some issues I would probably never understand. He needed a good shrink about as badly as I needed to stop avoiding mine. I broke from his penetrating dark gaze and trekked to the kitchen for a glass of water. The tap ran for a moment before I stuck one of the two glasses he owned under it.

This time, when I made it back to the bedroom, I tossed and turned and kept tossing. Why the hell was seeing Severe laying on the floor like that bothering me? Why did I care? *Because his trauma, whatever it is, and your trauma were horrific enough to make you both seek comfort on the hard floor?*

Occasionally, I slept on the floor, but it didn't mean Severe and I shared a tortured bond. *Did it?*

I tipped back into the living room like the crazy I was turning into and stepped across Severe's long legs. I positioned myself so my head was at his feet. I told myself I was doing this so we could share the covers when I could find no other logical reasoning behind my actions.

The other thin blanket from the back of the couch was all that protected him and now me from the hardwood floor. He didn't move when I eased down next to him and tossed the blanket I'd taken over his legs and torso area.

I lay there, my shoulder touching his ankle, and closed my eyes. What was I aiming to accomplish? Did I harbor an endearment to him because he had stood between me and his enemy's bullet? Was I unconsciously making an attempt to appeal to him to get on his good side, assuming he had one? Was I convincing myself we had a connection because we both had issues we couldn't escape?

I didn't know the answers to any of those questions. At this point, the longer I was away from my routine, the things that kept me sane, the more I discovered that work and alcohol may not have been the only ways to ward off my demons. Sleep came easier than I expected, sucking me into a dreamless trance.

CHAPTER FOURTEEN

Severe

A glance down revealed what was so pressing and annoying in my pants. My dick was hard and painfully distracting. I'd assumed the thing didn't work other than to alert me to a need to urinate and when poisoned by the rush of adrenaline that killing induced. As far as women went, it never stirred for them unless I was thinking about death.

I noticed attractive women like any man did, but I was wired so that I enjoyed watching rather than participating since my dick remained lazy unless blood and violence were involved in the exchange.

Now, the wretched thing was letting me know that it did work without the inclusion of life-ending scenarios, but it was apparently only interested in just this one woman. The only woman that I knew not to touch, that I was warned not to touch, and was forbidden for me to touch as far as the Order and its rules went.

She'd invited herself to the space next to me on the floor. Her feet were now comfortably tucked under my side and the front of her body pressed into the side of my leg like I'd given her permission. Her warmth covered me better than any blanket ever would have.

Why was she not afraid of me? Her lack of fear vexed me. Was she naïve, or was she one of those women who looked pretty on the outside while their insides were as dark and demented as hell itself?

I'd failed to pull the trigger when I'd had the green light to take her out. Now this. I glanced down once more, adjusting myself to relieve the pressure of being so hard.

"Don't say shit," I muttered before *he* started up.

***

Jade

"Oh, my God!" The words rushed out in a harsh whisper when my eyes popped open, and my vision focused on the two dark sets of eyes leaning no less than a foot from my face. I inched back, my hand covering my heart.

Severe didn't say a word. He just stared with a deep, dark, deviant gleam in his eyes, and Scrappy, the cat I was eager to meet, also hadn't been affected by my sudden movement. Like her adopted father, she sat staring like I was an alien from another planet.

I fought a sneaky little smile amid my thundering pulse the longer I took in the cat. She was still small for her age. She gave me the boost of power I needed to ignore the dark shadow of her owner.

Scrappy was a deep shade of black, her fur thick and shiny like her dark owner took good care of her. Her eyes were a sparkling shade of blue-green, and unlike any cat's eyes, I'd seen. And if an animal could smile, I'd say this cat was aiming a teasing smile at me right now.

"Nice to finally meet you, Scrappy," I said.

Her reaction was to lean her head down and lick my cheek. It was a swipe so swift it barely registered on my skin. I don't believe I'd ever seen a cat do that before, not that I'd been around many cats.

The action was also something new to Severe based on his raised eyebrow. I sat up on my elbows.

"Does that mean we're friends now?"

In true Severe-raised fashion, the cat turned and walked away without a response. She pranced over to her nice little bed in the sky, climbed the stand, positioned herself just right, and dropped her head between her paws.

My attention left the cat and lifted to the man leaning over the couch and staring down on me.

Blue.

His eyes were a brilliant shade of cornflower blue with gray flecks of color sparkling in them. The sun streaming in through the living room window was working in my favor to allow me to see his face fully and without any shadows. Even more so this time than the first time I'd seen him on the boat.

Wow!

He was beautiful, even with all the tattoos covering parts of his neck and at his temples. Was this why he always kept his face in shadow? His angelic features didn't match his dark persona.

"Good morning?" I murmured, not sure what else to say while being so close to his overpowering stare and dominating presence. Up close, he was overwhelming. His body was fit, lean, strong, and emanating the dark power he possessed.

I knew not to take offense to his non-responsiveness. I sat up farther to stretch and gather myself, taking deep meditating breaths to help ease the tension of sleeping on the hard floor.

Severe finally moved to sit up straight on the couch, pressing his back into the cushions while continuing to stare in my direction. I sensed his gaze on me while I stretched and breathed out my tension. Was he feeling put off about me invading his floor space or because I was wearing his clothes?

Despite an aching back, I stood on shaky legs and rolled my neck on my shoulders, sensing those cold dark eyes on me the whole time. I glanced down, taking into consideration that I was braless and flaunting my ample chest, tits bouncing all over the place in front of a stranger.

I dropped my arms and shot a quick glance in his direction before I stepped away toward the bedroom without a word. He remained silent, but I sensed him watching me until I entered the bedroom.

Once in the bathroom, I breathed a deep sigh of relief before taking care of my morning needs and freshening up as much as I was able to without my own personal items. I may have been captured or *something*, but it didn't give me an excuse to skirt my hygiene standards.

I returned to the living room, finding it empty, until I heard faint sounds coming from the kitchen. I took a seat on the couch. The glistening sight of the sunbeams bouncing off the water caught my attention through the open curtains in the large living room windows.

Severe approached. His steps remained silent as he closed the distance.

"I need to go out and take care of some business today." He glanced down at the couch but didn't take the seat next to me since I was sitting in the middle of it.

"Can I come? I mean, doesn't this business involve me too?"

"It does. But you're safer here," he said.

"Are you sure? What about the riddle you told me yesterday?"

His face squinted. "Riddle?"

"Yes. You said, and I quote, "With me is the safest and most dangerous place you could be." I still haven't figured it out yet, but if there is any sense to the statement, shouldn't I stay with you?"

"For now, this is the safest place. I have less control over what happens out there," he said.

The seriousness in his gaze let me know that he either anticipated trouble or would start some.

I nodded.

"Me and Scrappy will get to know each other better," I stated before letting my head fall back into the couch as I'd often seen him do.

He walked away and, a few minutes later, returned from the bedroom, dressed in his normal black boots, cargo pants, and a long-sleeved black shirt with his club's cut. He finished off the look with his black cap pulled low. He didn't offer a goodbye to me or Scrappy. He simply walked out and pulled the door closed behind him.

Four hours later, at one o'clock, I was starving and didn't want to see another peanut butter and jelly sandwich, much less eat one. So, I crept into the kitchen and nosed through the drawers and cabinets until I found some cans of tuna.

Scrappy came running into the kitchen as soon as I picked up one of the cans. They were the only canned items in Severe's cabinet. I'd never met anyone who lived like this.

Only a quarter of his closet space was used. He used one of the three drawers in his dresser. His bed wasn't slept in. I didn't understand him, but at the same time, I believe I understood him, which baffled me even more.

After finding the can opener among the pair of forks and spoons in the utensil drawer, I opened myself and Scrappy a can of tuna and forked each into the only two plates in his cabinet.

We stepped back into the living room, where I sat her plate on the floor in front of the couch as I forked some of the tuna into my mouth. It had a funny aftertaste, a tangy seasoning that gave it the taste of stewed tuna, but it was better than another peanut butter and jelly sandwich.

Once we were done, boredom hit me like a ton of bricks. Scrappy must have sensed my need to be needed, to work, or to do anything but sit there and stare out the window. She climbed onto the couch and sat next to me, positioning herself so her side touched my hip and her head was aimed at the view. She allowed me to rub her back, the touch warm and soothing.

"Let's get out of here," I told the cat, standing. There has to be something in this place to do. I couldn't keep sitting there hiding. I'd visited many dangerous places before entering this compound.

I slipped on a pair of Severe's black cargo pants that fit me perfectly, along with my borrowed shirt and shoes, and stepped nervously out the door.

The edgy tension that filled me wasn't due to meeting more biker-assassins, but it had everything to do with meeting more of those slithering monsters. I glanced up at the low-hanging trees, snapping my neck side to side to see if any were lurking.

Scrappy led the way. Since it appeared she knew her way through the bridge maze that led us away from Severe's cabin, I followed.

A smile crept onto my face when the congestion of vegetation and trees thinned, and the landscape began to open up. The first people I saw were two big bikers standing at the steps of a cabin. They abandoned what they were talking about when they spotted Scrappy and me.

"Hello," I greeted when I was close enough.

They stared, unspeaking for an edgy moment before smiles, thankfully, emerged on their faces.

"Well, hello," one said, reaching down to brush a hand over Scrappy's head but never taking his eyes off me.

"Hi, there. You must be Severe's old lady."

I was about to shake my head and correct him but thought it best to let them think whatever they needed to think to justify my presence. And since most of the compound feared Severe in some capacity or stayed clear of him, me being the scariest man in the area's old lady may not have been a bad idea.

My smile deepened, and I nodded, preferring to give a nonverbal reply.

The other man, who stared like I was a walking miracle, finally reached out a hand. I took it. His big hand swallowed mine.

"I'm Hangman," he said with a hint of pride in his tone.

"Nice to meet you. I'm Jade," I said, doing my best not to flinch at his name because I had a feeling it had something to do with the way he assassinated people.

Once the other who had petted Scrappy saw that I was friendly enough, he reached out his hand.

"Toe Tags," he introduced.

His teasing smile flashed when both my brows arched at his name.

"Mace is my old lady. She told me she met you yesterday."

I nodded. I'm sure she told him more, but I kept my smile friendly.

"Okay, so you guys have to tell me how you got those names," I said, sounding more casual than I felt.

Toe Tags was bulky and muscular, with short dark hair and a thick beard. He was a least two-hundred-fifty pounds and six-foot-six, the kind of good-looking big guy that could get a lot of female attention.

Hangman was a redhead, lean muscle and fit, and sported a long beard that brushed the top of his chest. He had a certain charm about him that would lure you into trusting him, despite him looking like a sexy offspring of the grim reaper at first sight.

A quick glance showed me tall, well-built men in the distance, not hiding that they were gawking. Some waved in our direction, and some tapped others to get them to close their mouths or stop staring so hard.

Hangman aimed a big hand toward a picnic table sitting at the edge of a stand of trees. The sight of Scrappy remaining at my side made me feel special. The notion that the guys were willing to talk to me made my heart swell with a sense of unexpected hope.

Once we were seated, they took up one side, and I sat in front of them with Scrappy on the seat next to me like my faithful little guard cat and protector.

"Since you're on this compound and, from what I hear, living with Severe, you must be official," Hangman stated.

I didn't know how to respond because I didn't understand what he meant by *official*. I'm sure news of my arriving yesterday with Severe was the talk of the compound. I'll go as far as to say some may have placed bets on if I would survive the night based on the way they regarded Severe.

"Before we officially introduce ourselves, there is something I'm dying to know," Toe Tags said, saving me from having to make up a lie.

"What?" I questioned. The intrigue in his brown gaze replaced the natural sting that had rested in his eyes earlier. The expression was unexpected on such a dominating presence.

"You're beautiful. Stunning, actually," he stated, not flirting but paying a genuine compliment.

"Thank you," I replied while he scratched his head. The dent between his eyes revealed his reluctance or perhaps his lack of understanding of my situation with his MC brother.

"How the hell did you get someone like Severe to claim you or to be with you for more than a few minutes at a time? I love my brother. Would lay down my life for him in a heartbeat. He's one of the most loyal Reapers there is and can be pretty damn convincing when he's playing a role, kind of like the devil tricking his prey into believing he's a saint. However, Severe's not a *people* person. He's not holding you hostage, is he?"

He leaned over the table slightly, his brows lifting while awaiting my answer. I gathered my words carefully before releasing a chuckle to lighten the burning curiosity aimed at me.

"Severe and I are complicated, but we work because I'm not afraid of him."

I shrugged, keeping my shoulders elevated. The men stared at each other with knitted brows before they put their gazes back on me.

"You should be afraid," one said.

"And you *need* to be afraid," came the other's comment.

Their words were a warning, their faces serious. Was Severe truly the monster everyone was making him out to be? I didn't meet a monster in that garage. I met a man who saved me from another monster. Therefore, my point of reference where it concerned Severe was not the same as anyone else's.

"So, I keep hearing. But the fact that I'm not afraid is probably the reason we work," I pointed out with more confidence than I possessed. Truth was, I didn't know how to decode my unusual relationship with Severe. We weren't a couple by any stretch of the imagination, and our communication could have used a steroid injection. However, we did have the ability to tolerate each other for long periods of time.

"Now, if you will, I would love to hear the stories behind your names," I reminded them. They lifted intrigued brows before smiles crept into their eyes and made it to their lips.

Getting others to talk about themselves was the first step in gaining trust. If not trust, at least lay the foundation to start building a rapport with them.

They must have spotted the interest in my gaze. I noted a hint of reluctance in theirs. They took their time eyeing me, assessing me to determine if I were worth their words, I imagined. They recovered from the sliver of hesitancy that edged across their attractive faces, and the looks of caution disappeared.

"I was shot in the head," Toe Tags began. "Third major assignment. The coroner got to the crime scene and pronounced me dead. I was taken to a morgue. I awakened from my near-death experience when they removed me from the freezer and placed me on the autopsy table. Stripped naked and freezing my ass off, the first thing that came into focus when I opened my eyes was my toes, specifically my right big toe, sporting a toe tag."

My lips remained parted through Toe Tags's story up to where he knocked out the medical examiner, stole his clothes, and snuck out of there with the bullet still in his head.

Who knew such hard men could be so interesting to look at and to get to know? Or was it that I was more into the bad boys than I cared to admit? Jana had teased me each time she caught me stare-drooling over a biker type or any good-looking, tattooed badass who crossed my path.

Hangman's story, like Toe Tags', was not at all what I expected. He'd actually survived a hanging after being left for dead hanging from a tree. Three more Reapers joined in the conversation, and I got to know Ribbit, Blue Meat, and Tetris.

They pulled up chairs, brought beer and pretzels, and told war stories and jokes. There were also some attempts to pry into my and Severe's relationship, but I wouldn't give up much because the last two days were a mystery, even to me.

Scrappy took off when she grew tired of the chatter. I got up to go after her, but Hangman stopped me.

"She'll be okay. She knows this place better than any of us. She makes her therapy rounds."

The line stretching across my forehead and my searching eyes spoke my question for me.

Tetris took over.

"She goes around to different cabins and lets us pet her. She has a knack for knowing who needs a little pet therapy. For her good deeds, she's often rewarded with kitty snacks."

As much as I hated to give up all of the hot male attention I was getting, it was time to find guest lodging, gather a few personal items Mace had informed me I could pick up, and get back to Severe's empty cabin.

I stood.

"As much as I hate to leave a good time, I need to pick up a few things from guest lodging and head back," I announced.

My eyes widened, and my ears perked at the responses I received to my statement. Looks of disappointment, a few groans of protest, and some friendly smiles. Did I possess a knack for dangerous men that I didn't know about? They liked being around me, and the notion of it tightened my chest in the best possible way.

I'd assumed I would be terrified of venturing out into this unknown city of biker-assassins on my own. I'd easily spent the better part of three hours surrounded by some of the deadliest men in the world, but oddly, I believed I was welcomed.

I was clueless as to how safe I was, but I didn't detect any type of malice from them. There, of course, were subtle hints of concern whenever Severe's name was mentioned that I didn't miss.

Toe Tags and Hangman exchanged glances before Hangman agreed to walk me back to the cabin where I'd met Mace.

CHAPTER FIFTEEN

Severe

I cruised the city with no helmet, using myself as bait. I wanted my face seen, knowing I would attract attention. If my hunch was correct, I was a mark now for not killing my target, and someone with the Order was behind the proposed hit.

This wasn't the way of the Six. They were direct. They would let you know that they were coming. They would offer you the option of turning yourself over to them so they could deliver a quick death or give you a head start on running. A dark and deceptive plot was playing out, and it was centered around Jade's kill order.

Now, the Order, or even an outside entity, had drawn my attention. I was persistent, but there was a part of me that, if it had its way, would kill everyone in its path just to make the problem go away.

"What did I tell you about calling me 'it,' mother-fucker?" He shouted loud enough to rattle my brain cells. *"You unleash me, and all your problems go away. End of fucking story."*

Ignoring its irritating words, I eased up on the throttle when I noticed the tan, darkly tinted sedan and a dark gray Acura in my mirror for the fourth time within the last ten minutes. They were following me, unaware that I was leading them to a location of my choosing.

I turned and rolled into the parking lot of *The Dirty Spoon* restaurant. I took my time climbing off my bike before feigning interest in checking it over. When I was sure one of the vehicles, the Acura, had parked, I dusted off my hands and marched towards the establishment before stepping inside.

The owner of the place was a racist asshole who'd gotten away with killing a fifteen-year-old African American teenager a few months back. He claimed the kid had broken into his restaurant. What the local cops didn't know was that the asshole had baited the young boy, hoping he'd break in so he'd have a target to kill. It was his third shooting in two years, and the local authorities were either too dumb or didn't care about the pattern.

All it took was me overhearing a few of his customers speculating about what they believed he was up to for me to become intrigued. It didn't take much research to find out that the speculations about him weren't just rumors.

My actions landed the man in the hospital after catching him in the dark alley behind his restaurant a week after the incident. He would never know it was me and would always be looking over his shoulders. I didn't want him to have another peaceful day for the rest of his life.

His restaurant was being targeted today in the hopes that the vehicles following me would start some drama that would end with his restaurant or him taking on some major damage. I sat with a view of the parking lot and front door.

Three men in neat button-ups, dress pants, and loafers exited the gray Acura and marched toward the restaurant.

Although they did a good job of hiding their weapons, I sensed them like a shark scents blood.

Once inside, one of the men strolled past me and headed to the bathroom while the others sat in a booth two sections ahead of mine. None of them made eye contact, but I was on sensory overload from the vibes I picked up from them.

I stood abruptly, causing one to straighten in his seat and cast an eye in my direction. When I turned to head to the bathroom, tension tightened their bodies while they concentrated harder on the menus sitting in front of them.

I marched into the men's bathroom and cast a fleeting glance at the third man standing at the sink washing his hands. Once the door was closed, I stood with my back against it, closing my eyes to soothe my demon, who sounded like a death metal band exploding in my head.

"Kill. Kill. Make it bloody. Impale him with his own arms. Make him bite off his own dick. Turn his asshole inside out and make him eat it. Feed him his own stomach contents. I want to see blood."

Since I was standing there not saying anything, my slightest movement made the man set his hands at his sides and closer to his gun.

"There is no need for a weapon," I informed him, glancing down at his anxious hand movement. "You answer a few questions, and we never have to see each other again."

His brow lifted while he assessed me, letting his eyes fall down my body, covered in black from head to toe. I'd pulled my cap down so he couldn't see the insane blaze of death flashing in my gaze.

"You answer one question for me first," he said once he was done with his assessment.

"Yes," I answered, my tone not giving away the hell playing out in my head.

"Are you Severe Sylas? Are you a member of the Carolina Hell Reaper's motorcycle club?" He'd stated my full name as well as of our club like he was a back-alley lawyer.

"That was two questions," I pointed out.

He shrugged and awaited my answer with a cocked brow.

"Yes to both questions. Got anymore?" I asked.

His brows lifted before he drew his gun and leveled a steady aim at me.

I smiled, pursed my lips, and set my gaze on his intense one.

He frowned, noticing right away that I wasn't bothered by him aiming his gun at me. His pinched expression revealed the level of his inexperience.

When I moved, he jumped back but maintained his aim. I pointed at the stall.

"I came in here to ask you some questions, but I also need to use the bathroom."

Instead of walking to the urinal next to his, I took steps toward the stalls.

"Hold it right there! Do you not see me standing here aiming a gun at you?" he questioned, his tone pitchy.

I yanked my zipper down before popping the button loose. "Did you not hear me say I needed to go?"

Hard from the anticipation of spilling blood, I gently pulled myself out. The sight made the man nervous enough to turn his eyes away.

"You're as crazy as they fucking say you are," he said, turning up his nose and keeping his eyes averted when a stream of my piss splashed on the floor.

When his aim wavered, I lunged at him, knocking the gun from his hand before my clenched fist landed square in his mouth. He stumbled back, sputtering and swinging wild punches that I dodged with ease. His attempt to try and kick me was another mistake. I shoved his off-balance body into the urinal, headfirst.

His head struck the slab of hard, wet ceramic, while his hand fell into the water, tumbling down the bowl, and making a thump-slash sound. He hit the floor, his face drawn tight with pain and anger that didn't last long due to my foot slamming into his head hard enough to take him out.

I made quick work of tucking and zipping myself back in and dragging my prey into the largest stall. His body landed atop the closed toilet with a hard thud. His head rocked to the left, and a line of drool slid over his bottom lip and stretched to his chest. He was hanging between consciousness and unconsciousness.

I yanked off one of his hard-tipped expensive loafers, sitting it on the top of the toilet behind his head. The hard slaps I delivered to his face drew him from the slumber in which he lingered.

"Wake up. I don't have a lot of time, so the faster you answer my questions, the faster this is done, and you can be on your way."

He glanced down at the silenced gun I'd shoved deep into his shoulder. Wide-eyed, he peered into my shadowed face.

"Are you here for me or the woman?"

"Both," he answered quickly.

"Why?"

"It was a double kill order placed by the Order," he gritted out, his eyes flashing murder.

"Why?"

"Your kill order was supposed to be fulfilled weeks ago. The Order wants you and your target gone as soon as possible. You know the drill. They are paying double to make it happen."

This bit of interesting news captured my full attention.

"Who do you work for?" I asked him.

"The Order."

"Which branch?"

"Law and Order," he replied with pride.

"Wrong answer. You are not a member of the Order. Who do you work for?" I asked again, allowing darkness to fill my gaze.

There was no way this weak and pathetic excuse for an assassin was a member of the Order under any of the

Six. I'd seen men wash out with more guts and grit in their middle finger than this man possessed in his whole body. Him spilling his guts so easily was a classic sign that he was not touched in any capacity by the same Order that had trained me.

I picked up his shoe and shoved the tip into his mouth before I pushed my gun harder into his shoulder and pulled the trigger. His loud groan was muffled by the shoe that I shoved deep enough to make him choke.

The harshness of the shove and the hard shoe bottom broke a few of his top teeth and uprooted one from the bottom. His sniveling cries, despite being muffled, would attract attention.

"Who sent you?" I questioned, placing the barrel of my gun in the center of his chest this time and removing the shoe so he could answer my question.

"Damage sent us to take out you and the target when your time ran out," he said, spitting blood between his gurgled words.

He'd dropped a name, another indication that he was not a member of the Order. Damage was the right hand to one of the Six—information I wasn't supposed to know. Like Micah, Damage was like a lieutenant or special liaison between members like me and the Six.

"How did you get your order?"

"Secure Message," he spit out.

"I knew you weren't a member," I said, disgusted that he would even pass himself off as one of us. This man was being played for a fool and had more than likely been tricked into thinking he was an actual member. Our kill orders were sanctioned by the Six and delivered on the dark web via a code taught within the Order.

"You're cannon fodder to get a job done that Damage doesn't want dirtying his hands or reaching back to his handler."

Was Damage working alone on this rogue operation, or was a member of the Six pulling the strings? Either way, this shit ran deep. Deep enough to know the body count would keep stacking up if I didn't figure out why they wanted Jade dead bad enough to involve a high-ranking member of the Order. There was no guarantee that Damage was pulling the strings either. He could have been a convenient scapegoat.

While the information was swirling around in my head, I lifted my gun to the man's temple and pulled the trigger. The side of the stall caught his brain splatter. The words on his tongue never made it past his lips.

"Not enough blood. More."

"Shut up and let me think. Can't you see he's already dead? We don't have enough time to play your kind of sick game," I muttered. My gun tapped at the side of my cap, the action assisting in allowing my brain time to attempt to piece together a puzzle in which I still didn't have enough pieces.

My watch's alarm sounded, alerting me that the two and a half minutes I'd allowed myself to extract information had elapsed. I left the stall locked and climbed over the top.

I took a moment to straighten my clothes, check for blood splatter, and quickly wash my hands. I exited the restroom to find two sets of eyes on me and sensed a few more tracking my every move.

After returning to my table, I waited for who would be the lucky one sent to check on his friend in the bathroom. It took thirty seconds for the one with the light brown military cut to stand.

The waitress narrowly avoided bumping into him. He allowed her to take the lead down the aisle, where she stopped at my table with my order of fluffy peanut butter and jelly pancakes.

The one standing kept glancing in my direction. His friend at the table had grown tense, his body posture too erect, his eyes too fixated on something on the table. He was waiting for his chance to gawk at me.

"Enjoy," the waitress stated, placing a set of utensils in front of me.

"Thank you," I replied before she stepped away.

The man walked past me, and as soon as he stepped into the bathroom, I threw down two twenties and headed back to join him, casting an inviting glance at the one staring me down from the table.

"Mack, you all right?" the man called, knocking on the locked stall door. He spun in a rush when I came barreling into the bathroom.

"Torture," my demon called, enticing me to enjoy the prolonged dread of death over a quick one.

"There's no time to torture him," I answered out loud, watching the man's wide-eyed reaction to my remark.

His hand moved quickly in an attempt to reach for his weapon, but I shook my head, warning him that he was making a mistake. He did it anyway. He reached for his gun and left me no choice but to put one in his chest."

"Blood. More blood."

I walked up and stood above him, observing the way he gasped for breaths as the sucking chest wound left him hissing and gasping with each inhale he took. His shirt was soaked within seconds, and he was hemorrhaging enough blood to temporarily appease my demon.

"The outcome in this line of work is you die. That's it."

I imparted my deathly wisdom while watching the life draining from his eyes. I dialed before lifting my phone to my ear.

"911, what's your emergency?" the operator called into the phone.

"I just saw the owner of *The Dirty Spoons* restaurant, Mr. Vernon Kale, shoot two men inside the men's bathroom. I believe he plans to cover up the murder. He's coming after..."

I clicked off just before the third man came barreling through the door. Since I was standing next to the door anticipating his arrival, I brought my gun down on the side of his head.

The sickening crack made him stumble on wobbly legs before he fell next to his friend on the floor. The back of his suit flew up, revealing that he hadn't even pulled his pistol.

Had these men had any training at all, or was money their sole motivator? It didn't matter now. They'd fallen victim to a traitor who was using them to cover up a scandal big enough to threaten the legitimacy of a two-hundred-year-old Order built on a foundation of trust, truth, and honor.

I shoved my gun deep into the side of the fallen man's forehead, my foot planted in the center of his chest to keep him down. "Tell me who hired you, and I can assure you that I'll seek revenge on your behalf for him getting you killed."

"Danger. He promised that we would be sworn into the Order if we completed this assignment for him."

They'd been duped. The few who knew about the Order would do anything to get into the organization, but cutting corners and breaking rules led you to death, fast. Many were killed for leaking secrets about the organization.

"How long have you been completing tasks for him?" I asked.

"A year," the man gritted, breathing harshly.

"How many of you work for him?"

"T-t-twen-ty," he spat out.

"Have any of you been granted access to the Order yet?"

"No," he choked out.

"Good."

Tap! Tap!

"You're welcome. I just did you a favor," I replied to the empty eyes staring up at me. I would leave at least one of them in pieces all over the bathroom floor, a small gift to shut up the asshole in my head.

CHAPTER SIXTEEN

Jade

Once we arrived at the lodging cabin, Hangman walked me inside. Waving at Mace, he bowed slightly in my direction with a wide smile, "See you later."

Mace jumped up from the couch she was perched on. Her wide-eyed stare bounced between Hangman and me before she waved absently and cast him a fleeting glance before he took off.

Mace stepped closer, peeked out the door after Hangman, and turned to me in a rush.

"They like you. It's already gotten around the compound that Severe's old lady has the men wrapped around her pretty little fingertips."

"What?" I muttered. "How? We were just sitting around talking."

"That's all it took. Those guys don't usually interact with anyone they don't know. The fact that you were able to tame Severe is probably why they think you're some kind of magic woman."

A peal of laughter escaped. "Believe me. I haven't tamed Severe. He's still as dark and untamed as his reputation suggests."

"If you say so," she said. "You do know he's famous, right?"

"Who?" I questioned.

"Severe."

"No, he didn't tell me he was famous." My curiosity was piqued. Mace owned every ounce of my attention now.

"Since you're here, it means you do know what he and the guys do for a living?" she asked, eyeing me cautiously.

I nodded.

"Yes. I know what they do, and believe it or not, I understand why groups like them are needed."

Her apprehensive expression remained the same, her eyes searching mine. My statement hadn't made an impact on Mace.

"Before I speak out of turn, I need to hear you say what they do for a living," she said.

She wasn't taking any chances, and I didn't blame her.

"I've been with Severe through seven, eight, nine kills so far. Therefore, I know what the Reapers do for a living," I told her.

This time she placed a hand over her open mouth. Her gaze locked on mine and she took me in deeper, assessing me with newfound regard. She didn't move or say anything for such a long space of time, I decided to reintroduce her to the conversation we'd never started.

"You said Severe was famous. For what?" I questioned.

"Oh," she said, breaking the staring trance she was in while assessing me. "His reapings are so vicious, they often make the news, local and national. And if you've seen it in person, then you know."

I shook my head. "He wasn't...particularly vicious. More along the lines of swift and brutal."

She cocked an eye at me. "Let me ask you this. Did he make you wait outside or go back in alone after you thought he was done?"

"No."

"Trust me, he was swift to spare you the gory details. The aftermath of his kills gets attention. Often. And the more vicious the target, the more he makes them suffer. One of his targets was a child molester of over a hundred young girls, a few of the girls he killed. Severe left the man in pieces, and I have no doubt he didn't kill him before he cut him up. And there were others. He turned one man into multiple wind chimes around his house. Then there was one whose head he blew up and took the time to piece most of it back together before he left the scene."

"I get the point," I said, cutting her off. Was it me, or was she proud of the gruesome scenes he'd left behind?

The door's chime drew our attention, and we turned to face it. This time I was the one with the parted lips and wide eyes.

A woman with the smoothest brown-toned skin I'd ever seen walked in. Her stylish shoulder-length bob, chic blouse, and flowing wide-legged pants made her look like she was gearing up to walk a runway. She had a sleek model's look about her.

She tilted her head at Mace, who waved her over, her grin wide and her body jittery. Mace was happy to see the woman.

The woman's face lit up when she saw me. She maintained her smile until she was standing next to Mace and facing me.

"Jade, this is Zyana, Israel's old lady," Mace introduced.

I reached out my hand, and she took it with a bouncing enthusiasm I didn't expect.

"Nice to meet you, Jade. You are all anyone around here can talk about."

She kept smiling and shaking her head like she was at a loss for words. She hadn't let my hand go, and I glanced down at our connection.

"I'm sorry," she said, finally releasing my hand. "I don't mean to stare at you, but you're Severe's...old lady?"

I nodded, going along with what they assumed.

"Please don't be offended. But. How?" She eyed me from head to toe like staring at me would give her a good answer. "He's so scary he makes the hair on the back of my neck stand. It feels like he can kill you without even touching you. The first time I met him, he was telling me about peeling the skin off skulls and dead wet pussy," she said, shivering at the idea and letting me know that Severe had left a lasting impression on her.

Slightly taller than me, she glanced down to make sure she could see clearly into my eyes. "You're okay. He's not holding you against your will or anything?" she asked, the crease in her forehead and tension in her body revealing the truth of her concern. She was the second or third person who'd posed the question.

I chuckled, the action sounding fake even to me. "I'm fine. I believe he purposely scares people to keep everyone away, but he's not like the persona he's convinced you all to accept about him. He tried, but I never gave him a chance to brainwash me into believing he was the devil."

Her unblinking side-eye said she begged to differ. "If you say so. And if keeping people away is his objective, it's working. He's not someone I'd walk up to and start a conversation with. Not someone I'd want to meet alone in the dark either, despite what the Reapers stand for."

Zyana stared for a while longer before she lifted the leather vest hanging across her arm to Mace. "Israel told me to bring this to you for alterations."

Mace's shriek made me jump and enticed Zyana's smile to break through the residual concern in her expression. Mace took the leather vest and lifted it up, checking it out.

"He gave you your cut," she told Zyana.

Zyana nodded with hints of pride flashing in her gaze. This must have been a big deal among this group.

"It's about a size too big, though."

While Mace was directing Zyana to try on the vest so she could see where to alter it, she glanced in my direction.

"Have you decided that you'd rather stay here?" she asked me, returning to the reason I was there in the first place.

"No. I wanted to see if I could pick up a few personal items and clothing. I didn't get a chance to pack anything before we came here, and Severe isn't exactly in touch with his feminine side enough to consider that I need more than one change of clothing."

"You're in luck. We have a small boutique in the back. What size are you, six, eight?"

"Ten, but thanks for the compliment," I replied, glancing down at myself. I'd been half-heartedly motivating myself to get back to a size eight for years now. Aside from going to the gym when I felt like it and eating salads a few times a week to trick myself into believing I was eating healthily, my overall diet and exercise program needed a major upgrade.

"You're a small ten," Zyana said, sizing me up and smiling. I didn't care that she was being nice. I enjoyed the compliment.

"Thank you."

Mace aimed a finger across her shoulder.

"Take the hallway. It's the last door on the right. Take whatever you need, and you can come here as often as you want. We don't get a lot of guests, so this place stays stocked. And despite what you may have heard about bikers and their old ladies, this group makes sure we have everything we need and a lot of what we want."

I nodded. The ratio of men to women here was at least ten to one. I supposed the men who claimed old ladies appreciated them more than the average guy on the streets. I imagined it was difficult to find a woman who respected and followed the biker's way of life and accepted what these specific bikers did for a living.

With Mace and Zyana's eyes following me, I marched past the desk and stepped into a hall that led to the back of the cabin. The area inside the cabin appeared much bigger than the cabin suggested from the outside front view. The first three doors were left open to neatly cleaned guest rooms.

Before I sprung open the door to the last room, I paused, smiling at the sound of Zyana laughing at something Mace was saying.

Stepping into the room, I was thrown off guard by the sheer number of items inside. There were racks and racks of all sorts of women's clothes, cubbies filled with new undies and bras, slippers, sleepwear, and stacks of female hygiene products.

Did Severe even know that this stuff was here? It wasn't lost on me that all of the clothing, including the bras and panties, were some variation of the color black.

There was even a rack of large shopping sacks hanging on a coat rack next to the door. I swiped one.

"I'm starting to get a newfound respect for not judging a book by its cover," I mouthed to myself while thumbing through some tops.

A laugh behind me sounded, making me jump.

It was Mace. She stepped inside, smiling.

"I was sold to Toe Tags's father to settle a debt when I was sixteen," Mace said.

My jaw dropped at her words.

"I was horrified, terrified, and assumed my life was over. But I was treated better and with more respect under the care of a Reaper than when I was at home. No beatings or verbal abuse. No more being treated like a maid or traded to different men to pay off my father's debts. Tags had discovered what was happening to me, and I believe he was who convinced his father to purchase me."

I didn't know how to respond. It appeared the Reapers were more than harbingers of death and did a fair amount of rescuing in their spare time.

"Long story short, when I turned eighteen, I was given the option of being set free, but by then, I was already head over heels for Tags. It took me a long time to adjust to being the old lady of a Reaper, but once I truly understood the depths these men would go through to protect their family, which is what they consider me, I developed a newfound respect for them. There are some rules that are difficult to process, but overall and compared to the way I grew up, I couldn't have asked for a better life."

This news was unexpected, but the genuine smile in Mace's eyes and the relief in her expression couldn't be faked.

"Take your time looking around," she said before leaving me to do my shopping.

After about forty minutes, I exited the little shop with a stuffed bag, not knowing if I would need the items for a few days or a week. Mace's face lit up at the sight of me.

"Got everything you need?"

I nodded, glancing around for Zyana, but she had left. Her vest was splayed out over the counter with pins in it.

"Are you hungry?" Mace questioned. I supposed she sensed that Severe wasn't the best host.

"Not yet, but I'd love to have something other than peanut butter and jelly for later. I ate a can of old tuna he had in his cabinet for lunch."

She offered a smile before aiming her finger at the couch.

"Set your bag over there. I'll show you our food pantry, little restaurant, and the bar if you ever need a *stiff drink.*"

"This place is remarkable," I complimented, impressed that the compound had all an individual's needs covered, including an effective means of therapy in Scrappy. I'd also spotted a few dogs cozying up to the men.

On our way out the door, a motorcycle was pulling up at a cabin in the distance, and the sight of Zyana greeting the big biker that climbed off made me grin. He scooped her up into a big hug, and I swore the sparks from their connection touched me across the distance.

"How did they meet?" I asked Mace while placing my hand up to my forehead to shield me from the sun.

"Her brother and Israel are good friends, despite her brother being a detective."

The information made me glance in Mace's direction with a brow stuck in the air.

She chuckled at my reaction.

"One day, her brother's cover got blown, and the bad guys after him threatened Zyana. Major sent Israel to protect her. You would never believe it, looking at the way they are with each other now, that she did everything in her power to get away from him. Now, there's nothing powerful enough on this planet that can keep them apart."

My smile widened while listening to Mace and watching the couple. When Zyana was finally set on her feet, she gripped Israel's hand and tugged him along, walking in our direction. He resembled President Micah, except his hair was short, and he was bulkier.

When we were feet away from each other, he observed me with an edgy scrutiny that made me nervous. A smile teased his lips and flashed in his green eyes, making the tightness I didn't know was in my shoulders evaporate.

"Israel. This is Jade. Severe's old lady," Zyana introduced as if he didn't already know the fake news circulating their compound.

Israel reached out his big hand, and I took it.

"Nice to meet you, Jade."

Zyana glanced up at him.

"Jade says she's okay, but I'm worried about her. No disrespect to your brotherhood or anything, but Severe—" she said, her forehead growing tight with as much concern as she'd shown earlier.

Israel rubbed up and down Zyana's back caringly. "Z, he's not as bad as he wants people to believe."

Based on Zyana's apprehensive facial expression, she didn't believe a word he said. Severe had done one hell of a bang-up job of making a group of highly skilled and deadly people afraid of him.

Mace excused herself before stepping off to the side to talk to her man.

"Sorry about your boat," I voiced to Israel when the small white font spelling out 'Snake Eyes' stood out on the front of his vest. My brain connected the name to the boat.

"I'll gladly pay for damages, if necessary, since technically, I don't believe we would have been there if not for me."

He waved me off, although my offer put a tight crease on his forehead for a few seconds.

"No need. Everything's already been taken care of," he replied.

Now it was time I reeled in my expression.

Mace stepped up after finishing the discussion she was having with Toe Tags. And I hadn't missed the long-parting kiss she'd given him that had him whistling and smiling as he walked away. I wanted that one day. The way these women regarded these men with generous affection and the way these men reciprocated it was something to be envied. All the death and deviousness the Reapers represented didn't live here on this compound.

"I was about to show Jade the food pantry if you guys would like to walk with us?" Mace offered.

"Yes," Zyana answered for her and Israel, who appeared ready to lift her off her feet and carry her off to where they were supposed to be going.

"I'm guessing Severe's not here?" Zyana asked while walking alongside Mace and me. Israel hung back, walking behind us.

"He had some business to take care of," I replied.

"How did you and Severe meet?" Zyana asked, her inquisitive eyes glued to my face.

The question kept Mace intrigued enough to trip over nothing in her path. She didn't even acknowledge the little stumble—she was so engrossed in what I had to say.

"He saved me from a mugging," I said, unwilling to reveal too much of the sketchy details since I didn't even know the full story of us yet.

Zyana released a long-winded sigh. "It's so hard to believe. It's like you're talking about a different person," she said, scratching her head.

We entered the cabin housing the food pantry, which was as impressive as the little boutique shop. It was a small grocery store without the freezers of meats. I picked up some fresh fruit, some dried goods, and a half dozen eggs. I even had the presence of mind to pick up a small shaker of seasoning, some oil, and a few bowls since I hadn't seen any of the items in Severe's place.

Thirty minutes later, a satisfied smile crept along my face as Mace and I said our goodbyes to Zyana and Israel. She walked me back to the lodging cabin to pick up my other bag.

"Scrappy," I said, glancing around when it was time to head back.

"Don't worry about her. She knows her way back home. I believe that cat was once human," Mace said, chuckling.

"The cat was my guide. I'm not sure I know how to get back," I admitted.

Mace agreed to help me carry one of the bags back as well as show me the way.

Once I sprang Severe's door open, she didn't step inside. She offered a genuine smile after taking a quick peek inside and handed over the bag of groceries.

"The door to the guest house is always open," she said. She wanted to say more but left it alone.

Once Mace left, I unpacked the groceries and my newly acquired clothes and toiletries. A quick shower followed, and I finally relaxed with one of Severe's books, *Lord of the Flies*.

CHAPTER SEVENTEEN

Severe

"Severe," the familiar voice of Pressure sounded. "It's good to see you, brother," he greeted before opening the gate to allow me entrance into Ground Zero. He was camouflaged within the vegetation covering the gate and trained to stay hidden in plain sight.

I offered a nod in the direction of his voice before I revved my bike's engine to continue traveling along the passage that would lead me deeper into the compound. Why did it sound like Pressure had a certain spark to his tone that he'd never used to greet me with before?

"He acts like he wants to lick your balls or something. What the fuck is up with him?" my demon asked.

"I don't know," I muttered while glancing back in Pressure's direction. In my opinion, we all harbored sociopathic tendencies, which I believed were necessary to perform our job duties. However, the guys regarded me as the loyal but psychotic brother they respected but left alone because they didn't want to rub me the wrong way.

When I parked my bike, Toe Tags and Hangman broke away from a crowd of about ten gathered outside the clubhouse where they were barbequing and drinking. They rushed in my direction.

"Oh fuck. Here they come. And they look like they want to talk. Get rid of them," my demon spat.

"Severe!" Toe Tags shouted, toasting in my direction with his open bottle of beer. I nodded, but the uncharacteristic behavior put me on edge.

What the hell was his problem?

"We met your old lady, and I must pay you a compliment," Tags nodded, his head gesture a part of his compliment, I supposed. "She is one bold fucking choice. To say you are unpredictable is an understatement," he mouthed, with a wide grin plastered on his tipsy face.

Old lady?

"I told you to kill her. Now here we are, married and shit all of a sudden. If I had a mouth, I'd spit on you for putting me through this shit," my demon grumbled.

My deep frown had Tags and Hangman lifting defensive hands.

"No disrespect, man," Hangman said, keeping his hands lifted in surrender. "Me and some of the others who don't have an old lady yet wanted to say that we're damned proud of you for setting a standard the rest of us can follow. All those times you scared women off, brushed them off, and not showing any interest whatsoever, and now, we understand why. You were biding your time, waiting for her. Will you share with us how you did it, one day?"

His words and questions made my frown deepen.

"Did what?" I questioned while finally slipping off my bike. What the hell was he talking about?

I jerked the bottle from Hangman's hand and sniffed it to make sure the shit they were drinking wasn't spiked with PCP or something before I handed it back. He glanced down at the bottle in his hand before pinning his expectant eyes back on me.

"How you met your old lady, Jade?" he reiterated. "We never saw her at any of our parties or events. She is, like I said, no disrespect, but she's beautiful and down to earth. She's not all prissy and closed off as you'd expect. I'm sure she made more than a few of us liars today for pre-judging her."

I nodded once in their direction and headed into the clubhouse, leaving their questions unanswered. What the hell was going on? Had I been gone long enough for Jade to spread her lies around the entire compound?

She'd left my cabin, proving she wasn't as naïve as I assumed. I'd have thought her too afraid of snakes to venture out and spread rumors. Was she telling people that she was my old lady, or were they assuming it since she'd volunteered to stay with me?

"The next time I tell you to kill her, do it, jackass," my demon shouted.

As soon as I stepped inside the clubhouse, a set of serious hazel eyes landed on mine. The tight set of his jaw and the tension in his body let me know that my situation had him under a lot of stress.

"All I've been hearing on this compound all day is your old lady this and your old lady that," Micah said. "All I've been reminded of from the Six is the target that needs to be taken out within the next ten days. Did you find anything new that we can take to the Six?"

He didn't give me a chance to answer any of the questions, further proof that he was stressed.

"I requested an emergency meeting with them, and they've agreed to next weekend. It's the soonest they're available. They want to meet before the contract officially expires."

I nodded at the update. If they were willing to meet, it meant they may not have been aware of the side operations taking place.

"My source believes the recordings linked to Jade's kill order are high-priced fakes. They are currently piecing together enough evidence to prove that it was doctored. And it had to have been done by some of the best in the business for it to take this much time to dissect."

"How long before you have irrefutable evidence?" he questioned.

"Two or three days at the most," I told him.

"We don't have much time to figure this shit out. I haven't mentioned any of the shit you encountered today or what you found out about Danger to them. What if a member of the Six truly is pulling the strings, and Danger is the fall guy? At that level, trust me, any fucking thing is possible."

We released deep sighs.

"We have to prove without any doubt that her contract shouldn't be executed because when they vote and make the final decision, that can't be undone," he said.

Micah lifted a hand, already knowing what I'd ask.

"I haven't given anyone any updates, not even our closest brothers. Plausible deniability. I don't want them taking any blowback if this shit gets any messier."

Silence filled the space for a long stretch of time.

"She doesn't even know that she's a target, does she," Micah asked.

I shook my head.

"You need to tell her the real reason why she's here and what you are to her," Micah urged.

His sharp-eyed gaze was locked on mine, an addition to the order he'd just given. There was a tightness around his eyes that I wasn't used to seeing. I believe his attention was torn between his duty to our club and to the Order.

"If you say that she doesn't know anything, I believe you. If you believe there's a traitor among the Order, I'll believe you over what any of them has to say. But my hands are tied unless we can prove without a doubt that what you believe is true and that the information you're discovering is also true."

My cousins had proven to me multiple times that I was like a younger brother to them. Micah believing me over the Six proved how much I truly meant to him. I didn't know how to express my gratitude to him, other than saying thank you, but I sensed he knew.

"I didn't mean to put you in a tough position, but I *can't* kill someone that doesn't deserve to die," I gritted out.

"Yes, you can!" My demon roared in my head.

I rolled my eyes. The demon living inside me had never gotten on my nerves so badly. I'd killed many people who weren't sanctioned hits, but there was never any doubt about the legitimacy of their executions.

"Will you be able to kill her if we can't prove what we believe?" Micah questioned. This was the second time he'd asked me the question.

I nodded, and for the first time since I was a kid, uncertainty paid me a visit.

"I'll do it for the both of us," my demon volunteered, his blunt words echoing in my head. Even if I couldn't pull the trigger, I knew that *he* would, even if he believed Jade was innocent.

The worried expression on Micah's face wasn't something I was used to seeing, especially where it concerned me.

"I know you, cousin, better than anyone here. I know that you have a mental fail-safe that will allow you to make a decision that a lot of others won't. However, she left an impression on half this damn compound in the hours you were gone today. If someone tries to touch her while our brothers are around, they will defend her despite the circumstances. After we have this meeting with the Six this weekend, we may have to hash this shit out in church. I can't have Reapers going against the Order. It's suicide despite us not giving a fuck about dying. However, I want for all Reapers what I want for myself, and that is to go out in battle, not disgraced by a firing squad or some other quick method the Order may choose."

I nodded, but my mind was in a never-ending battle. Were we willing to let our brothers die for a woman we barely knew? Were we willing to allow an innocent woman to be sacrificed by a corrupt organization?

CHAPTER EIGHTEEN

Severe

Finding Jade curled up on the couch with Scrappy snuggled in next to her was an unexpected sight. It seemed Scrappy was as drawn to her as everyone else. Even though she appeared naively fearless, I didn't know if it was an act or her personality.

Most women left alone in her situation would have been afraid to explore, but she'd done the opposite. It was a small test I'd put in place, and didn't know what the outcome would be because, like many couldn't figure me out, I couldn't figure her out.

She'd made an impression on the guys as they'd been singing my new *old lady's* praises since I stepped through the gates. I was "One lucky motherfucker," according to a few of them. I'd even been asked where they could go to find another like her.

I'm the broken one. I know and accept that about myself and learned to work with the scattered pieces, picking out the one or two I wanted when I needed them. I functioned efficiently enough to exist, to matter, and to fulfill a purpose, even if that purpose was wrapped in twisted but sensible logic.

Life for me was a constant test. What would finally make me snap? What vicious act would I commit that would finally lead to me having to be put down like a rabid dog? Was I being tested for redemption or to solidify my already established and deviant nature?

The longer Jade was around me, the more I believed she was picking up the shattered pieces of me and connecting them to the parts to which they once belonged.

She lifted from the spot she'd curled into on the couch, and when she noticed me sitting on the other end, she gasped, placing a hand over her chest.

"You have to stop that. How do you do that anyway? It's like you don't register until I see you."

"You've been out," I stated the obvious.

A smile crept across her face, despite the quick rise and fall of her chest. It pleased me to see that I'd scared her.

"Yes, and some of the guys think you have me here against my will. A few were genuinely afraid for my life. The rest think that I'm your old lady, and I let them believe it." She showed me a tight smile. "What am I to you?" she asked.

"You should be afraid," I warned her honestly, ignoring the other questions she'd asked because I didn't have an answer.

"After you left me here with nothing to do and no real food, I ate a can of your tuna, got bored, and decided it was time I took the tour that you didn't give me."

I noticed she'd ignored my comment. She also had a knack for ignoring my threats, unaware that I wasn't being sarcastic when I made them.

"You ate tuna?" I questioned, my squint deepening the longer I thought about it.

"Yes." She pointed at my kitchen cabinet. "Before Scrappy and I went on our journey, I opened a can for me and one for her, and we ate together."

My gaze dropped to Scrappy, who lifted a nonchalant brow. If she had shoulders, I'm sure she would have shrugged them.

"What?" Jade lifted onto her elbows while aiming her sharp, expectant gaze at me.

"I don't have tuna in my cabinet," I told her.

"Um, yes, you do. It was tangy and had an earthy flavor to it, but there were six cans in the cabinet."

Scrappy lifted her head higher like she wanted to but was unable to voice her two cents.

"The unlabeled cans in the cabinet? That's not tuna. I don't eat meat," I said.

She swallowed hard, her unblinking gaze pinned on my face. Her vibrant brown completion was paling before my eyes. Her gaze dropped to Scrappy before she shot it back up to me.

"What is it? What did I eat?" she questioned, her breathing heavy enough to make her chest resume its rapid rise and fall.

"Those cans are Scrappy's cat food," I informed.

Her eyes slammed shut, and she swayed. Her body went still and rigid like she was attempting to send herself back in time to skip lunch.

She jumped up to a sitting position, forcing Scrappy to scramble out of her way and into my lap. The cat stared, no doubt questioning what was wrong with the crazy woman.

"Now, she's eating our cat's food. She's gotta go! Now!" my demon squawked.

Jade's mouth was wide open as she raked her nails over her tongue, attempting to scratch out whatever residue of the cat food was left from there hours ago. Scrappy sat up in my lap. She released a low meow, as if asking a question. She glanced back and forth between me and Jade no doubt questioning her behavior.

Jade made spitting sounds now, and the frown on her face could have passed for a whole conversation about her displeasure of having the cat food inside her body.

"No. Oh, God. I didn't eat cat food," she muttered.

She shook her head rapidly like that would cleanse her of what her body was already converting into energy. The sight was so funny. I couldn't help releasing a chuckle. My chest bobbed up and down at the panicked sight of her. Genuine laughter spilled from me hardily.

"Severe!" she yelled, her stare sharp and her mouth hanging open at my reaction. "I know you are not laughing. I ate cat food, and you think that's funny? Oh, my God. I think I'm going to be sick."

She stood and sat back down, gagging with her mouth wide open. Scrappy glanced up at me before putting curious eyes back on Jade, who was putting on a performance.

She stood again. "I need to go throw up." I stopped her, gripping her wrist before she could take off.

"It's okay. It won't make you sick," I assured her.

"It's not okay," she shot back. "I ate cat food. How is that okay?"

She spat into the air a few times and opened her mouth to air out her tongue. The little crease that formed between the cat's eyes revealed that she may have been offended that Jade would be so prissy as to try to throw up her food.

"Scrappy's food is as healthy, if not more so, than ours," I reassured her while failing to keep my laughter at bay.

"If it's supposed to be so good for you, have you ever eaten it?" she asked, pinning me with a deadly side-eye.

"No," I answered quickly. "I've never had a taste for it."

The vicious slap she delivered to my forearm for that comment was warranted, but I couldn't help myself. This was the first time I'd laughed out loud in years or ever.

She sat and cast a mean glare like she wanted to roast my insides over an open fire as she aimed an angry finger. "It's your fault I was forced to eat cat food. You left me here with no food or direction."

She sounded hurt.

"There's…"

"Don't you dare say that there was peanut butter and jelly in there and that it's a balanced meal. If you say it, I promise you, Severe, I'll scream my head off."

My lips snapped shut. Scrappy took this as her opportunity to get off my lap and go to her bed. The cat had seen enough, but I enjoyed seeing Jade drive herself mad over mistakenly eating cat food.

She gagged and burped before staring up at the ceiling.

"Lord, will I grow fur now? I believe I can already feel the fur balls forming in my throat."

She coughed into her hand for effect, the sight making it difficult to contain another outburst of laughter. Once I calmed enough to control the unfamiliar urge to laugh, I placed what I hoped was a calming hand on her back.

"You're going to make yourself sick for no reason," I said.

"Easy for you to say. You've never accidentally eaten cat food."

My teeth sank into my bottom lip to suppress another laugh. Childhood memories flashed in my head and sucked every drop of laughter from my soul. My eyes fell closed, and the weight of my past made it difficult to reopen them.

"I know, but I've been forced to eat much worse," I told her. This statement drew her attention. She must have noticed the seriousness in my tone because she placed a tender hand on my forearm.

"You'll tell me the story?" she asked. "If you feel like it," she quickly added, knowing me well enough by now to know talking about myself wasn't something I did. However, in this case, I believed she deserved a piece of my story since it was my fault she'd eaten Scrappy's food.

CHAPTER NINETEEN

Jade

I believe I'd eaten much worse than cat food throughout my life, but seeing Severe laugh, and hearing the jovial sounds coming from him was enough to make me keep up my little show.

It appeared he wanted to expand on his statement about being forced to eat worse than cat food, but he was such a closed-off person that I knew it was difficult for him to share parts of himself in that way. The knowledge that he'd mentioned as much and considered sharing was a big step.

Why did it even matter? We weren't friends, yet I wanted to know more, a lot more about him.

I sensed his warmth despite the distance between us on the couch. The fresh scent permeating from him indicated that he'd been home long enough to shower and jump into his usual black tee and shorts.

Why was I so aware of him all of a sudden? My eyes were all over the man. Was I hormonal? It wasn't time for my cycle to pay me a visit and stir them up. I slid closer despite all that was swirling around in my head.

"Can I ask you something, Severe?"

"Yeah."

His cap was blocking that beautiful face I was desperate to see again.

"Why do you hide yourself, specifically your face?"

"There is no reason anyone needs to see me unless I want them to," he replied.

"I want to see you. Will you take your hat off?"

His gaze remained aimed in my direction for a long stretch of time, and when I kept my attention aimed at him without backing down, he swiped the cap off his head and tossed it on the coffee table.

The beautiful shoulder-length, dark brown hair the cap was pinning down now framed his face, the strands still damp from his shower.

"Can I touch your hair?" I asked, sliding close enough for my hip to brush up against his toned thigh. Indecision sparked in his gaze, but he answered.

"Yes."

I'd asked to touch his hair because it was the first thing to come to mind. The truth was, I wanted to get closer. I didn't consider myself a shy woman when it came to men but was finding that I was like a teen experiencing some of my firsts with Severe.

I turned to get closer, making my knee inch up his muscular thigh.

"Turn this way," I suggested, smiling when he shifted in my direction to allow me access to his hair. I reached up, and our gazes connected and locked. The depth of the connection made my hand stall mid-reach.

Everything stopped.

My next breath stuck in my throat. Sound no longer existed. The cabin, our surroundings, no other matter existed accept him. I choked down the supercharged energy flowing through me.

Neither of us possessed the ability to break the powerful hold of the connection we were sharing. Severe stared hard like it was the first time he'd ever seen me, his eyes searching mine, his breaths rushing out in quick spurts like mine. I swallowed hard, forcing a smile to get a part of me moving again.

Finally, my arm decided it wanted to work again, and my fingers flirted with the ends of his damp hair before I sent them farther, shoving them into the soft, silky tresses. Our eyes wouldn't let go of the tense connection that had me edging closer and digging my hand deeper into his hair until my nails raked his scalp.

I didn't notice how close I'd gotten, how close my mouth was to his, until he eased back.

"What are you doing?" he asked.

"I'm trying to kiss you." I leaned closer, no longer controlling the urges that were rushing demandingly through me.

He reached up and pulled at the hand I had curled against his scalp and tangled in his hair.

"We're not going there," he said with finality, shaking his head.

"Why not? You're attracted to me. I'm attracted to you. We're stuck here for an unspecified amount of time," I said, like that was all the explanation needed.

"You're experiencing heightened emotions due to the events you've been exposed to while with me. This close proximity environment is feeding your hormones lust. You feel gratitude towards me for saving you. It may also be transference," he said.

My brows drew tight at how he'd interpreted my feelings, sounding like a shrink talking to his patient. It was a misdiagnosis as far as I was concerned.

He hadn't released my wrist. The pressure he applied shot up my arm and sent an enticing mix of desire and panic through me.

Was I sexually starved and desperate for male attention? I don't believe I was. However, there was something about Severe that turned me on in a way I'd never expected and certainly had never experienced.

He made things sizzle. There were sparks of uneasy tension that deliciously coursed through my body and kept me aching for more of the addicting stimulation.

Severe brought to life a passion within me that had never revealed itself before—something I didn't know I possessed. In my twenty-nine years, he was the only one to pull the aggressive vibes from me. He unknowingly made me want him, despite the unprecedented and unpredictable setting in which we were currently stuck.

He applied more pressure to my wrist, and his gaze bore into mine intently, pulling the intense urge I possessed to be near him to the surface. As unintentional as it was, his actions were making me want him more.

"You're bored. You're used to working twenty-hour days. Now, you're stuck sitting around all day. I'm just something for you to do," he added, and at this point, I wasn't sure if he was convincing me or himself.

My head shook fast. "No. I've been bored before, and I don't believe it's boredom that has me on edge. Being around you is hyper-intense. I don't want to use our circumstances as a convenient excuse to keep suppressing what I feel and would like to explore further."

He released my arm and backed away. His strong touch was noticeably missing. I believed he might have been experiencing a rare moment of confusion based on the way his hand massaged his forehead and the other was squeezing his tense shoulder.

Did I affected him as much as he didn't know he affected me? He knew how to keep his emotions hidden, but every once and a while, I spotted the little sparks of interest that peeked through.

"Can I?" I asked him, placing my hand over the one he was using to squeeze his shoulder. He went still under my touch, the vibe between us even more vibrant now that we were somewhat acknowledging there *was* an attraction between us. He slid his hand from beneath mine but didn't pull away.

"Turn a little," I suggested. Surprisingly, he complied, turning and giving me access to his shoulders. I eased up higher on my knees, unable to help drawing closer to the warming pull he emitted. A sneaky smile swept across my face at the access to him he was allowing.

My fingers pressed into his tense shoulders. The knotted muscles in them were like sinewy cords of metal. I squeezed harder, getting a better grip until the tension eased and released the tight grip it had on his muscles.

"You're very tense. When was the last time you had a good stress reliever?" I asked.

"Today," he answered.

I immediately knew we weren't talking about the same thing.

"What happened out there today? Will you say?"

The tension was easing the more I squeezed. My questions distracted him from my touch and close proximity.

"I ran into some trouble. The kind of trouble you witnessed on the boat and at the car dealership in New York."

I lifted higher on my knees, pressing the front of my body into his back to glance at him over his shoulder.

"Are you okay? Did you find out who these people are? What's going on that you're not telling me?"

He blew out a heavy sigh. I didn't expect him to say anything, so relief swept through me when he began to speak.

"We believe there is a traitor in our organization that is using his or her power to manipulate the system. We believe they are using our own system against us to make unsanctioned kills."

My face squeezed into a tight knot.

"I kind of don't understand it all, but for the parts that I do, it sounds like you guys are in conflict with your organization and have to flush out a traitor in order to restore order to what I presume is a complex system of honor when it comes to the people you assassinate."

"Sounds about right," he stated, letting more tension fall from his shoulders.

"Thank you for sharing what you can about what's going on. I've accepted that it's complicated and that you're governed by guidelines I may never know or understand."

I continued to squeeze his toned shoulders, noticing how close we were, how close he'd allowed me, so soon after my thirsty little attempt to put my lips on his.

"I can see and feel the stress you've been under since we met. At first, I was upset about being dragged into this, but after talking to some of the guys today and after spending time around you, I'm starting to understand the concept of necessary evil and that it's not all evil."

I thought about the twist and turns my life had taken over the last few days.

"Is there anything I can do to help? And not because I'm angling for any rewards like getting back to my life, but because I genuinely want to help."

He shook his head.

"No, but it doesn't mean we won't need you in the future," he said. The statement meant progress. The version of him I met in New York would have given me a two-word riddle for an answer.

An easy smile surfaced and remained on my face. My focus slipped back to how close we were and how my body flirted with and pressed into his strong back.

I leaned in, intending to apply more pressure to his shoulder, but somehow my lips found their way to his neck, placing a soft kiss right in the center. The action made him suck in a hard breath.

He smelled good, like fresh soap and sun-kissed pine. Like everything else about him, he was either clueless or didn't care about his allure.

My lips on his hot skin made me want to explore more of him. A few more pecks left goosebumps on his skin, the sight putting an instant smile on my face.

He turned so rapidly that I fell into his lap, gripping his arm and opposite shoulder to steady myself.

"We shouldn't cross lines that are put in place for a reason." His expression implied more than his words.

"It's too late. I don't believe the lines exist anymore."

I reached up, and he leaned down until our lips collided in a hard, hot kiss that made me melt in his arms. At my angle, I was off balance, fighting to enjoy the lip-tingling kiss that reached past my lust and delved deep enough to captivate my senses.

The first swipe of his tongue across my lips sent my heart galloping in my chest and my body flailing and thrashing for more. The best I was able to do at my angle was to get a good grip on his hair and use the pull to center myself.

He stopped. So abruptly, my eyes snapped open, and my reeling mind stopped spinning. Our breathing filled the space with the only sound. I sat up, but not to separate myself from him. I shifted to a more comfortable position across his lap.

When I drew closer to his face and reunited our lips, he accepted my kiss, allowing his soft lips to melt into mine like he was testing the sincerity of my actions.

"You're a good kisser," I whispered against his mouth. "I like kissing you. A lot." The warm, soft firmness and the snapshot of his lips on mine so kissable kept me tuned into him.

His tongue, when it stroked mine, was the same, and he used the right motions to make me want more, crave more, and seek out more. Most men were too sloppy with their kisses and left me frowning, swiping away extra saliva, and even turning away. Not Severe.

I had to stop myself from following his lips when he eased back. My compliment had him studying me, or maybe it was that we were crossing the shaky line he'd drawn.

A hard swallow made my throat bob. Our closeness was hot and heady, a living emotion verging on insanity. I wanted to kiss him again, needed to so badly that I leaned closer and stretched my neck until our lips reconnected. He didn't respond at first, letting his lips sit against mine, unmoving.

The exhilarating rush lingering between us exploded when he returned the kiss hungrily, devouring my lips, tasting my tongue, and exploring my mouth.

When we separated this time, I couldn't bear to stray too far away. I needed to lengthen the connection that drew me to him. I needed to explore it so that I could see if I could figure out what lured me to him this desperately.

His earlier diagnosis of us was wrong. There was no way this was induced by transference or gratitude. This was the moment when I acknowledged that I had feelings, ones that had shown up despite the time or my circumstances. Deep and demanding, these feelings had lingered and was now revealing themselves when they could no longer be suppressed.

There was a lot more to get to know about this mysterious, scary, smart man, but there was no more denying our undeniable connection. He was good at ignoring. I wasn't.

We had chemistry, whether he admitted it or not. I knew what I was experiencing. I sensed what kept gnawing at my bones and pulsing through my blood like it owned me.

I'd had many flings, fleeting romances, and boyfriends I knew wouldn't last past a month. This wasn't that. This was the sky opening up and dumping everything but the kitchen sink at me. This connection between us was almost instantly there, and, circumstances be damned, it grew stronger the longer we were near each other.

I leaned in, letting my arms drape around his neck until I was wrapped around him, my nose snuggling into his neck, where his pulse thumped hard against my lips. He returned my embrace, not because he wanted to, but because like me, I don't believe he had a choice.

"It hurts," he whispered, his breath whispering against a few loose strains of my hair.

"What hurts? Are you okay?"

Glancing down at the way I was straddling him, I accepted that I'd lost control, another sign that this wasn't boredom.

"Being this connected. This close," he said, his words barely audible.

His brows squeezed tight while he stared, his gaze searching mine purposefully. The delicate way he stroked up and down my back was an affectionate action that I don't believe he was aware he was giving.

When our kiss reconnected and grew more frantic, he stood, taking me up with my arms slung around his neck and his under my hips. He eased me down until my feet touched the floor, but I didn't let go of his neck. I was too hot and needy.

"You have condoms?" I whispered. Breathy. Hot. Bothered.

He shook his head.

"Damn," I mouthed before I leaned in for another kiss he didn't turn down. My hard nipples ached. The peppery little pricks had me rubbing my chest against his hard one.

My pussy throbbed so hard it had its own heartbeat. Feeling him hard and hot against my stomach was the last straw.

"You don't strike me as the cat-chasing type. Are you clean?" I asked. There was no shame or hesitation in my question.

He nodded, but my question was something I believed I already knew about him.

"Aren't you going to ask about me?"

"No," he whispered, letting one strong hand run up my back. The other gripped my waist, and he pulled me hard against his body, making me gasp. Without allowing me time to think, my shirt was moving up my body. I lifted my arms willingly and allowed my top to be jerked up and over my head.

Button and zipper undone, I abandoned the task of getting my pants, his pants that I wore, off me to help him with his shirt.

Were we really about to do this?

"Shit," rushed out at the first sight of his tattooed body when we worked his shirt off. He had more mass than I first assumed due to the black clothing he always wore. He was toned, and tattoos covered his chest, his arms, and more.

My gaze chased my fingers down his happy trail, and I found my fingers fumbling with his pants on their own accord. I sent my tongue across my lips as I struggled to get my hands, shaking with anticipation, to work properly. The man was living art and had me so worked up and hot that I was melting.

"Aww!" I yelled out when I was spun away from my task and bent over the couch. My pants were yanked roughly down my legs. The tremble in me didn't register until I lifted each leg for him to take the pants off.

Once my legs were bare, the pants flew past my view, tossed away like unwanted trash. While he was bent and taking his pants down, I turned back, my eyes aimed at the area I felt earlier and desperately wanted to see now.

When he stood and kicked his pants and boxer briefs to the side, my lips fell apart, and my wide, unblinking eyes zeroed in on his thick, long, veiny, and inspiring work of manly art. The well-endowed piece sported a tattoo: a series of rings that, at first glance, looked like barbed wire.

At a closer view, one I had no shame in getting, the tattoos were small tribal symbols that ran into the larger bands drawn along the front of his right thigh.

His magnificent size had me squeezing my thighs together and fighting to keep from drooling. He was in my hand, hard and heavy, and being stroked before I even realized what I was doing. His harsh intakes of breaths lured me from the spell his dick had cast on me.

After he allowed me a little time to get acquainted with him down below, he spun me again, this time keeping his hand pressed into my back to keep me down.

"No," I called back, feeling his strong hand ease up before he lifted it. I spun back.

"I'm not one of those skanks you screw in a rest stop bathroom and face plant in a urinal. I want to see you, at least for the first time," I said, unable to help glancing down since his thick length was licking the area above my belly button.

He shrugged and said, "Okay," before he shoved his strong hands under my arms, lifted and tossed my ass on the couch. My back landed between the V that connected the arm to the couch back. The top half of me hung slightly over the arm.

Without giving me a chance to adjust myself on the couch, he was spreading my legs and lifting my bottom half, leaving me off-kilter and unable to straighten myself.

The sight of his thick length aimed at my dripping lips had me wide-eyed and breathless. I'd asked to see him, but the sight of his dark peach, thick, and tattooed dick nudging my lips apart and dipping into me had me near hyperventilating.

My elbows dug deep into the arm and back of the couch in an attempt to straighten myself, but he wouldn't allow it. He kept me helplessly unbalanced, with my bottom half lifted by his possessive hands.

The deeper he dived, the wider he spread my legs. The sensation of him stretching me open shouldn't have been so damn pleasurable, but it was the best ache of hard passion I'd ever experienced.

I kept admiring the way his thick length kissed my wet lips, spreading them to slide in, deep and unyielding. The way his length dragged against my quivering opening; I'd surely come from the visual alone.

"Oh!" I blew out, letting my head fall back when he was halfway home. "Shit," I gasped part of the word and sipped on the other half when he pushed the rest of the way into me. I was full, so very full I was afraid to move. Lying there, my mouth hanging open and staring at where we were connected, I finally found his heavy-lidded gaze waiting on mine and filled with purpose and confidence.

He moved with a dragging pace, in and out, pulling a desperate gasp from me with every possessive stroke. I ached to touch him, to have his strong body to hold on to as it may have been all that kept me from falling apart. I believe he was intentionally keeping me off balance as it kept me at a distance and allowed him maximum control over me.

When he picked up speed, the pressure of his depth gave off a pleasurable ache that swirled in my lower back before it zipped down to my toes. Each stroke drove me farther over the arm of the couch, and there was nothing I could do but take whatever he dished out.

"Severe!" I called out, gasping, panting, and struggling for each pleasure-driven breath.

He pulled out and thrust back in so hard my elbow slipped over the top of the arm of the couch, and I expected to go over the top too, but he had such a possessive grip on my hips, I wasn't going anywhere but where he wanted me.

Again, he pounded me. "Oh!" I yelled out. "God. I…" I don't know what I was saying because the good he was creating was causing a stupid, blubbering mess to spill from my mouth. Each time he hit deep and hard, the tingling ache in my back shot up my spine, and my pussy throbbed harder against his dick. The slow dragging rotation stimulated my clit, giving all my parts the combinations of sensations guaranteed to get me off in the best way.

He was so slick with my juices that his dick glistened against the lamplight shining over our heads. This was by far the wettest I recalled being for anyone.

"I want to. I need it. Oh! God."

Breaths escaped me, and my hard gasps and moans were the only reasons I hadn't suffocated. When I became convinced I couldn't take the punishing thrusts, he must have read my mind because he repositioned himself and aimed his dick upward. Each stroke allowed his slippery head to lick across my G-spot and make me see stars in the process.

Relentless.

Desperate.

Passionate.

His expression shifted from determined to confident to focused. Finally, a threatening glint appeared—one that scared the hell out of me and unexpectantly added to the high he was feeding me.

The change in his gaze made it appear he'd somehow morphed into a whole other person, one who might fuck me to death, his favorite pastime. He slipped his arm under my left leg and lifted it. The move spread me wider, and balance was lost as the arm of the couch pressed against my back, and the rest of me was being banged out so good that I was on the verge of passing out from the addicting aches of desire that was spoon-feeding me a heavy dose of pleasure and insanity.

The sound of his body colliding into mine added to the sexual rush invading me in the most delicious way possible. He leaned in and flicked his tongue firmly over my nipple before pulling the hard pebble between his lips and letting his teeth close around the hard tip.

"Shit! Shit! That. Shit!" I cursed. It hurt so damn good I almost came. He switched to the other nipple in the nick of time, never letting up on the hard pounding he was putting on my lady parts.

"I'm. Oh, God. I don't know."

One leg was pinned against the couch, and his strong grip held it in place. The other leg was spread wide and pinned under his shoulder, with the back of my heel bouncing about and striking the top of his back.

The man turned me into his pretzel, taking my pussy by storm and making me take whatever he felt like giving. The expression on his face said I better take it and acknowledge that his dick was not good, but the best. And the look wasn't telling me any lies. Severe made me his slut, whore, and bitch at the same time, and I loved every uncontrolled, unhinged moment of it.

The rush had me riding a high I didn't want to end. I knew my circuits were about to overload, and my brain would fry from the fire he'd set off within me.

"Severe. I'm...oh my... Se...vere," I hollowed and whined at the same time before I exploded. The orgasm hit me everywhere, overwhelmingly aggressive and dominating. I grew deathly still, fearing I'd cross over and meet my maker. There was so much sensation, so much energy, so much everything flowing into me, over me, and through me all at once.

"Oh! Oh, God. Oh," was what I spit out when my shivering body rode the wave of an orgasm that kept giving and giving and a dick that kept tunneling through the rush and stroking at a raging fire I didn't even know could be lit.

Another orgasm hit before the embers of the first went out, and at some point during the hazy ride, Severe released.

"Fuck. Fuck. Fuck," he kept saying, so low in my cloudy reality that I didn't know if I was imagining the sound of his voice or hearing it.

My pussy squeezed a tight hug around his dick, making the drumbeat of his pulse thrum through me like a band of lit fuses. He didn't move until I stopped shaking, and his dick had gone down enough to give my poor walls some relief.

He eased himself out of me and lowered me onto the couch. I sunk into the cushions like I didn't have a working bone in my body.

"Whew," I whispered while keeping my heavy gaze pinned on him, eyeing him like the sexual marvel he'd proven himself to be. The man was the walking definition of 'don't judge a book by its cover' because he had put it on me so good that, sore pussy or not, I already knew I'd be asking for more and looking at him all googly eyed until I got it.

CHAPTER TWENTY

Severe

What the hell had I gone and done?

"You fucked the shit out of your target, and it was good too. But it doesn't change the fact that we still have to kill her, just not before you fuck her again. Fuck her until she's calling you her God. I like that shit."

I ignored my demon. He wasn't helping at all. I believed he was the asshole who'd decided to let things go that far. My intentions were to deter her from where I knew she wanted to go the moment she sat closer and put her hands on me.

I hadn't even used a condom, not that I needed it since I knew she had a birth control device in her uterus.

"Kill her while you're fucking her. She'd never see it coming. Look at how she's staring at you now. She wants to fuck again."

I backed away and paused at the sight of my cum dripping from her still-pulsing pussy. A creamy shot drizzled down her brown lips while her pink center put serious stress on my ability to back away.

The sight of her so open and sexually ready for me had me getting hard all over again. I backed away from this addictive woman's splayed legs and stood on my own weak ones before heading to the kitchen for water. My dick, still wet, made a slapping sound against the front of my thigh with each of my quick steps.

I guzzled my water while walking back to hand her one. She hadn't moved an inch, and her eyes ran down my body and stopped on my hard dick. What the hell was wrong with me and my dick? And with her.

"Addictive spell-casting pussy. Just this one time, I agree with you on something, and fucking her was an excellent decision."

She took the water, not once breaking the stare-off she was having with my dick. There was no denying she wanted it again, and seeing it so plainly displayed in her expression was fucking with my willpower.

"Fuck willpower! Fuck her hard while choking..."

I sat down hard on the couch to shut him up and blind myself from the sight of *her.* They were driving me crazy.

She sat up and allowed her feet to slide off the couch onto the floor as she lifted the water again and drank. I slammed my eyes shut, and I took in deep breaths, easing my raging thoughts and thinking about...

"Pussy. Good, high-class, willing pussy. So sweet. And wet. And tight. And..."

"Severe," she called in a low tone, and I answered without glancing in her direction.

"Yes."

"That was...," she paused, searching for words, I supposed. "Amazing."

"We shouldn't have," I muttered.

"Yes, we should have. And we should definitely do it again," she said, sliding close enough for her body to scrape against the side of mine.

The moment she touched me, all my good sense exited my brain and evaporated. My dick morphed from hard to excruciatingly stiff. I couldn't take the edgy waves that ran through me so fiercely that I believed my mind and body were locked in a duel to the death.

There was nothing else to be said. I snapped up from the couch, startling her with my fast movement. After kneeling before her, I gave one hard tug that had her splayed before me like a buffet meal. I gripped her hips, my finger pressing hard into her supple skin, and spread her legs as wide as they would go before I buried my face in her pussy.

I didn't come up for air until she came all over my tongue, and her juices were spread all over my face like my new secret sauce. Without giving her a moment to breathe, I dragged her to the edge of the couch and fucked her until it appeared I'd fulfilled my demon's intentions of killing her.

To my demon's disappointment, she wasn't dead, just fucked until she was almost unconscious. However, the smile on her face when her heavy gaze did meet mine was all the confirmation I needed to know that she enjoyed my rough sexual handling.

Two more rounds were all I was able to pull from her until she finally fell asleep or passed out. I didn't know which but was grateful. Otherwise, I believe I would have kept going. Her light snores sounded, the noise relaxing like blood dripping from a fresh, dead body.

CHAPTER TWENTY-ONE

Severe

Six days later.

When I walked out my door this evening, I couldn't say for sure who the hell I was anymore. Jade and I—we couldn't get enough of each other. It got to a point where our parts couldn't physically take anymore. Me leaving for some of the day or night to work on building a case for her was the only break we allowed our bodies.

To say I knew my target better was an understatement. We attacked each other like addicts, three, four, five times a day or until she was too sore to continue. I had never been like this—had never had a craving I couldn't overcome.

I'd allowed myself to get so carried away that I would sometimes forget about the deadly situations she would face if I didn't find a way to put an end to it. I couldn't bring myself to tell her that I was the frayed piece of thread keeping her alive and, at the same time, the bullet that would have to end her life.

My walk to sanctuary to meet with the Six was a silent, ominous one that put me on edge in a way I'd never experienced before now.

"She's changing you. She's making you care. Don't fall for it."

A long table with a single leather rolling chair at the head and a large screen on the wall at the other end linked me to the Six. They sat comfortably at their secret locations. Their faces were hidden behind objects to keep Micah and me from seeing them, even on a secure video conference.

They were six of the most powerful people on the planet, and no one, including us, the people they governed, knew who they were or what they looked like. They were representations, much like living declarations of power that we followed because the system had worked up until now.

At some point in my training, I'd come in contact with one or maybe all of them as we were informed of the tricky ways in which they'd reveal themselves to us. They had mastered the art of keeping their identities hidden in plain sight.

Micah stood at the back of the room in the shadows, bearing witness to this official meeting. Voices and faces remained obscured from view, and everyone was addressed as Mr., so their gender couldn't be determined.

When the Six spoke in a setting such as this one, they identified themselves by the section of the Order they represented. They would state the part of the knife they represented: edge, point, tip, flat, blade, or heel.

Mr. Putter was the oldest of the Six based on the fifty-year stretch he'd served. He was the leader of the Shadows, the church and spiritual branch of the Order known as the Edge of the Knife. His movement made the screen reduce the other five screens and zoom in on him on the larger screen at the top of the page.

He wore a *Scream* mask, which suggested he at least had a personality. He was fit based on his build.

"This meeting has been called as an official proceeding of the Order. A sanctioned kill order has been called into question," he said. The tone of his voice was deep, confident, and strong. His time served was the only hint as to his age. "This kill order was voted on by each member and passed, but the Reapers, the blade and deadliest part of the knife in our organization are prepared to present a valid enough argument for us to come together."

The rest of the Six nodded from wherever they were in their prospective state, city, or town.

Mr. Murphey, the leader of the streets, weapons, and arms division, came on the big screen. They were known as the Point of the Knife in the Order.

"If you have any evidence, Mr. Sylas, this is your time to present it," he said. He appeared to look down on me like a god, although projected from a screen.

I stood and pointed the remote at the video. It was the evidence the Six had used to vote and pass Jade's kill order. It showed her supposedly committing heinous acts, including but not limited to child abduction and sales.

The first scene began with her picking up a screaming boy of about five years old. I ignored what the video appeared to show and paused at certain points that revealed a digital gloss over the film that was embedded within the video frames. A few brows lifted, but they would have to see much more evidence before they would become convinced that the videos weren't authentic.

I went further, showing them that her speech had been manipulated, although her own voice was laid over what was being said. The video was intricately edited, but small portions revealed her lip movements not matching the words being said. Other than a few grumbles, none of the Six commented on the findings.

Was this film manipulation enough to convince them that Jade wasn't the monster in which she was being portrayed?

Although it wasn't written within some text or contract, the Six assigned me these specific types of child abuse cases because of my past. I'm sure they, specifically the one behind the corruption, believed I would execute Jade without question after seeing the videos.

However, they hadn't considered *her* as evidence. Her personality was circumstantial at best, but as far as I was concerned, it was still evidence. I presented them a rundown of her character, of the person I studied.

Micah and I decided that we would hold off on presenting the rogue group of fake Reapers running around attempting to usurp my kill order before the time had elapsed.

If it were a member of the Six spearheading this corruption, revealing too much would inspire them to up the ante on killing Jade and their rogue mission. This process was a tightrope walking game that would end in death. I sensed it and sniffed the stench in the air.

After fifteen minutes of showing them more film manipulation, I believed it was enough for them to consider that the evidence was faulty enough to reevaluate the kill order.

Mr. Emmerson, the leader of the Tech and R&D division, also known as the Tip of the Knife, stood, and his obscured face appeared on the big screen.

"We understand that the film could have been doctored, but people were interviewed to legitimize her actions. It makes the video evidence obsolete, manipulated or not."

I nodded. "I figured as much," I replied. I knew it would take more than manipulated film to convince them. I stood, walked to the door, and called in the witness I'd found to come into the room.

Thankfully, Micah believed in me. He'd allowed me to use a few of his high-powered connections to track down one of the supposed witnesses that confirmed Jade's guilt.

The man, Howard, had succumbed to a thorough beating, so we'd had to invest some money in getting him cleaned up for this meeting. He walked in, and although the members of the Six suppressed their verbal responses, it didn't stop me from seeing subtle hints of tension in some of them: eyes widening, a sharp intake of air, tense shoulders. One placed a hand over his open mouth and attempted to play it off like he was swiping a hand across his face.

Micah noticed what I saw, his quick eyes reading their body language for any telltale signs of stress. The Six were being studied as hard as I'm sure they were studying me.

I swept my hand toward the seat, directing Howard to sit. It had taken some heavy-handed convincing to get him to first tell the truth and even more convincing for him to climb aboard a plane to come here. He released a low groan and winced but faced the large monitor.

"Why are you here? We've heard your testimony," Mr. Cromwell, the leader of the medical and psych division, addressed us this time. His division was known as the Flat of the Knife.

Howard cleared his throat. "I was paid a hundred thousand dollars to read some lines. I know Ms. McKenna from working with her in the past. I know she does some things that the rest of the world doesn't see, but I've never seen her do anything illegal. I've never seen her hurt children. I never knew she would be harmed by me reading from that paper."

I aimed a finger at Howard's head. "He received ten anonymous wire transfers, one from a different state every two weeks. The amounts were small enough not to be traced back to a bank account or business."

The way in which Howard had received his payments was more proof that a massive setup had taken place.

"You were paid a large sum of money to say things about a person that you weren't sure was the truth?" Mr. Wolf appeared on the screen, dressed in an all-black ninja costume. He was our division head, the Reapers also known as the Blade of the Knife.

Despite never having seen the face of the man who heads up our division, he was well known for fighting against the Six on our behalf. He knew intimate details about each of us and didn't hesitate to have bi-weekly secure teleconferencing briefings with us.

Mr. Wolf claimed to have laid eyes on each Reaper, and based on the way he made it a point to take care of our needs, whether it be to eradicate a threat against us or fight against the Six on our behalf, I believed him.

Howard eased up in his seat, preparing to answer the question, but Mr. Wolf continued before he could speak. "Wasn't there any part of you that considered how your words on the record could impact this woman's life?"

Howard nodded. "I didn't want to say it, but the people who took me said they knew things about my family, about me, and insinuated that if I didn't do what they said, they would start killing off members of my family, starting with my daughter. The money was to make me appear as guilty as them. They also pointed out that Ms. McKenna is wealthy, a lot more so than she allows people to see. She could overcome rumors and hearsay, murders and kidnappings."

This bit of news got the Six's attention enough for them to take turns questioning Howard extensively. After an hour, they requested a twenty-four-hour hold to continue the proceedings the following day.

They would communicate offline. I didn't know if that was a good or bad thing. If one of them were the traitor, it would give him or her the chance to manipulate the others.

Micah tossed a sack over Howard's head and personally escorted him back to the airport so he could return to the safe house in which we had relocated him and his family.

***

The next day.

Micah and I sat silently, awaiting the Six. I, as well as he, didn't know what they would decide. They were pulled into the secure conference, communicating with each other, blurred faces, masks, and one blacked-out screen were mumbling back and forth, the volume controlled by some tech guru who may well have been the person who doctored Jade's video.

Each took turns presenting their viewpoints on the matter. One believed the evidence was sound enough to pause the kill order and gather more evidence on Jade.

One presented a scenario that called into speculation that Jade had enough time and money to find out about her assassination and start manipulating people and events herself.

Another believed the original decision was based on enough evidence to remain in effect. The other three presented cases that didn't give you a hint of whether they were for or against resuming the kill order.

At this point, I was convinced that they would rather kill an innocent woman than tarnish their reputations.

"Once this boring shit is over, can we just go on a killing rampage? At this point, I don't care if it's people or animals. This 'trying to do the right thing' kick you're on is fucking up my whole vibe."

I ignored him.

When all was said and done, the Six were prepared to cast a ballot. Yes, to postpone and gather more evidence.

No, would declare the kill order valid, and I would proceed with the reaping.

"Thank you for bringing this to our attention, Mr. Sylas," Mr. Martin, the head of the Law and Politics division, also known as the Heel of the Blade, addressed the group this time.

"After careful consideration. We have all decided to write down our votes and display them here."

Clear white sheets of paper sat in front of each of them. They took as long as they needed and considered all that had been presented over the past few days before writing down their decision. A bunch of scribbled yeses and no's were what determined a woman's fate.

The first to go, Mr. Martin, lifted his vote with the word 'yes', indicating he wanted to proceed with Jade's assassination, despite the new evidence presented.

When the second 'yes' vote was lifted, my ability to stay calm began to slip. The third 'yes' was lifted, and as far as I was concerned it confirmed that one or more of the Six were corrupt.

"And there you go. Six more motherfuckers you need to add to our list. It's getting short anyway."

It had been a long time since I'd agreed with my demon. The evil laugh he was releasing inside my head made me wish I'd never had the thought.

There was enough evidence presented for them to cast doubt or change their minds. Jade had become the face of this deathly scandal, and I was convinced that she was clueless as to the danger surrounding her.

One of the most powerful secret organizations in the world wanted her dead. It didn't matter that the evidence against her was fabricated. Someone with a tremendous amount of power wanted Jade dead, and the only reason I could think of was that she was in possession of a powerful piece of evidence that could take one or more of them down.

I'd gone about this all wrong. Instead of attempting to change their minds, I should have figured out what Jade knew or had in her possession that could have landed her in this position.

My gaze moved over each one of them, searching for any sign that would give me a hint as to who might have been the true snake. I was convinced now that the Six was compromised, and if I didn't figure out how to expose them, Jade was dead. If her kill order wasn't carried out, the Reapers could face war against an organization large and vicious enough to swallow us whole.

The Order was responsible for producing killing machines like me, Micah, and the rest of the Hell Reapers as well as five other divisions, trained to the hilt with skills that would make the world's most notorious criminal and legal organizations jealous.

Micah shifted behind me at the sight of four yeses and two no's lifted on the screen. His eyes were aimed at the screen, but his face didn't give away anything.

He stepped closer, placing a firm hand on my shoulder, as he eyed each member. "Thank you all for your time. We know what we have to do, and it will be done."

He answered for me, knowing me well enough to know that I would tell them to go fuck themselves with the jagged edge of a dull blade. A few curt nods were offered before their screens began to go black.

Micah leaned down. His face hovered near my ear. "This shit isn't over. We have five days."

He turned and left the room, leaving me with those words.

CHAPTER TWENTY-TWO

Severe

Four days later.

"I'll send you the fucking evidence," I growled low into the phone, my face squinted so tightly, it ached. The distorted voice on the other end of the line was like glass raking across my last and very damaged nerve.

I didn't have a right to be upset about what the Order was asking me to do. I knew what needed to be done. I no longer had a choice. Jade had to die. The Six had made a decision, and my instincts, as well as findings, weren't enough for them to overturn the order.

A quick glance at my watch revealed that the countdown was edging closer. There was no use telling her that her fate had been determined by a vote. If she knew what was so near in her future, her survival instincts would kick in, and she would fight me and anyone else who came at her.

It was better that she believed the lie and lived the time she had left blissfully unaware that the Reaper she was starting to trust was the one who would take her life.

"It's about fucking time you take responsibility for what you should have done in New York," my demon pointed out.

"Shut up. I wish I knew how to pluck you from my head," I muttered.

Since the contract due date and time were close, the one warning phone call was all I would receive. I had to furnish proof of the kill or risk the Order bringing their wrath down on the Reapers, many of whom remained unaware of the unfolding situation. I couldn't allow them to get dragged blindly into something I'd initiated.

Micah was right. This was a mess. My gaze pierced the dim view from my porch. The natural sounds surrounding me, the moon shimming off the dark water, and the swaying shadows of the trees usually provided a small level of calm. This time the view had lost its magic.

The high of Mr. Tincher, the man I'd brutally murdered less than two hours ago, had worn off. I'd tracked him down and scratched him off my personal hit list. His death would make news highlights, something I would have been proud of last month.

Now, I was running on fumes. My mind had quickly returned to a wasteland of impure and demonic ideas that demanded action. I turned the knob and stepped into my cabin, stopping short at the sight of Jade.

She was asleep on the couch, facing the door with a book open and lying atop her chest. Scrappy was cuddled up beside her with her head lying on the right side of Jade's black, silk pajama-covered stomach. The cat lifted her head lazily and eyeballed me before brushing me off and laying her head back in place.

The silk shorts that matched Jade's top showed off her toned sexy legs. The memory of her legs being pinned deliciously open by me yesterday had me becoming hard and making the asshole in my head stir.

"Legs. Mmm."

My eyes fell closed in an attempt to ward off the lustful ideas crowding my brain. Everything about this was off, wrong, and fucked all to hell.

I spun toward the bathroom for a much-needed shower since I was sure blood had ended up in places I didn't remember it going, thanks to the asshole in my head who couldn't help taking things way further than was necessary today.

"You're welcome."

***

Jade

My eyes fluttered below my lids as reality trickled into my system and quickened my pulse. Severe was back. I sensed him even before hearing the shower. Over the last four days, he'd been drilling me hard about secret plots I may not be aware of, things I may not be conscious of knowing.

He'd questioned me about the powerful people I was connected to, who donated to or sponsored some of my non-profits. It almost felt like I was on trial, but he always managed to reel in the questions and make me forget he'd even asked a single one.

I dragged myself up, expecting to see Scrappy, but she'd climbed into her own bed. She took her close encounters in small doses and went about her business when she'd had enough.

When I was tossing my legs over the side of the couch to sit up, Severe walked in, and I fought to keep my eyes from dropping below his chin. For obvious reasons, my eyes were eager to stray lower, but I fought the urge.

"Hello," I said, aware that he was perfectly fine with dead silence.

"Hello," he returned, taking a seat on the couch, putting space between us. I don't know what I expected, but the silence and his actions made things awkward, considering we were more than acquaintances now. At least, that's what I wanted to believe.

Other than the odd questioning sessions, he would also go off in deep thought, and it would take me coaxing him back with light touches and sweet kisses that always led to the best sex of my life.

He wouldn't reveal much, but I believed his stress revolved around not figuring out who the traitor in their organization may be so he could root them out. Solving that problem was way more in-depth than he would ever tell me, and I believed far deadlier than he would let on.

If I was stuck and couldn't go home after witnessing the initial incident in the garage, I didn't want to imagine how long I'd be stuck after seeing all that followed.

"How did everything go? Are you any closer to being able to send me home?"

"No," he released a frustrated sigh. "Things are…" He shook his head like he was warding off an evil spirit. "…Complicated," he finished.

I slid closer until my bare leg bumped his solid one, my brows knitted tightly.

"You can let me help. I possess resources and reach. I have a lot more power than anyone would give me credit for."

The statement made him stare at me. The prolonged look, unreadable and intense, caused me to draw tighter with tension.

"I need to figure out a way not to kill someone," he glanced at his wrist to check the time, "all I have is twenty-two hours and fifty-two minutes."

"What did they do? Isn't death the livelihood of your club? Isn't that what you're supposed to do?" I asked.

"There is clear evidence showing the person hurting children, but I found proof that the footage was digitally altered. However, it wasn't enough to cast doubt on the order and get the contract pulled."

"It sounds terribly complicated, especially where it concerns life and death. Death is it. If you don't believe in the justification behind the hit, I can understand your dilemma. So, what happens if you don't do it?"

He released a low huff. "Mutually assured destruction."

My face wrinkled. "What?"

"A lot of death," he answered.

"Like a war? Just because you refused to kill someone that you don't think should be dead?"

He nodded. "It's rare that a contract gets questioned, even rarer that one gets overturned. So, a refusal is a slap in the face of years of trust, honor, and order," he said.

For someone like him to have doubts, the situation ran much deeper than he was saying. His motorcycle club was embedded with an order of assassins, something I was still attempting to wrap my head around. I vaguely recalled overhearing my father talking about a similar group when I was younger. Except they didn't have a name, as far as I knew.

"What are you going to do?" I questioned. I wanted to help him, but I didn't know how.

He glanced in my direction, holding my gaze in suspense before he answered.

"I'll think of something."

Silence filled the space with a thick pressing tension that had me rolling my neck. My eyes dropped and lingered on his crotch.

Why did he have to fuck me so good? Now, when I wasn't scraping up information around the compound and attempting to figure out what was going on for myself, I was thinking about him fucking my brains out.

I drew closer, a moth, not caring if the flames burned her alive.

My finger traced along the tattoo around Severe's neck. The snake's mouth was open wide enough to breach each side of his neck, the tongue sticking out under his chin. The snake's body was tattooed over his right shoulders and along his back.

"Why did you get this tattoo?" I asked him, curious.

"This is the kind of snake that bit me when I was on a mission in Honduras. I got caught slipping, and they threw me into a dark pit with one. The snake didn't make it, and neither did anyone on the compound. I ended up spending about a week in the hospital due to blood poisoning."

"You sound proud," I pointed out.

"I was supposed to die about ten minutes after he bit me. I carried out my mission and managed to drag myself to a hospital for the anti-venom two hours later."

His war stories were legendary, and although I loved hearing them, right now, my hormones were waging war on my uterus. And he had the one weapon that could slay my war-ravaged body.

"You look like what a hot, vicious, dangerous, killer vampire would be if such a creature existed. You are your name, a Severe threat to the life of all kinds."

He lifted a curious brow but didn't respond. I was sure he'd figured out by now that when I started mouthing off compliments, they were being pulled from desire for the real thing.

"You resemble beautiful death, alive and in the flesh. You terrify me as much as you turn me on, but there is something about you that you can't hide."

"What?" he asked.

"No matter how many tattoos, how crazy you talk to people, and how easily and viciously you kill, it still doesn't take away that you are an attractive man. I think you have done as much as you can to alter your appearance into something as horrific as that mind of yours could conjure, but guess what? It didn't work."

He cocked a brow at me, his eyes assessing.

"Considering your dilemma with your organization and all that you must have on your mind. I have a selfish thing to ask you." There was no way he didn't know what I wanted.

"Can we?" I asked, glancing down at the tick bulge in his shorts. I should have been ashamed of myself, but I wasn't. And not even he could deny that we were sexual soul mates.

Severe's eyes met mine. There was a glint of something I couldn't interpret shimmering in the depths of his gaze.

"Shouldn't have happened and shouldn't have kept happening. We can't keep doing that," he said, crushing my sexual hopes and dreams.

I rested my hand on his thigh, not giving him a choice but to put his eyes on me again. His eyes were mesmerizing when he wasn't thinking up ways to destroy people, property, or both.

"Let's not kid ourselves here. We…" I pointed between us, "We were an inevitable truth that was shelved in denial, doubt, and every other don't-do-it scenario."

He lifted a brow at the statement, and I couldn't tell what that little hitch over his lip meant.

"Me," I placed my hand over my chest. "If I'm stuck in a dangerous situation, and there's some good that could come from it, I'll take a big order of good, please."

Sarcasm dripped off each of my words. Severe's gaze rested heavily on my face like he was attempting to determine what to do with me. I was about to say something else, but there was something about the way his eyes narrowed that suggested I stay quiet and not make any sudden movements.

The man had a way about him that let you know when you might be in danger. Asking him for more sex may have triggered something, and I didn't know if it was a good thing or a bad one.

He took my hand and stood, taking me up with him. He walked me around to the back of the couch and made me stand in front of him. When I'd made him aware of my aversion to being put flat on my back while having sex, he came up with some inventive positions.

I swallowed hard, having no idea what he was about to do to me. His movements were deliberate enough to keep me on edge. He ruffled the edges of my blouse, rolling it up my sides with the ease of a thief.

With him behind me, removing my clothes, it increased the building tension and made my heart do spinning leaps in my chest. Anticipation and burning passion blossomed, and only he knew how to stoke those desires and turn them into a blazing inferno.

I lifted my arms while my skin prickled. My tits bounced free when he pulled the top over my head. There was no use putting on a bra unless I was going out. All I thought about throughout the day was him coming back and giving me a dose of this.

He dragged my pants down next, and not being able to see his face kept me curious, but I dared not turn around as it would poke holes in the heavy tension that had my sex pulsing, wet, heavy, and ready.

He twisted my underwear around his fist, the material pulling tight against my stomach and waist. He kept twisting until my wet lips were exposed. A firm hand was pressed into the center of my back, the initial touch making me suck in a deep breath. He pushed until I was bent over the back of the couch, my ass high in the air, my legs spread wide.

"Oh," I couldn't help the relieving cry when he palmed my pussy from the back, using his middle finger to massage my slick clit.

"Sa-ha," I said, sucking in a breath when he slipped a finger in and out, so purposely, the wet sounds of my lady parts slurping on his finger grew louder with every stroke.

He released the twist he had on my panties by snatching them off me with one hard, ripping yank.

With his free hand, he reached down and shoved it past my inner right knee, and when he lifted up his arm, it took my leg up, opening me and sending my top half over the couch. He did the same to the other leg, lifting my feet off the floor. I was at his mercy now, spread wide with the lower half of me angled down enough to keep me bent over the couch. I could hear him behind me shoving his shorts down.

His dick nudged my wet lips before slipping across my clit and making me squirm. The thrust that followed was a long and deliciously slow push that left me hyperventilating. I gripped whatever parts of the couch I could pull into my searching hands. He repeated the addictive strokes, coaxing me to open for him, to get wetter, hotter.

Despite feeling stuffed, my obedient body allowed him to pick up the pace and fuck me hard enough to drive me over the edge of madness. How could I be twenty-nine and not have had sex this good?

"Oh, Shit. Yes." Who needed complete sentences? My choppy starts were enough to let him know he was fucking my sexual world up in the best possible way. I wasn't ever going to want sex with anyone else, not after having a taste of this.

There was no bend over or turn this way with Severe. He picked me up and fucked me in a way that said, *you're going to take this dick, and you're going to fucking love it.*

For our second round, he put me in the reverse cowgirl that he controlled by gripping a handful of my hair and bending me so that I was a bow atop him. Despite me being in the more dominant position, Severe kept me off balance. I had no choice but to take it the way he gave and dammit if he didn't come correct. Pun intended.

In the third round, I became his portrait when he sat me against the wall of his chest and fucked me from the back. It was an angle I'd never even imagined being performed on me. The sensation of his dick sliding across my ass before being thrust into me from an upward angle was on a different level of erotic. I was open, helpless, and filled to max capacity with each thrust. This sex was a drug he created just for me. It was the kind of drug habit that rehab couldn't break.

Severe was a man to be respected. I believed he was the only one who could take this one-hundred-and-fifty-pound body of mine and beast fuck me from the back while standing and controlling how wide he opened my legs and angled his dick to maintain control of the pounding and the depth of each thrust.

What more could be said for a man who could do this to me and make me toss all inhibitions in the trash?

CHAPTER TWENTY-THREE

Jade

Later, after the dust had settled and the heat of our passion had cooled, I took a quick shower and laid my satisfied body on the couch. It was dark, and Scrappy hadn't returned yet. Each time we started ripping each other's clothes off, she had no interest in bearing witness to our love scenes, so she would leave and return hours later and sometimes still find us tangled up with one another.

Severe walked in from his shower and gave me the look, the barely lifted brow. I nodded at the look and smiled. I believed he felt guilty about us having sex, and I couldn't understand why. He always made a valid attempt to stop it before we blew each other's minds, but he and I knew the chemistry was too strong to fight.

I patted the seat next to me, sitting in the center of the couch, before he put distance between us.

"Do you feel guilty after we're together?"

He didn't answer but knew what I was talking about.

"It's okay to like me, you know," I told him.

He shook his head.

"It's not okay. It's impulse-driven, close proximity, gratitude, and projection. We shouldn't allow impulses we can control drive us where we shouldn't be going."

This was the second time he'd reduced us to impulses.

"I disagree with your assessment," I said before taking his hand. The soft kiss I placed to the back made his brows twitch, but he kept his gaze aimed at the wall in front of us like he was afraid of what he might see if he looked at me. I stroked the beat of his radiating energy, where my fingers rested against his wrist.

"When I kiss you, I taste more than your lips or your tongue. I taste acceptance, fear, and pain. I feel all the things that have touched your soul because you allow little pieces of what's been tattooed there to spill out and onto me. You know how to keep your emotions hidden, but when I can't see it on your face or in your eyes, the impulses between us are strong enough to leave traces of their existence.

His gaze met mine, unblinking, and his face was devoid of emotion.

"When you hold me. It's like you envelop my whole body. When you touch me, you are very deliberate. You watch where your hands are going and what they are doing. And you don't chase me away when I wrap myself around you or lay against you or climb onto you. You let me have that sense of connection for as long as I want it. You let me see you and feel you in other ways, and I'm not even sure if you're aware of it."

His eyes searched mine, his stare lingering. A flash of concern, curiosity, and another untapped emotion sparked within the depths of its gaze. It was a reaction he allowed me to see, as he was usually guarded when it came to his feelings.

I believe he was processing how I'd lost my mind and what had driven me off the deep end. I loved that look of uncertainty on him, someone who was always so composed, intimidating, and set to be offensive to keep me at bay.

"I won't allow you to reduce my experience with you down to a textbook definition or a probability. I see you better than you believe I do. I feel you deeper than you would expect me to. I'm even crazy enough to have feelings for you, more than you are willing to accept. Do I fall into the category that you keep looping me into: impulsive, close-proximity, gratitude-happy? I probably do, but I acknowledge that there is more. I accept that there is more. I believe there is more. You should too."

I backed off and repositioned myself on the couch, sitting Indian-style in the middle. He eyed me with lingering curiosity.

"I want you to lay your head right here. Your legs will dangle over the arm of the couch, but that's okay because all I want is your mind," I told him.

He didn't move, and the brow he lifted rose higher. His gaze dropped to the little pillow I placed in the fold of my legs before he pinned his gaze on mine. The tension in his forehead eased the moment he considered my request.

I patted the pillow again before stroking it with a tender touch, waiting. His movements were cautious, but he leaned in my direction. The hesitant glint he allowed me to see looked awkward on his face.

He always had an air of quiet confidence about him that let me know that not much, if anything, frightened him. The notion that I, my touch, and my affection for him introduced a level of fear to him gave me a sense of power over him.

He positioned himself in front of me, but he didn't turn and hadn't placed his head on the pillow.

"It's okay. You can trust me, Severe. I'd never do anything to hurt you, and even if I wanted to, I'm smart enough not to even try."

His lips twitched at the comment before he turned his back to me and allowed his long legs to stretch over the arm of the couch.

His broad shoulders lifted and dropped from the deep breaths he took before he laid back. My hands immediately stroked his shoulders while he adjusted. This was a big step for him to take. I knew it, and I saw it in the tense set of his body.

"Relax," I told him in a low, calm voice before I lifted my hands from his shoulders. I ignored the temptation of playing in all that silky hair.

"Relax," I coaxed again. "It's just us: me and you. This is our comfort zone. We can do anything we want within these walls, especially relax."

Finally, he closed his eyes, and more tension fell away from his body. His relaxation shifted the energy in the room, creating a safe haven to release whatever we wanted. My fingers worked in light circles until his full weight pressed into the folds of my legs.

Scrappy, who'd snuck back in, was cozy in her bed. Although her eyes were drooping, they were observant, like she was acknowledging that she was a part of this connection we were establishing. Her head rested against the comfort of her cushion, the sight enticing me to smile.

"I've mentioned it, but I've never told you about the worst thing to happen to me in my life. It was my scariest moment. It was torture, tragedy, and pain all rolled up into an eight-hour window that changed my life forever. It left me empty in a way that made it extremely difficult to connect with people, especially men."

I was saying a lot and talking in circles, but he remained relaxed while listening.

"Therapy has helped me over the years, but only to a certain point, a point that allows me to function but remain aware that I'm not fully healed. May never be. Seeing that you are struggling with something as heavy and have similar sleep habits as me, has made my time with you better than therapy, if that makes sense."

I paused.

Breathed.

"I never told anyone the details of what happened to me the night my father was killed, never intended to."

I sucked in another relieving breath. This session was for me as much as it was for him. He needed to get something off his chest, but I was certain he would never release his demons if I didn't release mine.

"You're the one person I believe I need to tell. The only one I believe I *can* tell," I told him. I gulped down my anxiety and blew out a long breath.

"When I was a girl, all I wanted was to be like my father. I was his little shadow, ready to follow him wherever he went. There were times I'd sneak into his car just to go wherever he was going. He'd punish me when he caught me, but it wasn't much of a deterrent. He was my hero and the only example I had to follow. And despite his job, he took his time with me, my sister, and my brother. He listened, read to us at night, cooked for us, went to school meetings, and made sure we were well taken care of when he wasn't around."

A glance down showed me Severe's closed eyes, listening to my words.

"Fast forward to me at sixteen. I'd sneaked into the back of his car and laid out on the floor. We drove for hours, him making the stops that I knew well from the many times I'd been with him. He'd told someone on one of his phone conversations that he was headed back home, except he didn't go home. Someone else had called him asking to meet up, which ended up being out in the middle of nowhere on a dark, deserted road. Things started going badly when his driving became erratic, and he began swerving. Next came the bullets. At first, I assumed it was rocks hitting the car, but when he let down his window and fired back, I had no choice but to make my presence known."

Severe's shoulders tensed, and his eyes trembled more rapidly under his lids in reaction to my story, but I had to keep going.

"My father made me climb over the seat and lay on the passenger side floor. The first bullet that slammed into him hit him in the shoulder and made him swerve hard enough across the road that the front of the car struck a portion of the metal railing on my side of the vehicle. He stopped me several times from getting up. Another shot caught him in the neck, making him drive with one hand and hold his neck with the other. The car kept getting pelted with shot after shot like they were throwing stones, and the rocks kept getting bigger and hitting harder.

"The cab of the car was dark, but the lights on the panel allowed me to see that my father was bleeding badly. He kept telling me he was wearing a bulletproof vest and that everything would be okay. I believed him. Another shot caught him in the chest. He lost control of the car, and we swerved off the road and ended up in a narrow ravine before plowing into a cement slab. I hit my head hard enough to black out. When I came awake enough to focus, we were positioned on a tilt so that the driver's side faced up. The car was surrounded, and I was under my father, who was wheezing for breaths. The men outside the car were taunting him, telling him that they were finally de-throning a king. They laughed and kept letting off rounds into the car, some hitting him. The whole time he was staring, telling me I would be okay, that he wasn't going to let anything happen to me. More shots were fired, each one echoing through me the moment they entered my father's body since I was pinned under him."

I breathed, fighting hard not to let my emotions take control of my first chance at releasing this nightmare.

"If I hadn't been there with him, I know my father wouldn't have stayed in that car to protect me. He would have fought. He would have found a way to stop those guys from killing him. He always said he didn't believe in giving up. He believed and taught me to believe there was always a way to beat the odds, no matter what. However, that night, he sacrificed himself to save me. He didn't fight because...of me."

I choked on the words, fighting back tears.

"The final shot came from someone who'd found a way to climb atop the car. He was right outside the busted-out driver's side window. My father's final words to me were, "The ones you love will hurt you most," right before the man aiming a gun at his head said, "Tip, Blade, Edge, Flat, Point, and Heel. A knife has many parts, but it's too bad the point wasn't sharp enough to scrape across the heel."

Severe's eyes popped open, and his gaze searched mine. His tension was back with a vengeance—his breathing kicking up a notch. He was digesting my words, and I got the odd sense that they resonated with him on a level I couldn't understand.

I rubbed his shoulders and returned to making gentle circles around his temples to calm him. Touching him, easing his stress away, also dulled mine, and I found the strength to tell him the rest of my worst living nightmare.

"The riddle has played in my head over and over for years. Aside from the fact that one of my father's killers listed the parts of a knife, I never figured out what the words meant. All I know is that it was followed up by the final gunshot. The bullet slammed into the back of his head so hard he head-butted me. The lick dazed me but didn't stop me from hearing him take his final breath or feeling it rattle through my own body. I passed out. When I came awake again, it was a constant drip that pulled me back into the nightmare.

"My father's wide eyes in the dark had glossed over. The sight of him so close, so stiff and lifeless, freaked me out. I panicked, feeling his blood on me, seeing his wide-open eyes, and knowing he was dead. I was empty, gutted.

My soul departed along with his. I couldn't move him and was too weak to lift him off me. His body had stiffened around mine like I was in a grave built of him. In the dark, cold wreckage, I screamed, and I pushed. I did everything I could, but I was stuck in a crypt made of my father's bullet-ridden body."

I lifted my hand from Severe and fingered my own forehead, hoping someone could one day come up with a way to extract memories. However, I knew my memories were life notes I had to carry, ones I needed to hone in on to pull the strength I needed to conduct the types of operations that kept others from suffering the same nightmare as me. Severe had a stressed frown in the center of his forehead, my story clearly bothering him.

"The next morning, a passerby discovered the car. By then, my voice was gone, and I was down to low murmurs and whimpers. The rescue team had to break my father's bones to drag me from under him. It took me three months to start talking again. Twice as long to start interacting with people again. When you asked me why I wasn't afraid of you, I told you that the worst thing that could ever happen to me had already happened.

"That night in the garage, that killer asked me why I wasn't freaking out when he was aiming his gun at my face, and I told him the same. The worst thing to ever happen to me was the night I died with my father. I felt each gunshot that ripped through him, heard his life dripping from him, listened to his last words, felt him take his last breath, felt his soul leave him, and remained caged under his stiff, empty body for hours. I felt every stage of his death, and I don't believe there is anything else out there in the world that can be worse than that experience, not even my own death."

Aside from my sniffing and hard breaths, silence flowed into the space like quick running water when I stopped talking. Severe's eyes popped open, and the gleam in them, the tortured expression on his face, revealed his empathy. He lifted up, but I pulled him back down.

"Please," I begged. "Will you tell me what happened to you and why you try so hard to keep people at a distance? For the most part, it works, but some of us, your cousin, and a few others can see through the thick walls you've erected around yourself."

I continued to rub his temples, my touch light, barely a caress, but it was keeping our energetic connection intact. He allowed his body to settle and his eyes to close, although they continued to move rapidly under his lids.

"From the time I could remember anything, I remember the beatings."

His first sentence was enough to close my eyes, knowing I was in for an emotional roller coaster of gargantuan proportions.

CHAPTER TWENTY-FOUR

Jade

I was already dreading this story. Abuse. It always left a person with the most devastating mental scars, some they didn't want to acknowledge, the memories carrying the echo of their pain. I sensed it early on when I saw the hurt hidden within the depth of Severe's gaze. He'd survived his own personal hell.

"From the time I could remember anything, I remember the beatings."

The sentence echoed in my head until Severe's next words replaced it.

"My father walked out on my mother when I was five. She would often lash out at him, and when he could no longer take her mood swings, he walked out and told her he was coming back for me. Until this day, I believe she killed him and disposed of his body before he could get away since he was never heard from again or found.

"Without my father there as a buffer, I became the abused, even expected it since it happened so often. Something as simple as me breathing or making too much noise when I moved. Me asking for food when I was hungry. The notion that I was even there was enough to set her off. It didn't matter what I did. She'd find a reason to unleash her anger on me. I'd seen her doing drugs before, but her drug use got worse after my father left. She wasn't reliable at paying the bills, so the power was often switched off. If it weren't for my cousins sneaking around to see me, teaching me how to fish and hunt, I wouldn't have had food most of the time."

I kept my strokes against his temples light, the touch easing the tension riding him.

"When she needed money for her drugs, she bartered one of a few things she had to trade. Sex was her go-to form of payment. When her pushers stopped wanting her for sex, she offered them the *last* thing she had left. Me."

I stifled a gasp and struggled to swallow the big knot of sorrow with my eyes shut tight to keep from pulling his attention away from telling me his story. Attempting to swallow that much tension caused my throat to bob with a series of hard swallows. A piece of my heart was being ripped out, each of his sentences the rusty nail doing the damage.

"She'd go out and find those who gave her money for me or dealers who didn't mind collecting their payment from my flesh."

It took a chorus of prayers to keep me from losing my shit so that Severe would continue. I squeezed my eyes tight to combat the tears stinging my eyes before I cleared my throat.

"How old were you when the sexual abuse began?" I managed to ask, although my voice was cracking like thin glass. His eyes were closed, and he remained relaxed, considering.

"The abuse from her came in a building progression: beatings, neglect, and severe verbal abuse from about age five to nine. I was ten when she started trading me for her drugs. She graduated to torturing me when I hit double digits."

He paused, and although he appeared calm, his anxiety radiated off him in waves of warm energy, and I wasn't sure if he wanted to continue.

"Do you feel like elaborating on what you labeled as her torture phase?"

Silence descended, pressing down on us, but it was welcomed. He needed the pressure of the silence to give him time to gather the mental strength to continue. He shifted, the movement an involuntary reaction to some horrific memory raging through him.

"One specific moment in her mental reel of torture was when she chained me up with my dog. I found a stray one day when I was hunting and scavenging for food. He followed me home. She hated that something seemed to love me and was willing to protect me. When my dog growled and snapped at her for hitting me, she punished us both, chained us to a tree, and starved us of food and water."

I did my best to keep my strokes light, but there was no way he didn't know I was losing my calming strength to his words because I was being sucked into his nightmare.

"She waited until we were at our weakest points and tried to force us to fight each other for a chicken leg. It didn't work. My dog wouldn't turn on me. It was the first time I understood what true loyalty meant. If an animal that couldn't speak understood the concept of caring for something else other than itself, then why didn't my mother have the same understanding?"

There was no way he didn't feel me losing it when my fingers started to shake.

"I eventually reached the chicken leg and dragged it close enough for my dog to grab before I collapsed from exhaustion. He ate half the leg and brought me the rest, teaching me another lesson my mother was too evil to impart. He taught me that others could be caring, loyal, and selfless."

At this point, there was no use attempting to stop the tears from flowing down my cheeks. He'd learned the basics of human decency from his dog. And I believed his cousins were his only companions as far as positive human interaction.

"What was your dog's name?" I asked, acknowledging that the dog was a part of the reason he understood compassion, probably better than most humans.

"Pope," he answered quickly. The sincerity in his tone when he said his dog's name wasn't missed.

"When she finally did feed me, I was so hungry, I didn't care what I was eating because I was ravenous. I ate two plates of the meat and rice she fed me."

I sniffed, sucked in a deep breath and held it, dreading what he'd say next.

"Not only did she tell me I'd eaten Pope, but she showed me what was left of his body after she'd skinned him. The night before, I'd heard him yelping and as close to screaming as a dog could get. I assume she was beating him as she'd done so many times before. She was doing much worse. Nothing else she'd done to me at this point had broken me. This broke me so badly that I stopped talking, even when my cousins would sneak and come and see me. I never ate meat again after that day. It was my fault Pope died because it was me who brought him around pure evil."

I lost it, sucking in a hard sob that left my lips quivering. Severe attempted to lift up, but I kept him down with firm hands on his shoulders.

"Please. Stay down. Ignore me, so you can cleanse more of this darkness from your system. Believe me, you'll feel so much better if you say it out loud and allow me to hear it and carry a little of the burden."

I sniffed and wiped at tears, attempting but failing to keep my movement discreet and gentle.

"I don't know if I should tell you the rest. It doesn't end well, and you'll probably think I'm a sick freak."

I leaned in, pressing a tender kiss to his forehead, one that he didn't flinch away from this time. He was getting better at letting me touch him.

"There is nothing you can tell me that will make me think less of you."

Silence filled the space. Our steady breathing and my occasional sniffs were the only sounds in the room. There was no way he could possibly tell me anything worse than what he'd already confessed.

CHAPTER TWENTY-FIVE

Severe

Fifteen years ago.

Hair swung past my face, my shoulder-length strands wet with sweat and dirt. The scent covering me was the rusted stench of blood and faint traces of the cheap shampoo I used days ago. The mouth of the shovel sank into the hard, packed dirt, the ground unyielding without my grunting efforts.

Hair, dirt, shovel, scoop, lift and toss. It was the cycle I'd been on for the past hour, digging a deep enough hole to return a monster who'd had no business roaming the earth.

The blood on my hands, and the act of violence I committed, left no guilt within my heart. I was finally free of the chains I'd allowed myself to be locked in all those years. This was the second grave I'd dug, and I knew it wouldn't be my last. This first life I'd taken was just the beginning. I already had plans springing up like weeds to take twenty more.

While digging, it was the first time I recalled genuinely smiling in my whole pathetic life.

Once the hole was deep enough to be level with my thin shoulders, I tossed the shovel out and gripped the

grassy dirt around the edges to lift myself from the per-
manent home I was creating for my tormentor.

I stood above her, staring down at the damage I'd
done to her body. Five hours, four minutes, and thirty sec-
onds. That's how long it had taken her to die. I loved every
minute of her dark, violent transition.

Since my skinny arms were burning from the digging
and from wielding the instruments I'd used to destroy her,
I didn't have the strength to lift her body. Weighing ninety
pounds, I sat on my boney butt and used my bare dirty feet
to move her.

I heaved hard on the first kick, my feet planted in her
side. One of her rib bones poked at the skin at the bottom
of my foot, broken and prickly like its owner. Even in
death, she continued to fight me, but I had finally won. I
had overcome the one obstacle that had made me a slave
in modern society.

I was born without love and bred without guidance,
care, or concern. Ruthlessness was my mother. Savagery
was my father. Loneliness was my best friend.

My cousins told me long before I fully understood
their advice, "We can't do it for you, Severe. You have to
find a way to unburden yourself of this nightmare on your
own."

The advice found its place within me while I was
standing over the open grave. My cousins, triplet misfits,
were the only source of connection I'd ever had to the
world. They'd risked coming in contact with my nightmare
to see me as often as they were able to, a blessing they
weren't aware they were bestowing on me.

If not for my cousins, I'd never know that real care existed, that concern was a concept people practiced, or that compassion was an emotion freely given. Israel trained me how to push myself past my breaking points and endure pain, mental and physical. Micah taught me how to meditate—to sit for hours at a time and let the universe come to me. He taught me how to harness my anger into a superpower. Eli gave me confidence. That no matter what anyone thought of me, as long as I believed in myself, no one would ever hold power over me. They all took turns teaching me how to read and write and how to act around other people. They all taught me various fighting techniques, how to hunt and take care of myself, how to use a knife, build a fire, and shoot.

At first, I was upset with them for not helping me escape my nightmarish situation, but it didn't occur to me that they were helping me all along, just not in the way I comprehended until I was standing over her dead body.

I heaved another hard kick at her, stiffened with rigor. She tumbled over the side and into her grave.

I stood in a rush, eager to see how she'd landed. Her one glossy eye remained, staring up at me, making her appear alive. She'd landed on her back with her head slanted slightly to the left side. For the first time, her deathly gaze was beneath mine, no longer above me mockingly.

She had treated me like shit—like I was no more than the thing she had to deal with. From my earliest memories, she'd always beaten me. The reasons didn't matter. The older I got, the more I understood that her abuse was more to ease her demons than it was to discipline me.

Because of her, I became a shadow, a thing that lurked in the background. Teased at school when I went, I was called a freak and mocked by those who crossed my path. I embraced my shadowy existence and stopped going to school. I lurked in the background no matter where I went, watching other kids interact and play, dance and sing with each other and watching grownups fight, make up, laugh and talk.

I'd been driven to suicide twice before I turned twelve, flirting with death before I fully understood the concept. Once, I was saved by my cousin, Eli. He pulled me from the lake and found someone in time to revive me. The second time, a stranger pulled me off a set of train tracks.

Torture. She had lavished me with enough that the lines between pain and pleasure and right and wrong were blurred into a single plain. Pain. She'd bathed me in enough for it to become my friend. Anger. I'd kept in enough to create a nuclear blast.

There was no sorrow in my heart for her, no guilt, nothing but satisfaction and a sense of accomplishment of finally breaking free of the prison she'd kept me in for fifteen years.

My cousins and my will to one day avenge myself were what kept me on this side of life.

A smile crept over my face while staring down into an eye, her eye, empty of life. My words were nothing but a faint whisper, but I sensed that she could hear me.

"Rest in pain...mother."

***

Jade

A jolt of awareness lured Severe from the memories. He glanced around himself like he'd forgotten that he was lying within the comfort of my touch. He'd gone in so deeply that he didn't notice me fighting to stifle my cries or even the light strokes I periodically brushed against his temples.

Now, he stared, waiting, expecting me to say how bad a person he was for killing his mother.

"I was sick. Depraved," he said, dropping his gaze. "I not only urinated and spit on her grave, I…"

He stopped, and the silence surrounding us loomed like it was a part of our session.

"You can tell me, Severe. I promise you I won't judge," I told him reassuringly.

"It was the first time in my life that I ejaculated. I never had urges before because, in my head, to do so meant that I enjoyed the only sexual experiences I'd ever had with monsters who didn't care that I was a kid."

"They weren't sexual experiences. It was abuse. Torture. And I don't believe for a second that you did anything depraved to the monster that abused you and brought in other monsters to abuse you too. I'm no therapist, but I believe you released some of the anger and rage you never had a chance to express against her before that day. It was years of pent-up anger and trauma compounded into a moment of relief."

He let my words sink in. His breathing leveling out again.

"I tried to hide what I'd done, that I'd killed my own mother, but my cousins extracted the information from me. They didn't judge me either, told me I'd finally freed myself from the demon that kept me prisoner. They said it was the only way I'd ever be free. They stood beside me while I burned down our house. Without me even telling them what I'd done over her grave, they all spit and urinated on the unmarked gravesite like they understood a part of what she'd put me through. They took me home with them, and my uncle, their father, took me in despite my serious anti-social personality, despite my habit of talking to myself, and despite all of the weird behaviors I exhibited. They never abandoned me. They taught me everything I was willing to learn. A few years after they became Reapers, they made sure I also became one."

There were questions and comments, but I kept them to myself. I allowed Severe all the time he needed to allow a piece of his mind to heal.

When his breathing deepened and eventually turned into a light snore, I smiled. He'd found peace in the release of all he'd been holding in all these years. I leaned against the back of the couch, my legs still folded under his head as he slept, his relaxed expression serene, peaceful.

I don't believe it was an accident, him finding me in that garage. We needed each other whether he believed it or not. All that we'd shared with each other was tying loops around us, knitting us closer together.

Severe faced hell at a young age, and it was a miracle he didn't break completely. He was broken—that much was true, but he'd managed to hang on to enough to heal one little piece at a time. I believe Pope and his cousins were the reasons he'd managed to hang on to his humanity, and for that, I was thankful for them.

CHAPTER TWENTY-SIX

Severe

The next day.

It was nearing noon. I'd decided to let Jade sleep in since we'd had a long emotionally-drenched night. She'd been right about talking about my past. I'd finally let go of a weight I'd been carrying on my back my whole life.

After we emptied ourselves of nearly every emotion, I fell asleep in her lap and woke to her placing kisses all over my face. I didn't discourage the sex that followed like I normally would because it leveled out the emotional fallout we'd unleashed on each other.

Her father's death was a horror I wanted to take from her and unleash on my future targets. The reference to the Order that was said to her father before he was shot had me seeking out Micah the first chance I got this morning.

Did her father have a kill order out on him? Was he a target, or could he have been involved with the Order in some other capacity? The mystery of Jade's kill order and everything surrounding it was a tangled mess of lies and deceit so vast and wide that we couldn't put the pieces together fast enough to save her life.

I opened the bathroom cabinet, took out some towels, and sat them on the ledge of the bathtub. Going back to the cabinet, I stared at the variety of bath bubbles and salts Jade had collected from her visits to the lodging cabin.

I couldn't walk around the compound now without someone stopping to compliment me on my *old lady*. My dark image, the one I'd perfected for years, was shattering like glass in a matter of weeks. She nor I corrected anyone when they assumed she was my old lady.

Soon enough, they would never see her again, and I would resume my role of being the black cloud that hung over the compound.

Lavender was meant to relax, so I poured some into the hot water swirling in the tub until it turned a pale shade of purple.

Jade trusted me now. I no longer had any doubts about it. Why else would she choose to sleep on the floor next to me every night versus sleeping comfortably on a perfectly good couch or bed? Why else would she ask to have sex again and again, although I wasn't gentle with her?

"Why didn't you turn her down?" my demon asked.

I ignored him. Besides, I couldn't worry about it now. The job still needed to be done. I headed back to the living room.

She was asleep, her feet up on the couch, and her head rested against the arm. She stirred when I sat on the other end of the couch. I tilted my head back and stared blankly at the ceiling, sensing her eyes on me.

Jade didn't wait until I acknowledged her. She climbed across my lap, the bottom of her hip dragging across my erection. As much as I wanted to, I couldn't form the words to execute a protest.

"I made you some water in the tub," I told her without glancing down at her. She lifted up, slinging her arms around my neck, perfectly at home with me and with her affections. She placed a quick kiss on my neck and cheek before she hopped up and took off for the bathroom.

"Thank you," she called back.

I gave it five minutes before I got up and stepped inside the bathroom. Her sincere smile greeted me as she lounged in the tub of near-boiling water.

"Severe," she whispered. "Thank you for the bath. This is sweet of you." Her words sounded as heartfelt as the smile that lingered on her lips. I slid the door closed behind me and took a few cautious steps closer, heightening her awareness enough for her eyes to pop open.

Her perky brown tits with their dark tips floated right at the water's peak while the purple-tinted water distorted the view of the rest of her body.

"What are you doing? Are you about to take nude photos of me or something?" she asked, tracking my movements. Her gaze dropped to my phone, gripped tight in my hand.

"No," I answered. "I'm about to record you."

"What? Why?" she sat up, her arms automatically crossing her chest.

I sat the phone in place on the lower shelf of the cabinet, adjusting it for the perfect view of her in the tub. I tapped the record button before turning to face her. Fear flashed in her eyes when she glanced down at the water surrounding her body and back at me.

A sad smile crept along her lips, but her eyes held fear, sorrow, and regret. The trust she'd given me so freely was about to be broken. Once I was close enough, I kneeled next to the tub, and she eased back, her chest already rising fast from her accelerated heart rate.

Whatever she saw in my expression took away the easy comfort she'd possessed minutes ago.

I wanted to tell her how sorry I was, that I didn't want to do this, that I didn't have any other choice, that I couldn't find any other solutions, but the words never came.

"Severe."

The sweet tone of her voice pulled at my heart, one I always believed was eternally dark.

"Severe?"

My name was a question this time.

"What's happening? This isn't you." She aimed a finger at the sink, but her eyes remained on mine. "I saw the medicine under the cabinet. I know you don't take it. I have prescription medication too. I don't take mine, either. Is that why you're looking at me like that?"

She sensed something was off. Her tight expression let me know her instincts were flashing her warning signs. I needed to get this over and done. Her knowledge about the medication I'd been prescribed and didn't take was an interesting revelation, one she'd never mentioned.

Blind trust. She never believed I was the monster, even though I didn't hide any of the evidence proving otherwise. I placed my hands on her tensed shoulders, and she startled.

Her eyes searched mine, and realization or some internal alarm made her jerk back. My grip on her shoulders tightened to keep her still. Water slushed and splashed over the side of the tub, wet the front of my shirt, and soaked into my pants, where I kneeled.

"Severe. What are you doing?"

I pushed down hard, shoving her under the water.

"Severe!"

She fought, hitting my arms and shouting my name, but I wouldn't answer her. I couldn't.

"Because I'm in control now!" My demon yelled.

"Severe. Please. You don't have to do this. I'll leave," she said, the pleading in her tone palpable, but I shoved her down again after she'd fought her way up, her words gargled, her screams sounding each time her face surfaced. She managed to fight her way up again, coughing, gaging.

"You'll never hear from me again," she promised.

She continued to believe the lie I'd fed her about why she was with me. It hadn't occurred to her that she was who I was talking about when I mentioned not being able to overturn the kill order.

She fought, knocking my hand away and shoving against my chest. She cried and screamed, her lungs working double time to fight for oxygen and to carry her distressed cries.

"Please! God. Please. Don't!" she yelled and continued to fight and splash water all over the place. Her legs kicked, and she twisted and turned in every direction, but it did her no good. She didn't have the strength to fight me off.

One hand I used to keep her chest down, the other I clamped around her neck, squeezing with enough firmness to control her movements against the slippery surface. I eased her farther down into the tub while she fought me for her life.

Her flailing limbs and jerking body proved how badly she wanted to live. She was begging me through the fear in her wide gaze not to take her life.

"Please," she choked out one last time before her mouth and nose sank below the surface and didn't come back up. Our eyes remained locked until she blurred under the water and faded the deeper I pushed her under. There was still some fight in her, kicking, clawing, and scratching to get herself free.

I tightened my hand around her neck, holding her under until her eyes grew intensely wide and bubbles began to fizz up from her nose as she struggled to suck in breaths that fed her lungs water.

Her kicks lessened, and her bucking grew less frequent. Her fingers digging into my forearms eased up, and she began to fade, fighting with the last reserve of strength that remained.

I glanced back at my phone and cast a devious smile into the camera when her hands fell away and slid into the water.

Why was my heart pounding so incessantly at the sight of Jade under that water? Eyes open, mouth parted, her naked body spiraled about after her struggle.

I stood and released her from my hold. Her chest floated to the top of the water, her lifeless eyes half-mast. I stepped back and turned the recorder off, but not before smiling into the camera again.

***

Once the camera was off, I rushed back to the tub, my heart attempting to punch its way from my chest. I positioned my arms around Jade's back and under her thighs before scooping her from the water and causing a large portion of the liquid to spill to the floor.

I laid Jade flat on the floor, her body limp and her head lulling to the side. Placing my ear against her nose and mouth, I listened for a breath I knew wouldn't be there before I proceeded to position her head to start administering CPR.

The edgy bite of uneasiness had never attacked me like this, making my hands shake while I pressed hard into her sternum to coax her heart back into a life-giving rhythm.

Fuck!

Nothing.

She was sixty seconds into oxygen deprivation, according to my internal clock's count. Her body remained unresponsive, unyielding to my demanding actions to drive life back into her.

I pushed hard, hand over hand, before repositioning her head to allow me to force air into her lungs. Ninety seconds and my anxiety was starting to get the better of me.

"I wasn't trying to kill you. I don't want you dead," I whispered. "I only want to help you, to keep you alive long enough to figure this all out. To buy you a cover against death order that can't be overturned."

The emptiness remained despite my hard compressions. It was the kind of emptiness people must feel when I went silent around them.

"Two minutes," I called out in a whisper. She was slipping further and further away. Her skin was starting to fade and reveal more of the deathly signs I didn't want to see.

"Come on. You're strong. Don't die. You've come this far. Don't fucking die," I muttered.

"Let her die. What are you doing?"

"Shut up! You did your job. Now leave me the fuck alone!" I yelled at my demon while attempting to push life back into Jade.

Two and a half minutes and her radiant brown was now being snuffed out by ashen gray. Death was here now, waiting to claim his prize.

"Come on, Jade. Fuck," I muttered. "You're stronger than you look. It was the first thing I noticed about you."

I pressed harder, forcing her lungs to do their job. She hadn't been under long enough to die.

"She's dead. Problem solved. I did you a fucking favor."

"Come on! I wasn't trying to kill you," I confessed.

"But I was," the asshole in my head taunted.

Another round of hard breaths made her chest rise high, but it didn't fall into the breathing rhythm I was looking for.

"Jade. Fucking breathe so you can keep irritating the hell out of me," I shouted, failing to keep the unfamiliar ache of panic at bay. At three and a half minutes in, it was getting close to the point when CPR was useless.

"Jade. Breathe. Come back."

Up and down, I pushed and kept counting.

"Please come back."

More breaths.

"Please, Jade. You have to fucking live. You're the only one I don't want dead. The one I want to save."

A sharp catch of breath sounded, and I stopped my frantic compressions. She gasped, taking in a big gulp of air, sucking so hard her chest rose and took a moment to fall.

When she began coughing, her chest vibrating and her body seizing, I rolled her to her side and pounded her back with my palm. Water shot from her nose and mouth, her lungs working with the flow of oxygen to push the fluids from her body.

I kept her on her side, rubbing a firm hand along her back until her hacking and coughing lessened and her mental focus returned from the brink of the horrific feeling of helplessness she must have been experiencing.

Her eyes flickered around wildly, not seeing anything familiar in her distressed state of mind. I rubbed her chest next, knowing it was burning. Waterboarded four times, I knew how it felt to drown. The sensation was like your lungs were burning over a steady flame, and the air you breathed was laced with acid that ripped your internal organs to microscopic pieces once it entered your body.

She gradually returned to herself, coughing, and gagging on the air she needed, taking it in too fast and likely thinking she wasn't getting enough at the same time. She spat water while some continued to seep from her nose.

I lifted her up, propping her against my chest until she settled, and the coughs came less frequently. I helped her to stand, and the tremble in her body let me know she was still in shock. I draped a robe around her shoulders and helped her push her arms into the sleeves.

She jerked away when I attempted to tie her into the robe, her thoughts clearing enough to recall what I'd done to her.

"Get away from me. You are the monster you've been claiming to be," she said before more coughs escaped, doubling her over. She staggered to the toilet. The lid slipped from her shaky hand and landed with a hard slap before she slumped onto the top of it, hacking and wheezing to get her breathing under control.

I took a step, and she lifted a trembling hand while shaking her head.

"No. No. Don't," her weak voice sounded when I continued to step closer and stooped before her.

"I had to do it. Had to make it as real as possible," I said, knowing she wouldn't understand what I had done, no matter how much I explained.

"Stay away," she coughed. "Get away," she uttered before shoving me, the push against the front of my shoulder so weak it hardly moved me an inch.

I left her alone, praying she would understand my actions and why.

I retreated to the living room and sat on the couch. For someone who'd prided himself on suppressing his emotions, right now, and at the moment I realized Jade was gone, I felt everything.

My trembling fingers made the necessary swipes over the surface of my phone, using muscle memory to send the recording.

It took thirty seconds to receive the standard reply. A single black reaper blade.

I dropped the phone on the coffee table and gripped my forehead. Was there such a thing as forgiveness for a person like me? This was the only time in my life I'd ever wanted it.

CHAPTER TWENTY-SEVEN

Severe

A loud crash had me rushing back into the bathroom. Jade had pulled the rack of toiletries from the top of the counter in her attempts to stand, and she'd landed back on the wet floor.

"Why?" she said between coughs. She jerked away from my hand when I attempted to help her. A look into her eyes revealed abject horror spilling from the depths of her gaze.

"Stay away from me," she yelled, her voice cracking before an outburst of hacking coughs took over. The coughing didn't deter her from her attempts to put distance between us. She crawled on her hands and knees and spun, putting her back against the tub before her shaky arms pushed against the wet floor until she was able to stand.

Droplets of water fell from her hair, shaken loose in her struggle, and drizzled down her exposed skin. She pulled the robe closed around her body before making several clumsy attempts to pull it tight at her chest.

She staggered, her mind speeding along, but her body had not yet recovered from the trauma it had endured. Her feet skated across a wet patch on the floor, and I instinctively reached out to keep her from falling. She stumbled into the door frame and caught hold of it to keep herself upright. Coughing, bent, and groaning, she made her way to the living room. I followed.

When she stumbled to the front door, I moved to stop her. She spun and swung on me, missing by a mile but sprinkling me with water.

"Stay away." Her weak voice didn't have enough volume to be effective, but she swung her arms repeatedly to keep me away from her. She swayed into the wall near the front door, hitting it with her left shoulder with a hard thud.

"Don't come near me!" she shouted. Her gaze was white and wild, her breathing erratic.

"I didn't want to hurt you…"

"You did. You tried to kill me. You wanted me around for your sick pleasure."

I shook my head, unsure how to explain my side of the situation.

My attempts to calm her and keep her from leaving in her condition didn't work. I did the one thing I knew to do when I couldn't figure out a solution. I picked up my phone from the coffee table and dialed one of the only people I trusted in this world.

***

A loud knock sounded at the door, making Jade jump since she sat near it. Instead of watching for who was at the door, her gaze remained pinned on me. Her shoulders were pressed back and against the wall behind her like she was attempting to push herself through it.

I never locked the door. Micah cracked it open and stepped inside. He stood in place, took in Jade's terrified eyes, her crumpled body, and me standing near the coffee table staring at her.

"Severe," Micah called.

I didn't have to remove my gaze from Jade to know his sharp gaze was fixed on me.

"What the hell is going on? *You* called me, so I know shit is fucked," Micah said.

"He. He. He tried to kill me," Jade said, pointing a shaky finger and glaring at me with big wide eyes.

Micah shook his head.

"No. If that man wanted you dead, then you would be," he assured.

He took a few more cautious steps closer to Jade, who dropped her chin behind her knees, tears falling fast down her face as she cast bloodshot eyes in my direction.

"I promise you, if he wanted you dead, you wouldn't be sitting here. Whatever the hell's happening with you two is outside of any norm, more so for him than you, but I believe the last thing he wants is you dead," Micah said, speaking on my behalf.

Without turning away from Jade, he asked. "Severe. What the fuck is going on? And this is your president asking, not your cousin."

"I wanted to help her, but you know I'm not good at dealing with *people*," I told him, not sure if my words were making sense.

"If you had only left her in the fucking tub, you wouldn't be dealing with all this 'people' shit," my demon pointed out.

"Helping me by trying to kill me?" Jade spat. She released another loud outburst of cries before she aimed her stiff finger like it was a blade. "I liked you. I trusted you. I believed you were a decent person," she heaved out the words. "You made me believe that I needed this place and that I needed you, but it was all a part of your plan so that I'd trust you and not see it coming when you decided it was time to kill me."

Another round of coughs stopped her rant. Micah reached out to help her up. "Let's go to the couch so we can sort through what's going on here."

Jade stared at his waiting hand for a while before she reached out and took it. Micah pulled her up, and I observed the way he handled her, his touch caring, his voice a delicate whisper of reassurance.

He assisted her onto the couch, on the side she usually sat on. She tucked her feet under her body and avoided my eyes. Micah aimed a stiff finger at me before aiming it at the couch.

"I believe I know what's going on because I know you, but I've let you go long enough in the dark with this shit. Now sit the fuck down and fucking start talking," Micah barked.

Respect. It was the one thing I didn't overstep to stroke my own ego, especially where it concerned my cousins. Only they could talk to me this way. Jade was the one person outside of my family I also respected, and I didn't understand why.

"They sent me the final warning. I needed to furnish proof, or they would send someone else," I told him.

Micah lifted a brow, and Jade's unblinking gaze found mine. We sat staring across the couch at each other. Her brows pinched while attempting to decode my words.

"Wait a fucking minute," Micah moved into position in front of us like a father preparing to discipline his children. "Does she know? You still haven't told her why she's here with you?" he asked.

A quick head shake was all I offered, avoiding the two sets of eyes I sensed on me.

"Tell me what? As far as I know, he liked playing me like I'm a ball of yarn and him the hell cat," she blurted.

Micah bit into his lip, fighting not to laugh. Jade's slick tongue was something that I liked about her.

"I told you days ago that you needed to tell her," Micah stated.

I shrugged. I wasn't going to tell him that I got a sick thrill from knowing that a part of her was wary of me, of what she believed I might do to her. I hadn't missed that curious glint in her eyes when she couldn't figure out some of my behavior.

"Tell me what?" she questioned, dropping her feet to the floor and angling her body to get a better view of me. "What are you keeping from me—have been keeping from me this whole time?"

Sound became a solid object in the room.

Jade rushed me, scooting closer to get in my face.

"What are you keeping from me?" she repeated and didn't back away. This was that brave side I admired about her. Micah's wide gaze bounced between us. Jade's ragged breathing made the only sound.

My gaze finally lifted to meet hers. "You remember I told you there was a target I didn't believe I should execute?"

She nodded, waiting.

"You like doing shit the hard way, don't you?" Micah shook his head.

Jade's expectant gaze was burning a hole through me.

"What?" she asked, gripping my arm and digging her nails into my skin so hard she was set to draw blood.

Our gazes locked. "You are my target. You always have been my target."

The words hung in the air like rotten fruit clinging to a dying vine. A sarcastic chuckle escaped Jade. Her nails eased from my skin, leaving compression marks. My words made the tension in her body draw tighter and the frown on her face deepen.

"You expect me to believe that someone hired a grim reaper from hell to hunt me down and kill me?"

Her laugh grew louder, the sarcasm in the sound filling up the room.

Micah lifted a brow at her reaction, his eyes bouncing back and forth between us. It wasn't every day a Reaper's target laughed at them.

I focused on the expectant unblinking eyes she flashed me once she stopped laughing and released another round of coughs.

"I was following you for weeks, studying you. It's why I was there when you were snatched in the garage. The man from the garage was also sent to kill you."

The crease in the center of her forehead deepened, her eyes working left to right in an attempt to make sense of my revelation. She shook her head.

"Why would someone want me dead? I'm no criminal. I am not even in the type of business that gains enemies. I don't understand. Make me understand," she demanded.

Micah stepped closer and stooped in front of her so he could get a better look into her eyes.

"Do you sell children into sex slavery and to pedophiles?" he asked her.

She gasped at the accusation, placing a hand over her heaving chest while struggling to catch her breath.

"Who said that? I would never. Someone is lying."

She looked between Micah and me twice before her gaze locked on me, despite Micah stooping in front of her.

"Is that why you tried to kill me? Is that why I'm here?"

Neither Micah nor I answered her, but I believed our silence was her answer. Tears began to leak from her red eyes.

She reached over and took a firm grip on my forearm, shaking her head like she needed me to believe her. I reached to pick up my phone from the coffee table with my free hand. My fingers swiped over the screen knowingly, but my focus was concentrated on Jade.

The sound of the recording distracted her enough for her to release my arm. Oddly, I didn't want her to let go, but Micah was right. I should have told her before now and at least explained why I took her.

"Those are the kids from the recreation center that I sponsor. Why?" Her head shook with a quick snapping motion. "No. No. Hell, no. That's not right. I'd never hurt kids. Where did you get this?"

The sight of the video had her breathless. I swiped it off and played one of the recordings.

"Yes. Put a bullet in his head. I pay you a sizable salary to do what I say without question. I want him dead."

She aimed a stiff, shaky finger at my phone. "That's me, but it's been rearranged. You can't believe I was abusing kids and ordering people's deaths."

"Acts of cruelty like this are why I'll take a job. But I always do my own research before I reap anyone. With you, I had second thoughts from the start. There was nothing I found that suggested that this evidence was true or that this level of cruelty belonged to you," I told her.

She stared intently, still breathing hard, her eyes flashing so many emotions that I couldn't decipher one from the other.

"Following and studying you showed me you didn't fit the crimes in which you were accused. My instincts wouldn't allow me to kill you unless I was sure," I said.

She squinted before a frown took its place.

"I help children get away from predators. When I receive a call that a child needs help, I do whatever it takes to help them, including breaking the law. It's why I keep that part of my life in the dark. The child you saw me picking up in that video was screaming because he thought I was his abusive mother. If they had furnished the rest of the video, you would have seen the same child hugging me when he realized I wasn't her and that I was there to help him."

She sniffed and swiped tears that fell harder. Her cries grew loud and broken as she struggled to tell us her side of the story.

"It doesn't matter to me if it's their parents, siblings, or guardian. If a child is being harmed, I risk my own life and provide the financial means to get them out of that situation and place them with people I trust and who can help them."

She cast her gaze between Micah and me again before she kept it on me, her hand tapping over her chest to still her heart.

"I'd never do to a child what was done to me," she whispered, her words as broken as the sorrow-induced glint in her eyes. Her watery gaze swept over Micah's before she pinned it back on mine.

"You guys might be Reapers, trained to send people to hell with a swiftness that can make death himself jealous. But I've been to hell. I know what it feels like. What it tastes like. I've heard the deathly howls, the screams of agony, the cries of endless and unrelenting pain. I've smelled fear, tasted it, choked on it. I know hell intimately, and not just because I was there when my father died, but I also lived through the most depraved, sick, and endless torture one could ever suffer."

Her words put dips between mine and Micah's eyes.

"When I was fourteen years old, and my sister was twelve, we were taken by my father's best friend and sold into a child sex trafficking ring as revenge against my father. This is the dirty little secret part of my life that no one knows about. My father was well-known, powerful, and scary to most people. He used his influence and power to track us down, but it took three months. They split me and my sister up before my father made it to us. She was never found."

She drew in a deep breath, letting her chin drop to her chest before shaking away the trauma she'd suffered.

"During those months, I was raped repeatedly, beaten, starved, and drugged. When they found out whose daughter I was, the abuse worsened. They spit on me. Urinated on me. Used objects on me."

She hit her chest with each word to emphasize how deeply the pain went.

"They used me like a trash can. I was in the trafficking ring for three months, so there's nothing I wouldn't do to get other kids out. There's nothing I wouldn't do to get a child away from an abusive adult. The few that I help are nothing compared to the many who become stuck in it, like my sister. Or those who die in it."

Face soaked with tears, she swallowed hard.

"If I'm here because you think I'm a monster, it's because someone wanted you to think it. Someone wants me out of the way because I probably took away the child they wanted to use as a toy."

My hand was clasped around hers now, and she didn't jerk it away. Micah noticed, casting a brief glance in my direction before letting it linger on our hands.

"You were right," Micah said, breaking up the silence as his gaze pinned mine. "I'm glad I never doubted you."

He never did, even when I gave him reason to, and neither did he doubt his brothers. If any of us told Micah that a purple unicorn had landed at Ground Zero, he would take our word for it and figure out the rest later.

"I've set some things in motion against the Six that can't be undone," he said, his expression unreadable and bouncing between Jade and me.

"You two keep talking and making up. We'll talk later. There should be a lead by the end of the day. It's why I wasn't worried about the time on the contract running out. But your plan was brilliant. It gets the Six off our back and keeps in play the element of surprise, among other things."

He glanced at Jade. "I'm in no way glorifying what Severe did to you, but we live in a world that doesn't get whitewashed. We experience the truth of this reality so others can live a dream." She swallowed but didn't reply.

"I'll send the doc over to check you out," he told Jade.

He nodded in my direction before turning and walking away.

CHAPTER TWENTY-EIGHT

Severe

Jade slept beside me every night. It was our routine and one I'd taken for granted until now. Now, I lay here on my back, staring at the moon-kissed shadows of the water playing out like a movie on my ceiling.

She remained on the couch tonight, curled into one of the tight balls I used to see her sleep in when I was studying her. The position was one of protection. At first, all I wanted was for her to fear me, but now that she did, I wondered if I'd lost something special that someone like me never gets an opportunity to find.

"Fuck me with a rusty railroad spike. I don't have a mouth or a throat, but I'm about to throw up. What the fuck are you saying? Thinking? Keep that kind of shit out of my space," my demon ranted.

I pretended I didn't hear him, praying he'd shut up already.

Only a few weeks marked mine and Jade's time together, but it was like we'd lived a lifetime within them. Jade was such an intriguing woman, so intuitive and caring, even for me. She made me forget that I didn't even like people.

She'd let down her guard, allowed me access to her deepest secrets, and I'd found a way to push her away. It was ironic how I'd spent most of my adult life keeping people away, ensuring they remained at arm's length, and the one I wanted close was afraid of me now.

Jade was the one who'd managed to make me appreciate human interaction. It was a breakthrough I never saw coming. I believe I was connected to her more than I was willing to acknowledge, the kind of link that defied all logic and reason.

Her movements were subtle, a twitch, a turn, a shrug. These were her unconsciousness revealing things that affected her physically.

"No, please," she mumbled.

I sat up, locking eyes with her tense back.

"Don't. Please," she begged, the desperation in her tone laced with the tears she must have cried when she was experiencing what was in the dreams.

Reaching out, I set my open palm inches away from her back, the warmth kissing my calloused skin. Her movements grew more intense now, her cries more frequent.

I placed my hand flat against her back, stopping her movement. I soothed her with easy strokes like I would Scrappy. My touch relaxed her enough for her to stop moving. Her breaths were quick, but I believe my touch was keeping the haunting memories away.

If someone had told me a month ago that I would be sleeping next to a beautiful woman every night, one who knew some of my deepest secrets, I would have probably cut out their tongue.

I leaned onto the couch, careful not to increase the pressure of my stroke. My head rested close enough to her back that her warmth washed over me, relaxing me as much as my strokes were comforting her.

I was afraid for the first time in my life. I feared I'd lost the one thing I never dreamed would touch me. Genuine friendship. Someone who truly cared to see past my demon and see me. She saw something in me that I didn't even know was there.

Jade saw my ability to care and my willingness to want something other than vengeance, death, and destruction. I'd assumed that becoming a Reaper, a member of the Order, and protecting my brothers was my purpose.

I was wrong. The sum of my fears, of my torture, of everything that happened to me, it equaled what I needed to become in order to be here, to be strong enough, to be everything she needed me to be to save her. And in return, she'd saved me from myself.

Even if Jade never again saw me as she once did, I would be eternally grateful that I'd experienced how it felt to be cared for, to be thought of as a hero, and to experience true affection. To be touched by...*love.*

***

Jade

His delicate strokes faded, but his hand remained on my back. The touch was so soothing, so relaxing, and so unlike him. He would never tell me he was sorry, not with words, but I'd be damned if he didn't know how to apologize with action.

"I am darkness. The unseen danger that gives you a chill. The icy prick that makes your skin crawl for no reason you can see. The hell that invades your dreams and gives you nightmares. Do you want to find out what happens when I get upset?" It was one of the first things Severe had whispered to me. He was everything he said he was, but so much more.

I couldn't get past him almost killing me or that he was my executioner, even though his actions may well have voided a kill order from a legendary Order that didn't do take-backs. Twice now, this man had saved me, yet there was a sickening distance between us that I didn't want there but also didn't know how to close.

I cared about him. He understood me in a way that no one else would. His disturbing childhood with his mother and mine witnessing my father's horrific death and time in a trafficking ring were the type of traumas that ripped a person's mind to shreds.

I didn't doubt that we were healing each other. We understood each other. Our psychological traumas were the axis that spun our bond into creation.

Sleeping on hard surfaces to feel grounded. No one in my life but Severe understood why I sought comfort in such an unusual place.

Would I ever find my way back to him? Back to the peace we'd found within each other—back to the calm that sprang from our connection.

He was a hard man to get to know, but once he let me in and allowed me to see bits and pieces of him unmasked, I loved what I saw.

He was the architect assigned to deliver my death. There was a divide as wide as the Grand Canyon between us now. Despite him threatening my life multiple times. Despite his standoffish ways.

I still loved him.

The realization kicked me in the chest with enough strength that it made me jump. My eyes popped open, and he shifted behind me like he'd heard my thoughts. He removed his hand from my back, his touch no longer the blanket keeping me warm.

I lay there for a long while, thinking and praying. I sat up, swiping the back of my hand across my weary eyes, and allowed my feet to drop over the edge of the couch when the sun peeked through the front window. My gaze darted to the kitchen first. He wasn't there, but he wasn't gone either. I sensed him. It was a sense of knowing I'd developed toward him.

His steps, silent, drew closer. His shadowy figure barely broke the darkness surrounding him in the hallway. His gaze collided with mine and held when he stepped into the living room. I swallowed. I missed him. Last night was the first night since we'd been here that I didn't sleep right next to him.

"Good morning," I said, my voice more a croak than a smooth sound.

"Morning," he replied before taking a seat on the couch. The other end of the couch. The space between us made the pangs haunting my heart rip the vessel into broken pieces that spilled into my chest cavity.

This wasn't us. This was a physical representation of hopelessness. Yesterday, we were us: smiling, teasing, and at peace with each other. Touching and kissing and relishing how good we could make each other feel.

This was the kind of heartbreak that came with a relationship. A real relationship and not his diagnosis of us: the heightened intensity of our situation, lust, close proximity, gratitude to my savior, and transference.

I never believed we were any of those labels, and these past twenty-four hours proved that my feelings for him were further along than even I assumed.

"I don't like where we are, but I don't know how to close this gap that's been ripped into us," I said.

He dropped his gaze to the coffee table and didn't reply for so long that I dropped mine too. Our hands were the targets in which we chose to express our anxiety, me wringing mine, him clenching his fists until they were white-knuckled.

"You've faced your worst fear, and it makes you a stronger person," he told me, and his statement made my brows quirk.

"You see, I like being the monster. I enjoy scaring people. I found out that even monsters have fears. Yesterday, I faced my worst fear. I survived a nightmare in which I was the monster to the one thing I wanted to protect the most. I…"

He dropped his head again, his chin dipping low. I reached out and jerked my hand back. He noticed. I reached out again until my shaky hand sat on top of his. He lifted his gaze to mine before letting it drop to our hands.

He flipped his so our palms met, and our fingers interlocked. His gaze fell to our connection, a new sentiment for him.

"We can get past this together. We can heal each other like we were doing before. Do you believe that?" I asked him.

He nodded, but he didn't hide the heavy weariness in his eyes.

"I can be more than a Reaper. I possess the capacity to care about something other than my job, protecting my brothers, and carrying out what I'm called to do by the Order. I've learned more about myself in the past month than I have my whole life."

He squeezed my hand and pinned my gaze with his unblinking one. I squeezed his hand in return.

"I believe you will be able to resume your life and heal others no matter where you go. It's your gift. I'll help you get back your life, even if it's the last thing I do," he promised.

The words '*no matter where you go*' caught my attention.

"Will I not be able to resume the life I once lived?" I already knew the answer but was hoping they would find a loophole.

He shook his head.

"You were an official kill order. If they find out you're alive…" He left the statement open-ended, which added a greater depth. I was sure the Order wasn't going to let me roam around free and clear when I was supposed to be dead. Keeping a tight grip on his hand, I allowed a companionable silence to fill the space.

I wanted to ask, '*What about us?*' but I sensed it was a subject he wasn't ready to talk about yet. I wasn't sure I was either.

The idea of leaving him, of not being around him, made the sickening sensation in the pit of my stomach return. No matter what happened yesterday, the idea of walking away from Severe didn't feel right.

CHAPTER TWENTY-NINE

Severe

When I walked into the sanctuary, there wasn't anyone but Micah in there, sitting at the head of the table. I glanced around for the rest of the attending club members.

"Have a seat."

His tone was even, and his expression didn't give away anything.

"The Six, the Handle, the Council, they have many names, but they are our leaders. Some have been appointed, a few inherited their seats, and some have climbed the ranks and earned their seats. Despite how they got their titles, we have to respect their decisions whether we agree with them or not."

He paused. "If they find out that Jade's alive, they will kill you and her, at the very least."

"I know. And I'm prepared to suffer the consequences," I told him.

He laughed.

"I don't give a fuck who's in charge. It could be the Six, the Seven, or the Eight. Do you really believe I'd let anyone, including the fucking devil himself, take you out? Especially after you've gone above and beyond to prove that they were wrong."

My lips parted and closed, but I couldn't utter a single word. I didn't know how to respond to the strong sentiment he expressed so easily.

"How are you going to protect your old lady?" he asked.

My eyes snapped up at his comment.

"She's very wealthy. She can go wherever she wants, be whoever she wants to be, do whatever she wants to do," I told him.

Micah tapped a finger to his lips, his thoughts playing out in his rapidly moving eyes.

"Danger was found dead, classically made to look like a legit fatal car accident. The only thought that crossed my mind at the news was '*scapegoat*'."

He said what I was thinking.

"I know you've heard this story, all Reapers have, but I need to tell it to you again. The condensed version," he said, eyeing me.

At this point, I couldn't imagine what was going through Micah's brain.

"Years before we were born, one of the Six killed the other five members when he believed there was corruption at their level within the organization. The Six are put there to make sure we follow certain rules, and when we skirt those rules, they deal with us accordingly. The Sixth member believed so strongly in the organization that he was willing to take them all out, including himself. That is all I'm going to say on the subject."

Was Micah considering attempting to do what many would say was impossible? Why was there a wicked smile forming on my face at the idea?

A smile, that devious one that reinforced that he'd already set some things in motion, formed on his face.

He slid a piece of paper across the table into my view but kept a finger planted atop it to keep it in place. A glance down showed me an address I quickly memorized. Micah pulled the paper back and slipped it into his pocket.

"The Six stopped revealing their identities after that one member decided that all of them dead was better than a poisoned organization." He tapped his pocket where he'd placed the address. "I believe the time has come to clean house again. If you can identify one, they may lead you to the traitor. And just because they hide from us doesn't mean they always hide from each other. Although there are only six, they still have to play politics. They are notorious for hiding in plain sight." He tapped his pocket again.

I nodded, knowing that Micah was pointing me to a member of the Six or at least someone who could lead me to a member. I didn't know the full details, but he was confident that I'd find whatever I needed at that address.

"Reap well, brother," Micah said before we gripped each other's forearms and shook.

"This is why I like this guy. He still likes to kill people," my demon said, content with knowing we'd soon have someone's blood on our hands.

Micah glanced up at the entrance to the sanctuary.

"I know it's going to break your heart, but you're going to have to miss this church service," he said with dripping sarcasm, right before the door to the sanctuary was opened and the group filed in to start church.

I stood, nodded once, and received a slight nod in return from Micah before I turned and walked away.

***

Jade

Severe wouldn't say where we were headed. He became closed off, reserved, and silent. He was in Reaper mode. This was the side of him that had frightened me most, the part of him that had learned to shut off his emotions.

This was also the side of him that I didn't see often. The one who could pull off being a regular person, his tattoos covered, his face beautiful and accepting, his smile inviting, and his clothing conservative and normal. He knew how to become a handsome man you could easily walk up to and carry on a polite conversation with.

However, if I were being truthful with myself, I believed it was the darker side of him that I was connected with on a deeper level. This was who saved me in that garage when we first met. The cold lifeless one with the disposition of a dead man. He was also the one who had the strength to nearly kill me in order to save me again. The twisted level of physiological entanglements between us was incomprehensible, but I was willing to muddle through to understand him and us.

He was doing this for me. He didn't have to tell me the details, but he was attempting to find a way around an order that couldn't be broken. Technically, I was dead in this organization's eyes. It meant I no longer had a life outside of hiding. If they discovered me alive, it meant Severe, and possibly many members, if not all of his MC's deaths also. He didn't have to tell me any of this for me to comprehend what would happen.

It's why I went to Zyana and asked her to cut my hair. Her being a stylist, she gave me a model's image. I had never worn my hair this short, but the short bob style brushed my cheeks and transformed me into a different person. I couldn't stop touching it and running my finger through the silky strands. It would take anyone who knew me a while to recognize me as they were used to seeing fancy updos, long springy curls, or bone straight and hanging over my shoulders.

Despite all that had happened, Severe hadn't given up the quest to find out why this secret organization wanted me dead so badly in the first place. The answer could potentially save me from a life in hiding. It could also preserve the integrity of an organization like theirs.

***

Evening was starting to set in, the sun leaving bright orange rays streaking across a dimming sky. We pulled around the side of a no-outlet street with a big brick house on the corner. Severe opened the center console of the new

Volvo sedan he was driving and pulled out a stack of pamphlets, handing me half.

Fifteen minutes later, we'd knocked on six doors and were walking up to the seventh now. Darkness had settled, and porch lights were switched on periodically.

Severe did all the talking when the people inside decided to open their doors. He knew the bible like he'd read it from cover to cover hundreds of times, quoting scripture and attempting to get them interested in what I believed was a legit church here in Charleston.

We were about to knock on another door, and based on the sharp edge of the tension rolling off of him, I wasn't sure the person who answered would be alive after we left.

Severe rang the doorbell twice. Although we could hear people inside, they didn't answer right away. The door sprang open when he was reaching to ring the bell again, and the sudden appearance of the owner made my brows hike high on my forehead.

"What do you want? Don't you people have something better to do than run around trying to save people who don't want to be saved?"

Severe lifted a pamphlet, preparing to speak, but he swayed, unsteady on his legs. I reached out to grip his arm before he went into a convulsive trance, his eyes rolling to the back of his head. The thick stack of pamphlets spilled from his shaky hand and landed at our feet.

He tipped over and fell against the side of the man's arms. The stunned man didn't think to catch him, so Severe ended up prone at our feet and halfway across the open doorway.

"Help him, please, Sir," I called desperately. Since Severe hadn't let me know what he was planning, the scene spiked my heart rate.

The man snapped to attention and dropped to his knees to help me with Severe. Another person, who I assumed was the man's boyfriend, approached.

"What?" the second one asked, not finishing his question. A towel was wrapped around his waist. His wide eyes dropped to the scene taking place.

"Help me get him inside!" The man, I presumed was the owner of the house, said to the one in the towel. I continued to play my part. This was the house Severe was probably about to turn into an above-ground graveyard.

I'd listened to too many stories about him around Ground Zero, and I wasn't sure if I was prepared for what was about to happen. Some of the stories were so gruesome that it was difficult to reconcile the Severe I believed I knew with the one who could send a chill up someone's spine from miles away.

Once the two men dragged Severe past the door, I stepped inside and pulled it closed behind me. I wanted answers badly enough to become a part of whatever was about to go down, even if I needed to shield my eyes from some of it. Finding out who set me up was the only true way to save my life.

My eyes bucked when Severe rolled his body in the direction of the man of the house, sending a punch to his throat, before sweeping his leg around and tripping the other from his stooping position.

While the first man was holding his neck and attempting to go for his cell phone, the one with the towel caught a quick elbow in the jaw and was knocked out with a swiftness he never saw coming.

"What the hell is this about?" the man choked out while holding his neck. His wide glare shot in my direction before he put his eyes back on Severe, who dragged the now-naked man over to the leather couch. The towel was abandoned at the front door.

Severe lifted and dropped the groaning man into place before turning back to the one on the floor, still gripping his throat. He stood over him before he reached down, gripped him by the arm, and snatched the well-built man up like he was a misbehaving child. He deposited him next to his sleeping boyfriend.

Finally able to move my eyes away from the men in the room, I noticed the fancy hand mirror on the coffee table lined with four rows of cocaine. A few blue pills added color to the white powdery lines. These men were getting ready to enjoy a night of highs and lows, and we had disturbed them.

The one who lost the towel had already popped his pill, and his unruly and bobbing erection was putting on a performance. It was like standing near an accident you didn't want to see but couldn't help watching.

"You must be the one who inherited your seat," Severe stated while standing over the man of the house.

I didn't know what that meant, but I believed I would before we left this house. Severe withdrew his phone and snapped a picture of the men before he turned his back on them to put his eyes back on me.

"Have a seat," he told me, putting his eyes on one of the two chairs facing his scene and separated by the coffee table. I sat, getting a better view of an erection that would probably pop up unwanted in one of my dreams later.

"Who are you? What do you want from me?" the man questioned.

"You have some information that I need. You're either going to give it to me the easy way or my way," he promised while walking around the couch the men sat on to stand behind them. The jittery man of the house jerked his neck around, attempting to see what Severe was doing.

He drew my attention as well. When he dropped his hand to his belt and began undoing it, I swallowed the lump that I didn't know had formed in my throat. I'd seen him kill before, but it was always in a live-or-die situation.

Was I mentally prepared to see whatever it was he was about to do now?

Once his belt was off, he looped it around the sleeping man's neck, pulling it taut while slapping the man in the face to wake him. The man's erection, if it were possible, grew stiffer.

"Don't do this? What do you want?" the other asked.

"I need you to tell me who, if not you, is training a team of phony Reapers. I also need you to tell me why you voted to put a death order out on that woman over there when there is evidence proving she's not guilty of what she's been accused of. You tell me that, and this ends quickly."

The man shook his head erratically, his eyes scanning me before he twisted his head around to Severe. His gaze dropped and lingered on his boyfriend, who was finally opening his eyes and clawing at the belt, tightening around his neck.

"I don't know what you're talking about."

The belt was drawn up another loop, causing the man to claw and reach for the leathery strap stretched tightly behind his head.

"Please. Please don't hurt me," the struggling man begged, his voice choppy.

Severe took out his phone, reading a message, I supposed. His face didn't give anything away before he clicked off and shoved it back into his back pocket.

"Please don't do this. I don't know what you're talking about."

"You don't?" Severe asked, his voice soft but edgy in that way it made my spine tingle.

"I just received confirmation based on your facial profiles that you enjoy the company of little boys," he said.

The closest thing to joy I'd ever seen rested on his face. It was like he needed to know how truly bad these men were to enjoy this more.

This would end in death, and he wanted me to see it all. He wanted me to see the monster he'd been warning me about since I met him.

What he didn't understand was that I knew what he was from the moment I met him in the garage.

Killing this man was a part of the work he enjoyed, the only job I believed fit his personality.

Click.

The sound of the blade springing free made the men jump and widened my eyes. Severe placed the blade under the man's ear, getting the wide-eyed attention of the one he wanted answers from.

"Don't do this," the man begged, staring at his boyfriend with blood dripping down his neck where the knife was sawing back and forth through the underside of his ear.

"Don't insult my intelligence by pretending you don't know what I am or why I'm here. Tell me what I need to know."

The belt was pulled harder around the man's neck, yanking his head into an upward angle.

Severe leaned down and whispered something in the man's ear, causing his eyes to open as wide as saucers. Pressure was applied to the knife under the boyfriend's ear, making blood drip faster and his screams grow louder.

Why didn't they just talk? Give Severe the answer he wanted in order to minimize their suffering. The man's wide eyes were on his boyfriend, who was choking while his ear was being knifed off the side of his head.

My eyes bucked, my lips parted, and my breathing grew ragged. As much as I wanted to, I couldn't look away.

"I was one of the ones who voted to keep her alive," the man blurted, yelling over his boyfriend's screams. His legs bounced while he wrung his hands so hard, I expected to see his skin flaking off.

I sat on the edge of my seat, my eyes traveling around the scene, waiting for the man to say more. He was one of the members who had voted on my death, despite Severe finding evidence that I was set up. Once Micah left Severe and me alone the day he drowned me, he told me everything.

This man saying he voted in my favor didn't mean anything because not only did I not believe him, I wanted to know who wanted me dead and why?

The naked man's screams grew so intense at this point that Severe paused the ear-sawing and placed an expectant gaze on the one we needed answers from.

"That's all I can tell you. If you know what I am, you know that I can't divulge anything about another member. It goes against everything we believe in. If it means I'll die here tonight, then so be it," he said. He was braver than I gave him credit for.

"Creating shadow executioners to execute official members like me and placing kill orders on innocent people is something you believe in?" Severe asked.

"Until you provided more evidence, every shred we were presented with checked out," the man replied.

"And yet, the order was not voided. I'm tired of this," Severe said. What was he about to…?

"Aww!"

The loud scream ripped through the air like a physical object being lifted and thrown. The man's ear fell to the couch and landed next to the shaky leg of the one who wasn't saying what Severe wanted to hear.

A strong hand was placed under the screaming man's shoulders before Severe pulled him into a higher sitting position. His world was crumbling around him, and he was losing body parts, but his erection remained.

"Take off your pants!"

My eyes snapped up to Severe, as did the man's.

"No. You can't do this. Do you know what's going to happen to you when they find out what you've done? They'll know that another member gave me up?"

"Aww!"

Another loud scream ripped through the air, this time from the knife sinking into the naked man's shoulder, deep enough for the handle to stick up in the air. The man's screams turned to groans, guttural and pain-soaked.

His tight-lipped partner stood, pulling at his loose-fitting pajama pants while shaking his head at his half-dead boyfriend. Once his pants were off, he appeared too ashamed to look in either my or Severe's direction. He hadn't had a chance to take his blue pill, so his member was shriveled like a prune sitting atop two walnuts.

Severe was doing something I couldn't make out behind the shrieking man. When he walked away, the man's head was pulled taut by the belt, indicating he was tied in place by his neck. He couldn't move the shoulder with the blade in it, but his free arm flapped about like a dying fish out of water in an attempt to free himself.

The one standing stared at Severe walking around the couch until they were standing face to face. Head shaking in protest, he kept his hands cupped over his dick while Severe locked gazes with him. The sound of his boyfriend's harsh breathing and loud whimpers floated through the charged air.

"Which one of you set her up?"

The man shook his head, refusing to answer and making things harder on himself. I believe he understood he would die either way.

"The hard way it is," Severe said before slapping his hand down on the man's shoulders and shoving him closer to his boyfriend.

The boyfriend grunted while attempting to pull the blade from his shoulder. Based on how his hand and body shook, he wasn't making any progress.

Severe turned the standing man to face his boyfriend so he was positioned between the groaning man's legs. His teeth were bared past his gums as he gaped up at the men standing above him. I leaned in to get the full picture of the scene. What could he possibly do to make the man talk? I was fairly certain the one with the missing ear didn't know anything.

Severe reached around the man, who I would have expected to have more fight in him, and jerked the blade from his boyfriend's shoulder.

The man, knowing Severe was a Reaper, must have figured his odds of escaping this situation were slim to none. Therefore, fighting was futile.

Severe kicked the man's legs apart before pushing him closer to his whimpering boyfriend, who stared wide-eyed and held up his good hand to wave off what was about to happen.

His dick remained stiff, a useless pole. The little blue pill was proving it could sustain its job through the worse kinds of trauma.

I yelled out, "Talk! Tell him what you know!"

Severe shoved him down harshly. He landed against his boyfriend with a hard slap, making the man's scream reach a decibel-breaking volume when his head landed against his bleeding shoulder.

The one in Severe's rough hold was helped with harsh yanks and pulls until he was straddling his boyfriend. And...

I slammed my eyes shut.

"Aww!"

They both yelled at the brutal penetration. No jelly, but hard and fast, the man's backdoor was violated. Severe stabbed a knife into the back of the one on top while his partner flopped around under him, both pleading mercy.

Talk. Talk. Talk. I tried to will them to give up some information, any information, because things would only get worse.

The scene was humiliating enough, but Severe took things a step further. He used one hand to keep the knife planted in the top's back and reached down and yanked the legs of the bottom, undoing the anchor he'd made for himself with his feet planted firmly on the floor. The scene finally began to take on its demonizing qualities.

Each time the man's legs were kicked or yanked, the movement pulled the belt tighter around the bottom's neck while the knife sank deeper into the top's back. Him squirming to avoid the blade drove it in deeper and made the belt tug harder around his partner's neck.

The stupid man still wouldn't talk. Severe walked away, and all eyes followed him, despite the pain and suffering taking place.

"No," I mouthed while watching him come back with a crystal object that resembled a cactus and, oddly enough, reminded me of an oversized spiked dildo.

Severe sat on the couch next to the two men, one choking and the other staring at the glass object, knowing where it was about to go if he didn't talk.

"The fucking Senator, okay. Please. Stop!"

The Senator?

"Give me a name."

"It's her uncle. Senator McKenna. He wants her dead because she wouldn't stop digging. She was getting closer to finding out how he was funding his future campaign for the presidency, and he knew he couldn't let that happen."

Severe shot a quick glance in my direction.

"How was he funding it?" he asked the man.

When he didn't answer right away, Severe shoved the knife deeper and kicked his boyfriend's trembling leg. The bottom man's eyes had rolled to the back of his head, his tongue hanging out of his wide, open mouth. He was reduced to sputtering gasps and hard body jerks.

"He auctions kids. Kids that he knows no one will search too hard to find," the top blurted, his voice jerky from his partner's convulsing body.

What did I just hear? Was I stuck in a dream? Was my uncle a member of this secret organization and wanted me dead? My uncle was trading kids for campaign money? Could any of this be true? Was the trafficking ring I've been dismantling for the last two years the same one being run by my uncle this whole time?

"No. No. No," I kept repeating, shaking my head.

The whole scene slapped me in the face. The scent of the blood, the men yelling and thrashing and begging. The bottom man dying while they were still connected. Severe, yanking the top man up, a suspected leader of his organization, positioning him and shoving him down on that spiked, hard, foot-and-a-half-long piece of glass.

The sound. The scent. The sight of blood sliding over the glass and the man's body jerking involuntarily like it was the only movement that made sense.

My uncle was responsible for everything bad that had ever happened in my life. I couldn't breathe. The bile I'd been fighting to keep down rushed up my throat. I was going to be sick.

I hopped up, causing Severe to glance back, but he didn't stop his deadly actions. His hands on each of the struggling man's shoulders, he continued to shove him down, determined to make sure every last inch of that deadly object entered the man's body.

I tore through the living room and ran to the kitchen. The sink caught the first chunks of vomit I released. I continued to retch until my stomach was empty, and dry heaves arched my back.

My mind was heavy with thoughts of how my uncle had betrayed me. Even while Severe was in the midst of performing one of his most monstrous acts, my uncle was still far worse than him.

Moments later, during the drive away from the burning house, I gave Severe one of the three known addresses I had for my uncle. I was going back home. We were going back to New York.

CHAPTER THIRTY

Jade

A sense of déjà vu hit me at the sight of Severe flying us back to New York. After our arrival, we picked up a car that was conveniently left for him at the airport. We drove in silence while I allowed my thoughts to roam free.

"The ones you love will hurt you the most."

It was all my father could get out before a final shot took his voice and left him wide-eyed and struggling for his last breath.

After driving for nearly two hours, we arrived at the second location on my address list, the offices that housed my uncle's recycling company. Now that I knew some of his secrets, I wasn't sure this was a recycling company. It was likely a front for some other shady operation. Another side hustle when selling children didn't net him the profit he wanted.

This building wasn't in the best part of the city. Therefore I had to go through security. First in the lobby when I entered, then again once I arrived at the floor that housed his office.

"Mr. McKenna will see you now," his receptionist announced after making me wait to check in with him and send him photographic verification. I wasn't sure where Severe was, but I sensed him nearby.

"I'm headed home," the woman called into her headset, picking up her purse. "See you tomorrow, sir."

We passed each other, her on her way out and me heading to my uncle's office.

"Jade," he called, smiling like he normally did. "It's not often I get a visit from my favorite niece."

I didn't speak or return the fake enthusiasm he'd perfected. He was a good actor. Not once did his face reveal the monster who'd framed me for some of the most heinous crimes on the planet. I was his scapegoat, kept around until I was of some use.

Me getting too close to his operation was the excuse he'd needed to point eyes away from him. If he was capable of doing this to me, he was capable of doing anything to anybody. And this was the kind of man who could get himself elected to one of the most powerful positions in the world.

My face remained impassive as I took one of the seats in front of his desk. Two of his security guys stood behind him, feet away and one at each shoulder.

"I'll get straight to the point. I know that I should be dead. But, as you can see, I've managed to survive in spite of some of the deadliest assassins on the planet coming after me. No thanks to you."

His forehead crinkled, but he didn't reply.

"I didn't survive among the infamous Hell Reapers because they are *yes* men who pull the trigger like lap dogs when members of the Six order them to do it. I survived because they are intelligent enough to spot a lie even when something looks like the truth."

He released a fake laugh. His men's posture stiffened, sensing the building tension in the air. It could have also been me tossing around words about a secret organization I wasn't supposed to know about that set them off. At this point, I didn't care.

"What are you talking about?" he questioned, chuckling.

"I know you either have some type of leverage over one of the members, or you're one of the Six. I know you initiated the order to have me killed with evidence you had doctored. You wanted me to take the fall for the trafficking ring you're running when you found out I was the one saving some of the kids you were trading. I must have been close to finding out all your secrets."

"Are you okay?" he asked, flashing me a wicked side-eye. "You're talking crazy, not making any sense. Why would I jeopardize my career to do something as insane as trafficking children? And why would I have you killed? It makes no sense."

He sounded so convincing.

"Being one of the Six is not enough power for you. You want to be the highest power. You want to be president by any means necessary," I stated.

If he was a part of this secret organization that believed I was dead, it meant I didn't have time to waste. I didn't know what kind of backup plan he had in place, but I was sure he put out the bat signal as soon as I walked through the door, and he saw I was still alive. I stood, and his men snapped to attention and placed their hands closer to their weapons.

"I don't have time for your lies. I know you've called for your people to come and take care of me, but not before I get some answers. I pulled the gun from my waistband and lifted it, showing him that his security hadn't done a thorough enough job of keeping him secured.

His men pulled and aimed, placing me in their crosshairs before I got a good aim at his head.

In my peripheral, I saw Severe walk into the room through the open doorway of the balcony. His silent steps didn't alert anyone to his approach until he was standing behind one of the men with his gun pressed to the back of his head.

The man opened his palm and dropped the gun without a word being uttered. Although he maintained his aim, the second guard didn't appear as confident as he was a moment ago. His eyes bounced between me, Severe, his friend with a gun to the back of his head, and finally to my uncle before he made the rotation with his eyes again.

My uncle may not have been afraid of me, but his eyes widened at the sight of Severe in his all-black attire and at his sudden appearance.

"Which one gave me up?" he questioned, picking up the brown liquor he swirled in the glass before taking a swig.

Severe didn't reply.

"How many of us have you killed?" he asked, staring into his glass but talking to Severe.

Again, no reply was provided, and I didn't miss the small tick below his left eye. The silence bothered him more than the gun I kept aimed at his head. He was used to running things and getting answers.

"You were responsible for killing my father. Your own brother," I whispered, gluing together an age-old crime while glimpsing the malice now shining brightly in my uncle's eyes. It was the first time he'd looked at me that way, disdain alive and pulsing in his gaze.

"Why?" I asked.

"How the hell do you think I found out about the Order? Jace was one of the Six," he said, spitting out my father's name like it burned his tongue. "He ran the street division for the organization. It was the secret behind all his power and how he could literally do anything and get away with it. I found out I was in line to inherit a seat if anything happened to him, so I took my opportunity. But, the motherfucker lied to me to test my loyalty. The seat ended up going to someone the organization appointed. However, I'm a McKenna, and I found another way," he said, no emotion in his tone.

"Tip, Blade, Edge, Flat, Point, and Heel. A knife has many parts, but it's too bad the point wasn't sharp enough to scrape across the heel," Severe said, getting my uncle's attention and distracting me form the devastating revelation he'd just unleashed. He'd blurted the riddle that was spoken before my father died.

"It was you who sent her father that message so he'd know that it was you or the Order behind his death."

Severe was stating what he'd pieced together, but I wanted to know how this devil that unfortunately shared my blood would respond.

"You're a lot smarter than you look dark Reaper," he said to Severe, chuckling.

I shook away tears. Not because I was sad but because of the anger building inside me. At how unemotionally he spoke of killing his own brother. The eyes I once trusted were cold, dead, and empty.

Jaxson McKenna was the monster that lurked over my shoulder my whole life. He was responsible for the worst thing that ever happened to me. If he was capable of killing his own brother, he was capable of anything. Him placing me under a death order was nothing more than a decision he'd had to make to get what he wanted.

My father and I leaned on him for support after my sister and I were captured and placed in that trafficking ring.

The trafficking ring.

I launched myself across the desk, not caring about anything but ripping this man's throat out with my bare hands. I managed an ill-flying fist to his jaw, but he skirted my next blow when he spun from my grasp in his chair.

Two more of his men entered the room while I was aiming to get at him. Severe had a gun aimed at my uncle's head, and another one remained at the back of the head of the guard he was using as his bulletproof vest.

My uncle's goons had their guns aimed at mine and Severe's heads. My uncle was smart enough to lift his hand up when the odds of us all catching bullets presented themselves.

"You evil, hell-infested, demon-eyed, black-hearted son of a sick twisted bitch," I spat at him. My fury had spit flying off my lips. I rarely cursed, so I must have been saving all of the words for this moment, for this man.

I aimed a stiff finger at him, wishing it could be used to shoot him in the face.

"When Jasmine and I were taken, you were responsible for us going into that trafficking ring, weren't you?"

He didn't have to answer me. I already knew the truth. His own nieces.

"You're worse than the devil himself. Do you have any idea how many times we were raped, how many times we were beaten, injected with drugs, and starved? It's men like you who make the Order necessary. But when someone like you is at the helm, helping to run it, you taint everything the organization stands for."

I hawked and spat in his face, making the guards aiming guns in two directions stiffen. He swiped at his face, and the disgust there may as well have been words. I wanted to cry and scream and kill him all at the same time.

My father had taught me a lot about killing, mainly about when to do it. However, it wasn't something I believed I was capable of doing until now. My hands shook because I needed them to be around Jaxson's neck so badly.

Severe hadn't said another word. He was a weapon without a weapon, and although I didn't know a lot about his training, I knew and had seen enough to know that he didn't need a gun to escape the deadliest of situations.

I glanced at him, and our eyes met for a second. He lowered his gaze, putting his eyes on the floor. I didn't know much about combat, but I knew at that moment that he was telling me to get down.

No sooner than I dropped to my knees did gunshots ring out. Severe was on the move, turning and shooting and throwing knives. I didn't know where he'd gotten the weapons but surmised he'd taken them from the multiple guys he'd come in contact with on the way up to my uncle's office.

One man reached into his inner holster for his backup after his first weapon was kicked from his hands. He found the holster empty right before his head exploded, and his body dropped. He fell to his knees, mouth open. His wide, dead eyes landed on me when his head struck the floor with a loud fleshy thump. Three more of Jaxson's goons came storming into the office when the commotion got their attention.

Lights flickered, bodies continued to fall, and screams sounded. Flesh pounded against flesh and metal scraped metal—all the sounds of death in progress wailed like alarm bells at once.

From the corner of my eyes, I saw something that made me smile amid all the mayhem and death occurring in this room. Jaxson glanced up and saw me looking, saw me smiling, saw me crawling closer. His expression grew more exaggerated, especially when I got close enough to kick him in his damn mouth.

He launched himself in my direction, attempting to throw a punch. I assumed someone that was sitting at the top of a legendary spy organization would have had some level of training, at least self-defense, but it appeared he lacked the proper skills required to defend himself. He was the type of man who ordered others to do the fighting for him.

The licks he attempted to land were blocked by my angry fist, and followed up with my fist to his face and my foot to his body.

The silence filling the space gave way to the sounds of me and my uncle fighting. Only when my fists began to slide over his bloody face did I stop punching and look up to find Severe staring. Of all the deaths that had been tossed around this office, the one visible sign that Severe was involved at all was the cut over his left eye and a few bleeding slices along his forearms. If he were injured anywhere else, it didn't show in his unbothered expression.

He reached down and easily pulled me to a standing position. I delivered a swift kick to my uncle's side before spitting on him again.

"How do you want to do it?" Severe asked, finally taking his gaze off me and dropping it to the piece of shit on the floor.

"Even if you kill me, you won't make it out of here alive," my uncle had the nerve to taunt us while spitting blood. "I borrowed a little trick from you Reaper assholes," he snickered before spitting out more blood.

He sat up, swiping at his bloody face and setting his evil eyes on me.

"Before your little Reaper pet started murdering my guards, I enacted my backup plan." He lifted his phone, shaking it teasingly.

He struggled to stand, his eyes bouncing back and forth between Severe and me. He took his time, turning in a circle before letting out a whistle at the sight of his office.

"I wanted you on this case because I expected your sick, murderous ass to kill a child molester on sight. Someone who was doing to kids what was done to you for so many years. I never expected or never saw any semblance of life within you. I saw a killing machine," he said, glaring at Severe like he was the monster. He swiped more blood from the corner of his mouth.

"Fuck," he muttered, cursing himself for choosing wrong. His logic was to set loose a killing machine on the only type of person I believe Severe enjoyed killing. However, his sick plan to use Severe as a pawn to kill me without question had failed.

Jaxson didn't care that I was tormented by what happened to me or that he was responsible. He didn't take into account that Severe would sense I wasn't the predator I was being made out to be but, in fact, a victim.

"You didn't count on him not being the heartless monster groomed by the Order. You assumed he would be complicit and swift due to his own past?"

The glare he aimed was filled with enough vicious intent to make me shiver.

When Jaxson's smirk appeared, my brows quirked. Did he not know that he was about to die? There would be no prison. There would be no slithering away from this because he was a member of a famous order of assassins either.

He aimed a finger at the door and then at Severe. "You may have killed the six guards on my personal protection detail, but like I said, I took a page from the Reaper handbook and incited an action that you deadly mother-fuckers perfected."

He laughed and nodded when Severe squinted.

"A Reaper Net. You're good, but you're not inde-structible. You will likely make it off this floor but let's see you take on a building surrounded by and filling with want-to-be Reaper misfits who are hungry and eager to prove themselves," he spit at us.

Severe handed me one of the pistols he'd acquired. I took it, checked that the safety was off, and aimed the gun at Jaxson without hesitation. His uncle title was revoked.

"Don't do it. You're not a killer," he said, spitting the words through the blood and saliva spilling from his lips.

"I'm not a killer, but killing you doesn't make me a murderer. It makes me a hero."

My finger flexed...

"I know where Jasmine is," he yelled, stopping me from sending a fast-moving ball of death toward his head. I sensed Severe's eyes on me.

"Where is she?" I asked in a voice that sounded like I had no breath in my body.

"You let me go, and I'll give you the location," he bar-gained for his miserable life.

Severe had gone into that mode where you couldn't tell if he was present. I didn't sense him, but my anger flared so fiercely it was like another person had entered me.

"You must think I'm crazy." I stepped closer, placing the gun a few feet from his chest.

"If she's alive, I'll find her, like I found out about you and all the dirt you've done."

I squeezed the trigger. The shot rang out, pounding into my ears. Jaxson flew away from me like the devil himself had snatched him before he slammed onto the floor. His arms were spread and flopping against the floor, his eyes and mouth wide, a silent, haunting cry lodged in his throat.

The shrieking yell he released was like nothing I'd ever heard. There was a sharp edge to the sound, the waves so potent they vibrated along my skin.

"I missed your heart on purpose. The next time I'll see if I can get a little bit closer without killing you, and I'll keep trying until you're dead. Now, where is Jasmine?"

"You'll kill me if I tell you," he spat out the shaky words.

"I'll kill you if you don't tell me. Now that you've turned me into something I never believed I'd be, I don't have anything else to lose while looking for her and cleaning up the mess you've made. I plan to turn your name, your legacy, and anything you have accomplished in this life to shit. From now on, when anybody hears your name, they will frown, spit, or curse."

The horror of me tarnishing his name was worse than the discomfort of him being shot in the shoulder.

"Aww!" he howled again when I sent another shot into his left thigh. It must have nicked an artery based on the blood wetting his pant leg and rapidly pooling on the floor. He didn't have much time left.

"Where is my sister, you evil troll?"

The deep frown made his face unrecognizable. "She was recruited into the Black Butterflies. You both were supposed to be. The trafficking ring was to break you before you were to be rebuilt by the organization."

"Female assassins," Severe whispered.

"You gave us to a trafficking ring to be raped and beaten before we were to be sent into some sort of assassin grooming?"

He didn't answer. His pain was winning out over my looming presence. His wide eyes found the blood pooling around his leg.

"Where is she?" I asked again.

"Even if you found her, I doubt she even knows who you are anymore."

"Where is she?" I asked through gritted teeth, right before I placed the heel of my tennis shoe over the seeping leg wound he was so concerned about.

"Aww!"

He kept yelling and didn't let up when I removed my foot. I turned to Severe.

"Let's go."

He lifted a brow but didn't protest my request. When I turned and walked away, Jaxson's shrieking cries died down into breathy groans. I sensed his evil eyes on my back. I stopped at the door and turned back.

"You know what. I've changed my mind. This world is better off without you in it. I'll find my sister without you."

I didn't hear the gun go off or feel it kick in my hands. It was like someone else had pulled the trigger.

Jaxson struggled, gasping, clutching at the air, fighting to drag in breaths. The blood on his chest spread fast, turning his light brown shirt black.

When I did come back to my senses and glanced down at the gun in my hands, I noticed I hadn't pulled the trigger. It was Severe who delivered the kill shot.

"Not him," he said, not wanting Jaxson McKenna's blood on my hands. His body had gone still, blood spilling like a red puddle around him. His hollow gaze was on me, the last thing he saw before he failed to suck in his last breath.

The quiet that crept into this scene spurred me to move while Severe went around the room, collecting weapons.

"Was Jaxson telling the truth about the Reaper net he's created? Are we going to die?"

"I put in a call for backup," Severe replied.

"We're in New York. Your MC is in South Carolina?" I stated the obvious.

"There are twenty Reapers in this city," he replied, locking gazes with mine.

It could have been paranoia, but I swore I saw something in his gaze that suggested that backup may not arrive in time to keep us from being ensnared in the death net my sadistic uncle had initiated.

CHAPTER THIRTY-ONE

Jade

Severe handed me a gun with a silencer attached. He'd revealed how often he'd spied on me and knew things about me that I didn't know about myself. He handed me the second gun because he knew I occasionally visited a shooting gallery. I took the Baretta, cocked it, and accepted the extra clip of ammunition.

"Shoot anyone you don't know. This is going to get bloody and messy, so you need to be afraid. I've seen your shooting record. You're a good shot. If you run low on ammo," he aimed a finger at his waistband, "don't hesitate to take one."

Swallowing hard, I nodded. Was I about to go to war? Nearly every tragic or bad occurrence in my life had been set into motion by Jaxson McKenna. Power had warped his frame of mind to a point where he would use and destroy anyone in his way to get it.

"Aim for the head or heart. They won't hesitate, and neither should you. Stay behind me, no matter what."

I nodded, glancing up at his impassive face. Guns hung from him like they were some sort of twisted jewelry. He wanted me to be afraid, but was he? Did he experience fear in the face of death, or had that feeling been trained and tortured out of him? It was a question that would have to wait because I sensed the death net tightening around us, and we hadn't exited this room yet.

Severe placed his body against the wall facing the door, aimed and prepared to take out whoever decided they were brave enough to test him. I was a few feet behind him.

He sprang the door open and aimed in each direction before he took off. I was right on his trail, my heart jackhammering in my chest.

Tap!

Tap!

Severe fired his gun so fast the bad guys were falling before I'd even spotted them. He picked up the pace, leading us closer to more loud, charging footsteps.

Another tap sounded before the glass in the window shattered. I didn't see that one until his body was hanging from a rope and swinging back and forth through the shattered window. These fake Reapers were climbing the walls like Spiderman, actions that would cause my heart to grow legs and run off if I wasn't with Severe.

As we drew closer to the stairwell, my heart and everything inside my torso were in my throat, and I prayed I wouldn't throw up again while keeping a steady aim. My eyes widened at the slight movement behind me.

I sucked in a deep breath, closed one eye, aimed, and fired. The man didn't go down, but took the shot, staggered back, and lifted his gun.

I fired twice more, taking him down this time with a headshot that sent blood splatter against the wall behind him. I didn't have time to think about what I'd done because two more appeared like roaches from a dark crack.

Aim.

Fire.

Aim.

Fire.

I didn't have time to think, just to react. Severe didn't even acknowledge me and my fight behind him because he was already ejecting and reloading a clip into his weapon.

"Stairs. You aim up, and I'll aim down," he said before he turned into the stairwell and immediately fired off rounds. The shots lit up the dim space, allowing me to see that there wasn't anybody approaching from the top.

We hugged the walls while Severe took the deadly risk of firing over the stairs sporadically. I believed he was taking men out each time as loud thumps, shouts, and curses sounded off among the constant tap of gunfire and the drumming beat of their boots. As soon as we were a least two floors down, Severe took us back inside an empty hallway on the tenth floor.

While I aimed down the hall, Severe smashed a table and used the leg to barricade the door. He unstrapped one of the machine guns from his neck and rigged it so that when they opened the door, the gun would fire off the thirty-round magazine. I didn't know where he'd gotten rope, but he was resourceful in the face of death.

His trap, though necessary in a situation like this, left me questioning how we would get down now without stairs. Surely we weren't taking the elevator.

He led me to the fourth room down the hall, and we entered. The room, a small and vacant studio apartment, was dark. Although I wasn't sure if I should be on guard, I aimed the weapon around the room anyway.

My eyes widened at the sight of the circular object in Severe's hand.

A hand grenade.

Where the hell did he get that? Had all of these deadly weapons been on him the entire time? The thump of feet marching closer drew my attention. If they opened that stairway door and came onto this floor, they would be in for a rude awakening.

Like the stairway door trap, he did the same in the doorway of this room with the grenade. The thin, barely visible string was right in the path where you wouldn't think to look when entering a room.

Now, where were we going since he'd sealed off our way out? I glanced back at the open balcony door. No way. I wasn't afraid of heights, but I wasn't at his level of combat tactics. I didn't know shit about scaling walls and didn't believe a quick lesson would do the trick.

Before I voiced my concerns, Severe took off in the direction of the balcony, and I followed, scratching my head and glancing back at the open doorway. The loud knocking must have been the men attempting to get the stairway door open.

As soon as I stepped onto the balcony, a gust of wind took my breath. Severe was already strapped into ropes and passing a metal-tipped rope in my direction.

Constant gun blasts sounded, alerting us that they had gotten the stairway door open and more fake Reapers were dead or dying. They would arrive soon and storm through the door.

Shit! The Grenade.

We needed to be off this balcony before they got here. I stepped closer, allowing Severe to encircle me in rope and metal rings until I was strapped to his back. He must have already set this all up before he climbed into my uncle's office.

"Same as we do on the bike. Hold on tight," he said.

"Severe. I don't know about..."

I lost my breath when I was lifted off my feet by him climbing atop the balcony's railing. The wind whipping around us released a low howl like it was warning me to stay on solid ground. I wasn't just wrapped around Severe. I'm sure I was glued around the man tight enough to put a spider monkey to shame.

"Oh my God," I whispered breathlessly and slammed my eyes shut when I peeked over his shoulder and saw nothing but open air.

"Oh! Shit!" I yelled at the top of my lungs when the bottom fell out of my stomach, and my body clenched into a knot so tight, I believed I might disintegrate. There was a jolt and a tap, the wind flirting with us the whole time.

My stomach lurched again, reminding me it was still inside me but attempting to make an escape if we went airborne a third time. I was strapped to a man who was bouncing off the side of a building like he was on a playground.

A loud bang sounded somewhere above before chunks of debris and, possibly, human parts rained down on us.

What was that *swish* sound? There it was again.

Why the hell did I look down? Three or maybe four bad guys were down there shooting at us.

No one made it out of this world alive, but I never imagined I would die like this—strapped to the back of a man known as death, scaling a wall, and returning fire to a group of death's prodigies who were determined to kill us by any means necessary.

"Oh!" I yelled out when I was whipped around, and we landed hard. I peeled my eyes open. We were on solid ground again—another balcony, about four or five stories up now. I lost count when at least the third method of death came at me. The worst part of the situation was that the ones on the ground knew what floor we were on now.

Within seconds, Severe had us unstrapped and was yanking rope down my shaky legs.

Aim. Stay on guard, I reminded myself before pulling my gun from my waistband, glad to see it wasn't lost in our wall-climbing expedition. I couldn't afford to have an oh-woe-is-me moment. These killers weren't going to stop until we were dead, and I wasn't ready to die.

Free of the ropes, we headed into the space, Severe shooting his way in. My quick prayer that no one was home was answered as we stepped through the shattered balcony doorway. This must have been a floor of individual office spaces and not suites and small apartments like upstairs.

"Can't we wait them out until backup gets here?" I asked.

"That's the worst thing you can do when you're in a Reaper net. Your best chance of survival is to take out enough to thin the net out so you can slip through the cracks. Waiting will allow them to tighten the net around you, and you'll be forced to fight many at once versus smaller groups later.

"Okay," I said, my heart sinking at his answer. This gave a whole new meaning to the term fight or die.

Severe took a quick peek through the peephole before swinging the door open and aiming quickly in each direction. Like the first hall we marched down, we headed for the stairs again. We were closer to ground level, but I didn't know how he expected to get there.

He kicked the door open next to him, snatched and shoved me inside, and then stood at the open door and waited. This space was someone's office.

"Lock yourself in the bathroom and stay low. Don't come out until I tell you," he said, his tone hushed but audible.

I needed to control my breathing, especially with him standing there with a knife in his hand instead of a gun. Nothing on Severe moved. I wasn't even sure he was breathing anymore. I tipped across the room and peeked around the corner, worried since it sounded like there was an entire army of men coming down that hallway.

I stepped inside the small half bath and left a sizable crack in the door that allowed me to at least see Severe's legs as I took a prone position on the floor. When the hairs on my arms began to bristle, my nervous system flooded with adrenaline.

I jumped at the loud bang that sounded before the tapping of multiple weapons sounded off. Muffled groans and screams sounded before they were replaced with the thumping of feet.

"Oh shit," I gasped when a body fell right in front of the crack I peeked from, the man's eyes and mouth wide, his face frozen in fear.

"Oh, God."

I scrambled back when I noticed his arm was missing. All of the thumping and bumping stopped, and an eerie silence fell over the place.

Severe appeared, standing in the doorway like the rest of the shadows.

"You okay?" he asked.

"Yes," I replied, standing. He turned and headed toward the front door, I supposed. I hopped over the dead man with the missing arm. How the hell had his arm been ripped off? I was glad I couldn't see the pool of blood that would be left from the detachment.

"Shit," rushed out when I tripped over another dead body. And that's when I saw the rest of them, some in shadow, sprawled out in the depths of the room, lifeless and bloody. Bodies draped across chairs, one halfway through the coffee table, another against the wall like a painting and stuck there by some object I was glad I couldn't see.

There had to be at least ten dead bodies spread throughout the office space. I was so busy ogling the dead men, I ran into Severe's back, his hard body absorbing the impact and making me bounce back and off him.

"Weapon ready," he said before stepping out into what could have been death waiting to take us. Since we were past the halfway point, we made it to the stairs in record time. The silence let us know that we may have had a cleared path to the first floor.

Fourth floor.

Third floor.

Second floor.

We paused outside the second-floor hallway entrance when voices came from the first floor. The longer we stood, the more sounds filtered up to us.

Severe cracked the door open and peeked into the second-floor hallway. He took down two as soon as he turned into the corridor. I edged around him in time to see the second man fall. They must have spread out over the building on each floor. It meant our wall-climbing expedition had allowed us to slip past some of them.

Severe took up a long stride, and I ran-walked to keep up, ensuring I covered our backs.

"Here," he said, cracking a door open. This office was right in the dead center of the long stretch of hallway. I believe he'd picked it with a purpose in mind. I didn't question it as I chose to believe he'd nearly gotten us through this Reaper net.

He closed the door behind us, propping a hard-backed chair under the door handle. He marched over to the window and lifted it.

"This alley leads to another that will get us close to where we parked. If I tell you to go, I need you to go a half mile west."

He handed me the keys.

"What do you mean? I'm not leaving without you," I told him.

I sounded like one of those annoying people from one of those cheesy movies. Severe didn't respond to my protest but proceeded to prop the window open.

"I'll climb down first. Pay attention," he instructed. He climbed out the window. This office didn't have a small balcony like the ones higher up. It was more like a metal ledge that Severe hung from and then dropped down into the dark alleyway.

I shoved my gun deeper into the back of my pants and found it difficult to do any of what I saw him doing. I was clung to the metal railing, attempting to turn around. How the hell had he gotten to the bottom of the railing when there was no place to plant his feet?

I stooped low before letting one of my legs dangle over the side. The loud thumping sound coming from inside the office let me know I was out of time. They were breaking down the door.

My other leg slipped off the side, and I nearly lost my tight grip on the bars. Why did it feel like this was much higher than it did when I was watching him?

My legs hung in mid-air while I held on for dear life, afraid to let go and picturing my shattered legs and bones splintering through my skin.

Severe. He wouldn't let me break anything. Faith in him was what inspired me to close my eyes and allow myself to drop. I landed with a hard thump, his strong hands gripping my waist to steady me. Upright on my feet and with my legs fully intact, I slung my arms around Severe's neck. He returned my hug.

"We have to move," he said, backing away and turning in the direction of the street. Multiple rounds of gunfire made me freeze. Severe snatched me down, and we crawled to a shadowy area of the building.

And then there was light. Bright lights lit up the alley, turning night into day. We were trapped, and I didn't know which way to go other than down, so that's what we did, staying low and inching closer to a line of tall metal columns that went up the line of the wall and created a little nook of protection. It was only a matter of time before they arrived now that we'd triggered the lights.

Severe aimed and fired, catching the first one that entered the open space before us. There was another and another and another. We fired nonstop, but they were an endless net of men wearing protective gear that assisted in allowing them to swarm the space.

There were too many. We would run out of bullets long before we took them all out.

This was it. The end of the road. At least I got to have some excitement at the end. Severe was the reason I'd gotten to experience the one thing I'd always dreamed of but never expected to find. *Love.* I loved him, and if we perished here in this alley, I believe we would carry on to the next life with each other.

"You may as well come out," a loud male voice called in the distance.

"We're closing the net, and there is no place left for you to go," another said, his voice sounding farther off than the first man.

Severe pushed me into the nook and turned his back to the dangerous fake Reapers closing in behind us.

"What are you doing?" I asked.

We were face to face and so close his warm breath danced along my skin and teased my lashes. The men behind us kept yelling for us to come out with our hands up, but I ignored their warnings and focused on Severe. He ran a delicate hand down the side of my new hairdo, staring with a caring glint like there weren't bad guys out there ready to turn us into shredded cheese.

"Even if you were as evil as your uncle made you out to be, I don't know if I would have followed through with reaping you," he said, thumbing my cheek.

That's when I saw the cuff dangling from his wrist.

"If I were as evil as my uncle and did half of what he was pinning on me, I'd have gladly let you kill me," I replied, but my eyes were on what he was doing with his hands.

He reached back and inserted the cuff into a rung of the metal column, cuffing himself to the fixture.

"Severe, what are you doing? You can't," I choked out when I understood what he was about to do. "Backup is on the way. If I weren't here, you would keep fighting, and you would kill everyone out there. Do that now. Please don't do whatever it is you're thinking of doing right now."

He didn't answer me. He simply stood there and stared. The shouting behind us grew louder, indicating the men were getting closer, closing in on us.

Severe was a stone wall. No matter how hard I shoved, he wouldn't budge.

"Severe, please. You can't. They will kill you on sight."

He was caging me inside the enclosure of this nook, metal on either side with the building's brick wall at my back. He was planning to use his body as a human shield to save me.

I shook my head, tears stinging the backs of my eyes.

"No, please. You have to keep fighting, no matter what. Save me that way. Not this way."

"I can't let anything else happen to you, especially after what I did to you. I can't risk you anymore," he mouthed.

"Severe, please. You have to know how much I care about you by now. You can't do this to me. We can fight. I'm a good shot. You know it. I'll hit every target," I promised.

"We're out of ammunition. You have two rounds, and I'm out."

"You're death himself. It's what Toe Tags calls you. Hangman said you've killed more people than tobacco products, and that's why you're the only Reaper who has two daggers in your skull. Fifty kills for each dagger. A full set of teeth, each tooth representing specialty kills."

His brow shot up at the reminder and how much I'd learned about him and his organization through his brothers. He lifted his other hand to close me in fully, and I fought harder to make him stop.

There were killers behind us, feet away and growing close enough to make visual contact while we were in the midst of our own fight.

"Please. Don't do this. You're a Reaper, you have a blade and your hands, and that is all you need. You can do anything."

"I know," he said, and the serene expression on his face said he'd already made peace with dying this way. Saving me. Leaving me.

He reached up and gripped the other side of the metal fixture, boxing me in. I pushed him. Shoved hard. Even made an attempt to knee him, but he was unmoved. He was a fixture before me. A shield of protection that would endure death to save me.

"You're flesh and bone. They will kill me, even if they have to go through you. Please, Severe. What about Scrappy? What about me? You're going to leave me in this cold world without anyone to relate to, without anyone who understands my pain, without anyone?"

I cried hard, tears spilling so fast I gagged on my sobs, the aching sounds being dragged harshly from my throat.

"Turn around and lift your hands. Right now!" A loud voice yelled. The fake Reapers were here. They could see us now. They had us in their sights. Defenseless. Vulnerable, and one of us ready to be sacrificed.

"You were right the whole time. We were more than adrenaline. More than a close proximity fix. You made me feel something other than rage, anger, or madness. You calmed my devil. You are the heaven I never believed I'd experience. I didn't see it until I was doing the unthinkable to you in that bathroom. And for that, I deserve whatever happens to me tonight if it means you get to go on."

He stood before me, hands lifted at either side like he was on the cross, his face aimed at me and his eyes on mine. I begged him. I begged so hard, but he wouldn't listen to reason.

"Where's the key, Severe? Give me the key so I can uncuff you. Please. Don't do this. You can't do this. You know how my father died. He did this. You can't make me live through something like that again. My father was the worst tragedy of my life, but if you do this, this will replace it. I can't let you die. Not for me. Not ever. I love you," I choked out, pressing my chest into his in an attempt to move him. "You can't do this to me, Severe. This would make you the devil that made me experience the worst trauma of my life."

Those words shook him from the sacrificial mentality he'd lapsed into. His eyes crinkled at the corners. His uncuffed hand came off the portion of the metal he gripped. He reached into his front pocket, dug out the key, and handed it to me.

A loud hiss sounded before the impact pounded into Severe's back like they had used a bat. His body was driven hard into mine.

"No! No! No!" I yelled while glancing into his unbothered eyes.

"Severe," I called, my tone low and shaking with fear. He didn't answer but stared deep into my eyes.

"Turn around and lift your fucking hands, asshole. Are you deaf and dumb?" a voice yelled. This one was close enough that the vibration of his voice touched us.

Pop!

Pop!

The impact of the bullets slamming into Severe sent him smacking into me hard enough to knock the wind out of me.

"Oh, my God. No! Don't do this, God. Please," I begged, sobbing and doing my best to reach out and find the spot I needed to get the cuffs off his wrist. I stopped my action when I stared into his face.

"I'm sorry," he whispered, his words causing blood to seep from the corner of his mouth. His eyes began to droop, his body swaying.

"No, Severe, please. You can't leave me. Not like this, please. I'm not going to survive this. I can't."

He slumped forward, but he managed to keep his uncuffed hand clamped around the thick metal beam to keep me caged. He came down until his forehead was nearly touching mine.

"Severe. You stopped fighting. This isn't you. Please," I begged.

"Turn around, motherfucker," a voice shouted, snatching him back and opening up the tight space I'd been pinned in. Severe hung limply by one arm that was pulled taut as his legs slid from under him, and the group of fake Reapers surrounding me took in the sight of us.

"Holy shit. This crazy bastard used his own body to save her. Can you believe this shit?"

I jumped out of the nook and stood in front of Severe's limp body. He wasn't attempting to pull himself up, and his arm was stretched so tightly that it was threatening to rip apart. It meant he was injured badly. Based on the number of times he'd slammed into me, he'd been shot at least four or five times.

He's not dead.

I kept repeating the mantra in my head as I stared down the barrel of at least twenty high-powered rifles and other weapons.

"We got ourselves a hero, men. Do you see this shit? This is what I call true loyalty. He sacrificed himself for her, and now she wants to return the favor."

Severe grew heavier against me, forcing me to lean back against him to keep him from spilling over and hanging by his wrist.

Movement crept down my shoulder. The warm flow and the rusted scent let me know it was Severe's blood spilling onto me. His blood flowed, which meant that he was alive and could still be saved.

I spun, putting my back to the man making threats against my life. At this point, I didn't care what any of them did. I would spend my time, whether it was five seconds or a minute, with Severe.

"Turn the fuck around right now. What are you doing?" the man shouted.

The hard thump of the man's boots pounded, and before I got the cuff key up to Severe's wrist, I was ripped away from him and slung around to meet the hard slap of the man's hand.

Severe fell forward. His body appeared suspended in mid-air, but it was his cuffed wrist ready to snap that kept him from tumbling to the ground face first.

Hurt. Pain. They were two of the most powerful motivators there were. The kick I delivered to the man's balls sent him down and had every weapon within range charging, cocking, lifting, and aimed at a part of me.

Like before, my mind was on one track. I turned back to Severe.

"The boss is dead," someone kept yelling.

"Kill her. She must die now too," another said.

I didn't have any training on how to undo cuffs, but I shoved my shoulder into Severe's bleeding body, holding up his weight while I worked the key into the tiny hole.

My shaking hand and my blurred vision worked against me, but I was determined. Silence stirred in the air behind me. They were about to pull their triggers and shoot me in the back, and at this moment, not knowing if Severe was all right or not, I didn't care.

I jumped at the sound of gunfire since it wasn't all silenced. Finally, the key hit the right area, and the cuffs sprung open. I worked and wiggled Severe's wrist free of them until I took on the brunt of his weight.

We staggered and nearly fell to the ground, but I grunted and heaved and prayed until I was able to lower him safely.

Gunfire sounded off all around me, the muzzles flashing like lightning bugs in my peripheral vision. I didn't know if these men were shooting up each other or what. I didn't care about what was taking place behind me while I worked on stopping the bleeding around Severe's head. There was so much blood. I couldn't tell where he'd been shot.

When a heavy hand clamped around my shoulder, I spun, bringing up the gun with my last two bullets. With my body over Severe's, I aimed at the dark figure above me.

"Don't shoot. It's me, Micah," the figure said.

It took my brain a long, intense second to piece together who was standing before me and why I hadn't been shot in the back.

"Micah," I whispered, letting the gun fall from my hands. "Severe. You have to help him," I begged, spinning back to face him.

CHAPTER THIRTY-TWO

Jade

Did his eyelids just tighten, move, twitch? Either they did, or my mind was playing tricks on me again.

"Come on, Severe, come back, please. Just because you're a Reaper, it doesn't mean you need to hang out and linger in the darkness. We love you on this side of reality also. We miss you. We want you around whether you believe it or not. I miss you," I coaxed.

There it was again. His eyes tightened. I stood, hovering over him like a crazy person. Squeezing and releasing the tight hold I'd taken of his hand and repeating the process.

Squeeze my hand. Please.

"Oh!" I cupped my free hand over my mouth to keep my shout in at the light squeeze of his hand around mine. There it was again. I wanted to dance, to shout, to scream. He was coming back. Severe was coming back.

His eyes started to move faster under his lids as his grip on my hand grew stronger. His foot twitched, his leg moved, and then there was a small jerk of his arm.

That's it, baby, come back.

For a second, time stopped, and so did my heart, the hammering beats muted, and then when the world re-started, his eyes snapped open while his hand squeezed around mine.

I'd sat at his bedside talking about everything and nothing, but now, at this moment, my motions were limited to smiling and blinking back tears. His eyes were on me, searching, focusing. His lips moved, and I leaned down to see if I could figure out what he was saying.

I jumped, my head snapping up when the door flew open, and the hospital staff, three of them, came barreling into the room. The machines Severe were hooked up to must have alerted them to his status.

Reluctantly, I released his hand and allowed the medical team to work on him. I waited in the background, my pulse in my throat the whole time. I breathed again for the first time in a month. I was finally released from the anxiety of waiting to see him open his beautiful eyes again.

I peeked around the crew of working bodies without hearing a word they were saying. My whole focus was on Severe, praying for his full physical and mental recovery.

***

Six hours later.

The hospital staff had run every test in the medical field on Severe. They informed us that there was no brain damage or memory loss from the head shot he'd taken and that the rest of his wounds would heal without leaving permanent damage.

At some point, when they had taken him from this room to conduct tests, they'd had to strap him to the bed to keep him from getting up and leaving the hospital. There were also five Reapers roaming the building.

I'd forfeited my alone time with Severe so that his brothers could spend time with him. Now, they were pacing the building and probably leaving chaos and mayhem in their paths.

They had revealed to me that this hospital was a part of some network that fell under the watchful eyes of the Order.

The moment I stepped back into the room, they all filed out so Severe and I could finally have our moment. Once we were alone, our eyes locked and never wavered. My breathing sounded over the hiss of one of the few remaining machines.

His eyes were on me, unreadable, and even in his injured state, they radiated strength. Uneasy steps drew me closer.

"I'm glad you're back," I said.

"Me too," he replied.

"That was a long nap you took. But, based on your sleep habits, I guess you needed it."

His lips twitched, but the smile didn't make it to his eyes. I reached out and took his hand.

"Are you up for talking about what landed you here, in this bed, and on my shit list?" I asked.

"Yes," he replied, nodding.

"First, Thank you for saving my life, repeatedly. There isn't enough time in this universe to allow me to show you how grateful I am that you saw something within me that didn't permit you to take my life but to save me instead."

He gave a little nod like it was no big deal when I knew how much effort it took to keep me alive, especially against an organization that dealt specifically in death. I squeezed his hand, wanting his full attention.

"Why did you give up? It wasn't you. It wasn't what a Reaper would do. The people I listened to, and all of those stories I was told when I was at Ground Zero said you wouldn't have given up. Your brothers talked about you like you were death himself, a living nightmare. A ghost. Indestructible."

My grip on his hand loosened, and his eyebrows twitched.

"Things are still a bit cagey within your organization. Micah wouldn't tell me much, but he assured me that I could go back to my life without any further threats from the Order."

I paused, unsure how to say what was so heavy on my heart. A deep breath and fighting back tears made him squeeze my hand.

"I wanted there to be an 'us' so badly. But you tried to leave me in that alley."

I paused, waited.

"You can stop me anytime I say something wrong," I said. "You could have fought, but I believed you wanted out. You wanted to die that night, and I believe I gave you a good enough excuse to do it."

Nothing. Only his keen eyes on me.

"You never believed that we were anything but adrenaline. A close proximity fix for each other. I didn't share that assessment, but I now have to accept that what I was feeling was one-sided."

He wasn't saying shit, and it was pissing me off. I was only saying some of this crazy shit to get him to tell me how he felt about me once and for all.

You'd better not cry. You swallow it and hold your head up.

I nodded, although he wasn't saying anything. My father's death was no longer the worst thing to ever happen to me, and this time, violence wasn't even involved.

His brows twitched, but still, he didn't say a single word.

"Is there anything you want to say? When I leave here today, I may never see you again."

"I..."

He paused, glancing down. "I'm glad you're okay."

I nodded, swallowing the boulder-sized lump in my throat. Despite him not making a single comment about us or about him sacrificing himself, I still cared about him. Still loved him.

"What about you? Are you glad that you're okay? That you survived this?"

He flashed me a quick side-eye before making his face unreadable again.

"I didn't try to kill myself. We're trained to believe we don't die. I wanted to keep you alive because you didn't deserve to die. The right people died," he said.

We fell into another long, silent stare, and I wondered what was *really* going through his head.

Say something about us. Tell me you want me.

"I'd better get going," I said. A swirling mass of emotions was about to take my will to be strong. I leaned down, closing in, and our eyes locked until my lips met his cheek with the lightest brush.

He still smelled like himself, despite being laid up in this place for so long. We continued to clasp onto each other's hands, and I inhaled deeply so that I'd remember. I pressed a few more lingering kisses until my lips were at his ear.

"You are the light that illuminates a very dark place for me, and you don't even know it. Once you figure it out, you'll finally be able to see yourself the way that I see you. I'm going to miss you for a very long time," I whispered.

When I lifted myself to walk away, I felt the lightest tug on my hand. His lips moved, eyes searched, and the little v formed on his face before he went stone-faced again.

Say something.

Say you'll miss me.

Say you want me.

That I mean something to you.

That our time together made you happy.

That I made you happy.

I walked away, heart shattered, mind in chaos, now knowing that he never felt the same way about me as I did him. Maybe I was his absolution, the one he believed he had to save at any cost.

As soon as I made it out of the room, I flung myself against the outside wall and allowed what was left of my heart to shatter into tiny pieces.

Mouth open, eyes leaking like runny faucets, and chest heaving up and down, I was a mess. The one man I wanted, the one who I believed understood me, didn't want me back. His only job was saving me, and he'd done it almost at the cost of his own life. I wanted more. He didn't.

CHAPTER THIRTY-THREE

Severe

"Wake the fuck up," the low steely tone of a familiar voice said while tapping each word into my aching forehead. My eyes snapped open to Micah, staring like he wanted to stab me fifty times with a flaming blade.

"What did you do? What the fuck did you say to Jade?" he barked the questions.

"Nothing," I answered quickly. I didn't recall seeing him this upset with me since I'd sneaked off and set a priest on fire in the middle of downtown traffic. It was his target, which made the act that much worse.

"Please tell me you said something or did any fucking thing but let her walk out that fucking door thinking you don't give a shit about anything other than doing your job."

He knew me too damn well. The shit fascinated me.

"You did, didn't you? She sat here in this fucking room..."

He stepped back and began pacing. His top teeth were grinding into the bottom, and his hands were in the strangle pose. He stopped and snapped around, causing my eyes to snap up at him. He wanted to kill me. I saw it in his eyes, in his stiff posture, and in that menacing expression on his face.

"That woman sat in this fucking room for a month, didn't even leave your side for one day, not even to go get food. We brought her food, or she ate whatever the hospital staff gave her. She bathed you. She read to you. She talked to you. Prayed for you. She even got Tags to bring Scrappy to see you a few times. She did everything but resurrect God himself to wake you up. And you let her walk out of this room thinking that you don't love her? Are you out of your fucking mind? Did you suffer some memory loss that the doctors don't know about?"

A deep frown formed on my face, a prelude to the anger flaring up inside me.

"You respect him. I don't and will curse him the fuck out. I don't care if he's the president of the fucking United States or cousin to the Pope. He'd better lower his fucking tone," my demon barked. It was like he'd been in a coma, too, and Micah had awakened him.

I cleared my throat so none of my words would be lost in translation.

"I'm a trained killer. I live in a one-bedroom cabin with so little furniture I can count the pieces on one hand. Let any doctor who examined me tell it—I'm diagnosed with enough mental conditions to fill up a fully functional psych ward all by myself. I'm not a conversationalist. I don't even like people, and it's not something I say to keep people away from me. After a while, people grate on my nerves, and I have to get away or risk losing it. And don't get me started on my unhealthy obsession with hunting down, torturing, and killing everyone who had a hand in my abuse. You want me to offer all that chaos to someone like her?"

His hands on his hips like a coach, eyes unblinking, and lips parted—Micah was rendered speechless.

"Damn. Since you put it that way, I see your flimsy point. But none of what you just said matters to her. Love is as much about what you can take as what you can give. Jade can take you just the way you are—no complaints, no judgment. She's been through just as much shit as any Reaper. Her father was a part of the Handle, one of the Six. This organization, in one way or another, ripped her family to shreds, and you just tore through the frayed pieces. Jade sees shit in you that you will never see in yourself. You..."

He aimed and shook a stiff finger at my face.

"You don't believe you deserve her, and that's your problem. Until you accept that someone like her, as you say, accepts you: faults, weakness, and the garage full of baggage you come with, then you will forever live with a fucking hole in your chest, and so will she. I've seen you two together. She loves you, Severe. You can tell yourself whatever the hell you need to remain in denial, but you love her too."

With that, he walked off in a huff and left me pressed under a mountain of emotions heavy enough to push me down to hell, where I belonged for hurting Jade.

CHAPTER THIRTY-FOUR

Jade

Two months later.

I walked beside Micah after calling him for this favor. He'd met me at the hotel I was staying at in downtown Charleston and had driven me out to Ground Zero. After two months of moping, of longing, of feeling like my damn heart would spill from my chest, I could take no more.

I needed to see him, to talk, even if it were to call him an asshole. Now that I was here, steps away from seeing him again, my nerves had my heart pounding and nausea climbing up my throat.

"When you called me, the first thing that came to mind was, it's about damn time," Micah said.

I chuckled, hoping it would help ward off my anxiety. I gripped Micah's forearm, stopping his easy stride.

"What if he doesn't want to see me? What if he doesn't want…"

"Stop. There's not a living creature on this planet who can't see the man is suffering and not from an injury."

Micah glanced at my trembling hand, which revealed my stress level. He pinned his reassuring gaze back on mine, and his bright smile gleamed with his piercing green gaze and enticed my lips to twitch with a little smile.

"Even when you were suspected of being the monster your uncle painted you out to be, he couldn't bring himself to hurt you. I knew you were someone special to him the day he brought you here. The way he was with you blew my mind. There was no doubt that he'd finally allowed himself to feel again, and you were the reason for it." He squeezed my hand.

"Ready?"

I nodded before Micah shoved the door open and allowed me to step inside. At first, no one paid us any attention until smiles, waves of acknowledgment, and even flashes of excitement greeted me on my return. The noise level died down with each step we took.

My gaze roamed the darkest corners searching for the first sight of him. I swallowed hard, my heart rate hiked, and my nerves were ravaged. Seeing Severe, silhouetted by dark shadows like a sexy dark avenger while sipping his drink was the best thing I'd seen in a long time.

*****

Severe

I've lost control of the new monster invading my chaotic sense of peace. There's no way to see around its ever-expanding view. No way to outrun its reach and no way to wiggle free of its deathly grip. It hurts and is the best sensation at the same time. It's confusing. It wraps you in the depth of the most blissful high. It rips apart your innermost desires and fulfills them. It lives to make you its most loyal victim. It can't be explained, and it has every meaning. It's life and death and hate and pain. It's more than an emotion. It doesn't see color or gender or anything other than what it wants. It invades your body down to the cellular level and controls your mind at will. It's stronger than death. It's your worst fear and greatest joy. It's chaos with no comprehension. It's a raging beast infinitely more devastating than me.

The new monster raging inside of me, one that trumps my demon and tortures my heart, my mind, and my soul—this monster wants the one thing it knows it can't have...*Jade.*

Over the last few months, I'd resigned myself to the compound. Leaving my cabin only when Micah used his presidential powers and ordered it. No one other than my cousins was brave enough to approach me about why I was losing weight and not scaring people off like usual. Now, the most anyone can get is a head gesture for a greeting, a brief dismissive glance, or a grunt.

Tonight, Micah had ordered me to come out to The Bar, our small watering hole on Ground Zero. Currently, I sat in the darkest corner atop a barstool, at the back wall, listening to everything from country to gangster rap and people partying and having genuine fun.

"I'd rather be playing Operation with one of the fuck-faced idiots from our list. This shit is making me sick. I think I'm dying, losing my voice, fading back into the black hole that created me," my demon spat, being dramatic.

My third drink hadn't put a dent in my unenthusiastic nature. I was sick of looking at my brothers, some with their old ladies, shouting, laughing, and dancing. Despite my mood, I studied their banter, their enthusiasm, and mannerisms, not knowing when I would have to mimic this type of behavior on an assignment.

I turned away from the crowd and propped my elbows on the bar, staring at the brown liquid swirling in my glass. My demon was better company than being a spectator to this joy festival.

A prickly sensation climbed up my back, faint and ghostly but very much present. I swallowed hard. This feeling took possession of me when my new monster was about to get what it wanted.

I was afraid to turn around, afraid my mind had taken on a new twist, and instead of a voice, it would upgrade to showing me images and make me feel things that didn't exist.

I sipped the drink, hoping it would tamp down the sensation that kept growing stronger and heightening my anxiety.

"Cousin," a male voice called.

Micah. I didn't glance at him right away, still kind of ticked off that he'd ordered me to come here.

"Someone's here to see you," he said, his tone teasing.

It was the familiar sensation marching up my back that made me turn my head and allow my eyes to find hers.

Jade.

I was frozen in place by the sight of her, my breathing erratic, and my mind blown in ten different directions at once. She was angelic, the one person with whom I had found true beauty and managed to forge a connection with that delved past my comprehension.

There was no longer anyone else inside this bar but me and Jade. Sound fled, and everything appeared brighter, like we were on a stage together.

"Severe."

Her voice, calling out my name, strummed some tightly pulled cords in my chest. She smiled, and her gaze dropped bashfully before she returned it to mine.

"Can we talk?"

"Yes," I replied, easing off the stool to stand in front of her. She lifted her head, her eyes searching mine.

"I know what I said at the hospital. And it took me some time to work through my emotions and to consider everything we experienced together. You saved me, and I'm grateful to you. I'm grateful for my life. I'm grateful I can continue to live free of one less nightmare. That I can resume helping the people who need it most. But, most of all, I'm grateful for the time I got to spend with you."

I stared, my heart pounding, my words a big wad of letters with no direction or formation. I wasn't good at managing my feelings, and having emotions was a new concept. I frowned, wanting to say something, anything, but the words wouldn't fall free.

"Will you answer one question?" she asked.

I nodded.

"Do you still believe we were acting on adrenaline, a close proximity fix for each other, projecting?

"No," I answered quickly. "I never believed we were, but I didn't want you to end up disappointed, hurt, and filled with regret."

I noticed for the first time that the silence surrounding us wasn't from Jade drawing all of my focus and attention. The music was off, the lights were switched on, and the laughing, dancing, and loud talking had ceased. All eyes in the building were locked on Jade and me like they were witnessing a miracle unfold.

"Do you still feel that way? Do you believe that I will be hurt, disappointed, or regretful if I chose you?" Jade asked, her eyes searching mine for the truth.

I peered deeply into her eyes, took a cautious step closer, and angled my head down to allow her to see every emotion I couldn't vocalize reflecting in my gaze.

"No," I said while leaning into our kiss. The first delicate touch made fireworks explode behind my eyes, and pulsing beats of energy zipped through me and set off bolts of thunder in my heart.

The loud shouts, the yelling, and *hot damns* at our reunion drew my attention and made a rare smile tease my lips.

Jade leaned her head against my chest, laughed, and peeked around at the crowd as they continued to clap, cheer, and send shrieking whistles our way.

"Let's get out of here," she said, the gleam in her eyes saying more than her words. We turned to walk out, and a round of applause erupted so loudly, the sound vibrated against my skin.

Claps fell against my shoulders and back, and whistling, yells, and cheers followed us out. Jade took my hand, and for a fraction of a second, mine went stiff before I closed it around hers.

My cousins and club brothers had made attempts over the years to pull me from my dark shell. Jade managed to make me poke my head out of the darkness to allow the light a chance to touch me. At first, I assumed she was the bringer of my end. Now, I knew better. Jade was my beginning.

EPILOGUE

"Oh my God," I cried hoarsely, dragging the last word out for so long, I choked on it. Severe knew every nook, fold, bend, and dimple in my body. He knew it so well that I believed he could get me off with eye contract alone if he tried.

Right now, I was relaxed, boneless. I couldn't move to climb off of him, so he was still inside me, not hard, but not soft either. I didn't have the strength to lift my head, so I propped it against his shoulder while my heavy breaths bounced off his neck.

I could feel his cum and my own juices seeping out of me and dripping all over him. He didn't care. His forehead was pressed into the front of my shoulder while he struggled for breaths.

Aside from him leaving his cabin to gather food, something other than peanut butter and jelly, we hadn't left since I arrived three days ago. The few reunions I'd had with Scrappy were short and sweet because her father and I couldn't keep our hands off each other.

"I've never had this much sex before," I admitted once my breathing leveled out. He squeezed my ass cheek but didn't reply. I could feel him growing harder and expanding inside me.

"What about you? Have you ever had this much sex before me?" I asked him.

He lifted his head and shook it.

"I've never had any sex before you? Not like this, at least."

I laughed, my chuckle ongoing. "I can't believe you finally told me a joke, and it's actually kind of funny."

"It wasn't a joke. It's never worked for anyone else. So when my cousins would send women for me to screw them, I would, but not with my body parts. I used sex toys, objects of opportunity, and even used a wine bottle on one girl. She came, so she didn't complain."

I jerked my head back, my breathing kicking up a notch because I was struggling to understand him and fighting not to squirm because he was hard again, and it was already giving me euphoric sparks without us moving.

"I'm not sure I understand what you're telling me. Are you saying you've never had sex because you couldn't get it up? Because that's what it sounded like you just said."

My face was creased into a tight knot, and my lady parts were down there humming a tune of praise and worship. He nodded while his hands slid up each side of my damp, naked body.

"I tried several times, but it only got hard when I was reaping someone or thinking about reaping someone. So instead of sending them all away when women approached, and so as to keep my cousins off my back, I improvised, used something that would get them off before sending them away," he said like what he was saying wasn't a big deal.

"Am I the first woman you've been with?" I glanced down at us because despite us having one of the most serious conversations of our relationship, our bodies were singing a different tune, and I couldn't help rolling my hips.

"Yes, the very first," he said, the words rushing out with the upward thrusts he delivered.

"How?" I breathed, losing the rest of the question on a deep inhale and a long exhale.

"How? Oh Shit. How do you know how to...to. Fuck. Shit, Severe!" I yelled, forgetting the question. I'd have to just figure out later how he knew how to screw me like a porn star, fuck me like I was his slut, and sex me up, down, and all around until I couldn't even say my own name.

I was confident now, more than ever, that I had become Severe's old lady. Never in a million years would I have thought I would end up with a bad boy, a Reaper, one who could make the devil himself reevaluate his priorities.

Death brought us together. Death kept us together. Death ripped us apart. But, life, the essence of it, the beautiful sparks we created together broke through all that darkness and forged the eternal flame of a bond that would never be broken. Severe was my spark, my light, my savior, and I believed I was his.

End of Severe

Acknowledgement

A special thank you to Author Siera London for inviting me into the Lunchtime Chronicles family. I'm forever grateful.

The novella, Carolina Reaper was written as a shout-out to my first motorcycle club romance series, Twisted Minds. The characters from Carolina Reaper, one of which was Severe, sparked readers' interest.

Thank you to all the readers who connected with me and shared your interests in reading more on specific characters. Your feedback is the sparks of motivation that feeds my imagination and breathes life into new stories.

Thank you to Unique Words, LLC. Your promotions/marketing services spotlights my new and old novels, gaining them social media visibility and reader engagement.

Author's Note

Readers. My sincere thank you for reading Severe. Please leave a review, even if only three words, letting me and others know what you thought of Severe and Jade's story. If you enjoyed it or any of my other books, please pass them along to friends or anyone you think would enjoy them.

Other Titles by Keta Kendric

The Twisted Minds Series:

The Chaos Series:

Stand Alones:

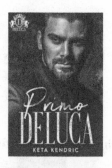

Novellas:

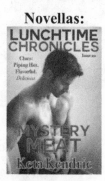

Paranormals:

Kindle Vella:

**Love Lied Series
(Seasons 1-3)**
Keta Kendric

Audiobooks:

Connect on Social Media

Subscribe to my Newsletter or Paranormal Newsletter for exclusive updates on new releases, sneak peeks, and much more.

Universal Link to all social media sites:
https://linktr.ee/ketakendric

Newsletter Sign up:
https://mailchi.mp/c5ed185fd868/httpsmailchimp
Paranormal Newsletter Sign up:
https://mailchi.mp/38b87cb6232d/keta-kendric-paranormal-newsletter
Instagram: https://instagram.com/ketakendric
Facebook Readers' Group:
https://www.facebook.com/groups/380642765697205/
BookBub: https://www.bookbub.com/authors/keta-kendric
Twitter: https://twitter.com/AuthorKetaK
Goodreads:
https://www.goodreads.com/user/show/73387641-keta-kendric
TikTok: https://www.tiktok.com/@ketakendric?
Pinterest: https://www.pinterest.com/authorslist/

Made in the USA
Coppell, TX
24 October 2023

23325869R00256